MD

Uncle Max

Books by Chris Kenry

CAN'T BUY ME LOVE

UNCLE MAX

Published by Kensington Publishing Corporation

Uncle Max

CHRIS KENRY

KENSINGTON BOOKS
http://www.kensingtonbooks.com

KENSINGTON BOOKS are published by

Kensington Publishing Corp.
850 Third Avenue
New York, NY 10022

Library of Congress Card Catalogue Number: 2001095185
ISBN 1-57566-847-5

First Printing: May 2002
10 9 8 7 6 5 4 3 2 1

Printed in the United States of America

For Bill Weller

Acknowledgments

Thanks to Chuck Mallory, Sean Wolfe, Craig Dietz, and Dave Leger for helpful and insightful critiques; to Nancy Karpan, Jennifer Marx, and my mother, whose never-ending redecorating kept food in my belly; thanks to Jeff Elliott for his help with antiques; and thanks to John Scognamiglio and Alison Picard for their insight and guidance with this manuscript. Most of all thanks to the powers that be for creating the central branch of the Denver Public Library, in which the majority of this book was written.

I never came across anyone in whom the moral sense was dominant who was not heartless, cruel, vindictive, log-stupid, and entirely lacking in the smallest sense of humanity. Moral people, as they are termed, are simply beasts. I would sooner have fifty unnatural vices than one natural virtue

—Oscar Wilde

The man seemed to know his way around households of this kind, he knew where everything was. He had made himself at home. This gift of being everywhere at home belongs only to kings, light women and thieves.

—Honoré de Balzac

Chapter One

If you don't know what you're looking for, Nguyen's is not easy to find. Unlike the hundreds of other antique stores that compete for space on the crowded Antique Row, Nguyen's does not have a flashy sign proclaiming its presence. Nor has the building in which it is housed been painted garish attention-grabbing colors. No, Nguyen's is in an unremarkable, two-story building of blond brick with a large storefront window facing Broadway.

In this window, there are no artfully arranged displays of furniture, no silver tea sets, or chandeliers (its owner being too concerned with theft and sun damage to ever display any of her treasures to the public). In this window, there is nothing more than a floor-to-ceiling black velvet curtain. A curtain that acts both as a sunblock and as a backdrop for her sign—an artist's easel on which rests a matte black canvas in an elaborate gold frame. On this canvas there are small, raised, gold letters spelling out *Nguyen's*, and then below, in identical, although somewhat smaller script, is the exclusionary phrase *by appointment only*. There used to be a telephone number on the sign, which the curious could call to gain entry; but lately even this has been removed and replaced with an e-mail address, since the owner, who is impatient with most of the buying public, now does most of her buying and selling online.

Nguyen's deals in high-end antiques, mostly of French or Asian origin, and is owned by Jane Nguyen, who is as minimal in appearance as her first name and storefront imply. On any day, in any season, she is invariably dressed in a simple, sleeveless black dress, the hemline of which, regardless of the current fashion, she keeps just above the knee. A simple strand of pearls or occasionally a gold brooch adds variety to what is otherwise a uniform. She is short, perhaps only five feet tall, and thin, and her long straight black hair is usually held back in a ponytail by a simple black band. Her one concession to whimsy is a pair of cat's-eye glasses, the corners of which are encrusted with small, almost imperceptible, rhinestones. In addition to her encyclopedic knowledge of French antiques, she is known about town, and with the dealers and clients around the country, for these glasses, whose lenses (unbeknownst to all but a select few) have as much prescriptive value as a window pane. They are completely useless as anything other than an accessory, and somehow I knew, even before she confessed it to me, that the glasses had been my uncle's idea.

Max was like that: always coming up with simple ways to make ordinary things extraordinary. His love of all things marinated or pickled is a perfect example of this. Okra, watermelon rind, cheap cuts of meat—anything that people usually wouldn't consider eating, would actively avoid or even discard—Max could dress up in some colorful vinegar with a few floating herbs, *et voilà!* The mundane would become a delicacy.

"The French are wise that way," I remember him saying (according to Max, the French were wise in just about every way). "They could pickle a piece of shit and make it edible. It's all about potential, Dil. Never mind what things *are*, the important thing is what they can become."

My name is Dillon, but he always shortened it to Dil, which is perhaps appropriate since I was nothing more than one of his very large pickles. An awkward, ugly, all-too-ordinary suburban adolescent who he marinated into something much more one summer almost a decade ago.

But, on this particular summer morning, it was to Nguyen's shop that I eagerly made my way. I work there on the weekends and on some evenings or on the days when I'm not in class. I was not scheduled to work for another hour, but something I'd come across in the newspaper that morning while paying for my order at the coffee shop had caused me to rush over, paper in hand, to show Jane.

"It's him!" I cried, breathless with excitement, dropping the paper on the desk in front of her, open to the page I'd been reading. "It's got to be him."

Calmly, Jane pushed the paper aside and neatly stacked the invoices on which she'd been working. She emitted an annoyed sigh and slowly put on her glasses. She was not yet forty, but her somber world-weary manner made her seem much older. She picked up the paper, scanned the articles, and then finally discovered the one I'd intended her to see. I watched her dark eyes behind the glasses as they darted across the text.

It was a small article on page two in the slender column devoted to celebrity news, which is, I have to admit, the first section I look at in the morning.

FORMER DENVER TYCOON AND WIFE ROBBED AT GUNPOINT IN SOUTH OF FRANCE, the headline blared. The article went on to detail how Lloyd and Beverly Boatwright-Stark, former Denver residents, had left St. Tropez early Friday afternoon en route to Monaco, where they planned to spend the winter. Roughly midway on their journey, their car was forced off onto a side road by another car and two motorcycles, all piloted by men in ski masks. The driver was pulled from the car, stripped, gagged, and tied to a tree. The frightened couple were then forced out and ordered by the leader of the gang—"in perfect, unaccented English," they were quoted as saying—to hand over the undisclosed quantity of cash and jewelry they were carrying. They were then similarly stripped, gagged, and tied up. They were discovered some hours later, frightened but unharmed, by a group of bemused schoolgirls.

When Jane had finished reading, she handed me the paper, gave a dismissive wave, and said, "They always were flashy. Remember their house, remember that ridiculous pink taffeta dress she wore to the Governor's Ball? Just like a blob of taffy! A woman half her age—and weight—couldn't have gotten away with that! And look at this, look here," she said, pointing to a line in the article. "*. . . an undisclosed quantity of cash and jewelry?* Christ! Who would drive around with a carload of cash and jewels? Only stupid ostentatious yokels like them, that's who. Serves them right."

"But what abou—"

"Oh, I know what you're thinking," she said, cutting me off. "But it wasn't him. You know as well as I do that he probably never even made it there." She then picked up her pen and went back to her invoices.

I was leery of her calm exterior. I had seen the sparkle in her eyes as they scanned the article and knew it had been caused by more than her gleeful distaste for the Boatwright-Starks.

"Oh come on! France! The Boatwright-Starks! Robbery!" I cried, naming three of Max's passions. "Who else could it be?"

Jane looked up from her invoices. She stared through the crowded shop at the small strip of sunlight admitted through the door. She had taken off her glasses and her face looked softer, less severe. I knew that she was thinking of Max, but what she was thinking I could only imagine. My own thoughts of my uncle went from one extreme to another, with very little in between that was neutral, and I was sure that she felt the same. Whatever she was thinking, I thought it best not to intrude for a while so I stretched out on the large Empire sofa and took one of the small madeleines from the paper bag I'd bought at the coffee shop. I chewed absently and stared up at the ceiling, the newspaper resting on my chest.

Maybe she's right, I thought. Maybe it's not him.

I remembered the picture of the Jaguar as it was pulled from the ocean. It had fallen two hundred feet into shallow water. The hood had been accordioned to one-eighth its original length and both doors had been torn off on impact. His body had never been found. It was assumed that it had been ejected through the windshield and that what was left of it had floated out to sea. . . . Fish food. But I didn't believe it. It was him in France. Somehow I knew it. I shut my eyes and tried to remember the last time I'd seen him; he'd been walking away, into the garage. I could see the outline of his lean body, his black hair; but try as I might, I could not make out his face. I remembered that his nose was crooked where it had been broken, that his eyebrows were enviably thick, and that his jawline was square and pronounced, but I could not see the whole picture. It was all in shadow. I tried hard to imagine him winding rope around the rotund, naked bodies of the Boatwright-Starks, as the paper had described, but I could see his features no better than they had through the mask.

"Dillon." It was Jane's voice. I looked up from the sofa. She had put her glasses back on and she was smiling. "Give me some of those," she said, motioning toward the bag of madeleines. "We don't open for another twenty minutes, why don't you go lock the door and tell me about your date last night."

I groaned and made my way to the door. Lately, I'd been trying my luck with personal ads in one of the weekly papers as a new way to meet guys who were hopefully a little less shallow and a little more intriguing than the ones I met in bars or at the gym. The results had been disastrous so far, but I have to admit, I did relish giving an account of the trauma to my friends the next morning. Bad dates, like disastrous vacations and injuries requiring stitches, always make for interesting stories.

I swung myself up from the sofa and handed her the bag. Then I wove my way through the maze of desks and sideboards and tables to the front door, turned the key in the lock, and went back to the sofa, dropping the newspaper in an elephant's foot trash can on the way.

"Let's hear it," Jane said, leaning her tiny body forward on the huge desk and rubbing her hands together in anticipation.

"What can I say?" I sighed. "He was very nice to look at: broad shoulders, slender waist, beautiful hands. He had a nicely shaped head in which, unfortunately, there was absolutely nothing."

"And you already refer to him in the past tense," Jane chuckled. I went on.

"Yes. When my life is made into a stage play, the actor given his minor role will be disappointed with his brief moment in the spotlight, but at least his lines will be easy to memorize since they'll consist mostly of one-word exclamations like Whoa! Cool! and Righteous!"

"That bad?"

"Oh, much worse. I had to drink just to get through it, but even that wasn't easy," I said, sitting up on the sofa, warming to the tale. "I was just a little bit late getting to the restaurant and when I arrived I saw that he had already been seated and had taken the liberty of ordering us a bottle of wine. It was an unnaturally pink wine that tasted awfully close to spiked Kool-aid, with a picture of some kittens on the label."

I knew this last remark would offend Jane, the wine snob, more than anything.

"No!" she cried, leaning back in her chair.

"Oh yes," I said. "And I couldn't drink it fast enough. But let me get to the meal. Every time I paused he'd look over at my plate and say, in his booming voice, 'Dude, you gonna finish that?' If I said no (and I did quite often. Imagine the food in a restaurant that sells wine with kittens on the label), he'd reach one of his hamhock arms across the table and scoop it up with his fork."

"At least he knew how to use one," Jane laughed.

"Oh God, I'm not even sure he had thumbs! It's too bad, really,"

I said, shaking my head, "because, of course, the sex afterward was quite good."

"So you slept with him."

"Of course. I didn't want the night to be a total loss."

"Will you see him again?"

"I don't think so," I said wistfully.

"What if he calls?"

"Ahh," I said, raising a finger, "then the phone will ring at the pay phone down the street from my house."

Later that afternoon, as I sat polishing a long neglected silver tray that Jane was preparing to photograph for eBay, I asked her when was the last time she'd gone out on a date. Her head remained focused on the camera she was mounting on the tripod.

"A long time ago," she said, curtly. "Aren't you finished yet?"

I knew I had hit a nerve, but I continued.

"Do you think you ever will?" I asked.

Her head remained down, as if she were looking at the camera, but her eyes were looking up and off to the side. "Maybe not," she said, and then went back to the camera.

"Is that because of him?" I asked.

"Because of whom?"

I didn't answer but let the question hang in the air. She paused, shook her head slightly, and returned her attention to the camera. I went back to rubbing the tray.

"Do you think he's ruined it for us?" I asked. "I mean, you not dating anyone and me writing off every new guy five minutes into our first date."

"You're still young," she said. "Don't be silly."

"I'm not *that* young," I countered, "and you're not *that* old. Do you think we'll ever find anyone like Max?"

"Not if we're lucky," she quipped, and got up and left the room. I knew then, despite her flip response, or perhaps because of it, that

I was right. He had ruined us. And the fact that now he was probably still alive made it even worse. In many ways a ghost of the living is much worse than a ghost of the dead, for there is always the possibility that he will come back, or that someday, walking in London or Prague or Paris, I'll meet him again or even catch a glimpse of him or someone that looks like him. Max will always haunt us, I thought, just like Rebecca, or Lara, or Ilsa, or any of the other ghostly movie heroines. But instead of a monogrammed hanky, or the balalaika, or a few bars of *As Time Goes By*, I'll think of him every time I have a date.

I went back to polishing the tray and tried again to imagine Max's face, but I couldn't. I could see it no better than my own murky reflection in the tarnished silver. And maybe that was what really scared me—not that I would always be haunted by him, but that I would forget him. That I *was* forgetting him. That slowly he was fading from my memory. Soon, I knew, it would be difficult to picture him at all; and the thought of that was like a hollow space in my life, a cartoon gunshot right through my torso leaving a perfectly round hole, an empty, hungry feeling.

Maybe he hasn't ruined me, I thought, maybe I just don't want to let go.

I finished with the tray, positioned it on the wooden stand in front of the black velvet curtain, and went to find Jane. As I walked through the shop toward the back room, past the elephant's foot trash can. I looked down. It was empty. A few feet ahead sat Jane, looking dwarfish in an enormous wing-back chair, newspaper in her lap, again staring out the window at the street.

But I'm getting ahead of myself. I've started raining from the clear blue sky, as Max used to say, meaning that I haven't let the clouds build up. I've cheated you out of all the thunder and lightning. I've started near the end of the story, and I've skipped the beginning and the middle entirely. I've left out the Balzac and the climbing and the egg, and everything, really.

But when did it all start? It's hard to say. I suppose I could start with the night Max arrived, but it really began earlier, when my stepfather left us and when Lana found God. The summer I was supposed to go to camp, but then at the last minute, thanks to Max, didn't . . .

Chapter Two

To say that Lana was vindictive would be saying too little. Add to that spiteful, jealous, bitter, selfish, neglectful, cruel, manipulative, vain, and hypocritical, and you get a much more accurate portrait. Granted those are not the nicest things to call your mother, but when you consider that *Mother* was the name she least liked to be called, the others really aren't so bad.

For those, and many other reasons, men have always left Lana. When I was five years old, my father left. When I was twelve, my stepfather left. Six years seemed to be about the limit that any man could stand to be with her. Somehow, I made it through eighteen, although certainly not by choice and not without scars.

She met my father when they were both very young and working as lift operators at a ski resort. At first, they were just casual friends, but that all changed one drunken night when they ended up together in a sleeping bag on the shore of Lake Dillon and I was accidentally conceived. That was their first mistake. Shortly thereafter, they made their second; they got married.

Jake, my father, was (and still is) a ski bum, which means that he has never wanted anything more from life than to search for untracked snow during the day and to drink beer with his buddies at night. Although that was sufficient for him, it was not nearly enough for Lana, who had read far too many Judith Krantz novels by then and expected her life to be full of champagne flutes, designer clothes, and yacht trips around the Mediterranean. Some of my earliest memories are of Lana giving very shrill vent to her material frustrations (reading Ms. Krantz had also given her an outline for dramatic tantrum throwing). My father would listen and nod his head, sometimes try to appease her, but usually he'd just grab his keys and coat and leave, not returning until the bars had closed.

One night, and unfortunately I was only about four years old at the time so I don't remember the specifics, Lana must have pushed him too far. They argued, and my father, as usual, headed out to the bar, but this time he did not return at closing time, or even the next morning. He did not return at all. She called the police and filed a missing persons' report, and the next day a massive search was begun.

Lana loved all the attention and gave several tearful accounts of his disappearance to eager television and newspaper reporters. About a week later the search was called off when we got a letter from Canada, which was, I suppose, as far away from her as my dad could imagine getting. He sent her all the money he had, said he would send more when he could, and that was it. He was gone. Out of our lives. I don't really hold it against him; I'm sure I'd have left, too, if I'd been married to her, but I've never stopped begrudging him for leaving me behind.

Years later I learned that he did try to call and did send me letters, but Lana was vindictive and mean, so I never knew. She hung up whenever he called and must have thrown away anything that he ever sent. Consequently, I did not see my father again until I was in college, and then it was an awkward meeting, in an airport bar, between two strangers who each felt as though they should have known more about the other. For the most part the conversation was slow and stilted, but on one topic it flowed like water down a hill; that topic was our mutual dislike of Lana.

UNCLE MAX

Alone after my father left, Lana bundled up all of her things from our trailer and moved back into her parents' tiny house in Littleton. Since I was too big to leave on the doorstep of a fire station or push down the river in a reed basket, she packed me up and dragged me along, too. My grandparents, recently retired and happy to have the house to themselves, were not thrilled to be our hosts. Nevertheless, my grandmother, ever eager to play the martyr, did open her door to us—although I think she did it just so she could practice her bothered sigh. She helped get Lana a job as a receptionist in the office of a plastic surgeon. And since Lana did not yet have enough money for daycare, my grandmother sighed and reluctantly agreed to watch me during the day.

What I remember most from this time are two things. First, I watched an awful lot of TV. Second, it was the first time I ever heard of Max.

From the moment I got up in the morning, I was plopped down in front of the television.

"Dillon," my grandmother would say, "why don't you take your cereal and go watch some TV. That Captain Kangaroo's on. Hurry now; you don't want to miss it."

My grandmother seemed to do nothing but sit at the kitchen table with her ever-present can of Tab, smoking cigarettes, doing her nails, and flipping through travel brochures for cruises of the Caribbean. My grandfather stuck to the small greenhouse he'd built behind the house, in which he was forever potting and repotting his orchids, and listening to talk radio on his Walkman. In fact, the Walkman was pretty much always on. From sunup to sundown, even during meals, he wore his headphones, which was fine because he never had much to say other than to shake his head every now and then and yell something on the order of "THIS COUNTRY'S GOING TO HELL IN A HAND BASKET" or "NUKE 'EM BACK TO THE STONE AGE!"

To which, my grandmother would nod, take a sip of her Tab, and reply, "Yes, dear."

After we'd eaten, he'd return to the greenhouse or retrieve his metal detector from the garage and wander the neighborhood, digging up stray dimes and bottle caps as he went, yelling salutations at the neighbors. On rare occasions, like my birthday or on one of his good-humored days when he'd been nipping from the bottle of rum he kept hidden in his workbench, I was allowed to help with the repotting or go with him on his treasure hunts. But usually when I asked, he'd just pat me on the head and yell, "WHY DON'T YOU GO WATCH SOME TV!"

So I watched TV. Hours and days and weeks of TV. Cartoons, talk shows, soap operas, reruns, local news, on and on, over and over again. On top of the TV were several framed family photos, to which my attention would sometimes drift when the morning cartoons gave way to the afternoon soap operas. There was my grandparents' wedding picture, pictures of Lana as a baby, and Lana on her first day of school, and Lana artfully posed and airbrushed for her senior class picture. Far to the left of these was a small hinged metal frame that opened like a book. On one side was a photo of Lana when she was about ten. On the other was a boy, about my age, with very black hair and a menacing smile on his face. I asked about him one day while I was helping my grandfather with the repotting. His brow furrowed and he stopped what he was doing. Then he shook his head and yelled, "THE DEVIL'S CHILD, THAT BOY."

I waited for him to elaborate but he just went back to his potting, shaking his head angrily.

My childish curiosity was piqued by this response, which I took quite literally, having recently watched a matinee of *Rosemary's Baby;* so later that afternoon when I was having my snack, I asked my grandmother about it.

"Nana, who's that dark-haired boy in the picture frame on the TV?"

She paused midstroke in her nail painting and gave me an angry look, like the one she gave me when I set my glass on one of the end tables without a coaster. She took a long drag on her cigarette and arched one of her penciled-in eyebrows.

"That," she said, her voice revealing her distaste, "was your mother's little brother, your uncle, but he's with the angels in heaven now."

"He's dead?" I asked, more than a little confused about how the devil's child could be with the angels in heaven.

"Mmm," she replied, and nodded vaguely. "Oh look, it's almost three o'clock already," she said, lifting me up from my chair and directing me toward the living room. "Isn't your show on? That one with all the little puppets in the colored neighborhood? Take your snack with you; that's a good boy. And be sure and use a coaster."

I went back to my spot in front of the TV but as soon as she left I took the frame down from its spot once more. It was odd to look at that picture—a picture of someone roughly my own age—and know that he was dead.

Later that night, during my bath, while Lana was perched on the toilet lid filing her nails, I asked her about him.

"How did your brother die?" I ventured, as gently and gravely as I could, afraid she might erupt in a flood of tears and wailing. Instead, her brow wrinkled and she looked confused.

"Die? He's not dead," she said, indignantly, "Well, probably not yet, anyway. Which one of them told you that?"

"Nana."

"Well, that figures," she sneered.

"But what happened to him?" I asked.

She stopped filing her nails and smiled devilishly. "Oh, he was trouble, that boy. He had some trouble—" she said and seemed just about to tell me about it, but then caught herself and thought better of it. "He, uh, didn't get along with Nana and Grandpa so he ran away, or they kicked him out, I don't remember which one it was that last time. I was away then, up at Keystone."

This was hardly a satisfactory response.

"But why did they say he was dead?" I asked. Again Lana started, but then stopped herself and her expression darkened.

"Look, kiddo," she said, stabbing at the air in front of me with the nail file, her tone suddenly serious and impatient. "You just zip your lips on the subject for now. We can talk about it all you want someday when we're out of here, but don't bring it up anymore. They're sick of us as it is so don't you go and make it worse. Got it?"

I nodded, and sunk down among the bubbles. We did not speak of it again, and the next day I noticed that the picture-book frame had disappeared from its place on the TV. I thought about it a lot after that, trying to imagine what he'd done that everyone was so afraid to talk about, but soon all thoughts of him were replaced by another man who appeared in our lives.

As I said, Lana was young then, blonde, blue-eyed, pretty, and prone to wearing tight sweaters, short skirts, patterned stockings, and lots of lip gloss. Indeed, that was why she had been hired at the plastic surgeon's office. The doctor she worked for was well into middle age and it didn't take long for him to take more than a professional interest in her. His midlife crisis had begun the year before and he'd treated the symptoms with the purchase of a vintage Jaguar. Although this undoubtedly made him feel young and free for a while, I'm sure, as with most accessories, the novelty eventually wore off. Lana, with her firm skin and youthful breasts, was surely closer to what he was looking for, so she soon became his next accessory. That she had an accessory of her own—namely, me—he didn't seem to mind. He had two college-age daughters and a wife himself, so I was hardly the biggest nuisance in his life. In due time, he shed his wife and replaced her with Lana. She became his new model, his upgrade, his trophy wife. I was the trophy wife's baggage, but as I said, he really didn't mind my existence.

Lana, on the other hand, came to mind it a great deal. To her I suppose I was a symbol of her youthful folly, of poor decisions she had made, of failures in her early life, of her advancing age. For those reasons, shortly after she met James, my future stepfather, she developed an aversion, an allergy almost, to the word *mother*, or any synonyms thereof. From then on, I was instructed to call her "Lana" and to keep quiet and stay out of the way as much as possible. She had always been neglectful and indifferent toward me, but when she met James that indifference transformed into an active dislike.

Like many people who were spoiled as children, I suppose Lana was incapable of loving a child, even one of her own. Sensing this coldness and hostility from an early age (if I'd been brain-dead, I could have sensed it) I naturally gravitated toward my stepfather, James. Over time, I like to think that James grew fond of me, too. He often took me swimming or horseback riding or to baseball games. And yet, instead of being happy that her son and husband were getting along, Lana was jealous of our friendship and never tired of cautioning James about spoiling me.

"I really mean it," she'd say. "You're making a brat out of him."

To which he'd just laugh and then haul me up onto his shoulders and ride me around the living room while Lana seethed, her eyes narrowing into angry slits.

In spite of that, for a few years after their marriage, we all lived more or less happily in a large condominium near downtown. James would have been perfectly content to stay there, but Lana had other ideas. She had a rich husband and thought that she should, of course, have a home reflective of that wealth. Over the years she'd made friends—women she'd met while volunteering for the Junior League and the Junior Symphony Guild—who were all leaving the city en masse and moving to the suburban communities of large custom homes that were then sprouting up to the south. It all sounded so attractive and new and clean and ritzy that Lana decided she just had to join them.

Initially, James was reluctant. He liked living in town and being close to everything—his office, the country club, the restaurants and sports stadiums—but over time Lana manipulated him into submission. She had an almost feline, little girlish way of whining and pouting that was, together with her tight sweaters and glossed lips, attractive to him. Usually, she got what she wanted. This time was no exception. She found a new development of massive houses and had James sign on with the developer to build a custom home. She then hired an architect, a general contractor, and an interior designer. Although initially, James had reservations, he came to share her enthusiasm for the early planning phase of the project. Night after night I'd find them sitting on the sofa sharing a bottle of wine and going over blueprints and floor plans and swatches of fabric.

No one could ever accuse Lana of being temperate, which became readily apparent in her plans for her new palace. At first, the design for the house and the surrounding property was grand, but with Lana in charge it quickly became grandiose, verging on gaudy. Armed with back issues of *Architectural Digest*, and with her nelly, bald decorator by her side, she envisioned marble entryways and elaborate iron railing. She laid out intricate tile patterns for each of the bathrooms and planned to fill them with tiny sinks and bidets and toilets and with huge tubs that would whirl and shoot jets of water from several different angles. Her kitchen was to be a vision of heart maple, polished black granite, and industrial-size brushed-metal appliances. It would have been more than adequate for even the most discriminating chef. For the rest of the house, she chose elaborate wood floors, Persian carpets, and window treatments all complemented by a lighting system that could be controlled with a clap of the hands.

Only later, when James began to get the bills for her plans, did he protest, but by then it was too late. Lana had tasted domestic luxury and it was ambrosia. She knew just the setting in which she wanted to live, and she would do anything to get it. Never would she return to a trailer, not even to a condo in the city. This was it. She had not "arrived," but she was well on her way; and like any addict, her needs only increased over time and her demands became more insistent and shrewish. It was then that she and James began to argue.

Being older then, I remember these fights much more clearly than those between Jake and Lana. They were always about money—money she needed to pay the architect, money for the developer, money for the interior designer. She needed deposits for the window coverings, for the upgrade to the nickle-plated plumbing fixtures, and to tear out and reinstall the kitchen cabinets because the initial plan, according to the designer, "just would not do."

Each morning before he left for work, Lana would corner James in the foyer of the condo and block the door with her body. She'd then present him with a list of people's names and the amounts they needed, and she would not move until she had several signed checks in hand. James grumbled and questioned, and Lana whined and whimpered and blubbered about how much work she was putting in, driving back and forth to the house, and how he wasn't helping at all, and how it would all be worth it in the end. Eventually, usually because he was sick of arguing and didn't want to be late, he would give in, take out his checkbook, and start writing.

One year, several hundred tantrums, and God knows how many tens of thousands of dollars later, the house remained unfinished. Nevertheless, Lana decided that we would move in as scheduled so she could keep a better eye on the day-to-day progress. This was another of her big mistakes. A very costly mistake that she paid for with her marriage.

The house, at that point, was nothing more than a cavernous, dusty, incomplete shell, in which noisy workers came and went all day long. It was filled with ladders and lumber and tools, and the air buzzed with the sounds of sanders and compressors. At night, Lana took over from the machinery and whined and pleaded and yelled at James. It was a miserable time for all of us but especially for James. He not only had to bankroll all of the misery, he also had to spend hours each day commuting to and from his office in gridlock traffic.

At first, I rode with him, since I was to finish out the year at my old school and then start junior high in our new neighborhood. On our mornings together I noticed how his mood would brighten (despite his invariable bout with Lana and the checkbook) as we drove toward downtown. He'd hum and whistle and talk to me about school and cars and golf. Conversely, in the evening, as we headed back home, he was always silent; if he did speak, it was only to give curt responses to any of the questions I might ask him.

About two months after we moved in, shortly after school ended and I began my summer vacation, a frustrated James informed us that he would be attending a two-week-long conference in Argentina. He went (with his secretary, we later found out). After the first week, he called to inform Lana that when he returned, it would not be to the house or to her. She could keep the house, he said, she could keep her car, she could even keep some of his money, but she could not keep him.

To vain Lana, this made absolutely no sense. That James had left his first wife for her was understandable. That he would leave her—for any reason—was incomprehensible.

"He must have been playing golf all day without a hat on," she said, chuckling confidently as she drove me to the orthodontist one morning. "You watch, he'll come crawling back. And when he does I'll be ready. He'll have to pay for this one! I'll get that Bisaza tile in the bathroom, just you watch me!"

But weeks passed and James did not come back. Lana was a little uneasy, but his Jaguar was still in the garage and if it was not entirely unthinkable that he would leave her, it would be folly to think that he would leave both her *and* his precious car. As a precautionary measure, she had the lock on the garage door changed and kept the only key on a chain around her wrist.

Meanwhile, the workmen, as insistent and as vocal for their money as a nest full of starving baby birds, feared a connection between James's long absence and their sudden lack of checks. Lana, clad in a skirt that was shorter than usual and a gauzy shirt with no bra, addressed their concerns one morning. She pooh-poohed their suspicions and told them, in honeyed tones, that James was just off doing some work in Argentina and had forgotten to sign any checks before he left.

"Those Argentines! They just love that reconstructive surgery! He's very busy," she cooed, shaking her own augmented mammaries.

On witnessing this pathetic display, the interior decorator immediately packed up all his samples and left. The contractor threatened to pull all of his men off the job, but like all the rest of the straight male workers, he was bewitched by Lana's feminine charms and said he reckoned it wouldn't hurt to wait a little longer.

A month passed and still no word. Then one day a perky young paralegal appeared on the scene and served Lana with divorce papers. This shook her composure a little, but still she held on, figuring that if he did actually intend to divorce her (which she still didn't believe), she could bleed him white in the process. She took the papers to her closet, stashed them far from the eyes of the workmen and emerged again in the gauzy shirt she planned to wear that evening for her meeting with the contractor. The same contractor who had telephoned more than once that day demanding, "A check! In my hands! Today, lady!"

Then something happened that Lana could not have foreseen and that all of her tricks were powerless against. The aforementioned contractor had come to our house, been unswayed by her tits, and collected the check (on which she had, in a panic, forged James's signature). He then disappeared. Forever.

Over the next few days, it came to the attention of the developer's accountant that massive amounts of money were missing from several different jobs, and that all of the accounts overseen by our contractor were empty. On closer inspection, it was revealed that the contractor's energy and enthusiasm (on which Lana had often commented) were largely drug induced, and for a long time he had been embezzling money in order to finance his little habit. Rather than face death or dismemberment at the hands of his dealer or prosecution at the hands of the bank, he had fled, taking Lana's hot check with him. The news of his departure spread among the workmen like the news of a coming tornado, and they wasted no time packing up their tools and materials and driving back down the hill.

And that was it. The end of the work and the beginning of our isolation. The next day our cul-de-sac was like a ghost town. All construction on our house and the houses around it came to an absolute halt and did not begin again for more than a year. Our house, due to Lana's impatience, was the only standing structure. The others were nothing more than driveways leading up to big holes in the ground. Some had concrete foundations; some had the skeletal beginnings of wood framing; but most were just eerie, lonely, muddy holes. There was no traffic on our street, other than the mailman, who came once a day. There were no streetlights. In fact, there was nothing but sidewalks and mud and empty prairie stretching off for miles in all directions.

Chapter Three

Of course, there were eventually phone conversations between James and Lana, as much as I'm sure James would have liked to avoid them. One in particular stands out in my mind. I remember it mainly because, for a while, it was the end of the phone and because it was the beginning of Lana's drinking.

"So greeaaat!" Lana said. She has a flat sarcastic way of saying "great" that makes the word sound anything but.

"Greeaaat. You're saying I can have the house but I can't have the money to finish the fucking thing! Greeaaat. No paint, no carpeting, no landscaping. Fucking fantastic! . . . Uh huh . . . uh huh . . . Well, here's what I think of you and your fucking pre-nup!" She yanked the cord from the wall and threw it and the receiver off the balcony and into the muddy field behind the house. At this point I crept off my barstool at the kitchen counter and moved to the relative safety of the living room. I watched her through the window as she paced angrily back and forth on the deck, puffing furiously on her cigarette. Then suddenly she stopped. She clenched her jaw and looked back into the house. She pitched the remainder of her cigarette the same direction she had pitched the phone, blew out a huge plume of smoke, and marched back through the kitchen to the hall closet. She opened it, selected one of James's titanium drivers from his golf bag and then marched off into the garage. A moment later I heard several dull thuds followed by the sound of breaking glass. A few moments after that Lana reappeared, her hair a mess, her face streaked with mascara tears, and the club (now bent in the middle) still in her hand. She dropped it absently on the floor and then walked slowly up the stairs to her bedroom. I waited a few minutes after I heard her door shut and then crawled out from my hiding space behind the sofa. Quietly, I made my way toward the garage. I opened the door slowly, so the hinge wouldn't creak and peeked in. The overhead light was on and I saw just what I'd expected but could still hardly believe. James's treasured Jaguar—the one Lana had always hated because she suspected (and probably rightly so) that he loved it more than her—now had a shattered windshield and several pronounced dents in its hood. I'm sure she could easily have done more damage, but I've always suspected that she was probably stricken by remorse in the middle of her deed, by the thought that maybe this was taking things a little too far, by the realization that if the marriage wasn't completely lost, this would ensure it. I shuddered as I looked at it: the cracked green paint and the exposed metal underneath, the tiny shards of glass, almost like thousands of tiny ice cubes, now covering the seats and the floorboards. I had rarely seen James angry, but I knew he would be livid when he saw this.

That's when Lana took to the bottle. It was an easy thing for her to do because instead of a basement, her custom home had been outfitted with an elaborate wine cellar, stocked with wines that someone (someone to whom James had written a big fat check, no doubt) thought were worthy of having in a suburban wine cellar. For months after the Jaguar clubbing, I never saw Lana sober. I would get up in the mornings, dress and feed myself, and then wander down the muddy street to the main road where the school bus would collect me. When I returned, she would already have started drinking. At least one bottle of wine would be open and she would be slumped on the couch, in the middle of her dusty palace, either watching TV or flipping through the pages of a magazine. I would kiss her on the cheek, ask her if there was anything she wanted, to which she'd usually respond by grunting and shaking her head, and then I'd go and fix myself a snack in the kitchen. When I finished eating, I'd go upstairs to my room and do my homework or my finger exercises on my clarinet, never daring to actually play it for fear of sparking her rage or annoyance. Later, when I was fairly sure she had passed out, I'd tiptoe back down and collect all the bottles and glasses and empty the ashtray. I'd gently cover her with a blanket and then, as quietly as I could, tiptoe back upstairs and read until I fell asleep.

I was so quiet and careful because to wake her, or to disturb her in any way was to risk unleashing a beast whose words were sharper than any teeth or claws.

"You know why he left, don't you," she seethed at me one drunken afternoon when she'd cornered me in the kitchen. I said nothing.

"Well, I'm 'onna tell you." She stood before me, swaying, wine bottle in one hand, cigarette in the other.

"He left a'cause a you!" she spat. "He was sick of having a brat around! Same reason your shitheaded dad left. Sick of you cryin' all the time in that fuckin shithole trailer, sick of the smell of diapers! Sick of it all! Sick of you! Nobody wants fuckin' kids around. Nobody!"

Shocking words, but it was not the first time I'd heard them and I knew better than to give any response. I had learned that responding at all only made things worse. Protest was useless. Indignation was useless. Crying was useless. I just stood there and took it, which is not to say it didn't hurt. Each blow struck me, destroyed little pieces of me, but I could never show it.

In elementary school I'd learned a game called Stone Face, in which two players square off and just stare at one another, each trying to maintain an expression that is completely impassive. This would go on until one of the two cracked, until someone twitched or broke into a fit of giggles. I never lost at that game. Life with Lana had made me a pro at Stone Face. Each time she went into one of her angry tirades, I immediately started the game and erected the blank facade, behind which my soul would quietly implode and collapse in on itself.

"It's a'cause you that we have to live in . . . this!" she shouted, gesturing at the huge, unfinished house.

"God! To think what I could've been if it weren't for fuckin' kids!"

Although my home life was miserable, it was, believe it or not, preferable to the wretchedness I was then enduring at my new school.

Junior high. That warehouse of raging hormones, angst, and acne in which society places it's twelve- to fourteen-year-olds. The place where differences are delineated and a caste system based on physical beauty, sports prowess, and popularity is established. Sadly, I found myself on the bottom rung of this new social ladder.

To make matters worse, my own hormones chose that point to release themselves in my body and wreak havoc. Seemingly overnight I was six feet tall, weighed a whopping 102 pounds, and wore a size eleven shoe. Acne bloomed on my chin, nose, and forehead, and my voice creaked when I spoke like an out-of-tune bagpipe. Add to that a new mouthful of braces and unwieldy headgear, and you've got a good snapshot of my adolescence.

But the worst part—the most torturous thing about it for me—was the fact that my newfound hobby, masturbation, did not at all involve thoughts of the opposite sex. The guilt of having thoughts about sex at all was bad enough, but the guilt of having thoughts about members of my own sex increased it tenfold.

Lonely, ugly, and afraid, I kept to myself as much as I possibly could in my new school. It was not all that hard to do except in gym class when I was forced to interact. This was torture. I was horribly uncoordinated, and it seemed that every activity involved some sort of a ball—hitting a ball, catching a ball, throwing a ball. I couldn't do any of it very well. I'd never had a dad or an older brother to do these things with. James had taken me swimming sometimes, but we had never played any games with a ball! In this gym class it was nothing but ball sports—football, baseball, basketball, dodge ball, medicine ball—and each day I was assaulted with the comments: "You throw like a girl!" "You dribble like a pussy!" "You couldn't catch that ball with a glove the size of the Grand Canyon!" Or, when they were feeling especially eloquent and succinct they'd just yell, "Fag!"

The class itself was agony, but what came after was a lower circle of hell.

"Okay, men!" the big-gutted gym teacher would bark. "Hit the showers!" and we were all prodded into the locker room and ordered to strip. It was torture. My body was not pretty. I was tall, alarmingly thin, and just beginning to sprout pubic hair, of which I was terribly embarrassed because there were only a few other guys in class who had any. I was also terrified because I really wanted to look at all the other bodies, but whenever even the vaguest thought of it crossed my mind, I could feel something stirring in my loins and, in the words of Lana's decorator, "that just would not do." That could not be. I could not be the "Fag!" they had branded me. So, every day when I stripped down, I kept my eyes on the floor. Then, lifting my head, I'd stare over the heads of all the nubile male flesh and march resolutely to the huge open shower room. I went quickly because from the time I got my underwear off to the time I reached the shower—a space of probably five seconds—I could already feel my dick stirring and I knew that I had to get to the shower fast, or else! Once there, I turned facing the wall and twisted the tap labeled *C* as far to the right as it would go. Only when the icy needles of water hit me, and I felt my balls retreat and my scrotum tighten up, did I relax and release the shuddering breath I'd been holding since dropping my underwear. I would thoroughly chill myself before returning to my locker, so that hopefully the cold would last at least until my dick was safely back inside my underwear. This procedure was effective, but it was also responsible for the charming little nickname that I was given and that stuck with me all through school.

Goose—on account of the fact that when I returned to my locker after my arctic shower, my skin was covered with goose pimples.

My principle torturer at this time was a boy named Aaron Lewis. Aaron was Italian-looking, with black hair and brown eyes, a square jaw and a Roman nose. I wish he had not been so good-looking because, if he had been ugly, it would have been even easier to hate him. In many ways he was everything I was not: he was good at sports; he was good-looking and well developed; and he had nice clothes that always seemed to fit him. By contrast, I was clumsy, ugly, skinny, and stuck with last year's fashions since Lana had been too drunk to take me shopping.

That my clothes were out of style was bad enough, but I'd also grown so much over the past few months that my pants never reached past midcalf and my shirtsleeves never covered my skinny wrists. Aaron had clear skin and straight teeth that didn't need braces let alone headgear with a hideous, robin's-egg blue, satin strap, which was the only color the orthodontist had besides pink.

Of course Aaron was popular and always had a group of boys or girls hanging around him. He was always talking, in his loud and cocky way, or laughing, or playing some sort of game, usually at my expense. At lunch, he held court at his table in the center of the cafeteria, surrounded by his gang and all the pom-pom girls. I sat alone or, if the tables were full and that wasn't an option, with the "special needs" kids, who were even more outcast than I, but within whose ranks I was easily camouflaged with my too-small clothes and my headgear. Most often, though, I would grab whatever food

I could carry in my pockets and go to the library or the band room. These two places were preferable to the playground, since I knew sand wouldn't be poured down my pants and my shoes wouldn't be taken and tossed around the playground while I made vain attempts to catch them as they flew back and forth above my head.

Looking back I see that I was like the chicken with the blood spot that all the others peck at. I don't know why I was singled out—perhaps because I was new, perhaps because I was ugly, perhaps because I never gave any reaction to being tormented. I just sat there, stoically, while Aaron wrung out a wet sponge on my head in art class or stuffed me into a hall locker. I never fought; I never cried out. I just let my body go where they pushed it and then waited patiently in the dark for the janitor to pry the door open. Aaron and his friends would trip me in the hallway so that I'd fall and send books scattering in front of me or sit behind me in history class and pepper the back of my head and neck with spitwads shot through a straw they'd saved from lunch. They'd grab my backpack in the morning and throw it on top of the school building or push my face down into the fountain when I leaned over to get a drink. But I never fought back and I never told.

I know I'm painting a pathetic picture here, I feel it myself. I'm putting things down as accurately as I can remember, and yet even I am thinking "How pathetic!" Even I am wondering why I didn't fight back, why I didn't tell anyone. But then I remember the fear: the fear of reprisals, both physical and mental; the fear of Lana hearing from someone else how pathetic and weak her son was; the fear of making things worse both at school and at home, which is all I could imagine would happen if I protested.

As awful as my life sounds then, it was not without moments of joy. In fact, two things made it bearable. The first was playing my clarinet, and the second—well, it will be apparent all too soon.

I had started playing the clarinet a few years before in elementary school, when I'd joined the band and was allowed to pick out an instrument. I'd wanted to play the flute, but Lana had squashed that idea, telling me I would just have to pick something else because the flute was "a girl's instrument." I tried the violin next, but after listening to a torturous five minutes of my practicing that first night she nixed that choice, too. I came to the clarinet by default, I guess, but I grew to love it so much I might have switched to it anyway. The band teacher at my new junior high, Mr. Sullivan, was a clarinet player himself so he favored our section and favored me because I was a good player. I wasn't especially talented but I did practice when I could, which was more than most of the other kids would do.

The first day, we were given several songs to take home and practice. One was "Rainy Days and Mondays." Later that night, as I sat in my room, silently doing the finger exercises so as not to wake up Lana, I noticed that underneath the bars and notes on the page, the words to the song were also printed out. Like most adolescents I was attracted to the dark, romantic, almost-doomed-but-ultimately-hopeful lyrics, but it went beyond that. I felt that someone had taken all the chaotic, jumbled feelings I'd had over the past few months and somehow made sense of them, given substance to the airy nothing. For the first time since we'd moved to the house, I didn't feel completely alone.

In class, the band was having immense trouble translating the notes on the page into anything resembling the song. After a week of listening to us wheeze and snort and squeak through it, a frustrated Mr. Sullivan brought in a record so we could hear what the song was supposed to sound like. I think I'll always remember that day; the sight of him lowering the needle onto the record, the faint sound of the scratches as it eased into the groove, the soft piano and mournful harmonica at the beginning, and then that voice! That deep, rich, impossibly low alto. It sent chills all through me and I had the feeling that all of my hair was standing straight up. By the end of the song I was swallowing hard and my eyes were watering.

Immediately I felt a kinship with that voice, not just the sound and how its low tones were so similar to those of the clarinet, but with the person singing those sad lyrics.

After class, after all the other students had filed out, I went up to Mr. Sullivan and asked who it was.

"Ahh, you liked that, did you? That was Karen Carpenter. Great voice, huh." I nodded. "Did it help you get an idea how the song is supposed to sound?"

"Yes . . ." I said, hesitating.

"You seem to play pretty well, though. I can tell you practice, and I appreciate it. Keep it up."

He started gathering up his papers and was getting ready to leave.

"Um, sir?" I asked, timidly. He looked up at me. I fingered my headgear nervously.

"Do you think maybe, if I was really careful with it, I could borrow that record some time, maybe make a tape of it?"

He chuckled.

"Here," he said, going over to the stack of records next to the small portable player. "You can have it. I got it for fifty cents at a used vinyl place. Not many people want Carpenters' records nowadays."

And he was right. The year was 1985 and I don't think the Carpenters were ever less in vogue. They had been relegated to the music world's Hall of Shame, right next to ABBA and the soundtrack to *Saturday Night Fever*. Of course, in later years, they were dusted off and made fashionable again; but in the eighties, they were not something spoken of with anything other than derision.

He gave me the record in its tan jacket, with the horribly dated photo of Richard and Karen on the liner, and I thanked him.

"It's too bad about her," he said. "They made such a good team."

I looked up at him, questioningly. "Too bad?"

"Oh she's dead," he said. "Anorexia. Starved herself to death. Never happy with her appearance, I guess, when her appearance was the last thing anyone cared about."

"Was that her husband?" I asked, pointing to the picture on the liner. He laughed.

"Oh God, no, that's her brother, Richard. They look pretty geeky, eh?" I nodded.

"Was she ever . . . married?" I asked, timidly.

"Who, Karen? You know, I don't know. Why? You carrying a little torch for our Karen?" he asked, teasingly.

I turned crimson. Me: nerdy band fag, standing there in my too-small clothes and my headgear with the robin's-egg-blue satin strap, clutching my clarinet case and a Carpenters' album. Since I couldn't disappear into the carpet, I switched the subject.

"I, uh, I can't really practice at home," I said. "It kinda bothers La-, er, my mom. Is there any way I could maybe practice here. Like, during lunch, I mean."

He looked at me, trying to read my face. He saw something there—fear, most likely—and his expression softened. He turned his attention to his teacher's book, resting on the podium, and flipped through the pages.

"Let's see, well, we have staff meetings here during your lunchtime on Mondays, and the choir rehearses here on Thursday, but you're welcome to come the other days. Are you sure you want to?" he asked.

I gave an eager nod.

"Okay then, it's all yours."

And so I was able to escape the cafeteria and the playground every Tuesday, Wednesday, and Friday, which was nice but still left me vulnerable to attack on Mondays and Thursdays.

One of Aaron's cleverest stunts happened one day as I was coming out of the band room. I was headed to the bathroom before my next class, but at the entrance, Aaron stepped in front of me. This was bad. I said nothing, did not try to go around him, but just looked down at the carpet and waited.

"Hey, Goose," he said. "Do you know what time it is?"

Nervously, I consulted my watch and mumbled that it was twelve forty-five.

"Are you sure, Goose," Aaron said, shaking his head from side to side, a savage grin on his face. "Cos I don't think so. It's not twelve forty-five. Check again."

My head down, I looked at my watch again.

"What time is it?" I said, my voice barely audible.

"What's that, Goose? You say something?" I kept my eyes down at my feet. My face hot with embarrassment and anger. He waited in silence.

"What time is it?" I asked again, hoping that if I cooperated it would be over soon.

"You hear that, guys?" Aaron said, looking around to his friends who were now circled around me. "Goose wants to know what time it is."

The friends laughed and moved in closer.

"It's time, Goose. It's time . . . to get wet!"

And suddenly, four of his gang took hold of me—two had my legs; two had my arms—and together they lifted me off the ground and hauled me into the bathroom. There, I was turned upside down and my head held inside the toilet bowl, which they flushed repeatedly. I emerged, gasping for air, my hair swirled on top of my head, while they all laughed. I stood dripping, as stoic and agonized as St. Sebastian, wishing I could just die and get it over with.

For a while after that, I made it a point to never drink anything during the course of the day so that I'd never need to go within fifty feet of the bathroom. If I had to go, I just held it until I got home. Then I ran up the muddy street to the house, as fast as I could, to finally relieve my poor bladder.

On one such day, I ran up the hill, whipped open the front door, eager to get to the bathroom, and was greeted by Lana's scowling head, peeking over the back of the sofa, which she was in the process of vacuuming.

"Hey!" she yelled. "Take off those muddy shoes before you come in here!"

I was shocked, not because she seemed concerned about me tracking mud onto a plywood floor, but by the fact that she was up, and appeared sober, and was using the vacuum—a machine I was not even aware she knew the location of. It was odd, but the next day was even more so: I came home, as usual, full-to-bursting, and as I reached the house I noticed a strange car in the driveway. It was not the Jaguar, or Lana's little white BMW, but a large boxy Oldsmobile. I approached it and peeked inside. From the rearview mirror hung a cardboard air freshener, but instead of being shaped like a leaf, or a flower, or a piece of fruit, this one was in the shape of a crucifix. I remember looking at it and wondering what smell they could possibly have assigned to that. I wondered also who the car belonged to and in what condition they had found Lana. I didn't want to go in, but my bladder bade me do otherwise. I opened the door and took off my muddy shoes as quietly as I could. Low voices were coming from the living room, but I had to pee so badly that I knew I'd have to wait to see who they belonged to. I ducked into the tiny bathroom under the staircase, the one in which the ceiling was so low I could barely stand. I did my business, zipped up my still-too-tight pants, and was about to flush when I heard voices just outside the door. I hesitated. The Oldsmobile owner must be leaving. I turned off the light and opened the door just a crack. There was Lana, and I was relieved to see that she was dressed and had combed her hair, although she still had not put on any makeup and looked pinched and tired. She was talking to a man, probably in his forties, not fat, but large and in clothes that fit him as tightly as my own. His hair was stiffly styled, like a newscaster's, and parted severely to one side, exposing a white valley of scalp. He was not unattractive, but there was an excessive neatness about him, and something synthetic in his tight-lipped smile and soft expression.

"Think about what I've told you," he said, taking Lana's hands in his. "Will you do that?" She nodded.

"And look over some of the literature? If you have any questions, we can talk about it next time, okay? Or you could call me." Again, she nodded.

"Thank you," she said, and for a moment they held eye contact. He gave her hands a final squeeze and left.

Although I didn't know it then, as I stood hiding in the little bathroom, Lana had found herself a new man. One who would always love her and never leave her, no matter how big of a bitch she became. No, it was not the Oldsmobile owner, but, rather, his boss. None other than Our Lord Jesus Christ.

The Oldsmobile owner was Wayne Blandings, and he was the assistant pastor at The Church of the Divine Redeemer. It was the church our cleaning lady attended, and she had sent him over after she had come by one day and found Lana so sauced she couldn't even speak. After that first meeting, Wayne came by frequently and often brought other "spiritual counselors" with him. Many days I'd return home from school and (after I'd peed, of course) would go into the living room and find them all huddled around the coffee table holding hands with their eyes closed.

I suppose in some ways Lana's rebirth was a good thing. She did quit drinking and even decided that she ought to go back to school and try to get a job. This she had been encouraged to do by her attorney months ago, since there was some loophole in her prenuptial agreement with James that could be twisted to make him pay for the majority of her education. Until then, she had not been sober enough to even consider it, let alone actually do it, but then, with Jesus behind her she applied, and was accepted to, a nursing program at the city college downtown.

With her faith, a shiny goal, and a new church to attend, Lana was much happier, which made life somewhat easier for me. Unable to share her happiness (I was not a "believer"), I tried at least to be happy for her, and several nights a week I would accompany her to "the Gatherings," as they were called, which took place in an old abandoned K mart that had been transformed into a church.

I was wary of the church and of Lana's conversion, for much the same reason I am wary of parties where everyone has done hits of Ecstasy. In each situation the participants are all so unrelentingly friendly, they hug you and pat you and smile at you as though you're an intimate friend, but it's a false intimacy that has left out the entire gritty step of getting to know someone. I wasn't buying it. Especially since I saw how easily Lana could put it on. The second we walked through the big glass doors of the church, she'd switch on her smile and happy demeanor and be nice to everyone, including me. You'd have thought there were cameras rolling. And yet, it seemed that somewhere along the line Lana had missed the part about God being all-seeing and all-knowing, because as soon as we left she switched it off and became her demanding, impatient, bitchy self. At least with me.

After my first few gatherings, I was, without my consent, enrolled in the YFC group. Youth for Christ was a group composed of kids, roughly my age, who sat around in a circle, singing alarmingly right-wing folk songs, and talking about the hellfire and eternal torment that surely awaited those foolish heathens who had not accepted Jesus Christ as their personal savior. And I was duly afraid, although more of the other kids in the group than of what might happen to my poor filthy soul on Judgment Day.

At the end of the five weeks in the group, I was to be baptized and receive my first communion. Not having been baptized, I was a big novelty.

"Aren't you afraid?" one pop-eyed girl asked me. "What if you get hit by a bus before the five weeks? Why you'll go to Purgatory then."

"I never met anyone one wasn't baptized," one of the boys added. "Well, no one but Jews, anyway, but then that's a different bird altogether."

The gatherings grew weirder and weirder the more we attended.

There were fire-and-brimstone sermons, of course, but occasionally, when the pastor had really whipped his flock into a frenzy, the service would climax with "the laying on of hands." This little piece of theater involved some of the parishioners lining up before the altar and waiting for the pastor to touch their foreheads. When he did this, it was like a spiritual jump-start, and the person would fall backward, apparently unconscious, into the arms of waiting ushers. At other times, the people in the pews would move to the aisles and fall convulsing to the ground, or they would look blankly ahead and start speaking in tongues, which I found more reminiscent of the possessed girl in *The Exorcist*, than of the presence of the Lord. I found it frightening, yes, but more than that I was afraid that I might be called on to participate, which for someone as painfully shy and self-concious as I was would have been unimaginable. The amount of audience participation required at the church—the singing, the hand holding, the hugging and swaying back and forth, the shouting, "Halleluia" and "Praise the Lord!" and "Thank You, Jesus!"—was about more than my nerves could stand. I would often look with sympathy up at the agonized Jesus on the cross and think, *I know just how you feel!*

My first communion, however, did mark a turning point for me, although not in the way you might think. I did not have a spiritual awakening; I was not born again, but I did, quite by accident, discover a way to make it all a bit more bearable.

Chapter Four

On the day of communion, the pastor made his way down the line dropping the host on our awaiting tongues repeating, "The body of Christ?" as he went and marking our foreheads with the sign of the cross. After I'd swallowed the host, I waited patiently as Wayne, carrying the large silver chalice, made his way down the line. When he got to me, he brought the cup to my lips and said, gravely, "The cup of salvation."

I leaned forward obediently and took a sip, but then I realized I was in trouble. I had forgotten about my headgear. The metal frame had slid easily into the metal cup, but when I tried to pull back, the frame expanded and the whole chalice came with it. Wayne, looking perturbed, shook the cup slightly, but this only sloshed wine up my nose and onto my shirt. I was terribly embarrassed and looked up at him over the rim with pleading eyes. He jiggled some more, but that just spilled more wine. Finally, I opened my mouth and took several huge gulps. It was cheap, chalky tasting stuff, and like all children, I had a natural distaste for alcohol. But there was no alternative, so I kept sucking it in until the cup was nearly empty. Eventually, it occurred to me to squeeze the sides of the headgear and when I did the cup slid right off. It fell to the ground with a thud, followed by silence. I coughed several times, picked up the chalice, and handed it back to a bewildered Wayne. With all eyes on me, I returned to my seat in the pew next to Lana. She wouldn't even look at me. She just closed her eyes in prayer and shook her head, but I knew I'd catch hell for it later. I slumped as far down in the pew as I could. The initial embarrassment passed, but in a few moments I noticed how warm I still felt. My ears were hot and I feared they must be bright red, but I felt relaxed, too. For the first time in so many months I felt less . . . self-concious, I guess. The tension drained out of my shoulders, and I even felt as though I might be able to sing the next song instead of just mouthing the words as I usually did. It was a wonderful sensation and I found myself thinking that maybe there was something to all this Jesus hooha after all. Of course, the spell eventually wore off. I realized it had been the wine and not the Lord that had invigorated me, and it was then that I really went to the devil. I discovered the second thing that could make me really happy.

You'll recall that I mentioned Lana's having built a wine cellar underneath the house. Well, after my first communion I skipped the middle man and took to administering the sacrament myself. Late at night, after Lana was asleep, I'd venture down to the cellar from time to time and sneak bottles back up to my room. I loved how easy it was to recapture that warm relaxed feeling with just a few glasses and, having lived with Lana, I was so good at being quiet and making myself inconspicuous, that most people never even noticed a change in me. Few ever came close enough to smell my breath, and I was usually so clumsy and awkward anyway that any effect liquor had on the way I carried myself could be easily explained by my inordinately large feet.

Yes, I became a teenage alcoholic, as trite as that sounds. My drinking started out slowly, just a few swigs in the morning to give me the courage to face Aaron's tormenting, and then a few swigs when I got home to help me face Lana and Wayne (who were by this time seeing a lot of each other) and to help get me through that evening's inevitable tedious gathering.

Since my twelve-year-old's palate was fairly unsophisticated, I gravitated more toward the sweeter wines, and under my bed there was a growing collection of stubby port bottles. I developed a particular fondness for port; it was syrupy and sweet and seemed to go into my system much faster than other wines. I favored a brand called Sandeman, although more for the name and the label than the taste. The name reminded me of the Sandman, which I thought appropriate since the wine itself was a very effective sleep aid. I liked the label because I found it strangely erotic.

The logo consists of a male silhouette—a mysterious, sinister-looking figure—wearing a cape and a wide brimmed caballero's hat, holding up a tiny glass of the port. The figure seemed enigmatic and sexy to me then and I invested it with all sorts of meaning and significance. As I drank I would stare drunkenly at the dark man, imagining him as several different people: sometimes it was Aaron, ready to jump out at me and attack, and sometimes it was the mysterious faceless male I imagined when I masturbated, the one who would take me away from the miserable life in which I was trapped. Other times it was the devil, who was surely in possession of my wicked, drunken, perverted soul, and sometimes it was my father, whose face I could no longer remember. Sometimes it was my stepfather, James, and sometimes I even imagined it as the dark-haired boy I had seen in the picture-book frame so many years before in my grandparents' house.

When I had drunk enough and had recorked the bottle and rolled it back under my bed, I'd close my eyes and abandon myself to these spinning images. All of the men in my life, cloaked and masked, and menacingly silent, would whirl and dance in my head like a mobile; each part moving independently but still somehow attached to all the others.

Of course my drinking was discovered. Despite my best attempts to maintain my public poise, I got sloppy. My schoolwork was late, if I turned it in at all, and I started cutting gym class. Some days I didn't even bother to go to school but just wandered out past the bus stop into the prairie until I found a sunny grassy patch out of the wind where I'd read, and nap, and play my clarinet, my thermos full of port beside me.

My truancy eventually would have been detected, but it was an instrument check in band class that exposed me. It was nearing the end of the spring semester and we were to have a final concert that coming Friday. Mr. Sullivan and his assistant decided they should take a look at everyone's instruments before then, just to make sure there weren't any missing pads or bent keys. They did this section by section, and as fate would have it they got to the woodwinds on a morning when I'd had a few morning shots of cognac. I'd recently made the discovery that the warm feeling from cognac lasted a little longer through the day than a few swigs from the port bottle, so I'd started experimenting with it. That morning I'm afraid I overdid it. I'd miscalculated the dosage. My head was spinning and it was hard to keep my eyes focused. When they got to me, I removed my pickled reed from the mouthpiece so that Mr. Sullivan could replace it with his own fresh one and give it a few toots. I handed the clarinet over to him and as he was attaching his reed he got an odd look on his face, as if he'd discovered something really wrong with my instrument. He sniffed at the mouthpiece and then abruptly pulled back his head. He looked directly at me, his eyes wide, and stood up.

"Miss Johnson," he said, his eyes still on me, "could you take over for a minute? Dillon, please come with me."

I knew I was in trouble, but at that point I really didn't care. I got up, with difficulty, and stumbled my way through the class to where

Mr. Sullivan was waiting just outside the door, my clarinet still in his hand. He shut the door, pulled me by the arm into the middle of the deserted hallway, and sniffed at the air around my face.

"You've been drinking!"

I wobbled for a moment but before I could respond, I threw up.

What followed was a trip to the nurse's office, my arms over the shoulders of Mr. Sullivan and Miss Johnson. There, it was debated at length between the nurse, the principal, the assistant principal, the principal's secretary, the band teacher, and the guidance counselor whether they should call an ambulance, a social worker, or my mother. An hour later Lana arrived, dressed completely in white, looking saintly and fresh and cooly concerned. Like a snow-covered volcano, she hid her simmering fury and managed to sound as bewildered and worried as her acting talents would allow.

She said nothing to me in the nurse's office and nothing as we walked out to the car. She got in, put on her large white-framed sunglasses, and started the engine. She drove until we were a safe distance from the school and then she pulled over to the side of the road, reached over and slapped me as hard as she could. But I was numb. It was like part of me was dead. At school with them or at home with her, which hell did I prefer? I was proud of the fact that I had almost never cried in front of Lana, but then I could not help it and a single large tear rolled down my cheek. That was evidently a sufficient reaction; when she saw it, she repositioned herself in her seat, put the car in gear, and continued driving.

Church took up a lot of my time after that, although it was hardly by choice. I'd been suspended from school, which wasn't all that bad since there were only two weeks left until summer vacation. For a week or so after that, I was literally the center of attention at the gatherings. I stood in the middle of prayer circles while all the parishioners formed a chain around me. With their eyes closed, first one, then another, and then another, would spontaneously ask God to help me or command the devil to stop tempting me.

Another time I was called to the front of the congregation and the pastor led his flock in a round of "We renounce him!" This started slowly; the pastor, with his eyes closed, kept one hand on my forehead while holding the microphone in the other.

"Lord? Can you hear me, Lord?" he'd ask, as if the connection was a bit fuzzy. "Lord, we ask your help tonight for one of your children, young Dillon, who's been tempted away by Satan. Tempted away by a weakness of the flesh. He's been drinking, Lord, and having impure thoughts, and falling down that slippery slope of sin! We're all gathered here tonight in your name, Lord, to praise you and ask for your help for brother Dillon. Hear our prayer, Lord."

"Hear our prayer!" the congregation boomed.

"Give him strength, Lord!"

"Give him strength!"

"To resist the forces of Lucifer!

"Give him strength!"

"To resist his impure mind!"

"Give him strength!"

"To resist what he knows is an abomination in your eyes!"

"Give him strength!"

"To cleanse his thoughts and get back on the path of righteousness!"

"Give him strength!"

Give me a break!

You see, it wasn't just the drinking they were worried about. In fact, that became almost a footnote. When Lana drove me home from school that afternoon after the failed instrument check, she immediately searched my bedroom. Of course, she found the stash of bottles under the bed and my collection of Sandeman's labels, all of which I had painstakingly removed from the bottles and arranged into a sort of spooky satanic-looking collage. But, worse than either of those things, her search revealed the catalogue pages! The ones I'd carefully cut from the hefty tomes of JC Penny, Sears, and Montgomery Ward and kept pressed between the mattress and the box springs. The pages and pages of headless male torsos, all scantily clad in briefs or boxers or pajamas, with whom I'd indulged in the most shameless of fantasies.

The slap in the car was only a preview of the blows Lana gave me when she found these pages. She was furious, and I still wonder how far she would have gone if the doorbell had not rung. It was Wayne. He was told all the details by a shrieking, hysterical Lana, but instead of shock or anger or disgust, he seemed strangely happy, almost glad to have another crisis for the Lord to fix. In minutes we had all joined hands and were on our knees in the living room while Wayne prayed and asked for guidance. My face stung from my beating, but it didn't hurt half as much as my hand, into which Lana dug her clawlike nails as we prayed. It was just her little way of telling me that although she was a Christian now, she was not above doing some things she might have to ask forgiveness for later.

After that as I said, the church-going became annoyingly regular. At night I'd go to gatherings, of course, but during the day, while Lana was at school, I was to go to the church with Wayne, and he would put me to work. In three weeks' time, I was to be shipped off to Bible Camp in North Carolina, where it was hoped, I would mend my ways. If, by the end of summer, I had not seen the light, Wayne knew of a wonderful military school in East Texas that he felt sure he could get me into.

Wayne came to pick me up each morning before Lana left, and together we'd ride to the strip mall where the church was housed. Once there, we'd pray with the aged pastor, attend the morning services if it was a Monday, Wednesday, or Friday, and then I'd work cleaning God's own Kmart. I straightened out the prayer books and the hymnals and made sure there were two of each for every pew. I sprayed and sponged off the vinyl kneelers, and swept, and dusted, and vacuumed all around the pulpit and the altar. I scrubbed the toilets and the bathroom floors, and even spent an entire day scooting around on my back scraping gum off the undersides of the pews. All of this was to keep me busy until it was time to go to camp, but then, thank God, something happened. Something really deserving of thanks, at least from me.

Chapter Five

Being a weatherman in Denver during the summer is quite possibly the least complicated job on Earth. Almost invariably each day begins with blue skies and sunshine. About noon, big, fluffy white clouds roll in off the mountains, and by three o'clock they have usually built up into a thunderstorm. It rains for half an hour at most. In the evening, the clouds move on and there is a clear sunset. A numbingly regular pattern that begins in May and repeats itself well into the middle of September.

The storm that began late that May afternoon was anything but regular. Oh, the morning arrived, clear and sunny, as usual, but when the afternoon clouds appeared from behind the mountains they were not cottony and white, but dark and low and accompanied by a cool wind. It was Monday. A week after my suspension and two weeks before I was to be carted off to summer camp. I had just finished my all-day-under-the-pew-gum-scraping and was getting into Wayne's car when the first drops of rain began to fall. He was taking me home briefly, only long enough to get cleaned up and eat some dinner, before Lana and I drove to the gathering later that night.

I remember thinking, as we rode silently through the suburbs, that my mood was as black as the sky overhead. I felt hollow and empty and lonely. I wanted a drink, but that was considerably harder to get since my suspension. My bottle under the bed had been confiscated; the wine cellar was off limits; and even during communion, the goblet passed by me and I received a blessing instead.

When Wayne pulled into the driveway, the rain was falling steadily. I flipped the door handle, but he had set the child-safety lock so I couldn't open it.

"Dillon," Wayne said, looking over at me with that sickly sweet smile he had perfected. I didn't respond, but I knew he was going to give me some long-winded homily before we parted or he would not have locked the door.

"Dillon," he said again, and took my hand, sandwiching it between his soft fat fingers. "I'm going to leave you now. On your own. Lana won't be home for another hour." He gave my hand a squeeze.

"Now, son, you're not going to do anything that will make me sorry I trusted you, right?"

"No," I said, shaking my head as confidently as I could and returning his squeeze. "No need to worry. That's all behind me now."

But what I thought was more like: *I have just spent eight hours scraping chewed gum and crusty boogers off of the underside of church pews, and in a little while I'm going to have to spend several more hours sitting on top of one of those very same pews watching people I don't even like as they sing and writhe and moan and make fools of themselves. If you think I am going through all that without the one thing that can make it tolerable, you are wrong!*

I knew that the very second I was safe inside and saw him drive down the hill, I'd head straight for the cellar. Maybe he made his comments because he knew it, too, but nevertheless he let me go. Probably because he felt confident that I could come to no real harm. The week before, he and Lana had mounted a cheap padlock on the cellar door and in their minds that made it as secure as the drug closet at the Betty Ford Clinic. What they didn't know was how easily I had outsmarted them, simply by removing the screws from the hinge of the lock and effortlessly flipping the whole mechanism, lock, hinge, and all, to the side. I had done this the first time just a few nights before and had almost succeeded in getting a bottle when I heard Lana coming and had to abandon my quest. I barely had time to replace the screws and stash the screwdriver in my back pocket.

"Shall we pray for some strength?" Wayne asked, raising an eyebrow. I nodded.

And so we prayed. Right there in the middle of the driveway with the rain tapping hard on the roof of the Oldsmobile. Wayne prayed out loud, and asked God to fortify me against the easy temptations of the flesh, against the seductive lure of liquor. I prayed silently, although no less fervently. *Please, God, please make him unlock the door. Please make him let me out of the car before I kill him.*

Eventually he released the lock, and I ran quickly up the walk to the house, not bothering to wave as he backed out of the driveway. The wind was stronger now and the rain blew almost horizontally. By the time I got inside and ran up the stairs to look out the small octagonal window on the landing, the rain was coming down so hard that all I could see were the Oldsmobile's red taillights as it crept slowly down the muddy river that was burying the street.

It was to be the storm of a lifetime—at least that's what the weatherman said—the kind that happens only once every hundred years, and sometimes not even that often. The rain turned roads into rivers and real rivers soon came up over their banks. Shingles were ripped off roofs and fences were carried away by the wind, smashing into the houses they once surrounded. Trees were uprooted and power lines snapped. Nature had suddenly and inexplicably chosen that day to show off.

Lana made it home, but just barely, as the street leading up to our house was so choked with water and mud and debris that her car had almost not made it up the hill.

"I don't think we'll go to the gathering tonight," she said, removing her dripping clothes and hanging them in the bathtub. "But, maybe it's a blessing in disguise," she continued, "because I've got a huge test tomorrow and I haven't even opened the book yet."

Since there was no power in the house, we ate a cold dinner together by candlelight. When we'd finished, Lana retired to her room taking the two remaining candles and the only flashlight with her, leaving me in the dark. But I didn't mind. Sitting alone in the dark was ten times better than having to go to another gathering. I felt my way up to my room, lay down on my bed, and did some silent scales on my clarinet. I finished off the bottle of Sandeman's that I'd stolen from the cellar and, at some point, passed into a boozy sleep.

Much later I was awakened by what I perceived as loud hoofbeats. With effort, I opened my eyes but saw only darkness and felt sure I must be dreaming. The hoofbeats continued, very loud, but never coming any closer and never moving farther away, like a herd of animals running in circles overhead. I sat up and tried to orient myself, but I could feel the thick heaviness of drink still affecting my brain. The noise, coming from outside, grew almost deafening, like handfuls of rocks were being hurled at the house. Unsteadily, I crept over to the window and lifted up the blind. The sky was still dark but the ground was covered with white pebbles that appeared to be popping like popcorn. I stared for a while, bewildered, but then I realized that it must be hail, since that often came with spring storms. But hail at night? I had never heard of that. I watched it for a while, as it popped and piled up on the lawn but soon, the steady rhythmic drumming became almost tranquilizing, and I returned to my bed.

The next time I woke up the room was white with morning light. I sat up, and a moment later my brain followed, clanging on the sides of my skull like a bell. I squinted at the clock, but it was flashing a meaningless neon red 12:00. My head hurt, and the brightness only made it worse. I was thirsty, too, so I decided to get one of the cold bottles of water Lana kept in the refrigerator.

On my way down I stopped again at the little octagonal window and peered out. The ground was still covered in white, but it looked less brilliant now than it had the night before, more soggy and transparent. I saw two narrow tire tracks leading in a graceful arc out from the garage and then off down the hill.

Lana must be gone, I thought, and felt relieved, but at the same time I wondered why she hadn't awakened me. It was surely past the time for Wayne to arrive. I looked outside again and figured from the angle of the sun that it was well into the morning, at least nine o'clock. Maybe he hadn't been able to make it, maybe a bridge was out, or something. I went down the stairs and into the kitchen. No note from Lana but, oddly enough, there was a guitar case propped up against one of the kitchen walls.

It's probably Wayne's, I thought to myself and shuddered as I imagined us all in a group at church singing an endless version of "Michael Row Your Boat Ashore."

I went to the refrigerator, got the water, and drank it eagerly. My head throbbed and the thought of the chores Wayne had planned for me that day made it even worse.

I've got to have at least a swig, I thought, so I went over to the kitchen drawer and took out the Phillips-head screwdriver. *I'll just take one good drink from the cognac bottle, just to get rid of the headache, and then I'll get dressed.*

I shuffled over to the entrance of the cellar but stopped suddenly and stared at the door. The padlock was undone! The lock was sitting on one of the steps and the hinge was open. I panicked for a moment and felt sweat break out all over my body.

Had I forgotten to put it back?! No, no, it was *unlocked* now. I had never unlocked it. I didn't have a key. Maybe Lana had gone down to inventory the bottles, or worse, maybe Wayne! But, no, no, there had been only one set of tracks and they were leading away from the house. Lana had probably just gone down for something, to trip the breaker, maybe, and had just forgotten to lock it back up. It was a good thing! A blessing in disguise, as Lana would say.

I crept quietly down the stairs, as if in danger of being seen or heard. There was a light switch, but I didn't turn it on. There was no need. I knew the exact location of the bottle I wanted, so I made my way confidently over the cold concrete to the tall rack at the far end. The cognac was up fairly high, but I was tall and could reach it if I stood on the tips of my toes. I had just grasped the neck of the bottle with my thumb and forefinger and was inching it out when I heard something scratch behind me. I spun around and the bottle fell. It hit the floor and exploded, sending glass and cognac all over my feet and legs.

It was dark. Silent. Had I imagined it? I could see no one, hear nothing. I held my breath and did not move. As my eyes adjusted to the darkness, I saw, from on top of one of the racks, the burning ember of a cigarette end. I shuddered but dared not speak. Silence. Nothing but the glowing ember and the mingling smells of smoke and cognac.

Although I liked to think I was above all the Christian nonsense to which I had so recently been overexposed, I could not help trembling and feeling I was in the presence of something not of this world.

"Can you keep a secret?" a voice asked and then a cloud of smoke drifted down toward me. It was a voice I had never heard before. A man's voice, gravelly and rough, but not entirely unfamiliar. I was still shaking. I tried to step back but stopped when I felt a sharp pain from the broken glass under my heel. I said nothing.

"I think you can," the voice said. I heard a click and a bare bulb illuminated. A shirtless man was reclining sideways on top of the wine rack, propped up on one elbow. In his left hand he held the burning cigarette, oddly between his third and fourth fingers. His hair was dark and long and quite curly, which contrasted with his pale skin and blue eyes. Smiling down, he assessed me and my predicament.

"Yes," he said, clearly amused by what he saw. "From this situation I think one could infer that maybe you are quite talented when it comes to keeping secrets. I am, too, and that's good. People talk too much. Less talk and more action; that's my motto. I'll need you to talk very little today, if you know what I mean."

I nodded, although I certainly did not know what he meant. He saw my confusion and added, "No one can know I'm here, and I'm afraid that very soon there are going to be lots of people looking for me."

"But who are you?" I asked.

He looked back at me, faintly surprised and confused, almost offended.

"Your mother didn't tell you?" he asked.

"No," I said, and shook my head.

"Strange. I thought she would have. No wonder you're scared." He took another drag on the cigarette but offered no explanation. He smoked luxuriously, like people in the movies, inhaling deeply and then pulling the cigarette away from his mouth so that a small white cloud appeared and then just as quickly disappeared up his nose.

"Is . . . Lana home?" I asked, tentatively, afraid of the trouble I'd be in if she found me down here.

"Your mother? No, she's gone to school, but what's—Why do you call her Lana?"

I thought about how to respond to this, as I did every time someone asked about it. I had been calling her Lana for years then so I really should have had a better response prepared, but I did not.

"She, uh, doesn't like to be called mother," I said and shuffled my feet in the sticky wetness beneath me. I had most definitely cut my heel, and as my fear ebbed away, I could feel pain take its place. He did not respond to what I said but just kept looking down at me, assessing me, and smoking. Again I asked, "Who are you?"

He put the cigarette in his mouth, sat up, and stretched his arms high above his head. He had made a sort of bed on top of the wine rack, with a flat board and several pillows and blankets. He whipped one of these blankets up into the air, like a bullfighter, and then, leaning over the rack, he let it fall on the ground so that it covered the broken glass, making a sort of path for me to walk on. That done, he grabbed on to one of the overhead pipes with both hands and swung his body in a circle, depositing himself as gracefully as a dancer on the floor some feet in front of me, lit cigarette still between his lips. He made an elaborate bow and extended one hand to help me across the blanket.

"Max is the name," he said, with an emphasis placed on the word *is*, as if Max was the only name any sane person would consider being called. I took his hand, very rough and calloused, and he helped me across the blanket. His grip was firm, which was surprising because he did not look at all strong. He was thin and wiry, with long lithe arms and legs, and a flat chest.

Once I'd made it to the dry concrete he released my hand, and only then did he take his cigarette from his mouth, again holding it between his third and fourth fingers. He noticed the bloody prints I'd left on the blanket.

"It looks like you'll need a bandage," he said, and in one movement he had swooped me up and was carrying me up the stairs. It was then that I realized who he was; he was my uncle, the boy in the picture about whom I had heard so annoyingly little over the years.

Emerging into the upstairs after being in the cellar was painful. The brightness and the ache in my head quickly eclipsed the pain in my heel. I had not gotten the cognac and realized, with a little pang of sorrow, that I probably would not.

Max set me gently in one of the kitchen chairs and propped my wounded foot up on the table. As he made his way around the kitchen, grabbing a roll of paper towels and filling a bowl with water, I examined him more closely. He wore a pair of red-plaid pajama pants with a drawstring at the waist, but his feet and upper body were bare. Again, I noticed how pale he was, so pale that blue veins were visible beneath the surface of his skin.

I directed him to the bathroom, where I told him he'd probably find a first aid kit, but he ignored me and proceeded to combine several odd ingredients from the kitchen in a tall glass. From what I could see these included olive oil, a raw egg, sugar, the juice of one lemon, half and half, several grinds from the pepper mill, a teaspoon of instant coffee, Tabasco, and vinegar. The glass was then three-quarters full, and he stirred it noisily as he carried it back down to the cellar. When he emerged a few moments later, he was still stirring but now the glass was full. He removed the spoon, cleaned it off in his mouth, and threw it in the sink. He set the glass on the table in front of me and then disappeared into the bathroom to get the first aid kit. I looked at the milky maroon liquid and the stench of it wafted up to me. It was a sour smell but underneath that odor was the spiky scent of alcohol. I picked it up and took a sip. Ghastly. Like rotten barbecue sauce. I stopped breathing through my nose and took another drink. I managed to get about half of it down but then had to stop as the feel of the grainy texture in my mouth made me afraid I might throw up. It burned as it made its way down, but I could not tell if that was the familiar burn of the alcohol or only the pepper. Max returned and began cleaning and bandaging my heel.

"What is this?" I asked, stifling a cough. He looked up and smiled, a cigarette in his mouth and one eye closed to keep out the smoke.

"Part penance," he said, "and part cure. I just invented it. Do you like it?"

I said nothing. I thought it was a mean thing to do, but I defiantly drank the rest of it and then set the glass on the table. He had dried the wound and was dabbing at it with a cotton ball soaked in hydrogen peroxide. I winced, but he held my foot firmly. I remembered Wayne and wondered if maybe he had already come that morning.

"I'm supposed to be in church," I said. "This guy from the church, the assistant pastor, Wayne, he usually comes to get me about eight."

"Not today," he replied, but then offered nothing further.

"Why . . . not?" I ventured, somewhat timidly, afraid that maybe I was in more trouble.

Without looking up he replied, "Let's just say there was some divine intervention on your behalf last night."

I looked at him, confused, and in my hungover state I must have looked sufficiently pitiable because he added, "The wind tore the roof off of the church. You're free for today."

I relaxed a bit in my chair. I was relieved, yes, but more than that I was glad that I would get to spend more time with such an intriguing stranger.

"You remember me asking if you were good at keeping secrets?" Max asked, his attention still focused on my wound. I nodded and watched as the smoke from the end of his cigarette rose up in a narrow stream and then ballooned out like a mushroom a foot above his head.

"And how are you at lying?" he asked, looking straight into my eyes. I hesitated for a moment. Was this a test? Had Wayne and Lana put him up to this? I decided that silence was the best response. He was now wrapping my foot with a long strip of gauze bandage.

"Well, let's hope, for my sake, that you *can* do more than just keep quiet because today I'm going to have to ask you to go a bit further."

As if on cue, the doorbell rang. We both looked up, first at the door and then at each other. He quickly taped off my bandage, pitched his cigarette into the sink, and wordlessly leaped over to the cellar door. He looked back at me for a moment. His face was grave but amused. He put his index finger to his lips, then turned and descended, pulling the door shut behind him.

I did not know what to do. Everything was happening so fast and my head was less than clear. I stood up. The doorbell rang again. In spite of what Max had said, I thought it might be Wayne, so before going to the front door I limped down the steps to the cellar and replaced the padlock on the hinge.

When I opened the front door, it wasn't Wayne but rather a man and a woman I had never seen before. The woman was short and plump, with an enormous blond hairdo. Her face was heavily made up and she was dressed in a pink skirt and jacket, with ropes of gaudy, gold jewelry dangling from her wrists and neck. The man, who was missing several front teeth, was absurdly large and his body, clad in a dark suit, filled the doorway.

"Good morning, young man," the woman said. Her mouth moved when she spoke but all of the sound seemed to be coming from her nostrils. I said nothing, but just looked up at them with my best stone face.

"Maybe you can help me," she said. "I'm looking for a man, could be he's your uncle or your cousin maybe, goes by the name of Max. He here?" she asked peering around me into the house.

I stared back blankly and then silently shook my head. The two exchanged tired glances and then focused once again on me.

"Has he been here?" the woman asked, her voice impatient. "You do know who I'm talking about?" I wrinkled my brow, feigning confusion and cocked my head to one side, like a dog when it hears an unfamiliar sound. She gave the man a nod and without a word he pushed me aside with one of his enormous hands and marched into the house. She followed.

"You don't mind if we check for ourselves, sweetie, do you?" she asked, not really caring how I responded. I followed behind her, leaving the door open in case I needed to flee. The man, who seemed to be missing a neck in addition to his teeth, headed directly upstairs while the woman walked casually into the kitchen.

"You home alone, today?" she asked. "No school?"

"I've been suspended," I said, feeling suddenly proud of the fact.

"Suspended, eh? Then you must be related to Max. What for?"

she asked, pacing the kitchen, her hands behind her clutching the handle of her purse and her large bust pushed out. She looked like an angry hen.

"For drinking," I said.

"For drinking," she said, but there was no surprise in her voice. Instead, I thought I detected a tone of disappointment. "For drinking," she repeated. I nodded. "Well then maybe you're not related because Max never drinks. That's part of the reason I trusted the little shit." She paused and chewed her gum angrily.

"Drink makes you sloppy. Remember that, er, what's your name?"

"Dillon, ma'am."

"Remember that, little Dillon. Drink makes you sloppy. You heard it from Doris."

The large man came back down and into the kitchen.

"Anything?" she asked. He shook his head. Together, they searched the study and then the living room, looking under all the furniture and opening all the closet doors. Finding nothing, they disappeared briefly into the garage. When they returned, they paused in front of the lower stairwell.

"What's down there?" the big man asked, pointing with one of his meaty fingers to the cellar door.

"Wine cellar," I said.

"Why's it locked?" the woman asked.

"Because of me," I said, trying to look ashamed. "Remember?"

They exchanged glances once again and she gave a nod to the door. Without a word the man charged down the stairs and threw his body against it. It didn't give the first time, so he backed up and positioned himself to charge it again.

"Wait!" I cried, imagining the trouble I'd be in if Lana and Wayne returned to find the door busted off its hinges. He hesitated.

"Wait," I said again. "I can get it open. Just a minute." And again

I got the Phillips-head screwdriver and began unscrewing the hinge of the lock. I did it slowly, hoping it might give Max time to find an adequate hiding place. When I'd finished, I went back up the stairs and let the man go down and open it. He did so and the pungent vapor from the evaporating cognac quickly wafted up the stairs. I thought for sure the game was over, and Max was caught. But a minute later the big man emerged alone, trudging slowly up the stairs and shaking his head.

"No?" she asked.

"No," he replied. They both looked dejected and stood for a moment trying to think what to do next.

She turned and walked toward the door.

"If he has been here," she mused, more to herself than to me, "he probably won't be back. And if he hasn't been here, he'll probably show up sooner or later. Hmmm. I'm gonna bet he has been here. Hell, he probably is here now, watching us." She looked up and around the ceiling, as if Max might be clinging to the chandelier.

"But, whichever it is," she said, turning to me and wagging a heavily jeweled finger, "if you see him, you tell him that I was here looking for him, okay? You hear that, Max!" she yelled back into the kitchen. "Doris is on to you!"

As soon as they left, I ran once again up to the top of the stairs and peered out the window. They were in a large blue Lincoln, Doris behind the wheel and her large friend in the passenger seat, his massive arm hanging out the open window. Almost all of the hail had melted now and most of the water had gone, so the tracks they left as they drove down the hill were in the thin brown mud that remained. I watched until I was certain they wouldn't come back and then I limped down the stairs, yelling, "They're gone! They're gone! You can come out now!"

But Max did not come out. There was not a sound in the house. Soon I found myself looking up and around the ceiling, just as Doris had done. I went down into the cellar and pulled the light string. There was the blanket on the floor, still covering the broken glass, but the pillows were gone from the top of the rack and Max was not there.

"It's okay," I called out. "They're gone."

But Max had vanished. I searched every corner of the cellar, climbed up on every rack, but he wasn't there. I went back upstairs, still calling out. Nothing. I stood in the middle of the kitchen feeling very self-conscious, as if someone was watching me, but I could see no one. Then the doorbell rang. I froze, not knowing what to do, like an actor on stage who was missing a page of the script. Was it the couple again? Was it Wayne? I ran quickly and replaced the lock on the door to the cellar. The bell rang again and then twice more before I'd finished replacing the final screw. I pocketed the screwdriver, ran to the door, and looked through the peephole. It appeared to be a woman with a large purse over her shoulder. She was kicking her boots on the step trying to get the mud off the soles. I opened the door a crack.

"Hello," she said, and smiled at me. She was a short chubby woman, maybe forty, with her hair cut in a pixie that only accentuated the roundness of her face. Her makeup was both inexpertly chosen and applied, with the end result that she looked a bit like a clown, albeit a somewhat soggy clown who had been through a rainstorm or who had just emerged from a swimming pool.

"Hello, I'm Meredith Brown, I'm here to see Max Naylor."

"He's not here." I said quickly and closed the door. The doorbell rang again, insistently, three times. Again, I opened it.

"Ex-*cuse* me," she said impatiently, "he had *better* be here. I spoke to him in my office just yesterday and he assured me that he *would* be here."

I shrugged and was about to shut the door again when Max suddenly swung into view. He had been on the roof just above the front door, and once he'd discerned who it was, he grabbed onto the gutter and swung down, swooping just over the head of

Meredith Brown. He landed in a somersault on the floor of the foyer.

"Here I am!" he said jovially, as he got up from the floor and bounced back to where Meredith and I were standing, open-mouthed. "Just as promised! Meredith, I'd like you to meet my nephew, Dillon. Dillon, my parole officer, Meredith."

We shook hands and she stepped inside, setting down her purse to remove her muddy boots.

"I'm so glad you *are* here," she said, unsnapping her coat, "It's been a real nutty morning, with this crazy Colorado weather and all. The first client I went to see was living in some grody crack house and I had to talk to, like, ten different people before I found one who'd even heard of him."

"Well, you'll find none of that here, Meredith," Max said reassuringly. "Here, let me take your coat. Dillon, could you get Miss Brown a beverage? What will you have, Meredith? We've got, well, I don't really know what we've got. I'm sure we must have water and coffee, maybe tea or soda . . ."

"Oh, why thank you, water's fine."

"A glass of water for Meredith," he said, giving me a smile and a wink. "And I'll have coffee. Black."

Still shiftless and shoeless, he took Meredith by the hand and gently escorted her into the living room. He sat her down on the sofa and then, instead of seating himself in the chair opposite, or even at the other end of the sofa, as might have been expected, he sat right next to her. I observed them from the kitchen, as I opened her bottle of water and waited for the coffee to brew; each time I looked up, Max seemed to have inched even closer to her.

"So this is your sister's house?" she asked.

"Yes, her husband left her a few months back. It's been hard on her, you know. I'm hoping I can help her finish the house, since she's going to school full-time and all, maybe help take care of the boy."

"That is *so* nice!" she said, beaming at him. "I wish I'd 'a had a brother like you when I got my divorce."

"Surely you're not divorced, Meredith," he said, his arm now creeping up the back of the sofa.

"Oh, yeah," she said. "Six years now."

"He must have been crazy!"

"No kidding!" she giggled, both flattered and nervous. Suddenly, she noticed how close he'd come to her on the sofa. She leaned forward and shook her head, as if to dispel some intoxication, then cleared her throat. Remembering the purpose of her visit, she bent down and dug a clipboard and what looked like a small radio attached to a Velcro strap out of her purse. Again she cleared her throat.

"Now, um, as a condition of your parole you'll have to have a full-time job within two weeks and you'll have to wear this," she said, holding up the radio. For a moment they both stared at the thing wordlessly.

"And what exactly . . . is that?" Max asked, looking concerned and leaning forward on the sofa.

"Oh, it's a new thing we're using called an in-house detention monitor. I strap it on your leg, like so," she said, leaning down and looping it around Max's ankle, "and every time it beeps you call in from a particular location and punch in your password and the phone number. It's real simple."

From Max's initial reaction to the thing, which I observed from my post in the kitchen, one would have thought she'd just wrapped a spitting cobra around his leg. But only for a moment. In an instant he had regained control. He took a deep breath and relaxed the muscles in his face. If I hadn't been watching so closely, I would have missed it. Meredith never noticed. She was too busy looking through his file trying to figure out how to activate the thing.

"This really won't be necessary," Max said, loosening the Velcro and removing the band.

"But it's in your file," Meredith cried, "you have to wear it!"

"Meredith, really!" he scolded playfully. "You should know better. This is me, remember? Max. I'm not going anywhere. I'll be right here helping my sister and her kid. I don't want to feel like an animal, all tagged and tracked."

He had taken both of her hands in his and was staring intently in her eyes. I entered bearing their beverages. Meredith looked up and nodded her thanks, but Max did not even acknowledge me. I sensed that my presence was neither required nor desired, so I retreated back to the kitchen and pretended to busy myself, all the while eavesdropping and glancing up now and then to see what was happening. Max stared at Meredith and she stared back, nervously. He raised one of his hands and gently brushed a lock of hair from her forehead.

"Trust me," he told her, his voice low and sweet. "Helping my sister will really be a full-time job. The boy's got troubles and he needs a father. Surely I don't need to tell you about that. *You* know. You've been through it. I thought that maybe I could be that father to him—the one he never had. I hoped that he and I could work on the house together, over the summer."

These last words were spoken in almost a whisper and when he said them his hand, which had been hovering near her forehead, drifted lightly down her cheek and rested on her shoulder. She blushed, and when she spoke, her voice was quiet and hoarse and flustered.

"I, uh, it's in your file," she said, and turned again, somewhat primly, toward the coffee table. Again, she picked up the Velcro anklet.

"Meredith," he sighed, grabbing her hand and bringing it and the anklet to his chest. He pressed them to his heart.

"Feel that," he said, staring once again into her eyes. "Just feel how frightened that makes me. Please, Meredith, let me be a human. Prison was so hard. Let me move on. Don't shackle me down again."

There was silence for several seconds after this, but then Meredith again released herself.

"I can't," she said, swiveling to face the coffee table again. "I really can't."

Max gasped and fell back on the sofa. "I understand," he said and lifted his ankle so that she could attach the monitor. She did so; but when she looked up, there were tears streaming down Max's face.

"Ohh, don't do that," she pleaded. "Please don't cry. I have to do this. It's in your file."

Max nodded, as if to say he understood, that he knew she was just doing her job. But the tears continued to roll and it appeared he could not speak. His crying was silent—the way babies sometimes do right before they let loose with a wail.

"Ohh," Meredith moaned, frantically waving her hands, "Please don't. It won't be that bad. You'll get used to it and if you wear longer pants you can pretty much cover it up."

This did not appear to appease him and his body began to heave with his sobs.

"Ohh, darn it all!" Meredith cried. "I'm not supposed to do this, oohhh, I'll tell you what I'll do. How 'bout this. I'll waive your employment requirement if you'll wear it, how's that sound? You can work here instead of going out and looking for a job. Is that fair? That's fair, isn't it?" The tears continued to roll, but Max looked interested.

"That way you can stay here and work on the house," she said brightly. He leaned forward on the sofa and Meredith patted him on the back. Max smiled.

"There. You see, I'm not such a meanie."

"No," Max said, and then grabbed her head in both his hands and kissed her firmly on the lips. "You're wonderful. Thank you."

Initially, she was too surprised to say anything. He released her head but kept one hand on her shoulder. She stood up suddenly, smoothing her shirt and trying to appear professional, not quite sure if she should be offended or not. She cleared her throat.

"But the next time I visit," she warned, "you have to show that some progress is being made on the house."

"Of course," he nodded, rising and once again placing his hand on her shoulder. "Yes. That makes perfect sense. Thank you. Would you like to see my quarters, here. Just so you'll know where to picture me when this, this . . . this leash electrifies me and I telephone you? Yes? You would? It's just right down these stairs . . ."

From the kitchen I watched as Max took her by the hand and led her downstairs, clicking the door shut behind them. I found this curious, and when they still hadn't emerged, several minutes later, I strolled over to the stairs and stared down at the closed door. I was just about to tiptoe down and press my ear against it when again the doorbell rang again. I jumped. My eyes darted back and forth from the cellar door to the front door. I was excited by who it could possibly be next, since the first three visitors had been so interesting, but then my excitement deflated as I realized it was probably just Wayne. He'd been busy all morning but now he was finally coming to pick me up to come help with the church roof. "Better late than never!" he'd cluck, or something equally stupid and cliché. It rang again. I decided not to answer it. I'd go up to my room, close the door and pretend I hadn't heard it. Oh, he'd figure some way in, but at least it would delay him. I ran up the stairs and looked out the window, but it wasn't Wayne's car in the driveway. Meredith's red compact was there, but next to it was an old black Volvo station wagon.

I ran back down the stairs and flung open the door. A woman was descending the front steps back toward the driveway, but she turned when she heard the door open. Unlike the other two, this woman was tall and elegantly dressed all in black, with long straight black hair pulled back from her face. She wore a matching skirt and jacket, the jacket accented with an ermine collar and cuffs, and on her left forearm, which she kept elevated by her side, a shiny black purse was suspended. Her groomed perfection was totally incongruous with the muddy, windblown landscape behind her, and it was only when I glanced down at her tiny shoes and noticed the mud that I realized she had not just materialized there. I could not see her eyes, as they were hidden behind a pair of large sunglasses, but on seeing me, her mouth widened into a smile and she approached.

"Good morning," she said, extending her hand, encased in a white glove. From the small amount of her face that was not hidden by the sunglasses I could tell that she was quite young, maybe in her early twenties, but her rich voice and calm deliberate manners made her seem much older.

I shook her hand, bowed my head slightly, but I did not say anything.

"I'm here to see Max. Is he in?" she asked, and peered over my shoulder into the house. Again, I said nothing. Something about her made me not want to lie as I had to the previous visitors so instead I said nothing. She regarded me calmly and waited for my answer, aware that I had both heard and understood her question. We both stood expressionless for several seconds, but then her lips widened into a smile and her head tilted slightly to one side.

"He's instructed you well," she said, both hands in front of her now, clutching the curved ivory handle of her purse. "You've done an admiral job. If I didn't know better I'd almost think you were autistic, or that I'd stumbled on the wrong address . . ." Her voice trailed off but her eyes were locked on me. She elevated the pointy toe of one of her shoes and rotated her foot back and forth slowly on the spiky heel. It was a feline gesture, the annoyed flit of a cat's tail when you block the sun in which it is lying.

"However," she said, leaning forward and peering at me over the frames of her glasses, "I'm afraid I do know better."

I noticed, when I saw her eyes behind the glasses, that she was Asian, and that surprised me. I suppose at that age I expected all Asians to speak with an accent, but her English was, if anything, far more clipped and precise than any I had heard outside of British movies. She reached in her purse and produced a white business card, which she handed to me with the following instructions:

"Be a friend, won't you, and give this card to Max. Tell him I'll be waiting tomorrow, ten o'clock, Paris on the Platte. He knows where it is."

I took the card and she snapped her purse shut. She was just turning to go but then paused and looked back at me. "You come, too," she said. "If you *are* able to open your mouth, they have lots of sweets and things that you might like."

My expression cracked and I smiled. That seemed to satisfy her and she turned and walked down the steps to her car, heels clicking on the concrete.

A half hour later, Meredith crept up from the cellar, her hair mussed and her cheeks like two rosy apples. Around her neck I saw what appeared to be a necklace of purple hickeys. In a fluster, she collected her coat and bag from the floor in front of the sofa and, without a word, went straight for the front door, pulling it gently closed behind her. A few moments later Max emerged, smiling and yawning and stretching, as if he'd just woken up. He wore only a pair of boxer shorts, and as he reached the top of the stairs, I noticed that both his ankles were bare.

Chapter Six

The next visitor arrived while Max was in the shower. It was after noon and my hangover, thanks to Max's cure, was gradually ebbing away. The doorbell rang and again my heart rose and then fell, fearing that it must be Wayne. I hopped to the door and peered through the peephole. It was not Wayne, so I opened it. A large man, well over six feet, stood on the porch. He was wearing a red fleece jacket, the arm of which had been patched with duct tape, and held in his hand a pale blue carton of cigarettes.

"Ah, hello," he said, in a voice that was heavily accented. "Max, is he here?"

I shook my head, no, and his shoulders fell.

"Has he left already? I mean, was he here?"

His face was weathered and tan, with white crow's feet around his eyes where the sun had not reached, and his windblown hair, once very blond, was now beginning to turn gray. He was wearing shorts, with lots of strange metal pieces hanging from a loop on the side and a well-worn pair of leather hiking boots. Something about him, his desperation or disorder maybe, made him seem harmless, so I did not lie. But I remembered what Max had told me and said nothing. The man waited expectantly for my answer and his brow furrowed. Then his face relaxed into a smile.

"Oh, but of course!" he said, and tapped his forehead with his palm. "To you, I'm stranger. I am Serge, a very old friend of Max's."

He extended his hand and I shook it, noticing that it was even rougher and more calloused than Max's had been and that most of the knuckles were covered in scabs.

"Can I come in?" he asked, his voice lilting up at the end of his question. "Maybe I could leave him a note, and I've brought him some cigarettes, *Gitanes*, his favorite kind."

Before I could protest he had marched past me and on into the kitchen, looking up and all around, just as the previous visitors had done. Not seeing Max, he fell into one of the chairs, as if the walk to the kitchen had exhausted him. He fished in his shirt pocket and removed a rumpled box of cigarettes, and then fished in his coat pocket for something to light it with. He found nothing, and then began to search all his pockets, patting himself down and removing bits of paper, more odd pieces of metal similar to those attached to his shorts, his car keys, a few pennies, but no matches. He looked up at me, a somewhat pleading expression on his face, his cigarette dangling lifeless from the corner of his mouth.

"Just a minute," I said, and went over to the kitchen drawer. I poked around but found no matches. Then I remembered that Lana had taken them up to her room the night before when the power went out.

"They're upstairs," I said, limping over to the staircase, "I'll be right back."

Up in Lana's room, I quietly shut the door behind me. The shower was still running. I gently knocked on the bathroom door.

"That you, Dil?" Max asked.

"Yes," I whispered, opening the door a crack. I was blinded by a cloud of fragrant steam.

"There's a man downstairs," I hissed. Immediately, the water stopped.

"Downstairs?"

"Yes."

"Why did you let him in?"

"I *didn't*," I protested. "He just sort of came in."

I could hear him frantically toweling off and I felt bad, as though I hadn't been able to keep up my part of that morning's pact.

"He sounds foreign," I added. "Says his name is Serge."

"Ohhh," Max sighed, and I could hear the relief in his voice. "I should have known. Tell him . . . Well, tell him I'll be down in a minute."

I retrieved the book of matches from Lana's dresser and made my way back down to the kitchen.

"Max will be down in a minute," I said, handing him the matches. "He's in the shower."

Serge smiled so broadly the white creases in his crow's feet nearly disappeared.

"Ha ho!" he cried, slapping his thigh. "I knew he would be here!" He lit one of the matches but as he brought it up to the cigarette, his hand shook so badly that the match went out. He lit another but this time he dropped both the match and the matchbook. I picked them up and struck one myself. He leaned forward, touched the end of his cigarette to the flame, and inhaled deeply. He nodded his thanks and then brushed away a few bits of tobacco that clung to his lips.

"I knew he was here!" he said, jovially. "I knew it! I had hoped he would come to me, I suspected that if he didn't, he would come to his sister."

He smoked quickly, but his hand was still trembling and he caught me looking at it.

"It's the morning," he said. "It usually passes by this time of day but today . . . maybe was the storm, it affects one, you know?" I nodded.

"You are the *neveu?* The . . . nephew?" he asked. Again, I nodded.

"I could tell. You look like him, the face is the same, and the same body." He looked around the kitchen, as if he were looking for something in particular. Then he looked at me. He started to say something, stopped himself, and then started again.

"You wouldn't have, eh, something to drink?" I knew what he meant. I nodded and went down to the cellar door, which had been left open when Max and Meredith emerged. Although the smell of cognac was still strong, when I turned on the light I noticed that the broken glass had been swept up and disposed of and that the pillows and a fresh blanket had reappeared on top of the wine rack. My adolescent mind was curious about what had transpired there so I quietly crawled up on the rack and examined the bed, wondering what tale the scene would tell, but all I saw was a rumpled blanket and a pillow smeared with some of Meredith's makeup. I stared at the makeshift bed for a few moments, not quite able to believe that two people had actually had sex there, and as I crawled back down, I had to reposition my erection in my still-too-tight pants. I went over to the rack that held the cognac, carefully slid a bottle out, and went back upstairs. Max had still not come down so I handed Serge the bottle and then got him a glass from the cupboard.

"Thank you," he said, pouring about two inches of liquid in the glass and downing it in one gulp. He then poured another inch and replaced the stopper in the bottle. He sipped from this and smoked and asked me questions about Max: When did he get here, and how did he look? Had I ever met him before? Did other people know he was here? I answered what questions I could with my limited knowledge and as I was talking I noticed Max tiptoeing down the stairs. He motioned for me to be quiet and not give him away so I kept talking.

"No," I said, "I hadn't met him until this morning actually, but I had heard a few stories about him from Lana and my grandparents."

"Oh yes," he said. "There are always stories to tell about Max! I remember one time, this was some years ago . . ."

At that point, Max was only a foot away from Serge's back. He leaned forward and whispered in his ear, *"Dans une bouche ferme, n'entrons pas les mouches."*

Serge rose up and spun around. Cigarette still clenched between his teeth, he grabbed Max in a bear hug and effortlessly lifted him up and around. He then set him down, pushed him an arm's length away, and exclaimed, *"Eh, mon petit, que tu es pale!"*

"Prison has that effect," Max replied. Serge then pulled him close and kissed him on the cheek.

"But why didn't you come to *me?*" Serge asked. "You know I would love to have you back, and there is plenty of room above the shop. You could teach and climb everyday!"

"How about I make us all something to eat," Max said, avoiding the subject. "I see it's already cocktail hour for you, but Dillon and I haven't even had breakfast yet."

For the next half hour, while Max made us an elaborate breakfast, I sat entranced and dizzy as the two of them talked. They spoke about the storm the night before and about Max's arrival, about Serge's business and about rock climbing, all in a language that seemed almost of their own invention.

"Did you bring any gear with you?" Max asked.

"Yes, of course," Serge said. "You know I always keep a few ropes in the truck. Why? You want to climb today?"

"Mmm," said Max, in between bites of food. "Harnesses?"

"Yes, yes," Serge said, becoming more and more excited. "I hoped you would want to; I even brought your old shoes! Where shall we go?"

"I was thinking," Max said, chewing meditatively. "Maybe we could try the house."

Serge and I exchanged confused glances.

"The house?" Serge asked. "This house?"

"Yes, there's a facade of sandstone blocks on the front," Max said. "It goes from the ground all the way up to the roof and seems to me it would be a good start for Dillon."

"Ahh, yes, yes, okay," Serge said, getting up and heading to the front door, "I'll go and see what I have. What size foot is yours, Dillon?"

"Uh, eleven," I said, somewhat timidly.

"*C'est vrai?* Fine, then you can wear a pair of my shoes."

Max poured himself another cup of coffee and lit a cigarette from the carton Serge had brought him. I began clearing the dishes and putting them in the dishwasher.

"Do you have any other pants?" Max asked me, turning around and looking me up and down. "Maybe some that aren't so tight."

I blushed again and shook my head.

"I only ask because it's easier to climb in loose clothing. You can borrow a pair of my shorts for today and tomorrow we'll get you some. Also, any chance you can survive without that contraption on your head?"

I fingered my headgear self-conciously.

"I'm supposed to wear it all day, at least for another six months," I mumbled.

"Oh yes," he sighed, exhaling a huge plume of smoke. "I'd forgotten about the suburban obsession with straight, white teeth. Give me a gap-toothed grin any day rather than another one of these bridled adolescents. Every time I see you with that thing on I keep expecting you to rear up and whinny."

I said nothing but could feel my face grow even more flushed. He got up and came over to me.

"Don't take it personally," he said, clenching his cigarette between his lips and lifting up my chin. The scent of coffee, shampoo, and cigarette smoke mingled around him. I looked into his eyes and saw a kindness there that I was not used to seeing.

"It's a sign of weakness to take offense. I didn't mean anything by it, really; it's just that I think you'd be happier if you were free of it during waking hours, don't you?" I nodded. Max sat down again.

"Think of it like a mud mask, or like hair curlers—Oh, they might make you look better, but do you really want anyone to see you while you have them on?" he asked with a wink.

I shook my head, no, and slowly removed the headgear.

"There now, much better! You look human!" Max downed the rest of his coffee, got up, and motioned for me to follow him downstairs.

"Come on, let's get you some more comfortable clothes."

A few minutes later, after I'd been outfitted in Max's shorts, we met up with Serge, who was busy winding up a brightly colored climbing rope in the sun on the front porch. Since there was no lawn, the yard consisted of thick sticky mud. For that reason we dared not venture off the porch, but there was enough of the rock wall going up from the concrete to give us a good start. Serge tossed me a pair of elfin-looking climbing shoes with smooth rubber soles and when I'd squeezed my feet into them, he laced them up tightly. So tightly that I could feel my foot throbbing where it had been cut earlier that morning, but I said nothing, afraid that maybe he wouldn't let me climb if he knew I was injured. He and Max showed me how to put on the harness and then both carefully demonstrated how to attach myself to the rope with a figure-eight knot.

"It may look difficult from down here," Max said, looking up at the wall, "but there are plenty of handholds and footholds between the stones, you see?" And he showed me how to take advantage of the tiny spaces of recessed mortar between the rocks. "You just work your fingers and the tips of your toes in there and keep looking up for the next place."

Then, as effortlessly as a spider, Max crawled several feet up the wall. He stopped, turned, and grinned down at me.

"You see?" he asked.

He made it look so easy, so possible. He then jumped down and explained the basics of climbing with a rope: Serge would stand at the bottom with the rope around his waist and release just as much as Max needed to climb, a technique called belaying; Max would then climb up to the roof, untie himself, loop the rope around the chimney, and then toss his end back down to me. I would then tie it to my harness and Serge would belay me to roof, pulling in the rope as I went up.

Max started climbing and Serge and I stood below watching him, Serge releasing the rope as he went.

"Just look at him!" Serge whispered, his voice full of admiration. "He looks like a dancer!" And indeed he did, a little, as he went up, and from side to side, with a steady, almost fluid rhythm.

"Your uncle, he is one of the best," Serge said, proudly. Max reached the roof in less than a minute. He anchored the rope and then tossed an end back down to me.

"Come on up, Dil!" he yelled. Serge helped me tie my harness to the rope and gave me a hearty pat on the back. I swallowed hard. My throat felt dry and my hands and feet were cold. I stepped up next to the wall and looked up at Max.

"Don't worry, I've got you anchored in up here and Serge is right under you." I looked over my shoulder at Serge. He was busy lighting a cigarette and kicking at a bug on the concrete. I made a coughing noise to get his attention. He looked up and smiled.

"Oh, sorry, I'm watching now. Climb when you are ready."

I looked back up at the wall. It seemed so steep and so far to the roof, when in fact it was probably only about thirty feet. I reached up and grabbed onto one of the stones. I placed first one and then the other foot into a little niche and stepped up. The rubber soles of the shoes were surprisingly adhesive and that gave me a little surge of confidence. I took another step and then another reach with my hand, pulling myself up even farther. Then again and again, hand, foot, hand, foot. The stones were irregularly spaced, but they were all rectangular and there were tiny ledges on the top of most of them, which made progress easy.

"Good job, Dil!" Max called down. "Keep coming!"

"Beautiful!" I heard Serge say and I looked back down to smile at him. It was then that it happened. I freaked. I realized how high up I was and just panicked. I pulled my body in closer to the rock and felt gravity take over. Both feet slid from their holds and my hands soon followed. I did not fall even two feet before Max clamped down on the rope from above. I dangled for a moment and then clung frantically to the wall. As far as I could tell there was no physical damage to me other than a small scrape on my knee, but psychologically I was almost ruined. I could hear and feel my heart beating in my head, and my stomach muscles were so tight I could breath only in short gasps. My hands and feet were frantic, each trying to find some stable surface to cling to.

"Ho la!" I heard Serge cry, and was disconcerted to look down and see that although he was watching me, he was too far off to the to side to catch me if I fell. Worse than that, he was still grinning and puffing calmly on his cigarette. I remembered, too, his shaking hands and the three inches of cognac he had consumed and that did nothing to help my state of mind.

"Dillon!" It was Max's voice. "Dillon! Look up at me!" I did so briefly and saw the shadow of his face, the sun shining brightly behind him. I squinted up, but then felt one of my feet slipping and looked down again to try and find somewhere to place it. I gave up trying to find handholds then and grabbed the rope itself.

"I don't . . . I don't think . . . I . . . can do it!" I cried, hardly able to speak.

"Sure you can!" Max said. "You were doing great, just got blender-headed, that's all."

I tried to breathe and avoided looking down.

"I want you to let go of the rope," Max said. His voice was stern but patient. "Do you hear me? Let go of the rope and lean back.

Don't worry, I've got you, Serge is right below, we're not going to let you fall. Trust me." I squinted up at him. His words took a moment to register, but there was something reassuring in his tone, not encouragement really, but an absence of worry or concern.

"Let go of the rope," he said again. "Let your arms relax a minute. Your legs'll hold you."

Slowly, tentatively, I did as he said and tried to put my arms at my sides, but it was like they suddenly had a will of their own and wanted to keep going back to the rope. I leaned forward.

"No, don't do that," Max said. "Lean back," he said slowly, "leeaan baacck. I know it feels wrong, but sometimes when something feels wrong, it's right anyway. You'll have to trust me on this one. Lean back. Put your weight over your feet and use your hands for balance."

Gingerly, against every message that my panicked brain was sending to my body, I did as he said. I leaned back a bit and tried to reach out to the wall. Again, I panicked and my hands went back to the rope.

"Good. Now stay back and let go of the rope. Just let go with one hand. Find a handhold."

I did so with one, and then quickly with the other, finding holds and clamping on to them with trembling fingers. I could still feel the harness held taut by the rope.

"Good. Now breathe and relax a minute," Max said. "Keep back and keep your weight angled in on your feet. Good. Now start again. You can do it. I've got you. Serge has got you. You're not going to fall. Good. Start climbing."

I looked up at the wall and saw that there were several possible places to go. *Lean back*, I said to myself. *You can. Weight over the feet, balance with the hands.* I moved one hand up, then one foot. My weight was on just one foot then, and as I went to switch it to the other, I felt the muscle in my leg spasm. I paused, took a deep breath, and told myself again to lean back. I did so and the weight on my leg stopped the tremors. I quickly lifted it up to the next foothold and stepped up. I looked up and saw that I was now only a few feet from Max.

"Come on, buddy, almost here. You're doing great!"

Step, reach, step, reach. I looked down and realized the rope was now slack and I was climbing under my own power. I reached the gutter and as I lifted myself up and over it I felt the sun on my face. Max took my hand and pulled me up.

"Welcome," he said, giving me a pat on the back. I did not reply. I felt sweat break out all over my body, as if it had been waiting until I was safe to release. I was exhilarated and relieved at the same time. My muscles and my breathing relaxed and went back to normal, but I felt recharged and excited—as if my blood had been electrified. Max put his arm around my shoulder and led me over to the other side of the roof. We looked across the plains to the foothills and then at the mountains beyond. I looked down. The tire tracks in the muddy street below seemed patterned and graceful, and even the dug-out basement holes, now nearly full of rainwater from the storm, sparkled and shimmered in the sunlight.

"It's beautiful," I said. Max's face relaxed into a smile.

"Yes," he said. "The world isn't nearly so ugly *à la distance.*"

Just then Serge crested the roof and pulled himself up. He was not connected to any rope, and he still had a cigarette clenched between his teeth.

"How do you feel, Dillon?" he asked, clapping me on the shoulder with one of his enormous hands.

"Better," I said, and smiled.

"Keep at it and you'll be a beautiful climber, just like your uncle." Then he came up behind Max and encircled him in his arms. They stood like that for some moments, just staring out at the mountains, both seeming to forget I was even there. I was so shocked that I nearly fell off the roof. It was such an intimate, familiar gesture, in which I instinctively sensed something sexual. My head, however, kept trying to dismiss it. It was probably just some French thing, like how they kissed both cheeks when they greeted someone. My head could try and dismiss it, but my heart, again beating like a drum, knew that it was something more. Max turned to look at me and I quickly looked away, embarrassed. Like I'd been caught looking at something I shouldn't. They separated and Max unlooped the rope from the chimney.

"Come over here, Dillon, and I'll show you how we set this up to rappel down."

When the rope was ready, first Serge, and then I, rappelled off the roof. Then Max tossed the rope down and followed after us, down-climbing with as much grace and agility as he'd gone up. At the bottom, they showed me how to wind up the ropes and how to organize the equipment in the back of Serge's truck, explaining the various functions of different metal clamps and carabiners. After that, the three of us sat in the sun on the driveway, and they showed me several knots to practice. I got so engrossed in the challenge of making the rabbit come out of the hole and go around the tree, and then back down the hole, and so on, that it was probably twenty minutes before I noticed their absence.

I looked around. It was late afternoon, and the sun was just moving behind the foothills. I got up, placed my bits of rope back in Serge's rusty red truck and stared back at the house. I went up the walkway and back in the front door. All was quiet. I closed the door and went into the kitchen. The cognac bottle was on the counter where I'd left it that morning, and next to it was a jar lid holding several of the filterless cigarette butts. Again, all was quiet.

I walked over to the basement stairs and looked down. The door was closed. My heart was pounding again and my throat felt dry. I had my suspicions about what was going on behind that door, considering what I'd witnessed on the roof, and yet somehow I could not believe it. It seemed too fantastic. I had taken about three steps down, just to see if I could hear anything, when the doorbell rang again. I froze. Then I scrambled up the stairs as fast as I could, afraid Max might suddenly open the door. I stood at the top of the cellar stairs and felt guilty, even though I had really not done anything wrong.

I cleared my throat and walked slowly over to the door. This time it was Wayne. His familiar round fleshy face appeared through the peephole, and he looked as big and pink and as tightly groomed as ever. I opened the door, but I did not protest or even question where he'd been. I did not speak to him at all. I stepped out on to the porch, closed the door behind me, and made my way down to the waiting Oldsmobile, smiling and nodding as he explained about the church and the delay.

"We've been scrambling like the dickens to get the roof patched in time for the gathering tonight," he said, backing out of the driveway, a smug grin on his face, "and it looks like Mother Nature was no match for the good Lord and his followers, because I'll be doggone if we didn't get her done!"

"Greeaaat," I said, adopting Lana's deadpan tone. The car backed out of the driveway and we drove away. Sadly, I watched the red truck recede and then disappear from view.

Chapter Seven

The gathering that night was brief. Many in the congregation had spent the day working to repair the damage to the church and were weary from their efforts. The "alleluias" were less numerous and more subdued; no one danced in the spirit or spoke in tongues; and even the singing sounded heartless and tired.

I sat on a pew in the front row in between two of the older ladies in the congregation. Ordinarily, I sat with Lana, but when the service started she still had not arrived. I kept craning around to see if she had arrived late and was somewhere in the back, but she hadn't come. Wayne, being the assistant pastor, was of course up by the altar and from the way he scanned the crowd I could tell that he was looking for her, too.

"I hope your mother's all right," he said when we met by the front door after the service. He wrinkled his brow and scratched his helmet of hair. "Not like her to miss a gathering, especially on a night like this when it's so important that we stick together."

I nodded and shrugged my shoulders.

"She probably didn't think we'd be up and running again so soon, but you'd think she'd wonder where you had gotten to," he said, patting me on the back. "Let me go get changed and I'll take you home."

When we arrived at the house, I was sad to see that Serge's truck was gone, and I hoped that Max had not gone with him. Wayne pulled gently into the driveway, shifted into park, and then, as was his habit, methodically shut off the lights, the radio, and the ventilation system. Only then did he release the door lock. We both got out of the car and walked up the path to the front door. As I opened it, I heard laughter. We went in, and Wayne shut the door behind us.

When we entered the kitchen, I saw Lana and Max sitting at the table, both talking and laughing, each adding parts to a story that it was clear they both already knew but were relishing retelling. I scanned the room, searching for the many wine bottles I felt sure must be fueling their mirth, but I saw none—only two water glasses on the table amid the remains of what looked like Chinese takeout. Lana was laughing and talking as happily as a parrot, but, more surprising than that, she was smoking! A habit she had given up after her conversion. They were both oblivious to our entrance and we stood watching them for some moments before Lana caught sight of us.

"Wayne!" she cried, popping up from her seat and quickly stubbing out her cigarette. He said nothing, but stared disapprovingly at the ashtray.

"I didn't hear you come in," she said, and scowled at me, as if I should have warned her that we'd arrived. "Have you eaten?" she asked, turning to Wayne.

"Yes," he said, and again patted my back. "All fed and taken care of. We grabbed a couple of corn dogs before the gathering, didn't we, Sport?"

I nodded. I looked over at Max and he gave me a wink.

"We thought we'd see you there . . ." Wayne trailed off, looking at Lana.

"Well, yes, uh yes, yes," she fumbled, "and I would have been there if I hadn't gotten out of class so late, and if, well, my brother here just got into town and I thought I should stay home and make sure he got all settled tonight."

Wayne eyed Max suspiciously. I could tell he was seeing Max's long hair and the cigarettes, the silver bracelet, and the pirate shirt, unlaced at the collar, and that he wholeheartedly disapproved of it all.

"I don't believe I've had the pleasure," Wayne said, advancing and extending his hand. Max put his cigarette in his mouth, got up, and shook Wayne's hand in both of his, much the way he'd done with Meredith earlier that day, holding on a bit longer than could be called acceptable.

"I hope we'll be seeing you at some of our gatherings," Wayne said. "The door is open to everyone. Your sister is usually so good about attending."

"Oh, Wayne," Lana purred, getting up and encircling Wayne's neck with her arms, "Now don't be that way. I tried to call you, I really did, but the phone lines are still out . . ."

This was a lie.

". . . and I knew you'd be bringing Dillon back tonight. How was he today?" she asked, trying to change the subject.

"Oh, he was great! He's a great kid, aren't you, Sport?" I gave an outward shrug and an inward groan. "I was pretty busy all morning repairing the roof, but I made it over and collected him a little past four. He was a big help raking the trash and getting it all bagged up. He's earned a good night's sleep, I'll say that much." And yet again he patted me on the back.

"Thank you, Wayne," Lana said, and again gave him a hug, pressing her breasts into his stomach. There was an awkward silence. I thought Lana would ask Wayne to pull up a chair, but she did not. Instead, she continued thanking him and slowly ushered him to the door.

"Hope to see you again soon," he called out to Max, as he was being led to the hallway. When they'd gone, Max came up to me and rubbed my head. He gave me a playful sock in the arm and said, "Sport!" I rolled my eyes.

"I wondered where you'd gone to," he said. "Serge was sorry he didn't get a chance to say good-bye, but he left a present for you on your bed and he wants to take us climbing next week—someplace real this time. Whaddya say . . . Sport!" and he fell back in his chair in a fit of giggles. I smiled, in spite of myself.

Lana returned and soon, believe it or not, we were all laughing, each of us taking turns telling stories about my grandparents while Max did riotous imitations of them both. I was happy about it all, but at the same time a little scared. I was so used to Lana's artificial public laughs that the hearty, genuine way she was laughing then made me ill at ease. It was as if, for once, she was not scripting it.

Of course, like all good evenings, my part in it ended too soon and I was sent to bed. When I got to my room I saw on my bed the climbing shoes I'd borrowed that morning. Next to them were several sheets of paper on which were drawn the diagrams of some knots to practice. "You can do these with the laces from the shoes," it said, at the bottom of the page. It was signed with a rather shaky *S*.

Again I heard the sound of Lana's laughter, echoing up the stairs. I knew I couldn't go back down, so I crept out into the hallway, lay flat on the floor, and peered through the spindles of the banister.

They were doing the dishes, standing side by side at the sink.

"Think about it," Max was saying. "I could help you with some of the work on the house and help keep track of Dillon."

"Oh, don't worry about him," she said. "He'll be going off to camp next week so he won't be in your way."

"I'm sure he wouldn't be in the way," he said. "I was thinking . . . maybe he could help me. I mean, I'm sure that camp you want to send him to costs money, and it's money that could be much better spent on finishing up this house, don't you think?"

"Mmm, but it's all arranged," she said. "Besides, he's gotten into some trouble. It's probably best if he goes. We're already looking into military school for him in the fall."

"We?" Max asked.

"Wayne and I, the guy that was just here, the assistant pastor from the church. He's been a great help with Dillon since James, that fucking prick, walked out!"

She paused here to let her venom dissipate before continuing.

"Wayne takes him to the church in the mornings. I don't really know what they do there, but he hasn't been in any trouble for the past two weeks, so whatever it is it must be good."

"When did you start going to church?" Max asked.

"Oh, after James left," she said.

I wondered if she was going to mention her own misadventures with the bottle, but she did not.

"I was feeling a little bit blue so some friends got me to go with them one night, and, uh, I've been going ever since."

I noticed that she said this nervously, as if she was suddenly a bit embarrassed by it all, and that she left out all the details of her conversion, which she usually loved to recount: how she had seen the light and stopped drinking, how she knew that light was the power of Christ driving Satan out of her heart, how she had accepted Jesus as her personal savior, etc.

"Oh," he said, and then let the silence hang between them. This made Lana uncomfortable and I could see her trying to think up something to say, some way to justify it to him, but she couldn't. Max knew her too well. He knew, like I did, that her faith was just something she had pulled out of the closet like a new outfit and was now realizing that it no longer really suited her.

"It's good for Dillon," she said. "It keeps him out of trouble."

"How long did you say you've been going?" Max asked.

"About six months, I guess, maybe longer."
"And when did Dillon get suspended?"
"That's different!" she cried.
"Of course, it is," Max said and started to laugh.

The next morning I was awakened suddenly. Max slipped into my room and whipped open the blinds, flooding the room with sunlight.

"Rise and shine, young man! We've got places to go, things to do, people to see! Up, up, up!" he yelled and whipped the sheet off the bed. Never a morning person, I lay there squinting like a newborn kitten while he danced around the room singing "Frère Jacques."

"Did you know," he said, coming round and perching on the edge of the bed, coffee cup in hand, "that there is a very exotic looking automobile in the garage? I've just come from there, and that, in addition to my consumption of several caffeinated beverages, accounts for my morning's exuberance!"

I rolled over and faced the wall.

"Don't you realize what that means?" he asked. "Freedom! *La liberté*, my boy! I was thinking we were going to have to thumb it downtown today, but now we can get there in style."

"Did you notice the hood?" I grumbled.

"Details," he said with a dismissive wave.

"There's no windshield," I added.

"As I was saying, young Dillon, details. Details that I have already dealt with over the telephone this morning, while you were up here sawing logs. However, I've reached the point in my plan where I require your assistance. Up, up, up!" he yelled and gave my ass a pinch.

"Ow! All right!" I cried, jumping out of the bed. He then strode out of the room and I followed him out into the hall.

"Now, we'll need a pair of nylon stockings and some golf balls," he said, checking the two items off on his fingers. "And I'll need some clothes. Some of your stepdad's clothes. He did leave some behind, didn't he?"

For the next half hour, we rummaged through James's closet, trying to find something that would fit Max. This was not easy. My stepfather was stout and short and Max was tall and thin, and Max was keeping me in the dark about what he needed the outfit to be appropriate for. In the end we found a pair of blue slacks (which fit only because they were new and had not yet been hemmed), and a blue-and-white-striped shirt. He tried on a tweed sport coat but his forearms stuck out a good six inches, so he opted for a tweed vest instead, and a smart little bow tie. The result was something like a young, long-haired Orville Redenbacher, and Max frowned when he saw himself in the mirror.

"This won't work," he sighed, so we returned to the closet. He tossed the vest and bow tie on the floor and selected a more conservative looking red necktie. In James's dresser he found a matching tie tack and cufflinks and to complete the picture he put on a pair of James's glasses. As he was brushing his hair and pulling it back into a ponytail, he told me again to round up a pair of nylons and some golf balls. I found the nylons in Lana's dresser drawer and then went down to the hall closet where James kept his clubs. In his bag I found a box of six golf balls. As I emerged with these Max was stumbling down the stairs, unable to see clearly through James's glasses but unwilling to take them off.

"Scissors," he said, and I led him to the junk drawer in the kitchen. He took the stockings, cut the legs off, and discarded the top half. He then opened the box of golf balls and dropped three of them in the leg of each stocking. He lifted the glasses and looked at his watch. His eyes widened.

"Yikes! We don't have much time, so we're going to have to hurry."

That said, he handed me one of the pendulous stockings and pushed me in the direction of the garage.

"But what are we doing?" I asked. "What do I do with this?"

"Ahh, be innocent of the knowledge, dearest Sport, till thou applaud the deed."

He switched on the light in the garage and walked up to the Jaguar. Despite the dents and the broken windshield, it still looked stylish, with its long hood stretching almost three times the distance of the cab. James had loved that car—worshipped it. It was his golden calf, his most prized possession, the thing most contentious in his pending divorce settlement with Lana.

He would cry if he could see it now, I thought to myself.

Imagine my horror then, when Max swung his golf ball–filled stocking and smacked the roof of the car, not once, not twice, but three times. He then paused and looked over at me impatiently.

"Jump in any time, Sport, we're on a tight schedule," and he gave it another smack.

"But . . . what? Stop!" I cried, grabbing the stocking from his hand. "What are you doing?" He looked at me, shocked for a moment, but then he smiled and whacked it again.

"Insurance, Dil. Insurance."

More whacks.

"What? Stop!"

"In-sur-ance," he said, prying my fingers off of his wrist. "Oh God," he sighed. "Remember the hailstorm?"

I nodded.

"Well that storm, to borrow one of your mother's platitudes, was a *real* blessing in disguise. She told me last night, rather offhandedly, about the car, and I must say, Dil, I was a little disappointed that you hadn't told me about it earlier, I mean, really! To neglect to mention something as vital as transportation! Anyway, I was reading the paper this morning while having my coffee and there, of course, were several articles about the storm and the damage it caused. Well, one of the businesses hardest hit, pun very much intended, were car dealerships! It only makes sense if you think about it. Almost all of their cars are parked outside, exposed to the elements. Well, that got me thinking . . . Are you following me yet?"

"I think so," I groaned, and rubbed my forehead.

"Good. Well, then, I thought to myself, I bet I could make that car look hail damaged. And then I thought, I bet old James has got a good insurance policy, and sure enough I was right. A platinum policy! With the premiums paid up through the end of the year. Not only will they come out and assess the damage, but they'll bring us a loaner until this one is fixed. So come on!" he said, tossing me one of the stockings and tapping at the face of his watch impatiently, "He's supposed to be here at nine-thirty."

And so, for the next five minutes we smacked the hood and roof and trunk of the car with the stockinged golf balls. When the damage looked natural enough we stopped, and Max hit the garage door opener. He put the car in neutral, and we pushed it out into the driveway.

"Okay, now go get dressed," Max said, pushing me back into the garage. "And make it look like you're going to school. Have your little book bag and whatever other accessories you school kids have. Go on. *Go!*"

When I returned, some minutes later, my clarinet case in one hand and my book bag thrown over my shoulder, Max and another man were talking in the driveway. The man, I gathered by his clipboard, was the insurance adjuster. Silently, he made his way around the car, carefully noting the damage, while Max examined his fingernails and tapped his foot impatiently.

"Certainly was quite a storm!" Max commented.

"Mmm," the man grumbled, running his fingers over some of the dents on the hood. "It's kept me busy. Say, some of these dents here look deeper than the others, like maybe they didn't come from the hail."

Max approached, lifted up his glasses, and examined the three gashes Lana had inflicted with the golf club. They were much deeper than the subtle impressions we'd made moments before with the golf balls.

"Well, yes, of course," Max said, without a moment's hesitation. "That's because they were not caused by the hailstones."

"Pre-existing damage?" the man asked.

"Ha ha ha, hard-ly!" Max bellowed. "As you can see we live in an area that is, how shall we say, a work in progress. The contractor skipped out, and, well, it's all tied up in the courts now, a big legal mess. Anyway, as you can see when the workmen pulled out, they left all their scrap lumber and crap lying around, so when the wind kicked up, of course, Murphy's Law, it all flew onto my property. Really did some damage," he said, shaking his head and fingering one of the gashes.

"Young Dillon here," he said, pointing to me, "certainly earned his allowance yesterday bagging it all up, didn't you, boy?"

I nodded, amazed at how quickly he was able to come up with a plausible explanation.

"Ready for school, I see, Sport," Max said, and then turned to the insurance man. "Listen, we're in quite a hurry. Any chance we could wrap this up? I'd hate for him to be late, it's the start of finals this week, and I was expected at the office over an hour ago. You do understand." The man nodded and made some more notes.

"Yes, yes," he said, handing Max a set of keys and looking at his watch. "Here are the keys to the rental," and he pointed down the driveway to a late model Ford parked next to the sidewalk. "I just need your signature here." Max signed. The man looked at his watch once again.

"The tow truck should be here soon." he said. "I'll catch a ride back into town with him. Here's my card. Give me a call this afternoon and I should have a time estimate for you on the repairs."

"Thank you so much," Max said, and ushered me down the driveway to the car.

"Oh, Mr. Sawyer?" the man called out. We were almost to the car. Max did not respond, so I elbowed him in the ribs. "I'm sorry sir, just one more thing." Max turned and gave a questioning smile. I got into the car, shut the door, and immediately rolled down the window.

"I'm sorry, I don't mean to sound suspicious, but it is my job and I have to ask. Uh, why is it that the car wasn't garaged?"

"Ahh," Max said, not missing a beat. "For that you can thank my wife. Terribly lazy, absentminded woman. Which is why, among other reasons," he whispered, cupping one hand around his mouth, "she's soon to be my ex-wife. But that's another story entirely. Any other questions?"

The man nodded, knowingly. "No, I don't think so," he said.

"Good. Well, I'll be off then," and Max got in the driver side and started the car. I was sweating as we drove off down the hill, and too awed to speak. Max was smiling and humming, still very much in character, swerving from side to side of the road, unable to see through James's glasses. When we had driven a few blocks away he took them off. He pulled the rubber band from his hair and shook it out, lit a cigarette and inhaled.

"You were very good, Dil," he said and gave me a pat on the thigh. "Do you think he suspected anything?"

I smiled and shook my head.

"You seemed pretty confident," I said. Max smiled at the compliment and exhaled a cloud of blue smoke.

"That's what it's all about, Dil, ninety-nine percent of the time. If you can appear confident people usually won't fuck with you, although I have to admit that was a little easier than even I had hoped. Poor guy!" Max said, looking in the rearview mirror. "He needs to rent a copy of *Double Indemnity.*"

We were about half a mile from the house when I saw Wayne's car headed in the opposite direction. He didn't recognize us because of the strange car we were driving.

"Oh no," I groaned. "I forgot about Wayne. He just drove past us!"

"You can thank me later," Max said, patting my leg. "But while you were snoozing this morning I was busy composing a note, which Wayne will find tacked to the front door, telling him about your early orthodontist appointment." He looked again in the rearview mirror and scrunched his brow. "I only hope he doesn't spoil things with our gullible friend back there."

Chapter Eight

After our performance with the insurance adjuster, Max drove us into Denver. I had not been downtown at all since I started at my new junior high, but I still knew my way around fairly well, having lived there with Lana and James for several years, and could orient myself by several different landmarks. The area of town that Max took us to that morning, however, was completely foreign to me: a run-down, forgotten strip of land between the highway and the Platte River. It was a single street, with old, mostly abandoned buildings on either side. There was a grizzly looking bar, crowded with patrons even though it was not yet noon; a fenced-in warehouse with two vicious looking German shepherds on patrol; an abandoned factory of some sort; and last, but certainly not least, a small coffee shop called Paris on the Platte.

Paris was a small low storefront, sandwiched between two much taller buildings, each of which were unoccupied and had their windows boarded up. In contrast, the small café looked inviting and alive, with its pink neon sign and tables and chairs spread out on the sidewalk. Inside, it was dark and cluttered. There were more tables and chairs, chaotically placed around the room, and nearly all the walls were lined with shelves of used books. To one side, there was a glass case from which they sold a variety of exotic cigarettes, and in the back, resting on another display case containing cakes and pastries, was an enormous antique espresso machine.

Paris catered more to the late night crowd so when we arrived, at ten o'clock in the morning, it had just opened and was nearly deserted. Its sole patron, Jane, was seated in a sunny spot by the front window, casually flipping through a magazine. She was dressed smartly, in a pale blue skirt and suit jacket with a simple strand of pearls around her neck. Her long hair had been twisted back tightly into a bun and was capped off with a pill box hat of the same hue as her skirt and jacket. As before, her eyes were concealed behind enormous sunglasses. She had not seen us come in. We wove through the labyrinth of tables and chairs and stopped in front of her.

"Good morning, Miss Nguyen," Max said, bowing deeply. She looked up and her mouth widened into a smile. She closed her magazine, got up and offered her cheek to be kissed. Max obliged. She then took both his hands in hers and gave them a squeeze.

"Oh, it's good to see you!" she said, and leaned back to take a look at him. Her brow wrinkled then and the smile disappeared from her face.

"What *are* you wearing?" she exclaimed, lifting her glasses and casting a disapproving glance at Max's borrowed outfit. "You're not actually thinking of going out and getting a job, are you?"

"God, no," he replied, "but you know me, always working! The clothes are borrowed, just until I can get something else."

She nodded and then turned her gaze to me and extended her hand. It was an extremely small hand, all the nails a uniform length and painted with a clear polish. On her ring finger she wore a large sapphire, encircled by small diamonds.

"Hello again," she said, smiling at me. "I don't believe I introduced myself last time. I'm Jane."

"Dillon," I mumbled, shyly taking her hand and looking at the floor.

"Well, Dillon," she said, leaning back and picking up her purse. "I'm starving! Shall we get something to eat?"

I nodded, and she took me by the hand and led me to the counter.

"The usual for you?" she called back to Max.

"Please," he said.

When we returned, with more pastries than we could possibly consume, Max was gone. He emerged from the shelves a few moments later carrying several books and a fresh pack of cigarettes.

"So," Jane said, addressing me, "has your uncle here been getting you into trouble?"

I looked at Max and smiled, but said nothing.

"Only potentially," Max said. "We haven't been caught yet."

Max and Jane then lapsed into a conversation I found hard to follow, speaking of things I knew nothing about. They had been friends a long time, that much was clear, since they were both at ease in each other's presence and spoke with a vocabulary full of their own slang and internal references. The conversation went on, lively and animated, and it was only when the tone changed that my attention returned to it.

"You don't look so good," Jane commented, reaching across the table and running a finger along Max's pale cheek. He pulled away and an impatient expression crossed his face.

"Yes, well, it wasn't a fucking picnic," he said.

"Bad?" Jane asked gravely. Max thought about this. He cocked his head to one side and gazed up at the ceiling.

"More like a long exercise in patience."

"I don't know how you got through it," Jane said, a pitying look on her face. "It must have been awful!"

"Oh, it wasn't so bad, really. It had a definite beginning and a definite end. That helped. You can get through anything as long as you know it will end someday. I knew I would get out, so I just put it on autopilot until then. Focused on what I'd do when I was released."

"And what might that be?" Jane asked.

"In due time, *chérie*, all will be revealed. But I'll tell you this much: it doesn't involve sticking around in this cow town much longer. But enough about me, let's talk about you. How's the family?"

Jane's expression clouded over at the mention of the word *family* and it was obvious that she didn't welcome the change of subject to this particular topic.

"The same," she groaned, and her shoulders fell, "only larger. New ones step off the boat every day and my father tries to get me to marry every one of them."

"And how's the shop coming?" Max asked.

"Still nonexistent," Jane sighed, and her shoulders fell even further. She pushed up her glasses and rubbed her eyes. "At least for the moment, anyway. I've got a booth in one of the antique malls. Me, and all the bored housewives and retirees in the city, arranging and rearranging the petty stock we amass from thrift stores and garage sales. Small potatoes, really, and it's just a wee bit degrading. Percy helps as much as he can."

"Percy?" Max asked.

"Oh, yes, I guess you wouldn't know about him, would you? He's one of my Tottering Ogres."

"Your *what?*"

"Tottering Ogres. At least that's what I call them, in private, anyway. They're all old and ugly and very rich, and I'm young and pretty and, how shall I say? hungry for a life I can't afford. There's a nice symmetry there, don't you think? A sort of yin and yang? Oh, now don't act all shocked!" she cried, shaking her head at Max, whose eyes had widened as she spoke. "You of all people."

"I didn't say a thing," Max protested.

"You didn't have to, I can tell by the way your brow went up. I should be used to it by now. Anyway, Percy is very nice, the nicest of all of the Tottering Ogres, and it gives me an excuse to get out of the restaurant and the nail salon. Of course my dad's livid and doesn't like Percy at all, so at first I told him Percy was just a business friend. When that wasn't enough, I'm afraid I told him he was gay. 'Like Maxey?' he said. 'Yes, just like Max' I said. 'Only older.' That quieted him down a bit, but I don't think he believes it."

When I heard this, I choked on the scone I was eating.

"Oh, my goodness," Jane said.

"You all right, Dil?" Max asked.

I coughed and smiled, took a sip of my water. What Jane said had jolted me as much as if I'd stuck my finger in an electrical outlet. Suddenly I knew my suspicions about Max and Serge had been right and my heart raced.

"Dil didn't really know about that yet," he said to Jane.

"About what? Your being gay? Please!" she scoffed, and then looked at me. "I guess I've known for so long it just seems obvious to me now. Well, Dillon, your Uncle Max likes boys," she said, matter-of-factly. "But don't worry, I think you're a little young for his taste."

They both laughed and then went back to the subject of Percy as if nothing out of the ordinary had been said. But I was shaken. I could hardly believe what I'd heard. My mind was spinning. I sat watching Max with a newfound sense of awe and respect and I couldn't wait to tell him that I was gay, too.

"And how is your dad's restaurant?" Max went on, taking another sip of his coffee.

"Booming," Jane said. "It has to be, really, to support our ever-expanding family of boat people. I've managed to weasel out of my shifts a few nights during the week, but he's still adamant about me putting in time on the weekends, and to tell you the truth, I need the money. I can usually get away with doing lunch on Saturday and dinner on Sunday, so that leaves my Saturday nights free. Which reminds me," she said, changing the subject and lowering her voice. "Doris came in last weekend. She wasn't happy. Asked a lot of questions about you."

"What did you tell her?" Max asked, leaning forward on the table, trying to appear unfazed. His lip twitched.

"Relax, darling. There was nothing I could tell her. You haven't been very communicative these past two years, never calling or answering letters. In fact, I probably learned more from her than she did from me. I mean, I knew nothing about your release."

In these last words there was a tone of angry sarcasm, and she paused after she said them, for effect.

"She's not pleased with you," she continued. "That much was clear. I *thought* you were done with her . . ."

"Yes," Max replied, but his tone was vague, and he casually lit another cigarette. She reached over and placed one of her hands on his.

"She's not one to toy around with," Jane said, looking straight at him, her tone level. "You do know that."

Max nodded.

"What is it she wants?" she whispered, looking around to make sure no one was listening. I continued eating my scone, trying to appear preoccupied, but aware that the conversation was moving into deeper waters.

"Oh, I have something of hers," Max said airily. Jane waited for him to elaborate, offered nothing.

"You're not going to tell me, are you?"

"No," he said, crushing out his cigarette in the ashtray. "I'm not."

"It's not drugs, is it?"

"No. I will tell you that. I'm not going there again."

"Then it must be money."

"What makes you say that?" he asked.

"Because Doris doesn't value anything else. Money for money's sake. That's Doris. It's money. Or drugs, which she'd just sell to get more money."

It took a moment but soon the significance of what she'd deduced sunk in.

"*You stole money from Doris!*" she whispered, her voice urgent.

"Not stole, really," Max replied. "It's more like I took what I feel I'm entitled to. A little something to compensate me for two fucking years of my life!"

"How much?" Jane whispered.

"Not enough," Max said bitterly. "But it's a start."

"But you can't stay here. She'll find you."

"She already has," Max said. "Dil met her. Didn't you Dil?"

I looked up, my mouth full, and nodded.

"She came to the house," I whispered, thrilled to be included in the conversation. "Just before you did."

Jane looked at me, her face troubled, then returned her attention to Max. "So she knows where you're living?"

"I suppose."

"What are you going to do? You can't stay. Where will you go?"

Max shrugged. He took a chunk of brownie and tossed it up in the air catching it on the way down in his mouth.

"What are you going to *do?*" Jane asked again, more insistently this time.

"I'll stall her," Max said. "At least until the end of the summer. Then I'll have enough money to get where I want to go."

"And do I even need to ask where that might be?" she asked, her voice tinged with sarcasm, but returning to normal volume.

"Probably not," Max replied, grinning.

Jane shook her head and rolled her eyes. She fell back in her chair, both hands clinging to the handle of the dainty purse on her lap. She gave an exasperated sigh and looked across the table at me.

"Your uncle," she said, shaking her head. "For as long as I've known him—and what has it been, my dear, ten years now?—has had an unnatural obsession with the country and people of France."

I looked at Max and then back at Jane.

"Confused?" Jane asked. "Well, you're not alone there, young Dillon. France is his brass ring, his promised land, his El Dorado. French fries, French toast, French movies, French perfume, anything having to do with the place, or even the idea of it, sends him into a swoon."

She leaned forward, picking up items from the table.

"Look here, Dillon, just look at these cigarettes, *Gitanes!* Look at the novels he's picked up." She reached over and plucked them off the table. "Maupassant, Balzac, Molière!" she said, reading the names off the spines and tossing them over to me. "Good Christ! I could have guessed without looking."

"What's there to guess about?" Max countered. "French writers are some of the best, most sophisticated, and most innovative in the world. France is the world capital of style and fashion, a notorious center for visual artists, a country that produces the most coveted food and wines in the world. I could go on and on—"

"And he will," she said, rolling her eyes, "*ad nauseum.*"

"It's a dignified, civilized country, full of educated and enlightened people," Max replied.

"Tell that to my father," Jane said. "They did wonders for his native land."

"I'm sure other countries were just as bad in their colonial practices, *chère* Jane. It was the U.S. and not the French that made a mess of it all. Why do you always have to be so cynical about it? Why is it so strange that I'd want to live there?"

"Oh, it's not," Jane said, and her voice took on a softer, almost sympathetic tone. "I know it means a lot to you; it's just that I think you may be unpleasantly surprised when you arrive, that's all. You want what you see in the travel brochures, when what you'll get is a lot of cheap souvenirs and crumbling architecture. Men who don't bathe often enough and women who don't shave their pits. Now don't get me wrong, I've never been there so I don't know for sure but I have a gut feeling that it's not all April walks through the grounds of Versailles. I doubt that every window in the city has a view of the Eiffel tower, and I'd be willing to bet that there are one or two women in Paris who aren't quite as beautiful as Catherine Deneuve."

"Of course I know all that," Max replied. "I'm not expecting a cultural Disneyland for Christ's sake, but I'm pretty sure it'll be better than this," he said, gesturing out at the city. "France will be less ordinary," he said confidently. "More exceptional and rare."

Jane gave an exasperated sigh and fell back into her chair.

"Rare!" she exclaimed. "Rare! You know what's really rare these days?" she asked, not really wanting an answer. "Well, I'll tell you. Being happy where you are. That's rare. Everybody wants to be somewhere else, thinks that if they pull up and go somewhere else, everything will be different, better, 'more exceptional and rare.' Well, it won't be. The dream is what you want, not the reality. The craving is always much better than the having."

"And you're an authority on this?" Max asked smiling at her.

"Yes," she said. "As a matter of fact I am. I see it all the time, especially with my relatives. They spend years and years dreaming of coming to America only to arrive and pine away for their homeland. They make their own little Vietnam right here and then rarely, if ever, venture out of it."

"Well, I won't be like that," Max assured her.

"Of course you won't," Jane sneered.

"When I arrive I intend to wallow in it! I'll set my feet deep down in the French mud and let them take root."

Jane looked over at me and rolled her eyes. Then she looked back at Max.

"And just how do you propose to finance your relocation?" she asked. "Or do I even want to know?"

Max grinned when she said this. He leaned forward on the table and rubbed his hands together eagerly.

"I'm glad you asked, Miss Nguyen," he said. "Because I have a plan. A plan that could be very profitable both for me and for you, if—"

"Oh, no!" Jane said, waving her gloves in front of his face. "I don't want any part of it. Your schemes tend to go awry and I can't afford any screw-ups right now. I've got my own means of financial salvation, thank you very much."

"But this is different!"

At that moment a large black Mercedes rolled into view outside. Behind the wheel an elderly gentleman was leaning over, peering through the passenger window, trying to see inside the coffee shop. Jane gave him a little wave and stood up.

"That's *my* plan!" she said, collecting her gloves and nodding to the man in the car.

"The Ogre?" Max asked, his voice filled with distaste.

"You bet! He's got more money than he knows what to do with and he thinks I'm the cat's pajamas. I've got to go," she said, adjusting her sunglasses and kissing Max on the head. "We're having lunch at the family place with his mother."

"His *mother?*" Max cried.

"Yes, she's ninety-three today, the dear," Jane said. "This is the first time I'll meet her so I'm hoping to make a good impression. If all goes well, a walk down the aisle may be in my future, and you know what that would mean, don't you?"

"Years of sex with the lights out and a hope for a vivid imagination?"

She scowled and slapped him playfully with her gloves.

"No, silly. It means I'd be on my way to getting away from restaurant hell, away from the nail salon, away from all of the eligible Vietnamese bachelors that my father wants to hook me up with, and far, far, far away from my little booth in the bourgeois antique mall. A walk down the aisle would help get me comfortably installed in my own posh little boutique! And that's why it is so important to impress Mrs. Geritol this afternoon. If she likes me, I'm a shoe-in with Percy. He told me she likes blue," she said, smoothing her skirt and assessing her reflection in the window. "And I certainly hope so because I spent a mint I don't have on this little Easter egg ensemble and it's making me nauseous to even see myself in it. Blue really doesn't suit me, does it? Anyway, wish me luck!"

She kissed us both on the head and clicked toward the door. She paused when she reached it, turned, and called back.

"Hey, I'm working at the restaurant Sunday nights. It slows down after eight. Why don't you two come by? We'll feed you, and I know my father would be thrilled to see you again, Max. Think about it."

Max nodded and blew her a kiss. She waved at me and went out to the waiting car.

When she'd left we sat in silence while Max smoked and finished his coffee. Now that we were alone I wanted to ask him about what Jane had said earlier about him being gay, and about what had happened the day before with both Meredith and Serge and how I couldn't really make sense of it. I was on the verge of speaking several times but was unsure how to start. Max sensed my frustration.

"What's on your mind, Dil?" he asked. I looked up at him and swallowed.

"You know what you guys were saying earlier . . ." I said my voice timid and low. The question was vague and he looked at me, waiting for me to continue.

"*You* know," I said, my face reddening. "About your being . . . gay."

This last word was whispered and I had to look down when I said it. Max laughed.

"Yes, why?" he asked. "Does it bother you?"

"No! No," I whispered, wishing he wouldn't speak so loudly. "No, it doesn't bother me at all. I mean, I, um . . ."

Max grinned, again waiting for me to continue and offering no assistance.

"I mean, I . . . I think I might be, too. Be that way, I mean. Do you know what I mean?"

I'm sure my face was the color of a brick.

"Yes," he said, and gave a little wink. "I know."

"And it's . . . okay?" I asked.

"Yes, of course!" he laughed. "Why wouldn't it be? In fact, in some ways you'll find it can be a real advantage. You'll see. But in the end it's not really a big deal, remember that. You're young now, but by the time you're my age, you'll be able to fill a book with the names of all the people who will tell you it's bad and that you're bad. Well, take it from me, it's not, and you're not. You heard it here first. You like boys. That's it. No good or bad about it. It just is."

I heard what he said and yet I almost couldn't believe it. For years, my whole life, really, I had kept my desires a secret. I'd kept them hidden for so long that when they were brought out into the open that day, in such a matter-of-fact way, and with no shame, I could not really believe it. It had the unreal quality of a dream from which I felt sure I would soon wake up.

I thought back to the church, and the hours of "We renounce him" that they'd subjected me to after Lana had found my catalogue stash, and I realized that the whole point of that exercise had not been to save me, but to shame me, to show me that what I was doing was bad and wicked and evil. And yet, in my heart, in the core of myself, I'd known they were wrong. I'd resisted. And that was why they were so persistent. Enough drops of water on a stone will dissolve it to nothing, and they poured buckets on me everyday. But Max had arrived, and suddenly I had the reinforcements I needed for my side of the battle. In him I found the one person who confirmed what I already knew: my desires were not wrong; the way I felt was not wrong; I was not wrong.

"When did you . . . know?" I asked, my voice, again, barely above a whisper.

"When did I know what?"

"That you were . . . gay?" I said.

He thought for a moment, raising one eyebrow and gazing off into the distance.

"Oh, I guess I thought about it the first time when I was six or seven," he said. "I was over at a friend's house and we were down in the basement playing one of those kid's games: Truth or Dare, or Spin the Bottle, something like that. There were girls and boys, and I remember wanting to kiss all of them and see them all take off their clothes." He paused and laughed at the memory. "I guess I knew I was different then because although the girls didn't really seem to mind kissing each other; none of the boys wanted to let me kiss them."

He lit another cigarette and puffed on it a while.

"But I guess I really knew when I was about your age. There was a neighbor kid, and, well, another guy I used to play around with. It was fun, but we should have been more careful. My parents found out and, well," he said, shaking his head and crushing out his cigarette, "they weren't happy."

"They found out!" I cried, remembering my own dismal stay with my grandparents.

"Yes," he said. I waited but he offered no more.

"What'd they do?" I asked, imagining that their reaction must have been even worse than Lana's.

Again, he looked off into the distance, but this time his eyes narrowed.

"What did they do . . ." he repeated. "Some things that were not very nice. I guess their names were the first I entered in the book of people who tried to tell me it was wrong."

He smiled, reached across the table and gave my hand a squeeze.

"But don't worry, Dil. You'll be fine. I can tell you already know what's true and what's not. You already know when to trust yourself. And that's a lot. That's a lot . . ." he said in a wistful tone, gazing down at the table. Then he looked up and his tone became serious.

"Just be careful when you do experiment, and I don't mean just about getting caught. I mean about AIDS."

AIDS. That was another word I could barely say above a whisper. It was a threat as frightening to me as any Lana could dish up, all the more so because I knew so little about it. So little, that is, except that it killed gay men.

"Do you know what to do so you don't get it?" Max asked.

"I think so, yes."

I really had no idea, but the frankness of the conversation was becoming almost too much for me to take.

"Hmm, that's not a very good answer," he said. "Do you or don't you?"

I looked down and shook my head.

In an unashamed and unhurried way, Max then went on to explain, in graphic detail, all that was involved in man-to-man sex. He told me what men did with their mouths, and what they did with their cocks, and what they did with their asses; how to use condoms and common sense to protect myself. In short, he gave me a primer on all the techniques and tools that were needed to have sex safely.

I wish I could say I sat and listened attentively while he spoke, asking pertinent questions in all the right places, and making mental notes, but I did not. I squirmed and writhed in embarrassed agony. My palms were sweaty: my face was red; and I was terribly afraid that the other people in the coffee shop might overhear him. Nevertheless, I took in much of what he said and am, to this day, grateful to him for making the effort and taking the time. It might be a bit much to credit him with my still being alive today, but, when you think about it, who else in my unenlightened world would have done even half as much?

"But enough of the free clinic for today, do you have any other questions about all things homosexual?" he asked.

I had thousands but I was so embarrassed I shook my head, no.

"Really?" he asked. "Nothing?"

I looked around the coffee shop. The other patrons seemed intent on their newspapers or their books. I leaned in closer to the table.

"What's it like?" I asked. He looked at me, confused. I tried to clarify what I meant: "When you're with a guy, and you're safe, and all that, what's it like?"

He laughed, leaned back in his chair, and grinned at me. "That's a hard one to answer." He took another cigarette from the box and tapped the end of it on the table to compact the tobacco. He lit it, inhaled, and puzzled over the question.

"What's it like?" he repeated, exhaling and gazing up at the ceiling. "What's it like? I guess it's like anything, really; like food, or an empty canvas, or what you see when you look out the window. It's what you make of it. It can be good; sometimes it's bad; sometimes it just is. A lot of it depends on how much enthusiasm, and style, and imagination you put into it. But most of all, it depends on who you've got to work with. That's important. I don't mean you have to be in love with them, or anything, but there does have to be a spark, a fire. If that's not there, then the love never really will be. Does that make sense?"

I gave a halfhearted nod. What I'd really wanted to know was what it felt like to kiss another man, what it felt like to do all of the things he'd so graphically described earlier in the conversation. Max sensed my disappointment.

"No? Well, that's about the most I can tell you," he said. "If I say any more it'll be like telling you what happens at the end of a book or a movie. Finding out is most of the fun."

"So you like being . . . gay?" I asked. "I mean, you wouldn't change it, if there was like a pill or something you could take?"

"You know," he laughed, "in spite of all the shit I've taken about it, I don't think I would. Being different has its advantages, I'm sure you can see that."

But I could not see it, and my thoughts immediately returned to Aaron and the other kids at school, and how they sought, seemingly above all else, to stamp out anyone who was different. In my experience being different had a distinct disadvantage. I tried to explain that to Max, giving a synopsis of my junior high agony, but before I could finish he interrupted me.

"That's different. It was the same for me when I was your age. It's the same for kids the world over. As you get older, though, you'll see what I mean. Being different gives you a clearer view of things and you don't buy into as much bullshit. I'm sure, knowing that you're gay, you don't buy into all the stuff they feed you at church. You're smarter than that, I can tell. Well, maybe not smarter, really, but being different has made you able to see. You see that a lot of what they say just isn't true. You see that the message they preach isn't the same as what Jesus said."

I nodded eagerly.

"So being gay is a good thing," I said.

"Like I said in the beginning, it's not good and it's not bad, it just is."

I shook my head. I couldn't believe all that had happened that morning, even in just the past half-hour. I felt so relieved to know that I wasn't alone. There were others out there. Others who had gone through the same trouble and had lived to tell about it. Max was one of them, and I felt grateful that he had appeared in my life.

"But remember," he added, "being gay is just a part of who you are. Do remember that. There's no need to make a career out of it."

I didn't understand this and looked at him questioningly.

"Hmm, how to explain?" He took another long puff on his cigarette. "It's like this, Dil: there are some people in the world who love to see themselves as victims. They get off on being martyrs. Does that make sense?"

I nodded, but could not see where he was going with it.

"Your mother is a bit that way, and your grandmother! Oh, how that woman *loved* to drag the cross around. Well, don't you be that way, Dil, because a lot of gay people are. They wrap themselves in the rainbow flag and cry and whine about how tortured and oppressed they are. It's a bit much. Don't be that way," he said. "That's the best advice I can give you. Life might toss you some turds but self-pity, no matter how justified it may be, is never very productive, or, for that matter, very attractive."

I nodded, not really understanding all of what he'd said, but feeling glad he'd said it.

"No, self-pity is not very attractive," he repeated, and then stood and looked at himself in the mirror. "And neither are these clothes. What do you say we get out there and fix what we can, Dil?"

Chapter Nine

Stealing, for those of you not familiar with the practice, can be highly intoxicating. The rush you get from theft is almost narcotic, and I can see how someone could become as obsessed with stealing as, say, skydiving, or snorting cocaine, or wrestling crocodiles. It is the risk, really, that is so attractive, the very real possibility of arrest and imprisonment, the possibility of profound embarrassment. As Jane said, the getting is often much more satisfying than the having. The risk of being caught is often far more exciting than acquiring the object you are after.

Maybe none of this is really news to anyone. It may seem obvious and fundamental, but to me at the time it was a novel discovery.

In addition to being novel, stealing was also empowering. It gave me a sense of superiority, a feeling of vindication, a means to redress wrongs, a way to obtain compensation from society for the slaps it had inflicted on me. A successfully executed theft gave me an almost smug feeling, and more confidence in my abilities than a library full of self-help books. After I'd done it a few times it became a sport, like any other, at which I wanted to improve, to perfect my stroke, or serve, or shot. I practiced whenever I could and was always trying out different tools and equipment to help me improve. Best of all I had a terrific coach.

"Have you ever stolen anything, Dil?" Max asked, as we walked away from the coffee shop that morning, headed under the railroad tracks toward downtown. I thought about it for a moment. I had stolen Certs and small change from my grandmother's purse, some pens and promotional items from James's desk, but other than that, nothing really.

"What about the wine cellar?" Max asked, looking ahead and continuing to walk. I reddened. I did not know how to respond or where this was leading, so I said nothing and we walked in silence. He seemed to want me to think it over. I stopped walking. He turned and looked back.

"Oh, don't worry," he said, returning and taking me by the hand. "It's our secret. Just like my being at your house is our secret. We can trust each other, right?" I nodded and resumed walking alongside him. We went on in silence and Max started to speak several times but then stopped himself. It was clear that he wanted to say something but was troubled by the best way to go about it.

"I don't know how much you've heard about me," he said, his pace quickening. I struggled to keep up. "But I am what the French call *un voleur.* A thief. A cat burglar. A larcenist. I pilfer and purloin for a living. I am, as they say, fond of taking the five-fingered discount. Are you following me?"

"I think so."

"Good. So here's the way things are today," Max continued. "We are both desperately in need of clothes, are we not?"

I nodded and looked down at my clownish pants.

"But neither of us has any money, right? Well, we're going to get some new clothes but we aren't going to pay for them, are you with me?"

"Yes," I replied, without any hesitation. He stopped walking and there was a somewhat surprised expression on his face. I think he expected me to be shocked, expected that maybe all the churchgoing had rubbed off on me and that I would start proselytizing and warn him of the dire punishment that awaited those who disobeyed the seventh commandment. But there was certainly no danger of that. I did not think stealing was all that bad. In fact, my time at church had, if anything, the opposite of its intended effect. Instead of giving me a moral framework to govern my life, going to church only made me feel that I was absolutely beyond redemption. I was damned, I figured, so what I did really didn't matter.

Let me try to explain: there was no question that I was a sinner. I drank and got in trouble and had impure thoughts about boys, and I knew that all of those were damnable offenses. Nevertheless, Wayne and the pastor and all the parishioners assured me that no matter how grave the sin, God was always willing to forgive, and they never tired of encouraging me to repent. The problem was, although God may have been ready to forgive, I was hardly willing, or, more significantly, *able* to repent. I knew that even if my sexual desires were wrong, they were so strong that they completely overwhelmed any concerns for what might happen to my soul. I knew that the way my dick reacted when I was in the showers at school had absolutely nothing to do with being an upright God-fearing Christian. I had tried everything in my power (ice-cold water, averting my eyes to the heavens, even pinching myself) to control it, but my body instinctively rebelled and the mast went up. When that happened, and it happened with an annoying regularity, it almost made me want to curse God for what seemed to me his wicked sense of humor. God was playing a game with me. A game with rules he had made that were impossible for me to follow. For that reason, my moral sensibility was not shocked by what Max was saying. I knew it was wrong in God's eyes, but then so was I.

That stealing was wrong in the eyes of society bothered me even less. In a way I actually felt good about it. I felt that society owed me something, much the way Max thought that Doris owed him something for his taking the rap and spending time in prison. Life was not fair, that much was clear, and if that was the case then what was the point in playing fairly.

Add to this the fact that Max was stealing to help me and you'll see I had even less resistance. He was doing it to get me some less ridiculous-looking clothes, to get me some acne medicine, to get me some shoes that fit. He was doing it to do all of the things that Lana had neglected to do and I was so grateful that I felt I ought to help him. It was the least I could do.

"Now today," Max went on, "you just watch and learn. I'll need you to play along with my lead, okay? The most important part of stealing is confidence. Remember that. Be confident. If you can't *be* confident, *act* confident, and if you can't act confident, then you nonchalantly make your way toward the exit and wait outside, you follow?"

"Yes."

"Excellent. You play the clarinet, right?"

I nodded.

"Jazz?"

"Sometimes."

"Good, because stealing has a lot in common with jazz; you've got your basic tune every time but you vary the melody, improvise. Like I said, follow my lead at first, play along, but then, as you see fit, jump in and add your own notes."

We started out quickly that day, with a trip to a cluttered army surplus store on Larimer Street, where I watched, awestruck, as Max deftly pocketed several items: a retractable razor knife, some sunglasses, a small tool set. The first time I saw one of these things drop into his pocket I nearly gasped. I thought if *I'd* seen him take it, surely someone else had too, but the fat man behind the counter was too busy chuckling at the comics he had spread out before him to notice, and the lanky stock boy was busy trying to look busy with a broom, so neither one paid any attention to us. When Max had all that he needed, we headed toward the exit. Then, to my dismay, Max turned to the right and approached the counter.

"Do you have airplane glue?" he asked the man.

Why is he doing this? I wondered.

"It's for my son here, he's building a model."

"Nope!" the man replied, not looking up from his paper. "Used to. Drunks were always coming in and stealing it. To sniff. Bunch a crazy coots. Whatcha building?" he asked, looking down at me. I gulped and looked at Max. He was gazing at me like a proud father.

"Don't be shy, Sport, tell him what it is."

I knew nothing about airplanes or models, but I did know that most of the models other boys in my class had built were cars.

"It's, a, uh, Oldsmobile," I sputtered.

"An Olds, eh? What kind? An SS? A Cutlass?"

"Um, neither," I said, trying to picture Wayne's car in my mind. "It's, uh, a, Delta Eighty-eight!"

"A Delta!" he exclaimed, raising an eyebrow above the frame of his glasses "That's not very sporty."

"No. No, but it's an easy model," I said, "and, and, and I thought it would be good to start with an easy one. It's the first time I've done one. A model I mean."

"Ah," he said nodding. "Start out easy till you get it figured out. Smart boy," and he reached over and gave me a pat on the shoulder. "Try the Ace Hardware. There's one up on Corona or over off of Thirty-eighth. They should carry that kind of stuff."

"Thanks," Max said. He smiled at the man and gave me a gentle nudge out the front door.

When we had walked a safe distance away, Max spoke. "Not bad, Dil. Not bad. You still with me?"

"Yes," I said, and wiped the sweat from my forehead on my sleeve. "But why did you stop to talk to him?" I asked. "We could have just left."

"Ahhh, it was a little test," he said, "and I'm glad to say you passed. Oh, your performance can definitely use some polishing, that stuttering was a bit out of control, but overall you did well."

From the surplus store we walked over to Sixteenth Street, and without a word of direction I followed Max into Fashion Bar. The store was crowded with people on their lunch break, and all of the clerks appeared to be busy helping customers or ringing up purchases. Max wandered slowly around the men's section, selecting clothes for us both and now and then asking my opinion. When he had amassed six or seven things, he walked by one of the vacant counters; as he did, I noticed that he dropped one of the shirts he was carrying.

"Hey," I whispered, bending down to pick it up, "you dropped one." He turned, a somewhat flustered look on his face, and knelt down to pick it up. In a flash I saw the razor knife come out from under the pile of clothes and slash through a metal cord. It was the cord tethering the device for removing theft protectors to the counter. When it was cut, Max quickly concealed the device and the knife under the clothes, got up, and continued walking. We went on browsing for about ten more minutes, and when we had a large pile of clothes, we headed toward the dressing rooms.

Fashion Bar was never very strict about their dressing rooms. There was no attendant watching to give you numbers or direct you to a particular booth, so we wandered in together and Max handed me several pants and shirts to try on.

"Pick the ones you like best and put them on," he whispered, his voice firm and clear. "Remove the clamps and any tags, and then put your own clothes on over them." He then pushed me into one booth and took the one next to it for himself.

I was sweating from every pore and my breath was coming in short gasps. I bit my lip and tried to relax. I took off my clothes and put on a pair of new khaki pants and a blue-and-white nautical sweater. I had barely pulled it over my head when I saw Max waving the remover under the partition separating the two booths. I bent down and took it. I tried to remove the clamp from the sleeve of the sweater, but my hand was shaking so much that I couldn't get a grip on it. I took the sweater off and set it down, to use the floor for leverage. I attached the remover to the clamp, gave it a squeeze, and it popped open like the mouth of an alligator. Sweat dripped down the bridge of my nose. I put the sweater back on, popped the clamp on the pants and then passed the remover back under the partition. I pulled my sweatshirt on over the sweater easily, but when I tried to pull my pants on I discovered they were far too small and tight to fit over the khakis. I thought my heart would beat right through my chest. I wanted to ask Max what to do, but there were other people in the dressing room now so I knew I couldn't. I took off my old pants, wadded them up in a ball and shoved them under the small bench in the corner. I hoped I could get out wearing the khakis, but they were deeply creased where they had been folded and looked new.

Confidence, Dillon, I told myself. *Act confident.* I looked at myself in the mirror. I was still sweating, but the air-conditioning had kicked on and as my sweat evaporated I felt myself cooling down. I focused on breathing normally. Max's door opened and he knocked on mine.

"Any of those gonna work for you?" he asked. I opened the door. Max was dressed in the same conservative clothes that he'd borrowed from James's closet that morning, and, if anything, the layers he had put on underneath filled out the clothes and made them look more natural. He assessed me and did not look displeased. I pointed to my pants in the corner. He nodded and then motioned for me to kick the clamps I'd removed under there, too. I did so and together we walked out of the dressing rooms. Thankfully, the store was still crowded and it appeared that no one had noticed us. Max hung several garments on the rod outside the dressing room, and we browsed around the store for a few more minutes, idly commenting on the cut of this jacket or the color of that shirt. He then looked at his watch with an expression of surprise.

"We'd better go," he said, and we did just that, walking through the front doors and out onto the street without setting off any alarms.

When we'd made it about a block, I could not help but grin. I was so elated that I wanted to break into a run. I felt like all the anxiety I had dammed up inside of me had suddenly burst out and was coursing through my veins.

"We did it!" I said, unable to conceal my excitement. I looked up at Max, wanting to take him by the hand and skip up the street. He brought his index finger up to his lips and shook his head. We turned off of the crowded shopping street and walked down the comparatively deserted Seventeenth Street. Only then did he speak.

"Not bad, Dil. Not bad at all. You nearly choked in the dressing room but you got it under control. I could see you were nervous, but you did all right." He lit a cigarette and inhaled it deeply, shaking out his shoulders.

"You had it all figured out!" I gushed, jumping in front of him and walking backward so I could see him as we were talking. "I never would have thought to steal that clamp remover, never in a million years, that was so great!"

He grinned and smoked, clearly relishing my admiration.

"And the razor, I never would have thought of the razor!"

"You flatter me," he said, but then his tone grew serious. "But flatter me more by remembering it. The order of things is perhaps the most important, Dil. Before you can go to the party and loot the cloakroom, you first have to steal the invitation."

I gave him a confused look.

He offered another comparison: "Get the ring before you announce the engagement. Get the clamp before you steal the clothes. It's the order of things. Understand?"

I nodded.

We walked back to the car, took off some of the clothes, and then Max drove us up to Capitol Hill where, for the first of many times that summer, we went to the movies. The theater was called the Ogden and, at the time, it was a run-down, art house cinema with movies that changed daily. Max loved it because they showed a lot of older movies that you couldn't see anywhere else and, perhaps more important, because you could smoke in the balcony.

The movie we saw that day was, appropriately enough, Hitchcock's *Marnie*, in which Tippy Hedren portrays a crafty kleptomaniac. The Ogden was in the middle of a Hitchcock marathon, mixing up the chronological order of the director's films, until they had shown them all. I know this because, with few exceptions, we saw each one that was shown over the next few weeks, although we saw very few of them in their entirety.

One of the more peculiar and annoying things about Max was that he often got up and left before the end of the movie. We'd be sitting in the dark and suddenly he'd nudge me, motion toward the exit, and out we'd go. At first I thought this was because we had someplace to go by a certain time, or because maybe he'd seen someone down below that he wanted to avoid, but then we'd make it outside and his urgency would disappear. He'd suggest getting a hamburger at the Wendy's next door, or even hanging around to get tickets to the next movie. This made no sense to me and I asked him why he always left. He just grumbled something about needing more cigarettes. After the third or fourth time I began to protest, but Max would not stay. Even when I refused to leave, usually at the point when the climactic violins started up, Max would just shrug, grind out his cigarette with his toe, and say he'd wait for me outside.

It wasn't until years later that I understood. I was watching a movie by myself. I think it was *To Catch a Thief*, and it was at the end, when the young French girl is revealed as the cat burglar, clearing Cary Grant of suspicion. Instead of feeling happy, I remember feeling almost deflated by it. I realized that I'd really wanted him to be the burglar all along, and that I had wanted the young girl, who was in love with him, to win him over. But, of course, Cary Grant could never be the bad guy, and what female, young or old, could possibly win out over Grace Kelly. I understood then why Max would often leave. Although he loved the style and the manners, the witty dialogue and the glamorous locations of old movies, he could never take the Hollywood endings. He could never take the way everything was tidied up and sanitized. The way conventional morality always triumphed.

In *Marnie*, for example, the movie we saw that first afternoon, the main character's motivation is so completely explained that the ending is completely forgettable. Instead of just having her steal and connive because she's greedy, or because her equestrian hobby is too expensive, her kleptomania is all explained away in the last five minutes of the movie by a flashback reference to a childhood trauma. She had killed a man who was attacking her hooker mother—which is not to say that childhood trauma is an entirely implausible cause. After all, I've just finished saying how I stole as a sort of compensation for my own miserable childhood. Still, psychological explanations (especially when they come in the last five minutes) are sometimes just so disappointing. Especially when you consider that through most of *Marnie*, we are manipulated by Hitchcock into rooting for her. She is strong and capable and shrewd. She dyes her hair and reinvents her identity, embezzling from one bumbling employer and then moving on to the next. She's so classy and self-assured that you actually want her to succeed.

But of course she doesn't. Her behavior is shamed in the end and blamed on a psychological disorder, and it's all just so lame.

So, any time the ending of an otherwise great film threatened to get sappy, or happy, or just too tidy (as most of the old ones do), down the balcony stairs Max would go. In *Rope*, when the killers break down and confess their crime, Max walked out. In *Spellbound*, when Gregory Peck's craziness is pinned on childhood trauma (in a scene almost identical to *Marnie*'s), Max walked out. *Rebecca? Psycho? Dial "M" For Murder?* Out, out, out. Nor was his disillusion limited to Hitchcock—he did not stay to see the end of *Gilda*, *Mildred Pierce*, or *Suddenly Last Summer*. Crime in classic cinema rarely, if ever, goes unpunished or unexplained, so Max would walk out. A hollow protest against all the easy endings, the pathetic weakness of the criminals, the lovers hurled together by a contrived fate.

Or maybe, just maybe, it was fear that made him walk out. Fear that their weakness might be contagious, and with Max sentimentality was a weakness he could never afford to have. Then again, maybe I'm falling into my own trap here, trying to explain Max and his motivations with simple psychology. I suppose this is the point in my story where he would, once again, shake his head and walk out.

Chapter Ten

After our day of shoplifting, we didn't get back to the house until nearly seven-thirty, by which time Lana had already gone to the gathering. The house was empty and quiet, which was good, because it would have been difficult to explain where all our newly acquired clothes had come from. After the movie we had again hit the shops along Sixteenth Street, stealing shoes, an antique cigarette lighter, some cheap watches, acne medication, and anything else we could get our hands on, more for the practice and confidence building than because of want or need.

As we pulled into the driveway, Max commented on the fact that the gas gauge was near empty. Gas was something he did not want to risk stealing.

"We're going to have to get some cash somehow," he said. "I'll have to think up some way to get it from your mother. Try and be especially agreeable tonight," he said. "I do have a plan."

When Lana returned, she immediately questioned Max about the missing Jaguar and about my supposed orthodontist appointment. He told her about the Jaguar first, which was a good strategy because she was so relieved to find out that James had not taken the car and so happy that Max had found a way to fix the damage she'd done that she completely forgot about the phony appointment.

"So how was the gathering?" Max asked, quickly steering the subject in a different direction.

"Oh, all right," Lana replied.

"Just all right?" he asked. "Is that boredom I hear?"

Lana frowned.

"No, it was okay, really, I just wish some of those people would put a little more effort into their appearances. I mean, this woman next to me was clearly at least a size ten and she'd somehow squeezed herself into a size six dress. It was so tight she couldn't breathe and just sat there wheezing and whistling through her nose all night."

The irony of this struck me so hard I almost screamed. I thought to myself how my own ridiculous looking outfits that were several sizes too small had never bothered her. But I remembered what Max had said about being agreeable, and I said nothing.

"That doesn't sound very Christian of you," Max scolded.

"No, I know, but don't people usually dress up for church? I mean even Wayne, who's usually so neat, was a mess. He actually wore these bright plaid golf slacks under his pastor robe. Can you imagine? It's not like we couldn't all see them poking out the bottom. He looked like a clown."

I could sense Lana's disillusionment with the church; like most everything in her life, she had grown bored with it quickly. Max saw this, too, and carefully fueled the fire.

"Yes, it seems to me people should dress up for church," he said. "Or at least try to, since it is God's house and all. But didn't you say they meet in an old Safeway or something?"

"No," Lana chuckled, "it's a Kmart."

They both laughed heartily at this, Lana trying to stop herself.

"The place shouldn't matter," she said, adopting a serious tone, but her attempt at gravity was betrayed by her smile. "We've met some really good people there, haven't we, Dillon?"

I nodded, and tried to appear serious, but soon Max was imitating the woman's wheezing and her nasal whistle, and all three of us were laughing.

Later that night, after I'd been sent to bed, I again crept quietly to the stair rail and eavesdropped on the conversation between Max and Lana.

"It's not just the drinking that was the problem . . ."

There was a long pause as Max waited for her to elaborate.

"I mean, there's a reason I've been so stubborn about him going to church." Again she paused. "How do I say this? He's, well, he's not like the other boys," she whispered.

"What makes you say that?" Max asked.

"Oh, come on! Look at him. He's not the most masculine kid in the world, always skipping around humming Carpenters' songs, and, well, just other things."

I knew that she was thinking of the catalogue ads but was too ashamed to say.

"It must be hard for him without a dad," Max went on.

"Oh, I'm sure," Lana said. "And that's where Wayne comes in. He's been great. He knows all about, uh, Dillon, and thinks we better nip it in the bud before it gets out of hand."

Nip it in the bud. It was exactly what Wayne would have said. Exactly what he would have pulled out of his never-empty bag of clichés.

"He's really taken to the kid," Lana went on, "and I think Dillon's warming up to him too."

Guess again, I thought.

"Hmmm," said Max.

"What?" Lana asked.

"Oh, I just wonder why you think Wayne is such a good role

model. I mean, I was sure picking up some strange vibes from him the other night."

"From Wayne?" Lana cried. "Like what vibes?"

"Oh, I don't know, just the way he looked at me, I guess, and the way he held onto my hand when he shook it. Doesn't it seem strange to you? I mean, how old is he and he's still not married? Is that really the type of guy you want spending time with your son? They disappear all day long. Where do they go? What happens when you're away?"

There was a pause.

"No, no, you're barking up the wrong track," Lana chuckled. "Wayne's just geeky, a little bit nerdy, he's not *that* way. And anyway, Dillon will be off to camp in another week and then he'll be in a strong, moral environment with lots of other boys his own age."

"And you think that will be better?" Max asked his voice full of derision.

"Well, yes, of course I do."

"Uh huh."

"Wait a minute, what does that mean?" she asked.

"What?"

"That uh huh."

"Oh, come on, Lana. Do I have to spell it out? A bunkhouse full of hormonally charged boys, communal showers, lots of chances to be off in the woods alone. I wouldn't be surprised if the kid came back in worse shape than when you sent him away."

"It's Bible Camp!" she cried.

"Mmm, Biiiible Camp," Max sneered. "Full of lots of namby-pamby counselors who will be cookie-cutter versions of Wayne. You know how those preachers are. You read the papers. They're just waiting for some confused boy like Dillon to come along. Prison was full of 'em, I can tell you that, and the stories they told . . . It'd curl your hair!"

There was a longer pause this time.

"Why don't you let him stay?" Max said, "I'll put him to work on the house, toughen him up a bit, give him a good, solid role model to follow. Really, it's safer to leave him here. Not to mention less expensive." He paused. "Think about it. Will you promise me you'll think about it?"

I heard no response but assume she must have nodded because Max moved on to a different topic. As for me, I went back to my room, closed the door, and beat off, imagining myself as the center of attention at the marvelous camp he had described and feeling a bit sad that I might not get to go after all.

Later that night, I got up to go to the bathroom, and as I headed back to my room I could hear music playing, softly, like someone had left a radio on with the volume turned down low. I went to the top of the stairs and listened. It was coming from below. I crept down the stairs. It sounded like a guitar and someone singing or humming. I went around to the cellar stairs and saw a light from the crack under the door. I could smell cigarette smoke, so I knew Max must be awake. But was he alone? The question lingered in my mind. I tiptoed down the stairs until I was two feet away from the door, and then stopped to listen. I heard only Max's voice and the guitar, but he was singing in French so I couldn't understand any of the lyrics. The guitar playing stopped but the singing went on, low and gravelly. Then the handle turned and the door was pulled open.

"I thought I heard something," he said. I looked up, but I could not see his face since the light was behind him.

"What are you doing out there?"

"I didn't know you played the guitar," I said. "I heard the music, and . . . I just came to see what it was."

Looking behind him I could see that the cellar had been made much more inviting since that morning. Max had brought down a few table lamps and a chair from the living room. His guitar was propped up next to the chair and a large ashtray was on the floor along with several empty coffee cups. He had evidently been smoking a great deal because the air was thick with a blue fog, and I could feel it in my eyes and in my throat.

"Got kind of rusty in prison," he said, turning and picking up the guitar. "So it's taking me awhile to get it back. Close the door. Sit down; sit down."

I took the chair and Max crawled up on the wine rack, where he had his bedroll. He propped his head against the wall and strummed a few chords, trying to recall a certain melody. He found it, and started playing the chorus of the Carpenters' "Superstar." It took me a moment to recognize it, but once I did, I looked up at him and smiled. He smiled back, cigarette clenched between his teeth, and winked at me.

"Thought you'd like that one," he said, and then closed his eyes and went back to playing. When he'd finished, he fumbled through a few other Carpenters' songs, but "Superstar" was the only one he really knew, so he played it again, much better the second time. He sang along when he knew the words and hummed the parts that he didn't. I was touched, and just like the first time I'd heard their music, back in band class, I got goose bumps. He put the guitar aside and took a sip from one of the coffee cups.

"I think I may have a way to keep you out of camp," he said, eyeing me over the rim as he drank. I didn't let on that I'd eavesdropped on his conversation with Lana. "I put the idea in your mom's head, now we'll just sit back and see what she does with it. But it looks good, Dil. The odds are definitely in your favor."

I nodded my head and leaned forward on the chair.

"I think she may be getting tired of the church thing, too, but until we're certain you just play along, okay? Just go when she tells you and maybe be extra nice to Wayne, maybe ask if you could even spend the night there sometime."

My face registered my sour reaction to this proposal.

"Trust me," Max said. "The more enthusiastic you are about spending time with Wayne, the less likely you'll be going to camp."

"Okay," I said.

Max hopped off the rack and set his coffee cup down. He squatted down in front of me and put his hands on my knees.

"Listen," he said, looking me straight in the eye, his expression serious. "If I can work it so you'll stay here, do you promise to help me? To do whatever I might ask?"

"Of course," I said, and swallowed hard. There was nothing all that peculiar in his words or in the fact of his hands on my knees, and yet I found the situation strangely erotic. I tried to dismiss the feeling, to shut it out of my mind, but my body betrayed me, just as it had in the showers at school, and I felt the mast going up under my robe. I suddenly remembered that I was in the room where Meredith and Serge had passed eventful times with Max and that made it even worse.

Oblivious to my trouble, Max went on: "Life is like a seesaw sometimes, Dillon. If I do this favor for you, it's like I'm taking all the weight off your end and letting you go up, you see?"

"Yes," I said, my voice creaking.

"Eventually I'm going to ask you to do the same for me. That sounds fair, doesn't it?"

"What do you want me to do?" I asked. Max smiled.

"Nothing worse than what we did today. Don't worry. Nothing bad, really. I just need to get some money, you know, and with my record most of the traditional routes to success are closed, do you follow?" I nodded and shivered again.

"Come up here," he said, climbing up onto the wine rack. "Either you're cold or this is making you nervous. Come up here and let's read for a while. We'll forget about this and talk about it later. Do you like to read, Dil?" I nodded and creaked out another "yes." I was so flustered and confused. I repositioned my bathrobe so it concealed my erection and then climbed up on the rack and sat at the far end, near Max's feet. He was using the empty racks below us as a sort of storage unit for his things, and he reached down and grabbed one of the books he'd purchased earlier that day at Paris on the Platte.

Max read aloud to me that night, as he did nearly every night after that. He was a great reader, which is not something many people can do well. It requires intense concentration and a quick intellect because the reader must be able to anticipate who is speaking, what tone of voice they are using and at the same time must concentrate on his own comprehension of the text. Max was a pro.

The book he read from that night, and for the next several nights, was Balzac's *Père Goriot.* As with all the movies we saw together that summer, I have in years since revisited this book, always looking for answers, for some hidden key to what made Max tick. But during those summer evenings my understanding of the story was more impressionistic. It was difficult for me to follow, as it was a bit beyond my reading and vocabulary level, and because it dealt with foreign situations in a foreign land, almost two hundred years ago. And yet, the beauty of Balzac is that his books are accessible on many levels. They may be great art, but they are, first and foremost, great stories, full of carefully fleshed-out characters in dramatic, exciting situations.

In Balzac, characters who appear in one novel often reappear in another one, so reading his books is a lot like watching an episode of *Happy Days* and suddenly seeing Laverne and Shirley in the Cunninghams' living room. It is strange to see them there, but you're not really surprised by it.

As I said, the book Max read from that night was *Père Goriot.* It is the story of Eugene, a young man from the French provinces who has come to Paris to study law. He has grandiose ambitions to launch himself into high society, but he is poor, and his poverty forces him to live in a grimy rooming house with several shady characters. One of these is an old foolish man called Goriot.

Goriot has two beautiful daughters whose material happiness has been his life's only concern. Consequently they have grown into spoiled brats with expensive tastes. They return, several times throughout the novel, only to leech money from their poor father. He lives in rags so that they can have new party gowns.

Eugene witnesses all of this greed and sacrifice, and the story is really about his own struggle between the two. A classic literary boxing match between the forces of Good and Evil.

All that was interesting enough, but what really piqued Max's interest in this story and drove him to plow on through the rest of Balzac's novels, was the appearance of a character who boxes in Evil's corner. A character called Vautrin.

Vautrin, aka Jacques Collin, aka *Trompe la Morte*, is a notorious criminal, a master of disguises, a sharp, incisive wit, and, best of all, a homosexual. When we first came across him in the pages of *Père Goriot*, he has just befriended Eugene. He pulls the boy aside one night after dinner and gives him a long talk on how to succeed in Parisian social circles, by playing false and abandoning his principles. It is an interesting conversation, but what is really interesting is that during the course of his speech, Vautrin makes some subtle attempts to seduce Eugene.

I still remember Max pausing at one point and wrinkling his brow. He glanced at me over the book and saw the same question in my face.

"Are you getting what I'm getting?" he asked.

"I think so," I replied, but thought maybe it was just my own hypersensitivity to even a hint of anything gay.

Max read on, and there were more subtle hints about Vautrin's sexuality, which we were both, at first, reluctant to believe. After all, this was the nineteenth century we were reading about. Things like that were presumably not discussed, let alone written about. Max reread the parts again and the second time the hints were less subtle. Of course Vautrin's attempts at seduction, both physical and moral, are unsuccessful with Eugene (It was, after all, the nineteenth century). But with both Max and me they were a hit!

After that, Vautrin became our mythic hero, our mascot, our idol. And we became his disciples, spending many evenings that summer searching through volume after volume of Balzac, elated whenever he would reappear.

The reading became part of the nightly ritual, but it was not the only part. On the contrary, reading was just the preface to the events that would follow, but more about that later . . .

Chapter Eleven

The next morning, at Max's suggestion, I went to the church. I knew what he was implying when he said I should appear eager to spend time with Wayne, but in spite of the lusty picture Max had painted of Bible Camp, I thought that given the choice I would rather stay home for the summer.

I got up early and had breakfast with Lana before she went off to nursing school, all the while doing my annoying best to mince and flit around the kitchen, humming an endless stream of Carpenters' tunes. When I sat down to eat I made sure to cross my legs, which she was forever telling me not to do, and to comment on how nicely her nail polish matched her lipstick.

"I wish I could paint my nails," I said, taking another spoonful of cereal and turning my attention back to the issue of *Woman's Day* I was flipping through. She gave me a hard look, grumbled, and went back to her coffee.

When Wayne arrived I made sure to appear enthusiastic, running to the door to let him in and then giving him a great big hug.

"Well, good morning, Sport!" he said, somewhat surprised. "Missed you at the gathering last night."

"And I missed *you!*" I said, getting my windbreaker from the closet.

Wayne approached Lana and touched her on the shoulder. "And how's the prettiest little lady in the city this morning?"

"Fine," she said, flatly, and took another sip of her coffee. She turned to look at him and her dismay registered on her face. Wayne was dressed in khaki pants and a pink polo shirt with the collar flipped up. He had tucked the shirt in, and this only emphasized the tube-like shape of his body. On his feet he wore penny loafers with no socks. This outfit was nothing out of the ordinary for him, but I could see that in the light of her conversation with Max, Lana saw him differently now.

"Something wrong?" he asked.

"No. Just tired, that's all. What, uh, what will you two do today?"

"Well, most of the day we'll probably spend shopping," he said.

"Shopping . . . ?"

"Yes, I've got Mother in the car and I promised to take her shopping today. We've also got to stock up on some things for the church since so much was ruined in the storm. That's about it, really. We'll run some more errands and probably break for lunch at Furrs. Mother loves Furrs."

I knew then, perhaps even before she did, that our churchgoing days were numbered.

"I'll have him back about four. Then I'll have to take Mother home and get ready for the gathering. You'll both be there, of course."

"Mmmm," Lana said, nodding her head. "If I get out of class in time. Traffic's bad sometimes. You know how it is."

"Well, let me know. Dillon could certainly come to church with me and I could bring him home afterward," Wayne said.

"Or maybe I could stay," I blurted out, almost without thinking. "I mean, at Wayne's." They both looked at me. Wayne smiled; Lana did not.

"I'm sure Wayne is busy," she said. "He is the assistant pastor, after all, and he has a lot to do."

"Oh, poppycock! If Sport here wants to stay with me," he said, putting me in a headlock and rubbing my head with his fist, "he's welcome anytime."

"Just bring him home," Lana said. "I'll try and make it on time."

"Well, okay then. You all set, Sport?" I nodded, and we left.

Out in the Olds with Wayne and his mother, I reverted to my usual surly silence, but neither one of them noticed, each intent on getting to the mall and the subsequent lunch at Furrs.

All through the morning, as we wandered the depressing Cinderella City mall, I kept contrasting this trip with Wayne and his mother to the trip the day before with Max. It was like comparing dry toast to chocolate cake. The day with Max had been so fun and new and exciting, whereas this never-ending stroll through the Muzak-filled worlds of Sears and Wards and JCPenney's on a fruitless quest for a girdle was almost unbearable. I was so bored I decided to practice stealing, which was fairly easy because no one was really paying any attention to me.

Since I was confined to the women's department, the selection of items to take was rather limited, and most of the things I took were rather stupid—a pair of stockings, a cheap necklace, a scarf, sunglasses. I didn't really want any of them but I made a game out of it, eyeing something when we first walked in and then analyzing the best way to slip it into my pocket. I was successful six out of the seven times, but then, in Montgomery Ward, as I was sliding a pair lace panties, of all things, into my pocket, my luck ran out. A huge hand gripped my shoulder and I turned to see an enormous security guard.

An hour of trouble followed. The guard hauled me into a back room where I was photographed, and scolded, and shamed, and then scolded some more by the store manager, Wayne, and Wayne's mother. But the thing I remember most, the thing I was most afraid of, was not that I would be in trouble, not that this would go on my "permanent record," as they threatened, not even that I'd probably be beaten to a bloody pulp by Lana. No, what really frightened me was how Max would react. What would he say about it? Would he ever trust me again after I'd shown myself to be so inept? The thought of his disappointment brought tears to my eyes, and that was evidently what everyone had been waiting for, because as soon as I started crying, they all stopped scolding. All they had wanted was to see a little remorse on my part, and when I realized that I really played it up.

"I'm so, so sorry!" I bawled. "I don't know why I did it, I'm just stupid! I'm a stupid, awful boy! Oh, I wish I was dead!"

The room went silent except for the sound of my choking sobs.

"We'll keep him on file here," the store manager told Wayne. "I think he's been scared enough. He won't try it again."

Wayne nodded.

"But next time," the manager said, waving a finger at me, "we'll have to press charges."

"There won't be a next time," I wailed. "I promise! I'm so sorry!"

That night was tense. Max was out when we got home and I crept quietly up to my room. I still had a bottle of Sandeman's stashed in the closet and I went for it. I uncorked it and was about to take a drink when suddenly I decided maybe I'd better not. Wayne had gone to drop off his mother, but I knew he would return and I had to be sharp to try to figure out how to handle this. A drink would only make me slow and stupid and probably get me into more trouble, and I didn't want that. I replaced the cork and put the bottle back in the closet.

When Wayne returned, he let himself in and came up to my room. It was almost six o'clock and I wondered if he'd come to take me to the gathering.

"Dillon," he said, poking his head into my room. I was lying on my bed facing the wall. "You awake?"

"Yes," I said, my voice hoarse from crying. Wayne approached the bed. He sat down and rubbed me on the back.

"Why don't we pray?" he said. "God will always listen, and I think if you'd just open your heart and let Him in, He'd forgive you. He'd help you. All you have to do is ask, son. Shall we give it a try?"

His sincerity could be touching at times. I sat up and he took my hands in his. He closed his eyes, and in his booming, assistant pastor voice, he prayed. It went on for a very long time. I opened my eyes at one point and saw Lana standing in the doorway, her book bag on her shoulder, staring at us.

"What's going on?" she asked, looking to one, then the other, for some explanation. Wayne turned and gave her a grave look. He then turned back to me, shook both of my hands and said, "Amen."

"Why don't we go downstairs?" he said, rising from the bed and walking toward Lana. "I'll tell you all about it."

Before Wayne closed the door, she shot me a burning scowl.

I waited for a few minutes after they left and then opened my door a crack. I could hear them talking below, but I couldn't hear what they were saying. I went out once again and crept over next to the banister.

"You shouldn't smoke," he said. They were in the kitchen, right below me.

"Well, my kid shouldn't drink, or fucking shoplift! Or fucking be a fucking faggot! Stealing *women's panties!*" she shrieked.

There was silence after this. Wayne was unaccustomed to profanity and so far Lana had managed to hide that aspect of her vocabulary from him.

"You're angry," he said. "That's natural in this situ—"

"You're right I'm fucking angry! He's more fucking trouble than he's worth. God damnit!" This was followed by the sound of a cabinet door slamming shut.

"Listen," Wayne said, "he'll be going to camp next week. That'll do him wonders, you watch. Just wait and see. It's been a difficult time for both of you. You need a break. Why don't I have him stay with me for a while, until you cool off, or until he goes?"

From the sound of breaking glass that followed, that option clearly did not appeal to her.

"He's not going to fucking camp!" she screamed. "And he's not going to your house. And we're not fucking going to fucking church anymore because it doesn't fucking do any fucking good!"

I gathered that while she said this she was pushing Wayne out because when she'd done so I heard the front door slam. Then all was silent. The dead bolt clicked and I heard her set the chain. I got up off the floor. The doorbell rang, again and again, and I knew it was Wayne trying to get back in. He was pounding on the door with his fist. Lana's heels clicked across the floor and I saw her charging up the stairs. I turned and ran back to my room. I tried to shut the door, but she was already behind me and blocked it with her body.

I'll spare you the description of what followed because it wasn't pretty. In a way I was glad that she did some visual damage (there was a black eye, and bloody scratches on my neck, a gash on my forehead where the clock hit me), because it was the real guarantee that I wouldn't be going to camp or back to church for a while. I think she was afraid, too, about what I might do, because she was quite civil to me for weeks afterward. Needless to say, Wayne was not allowed back. He called and called all that evening, and Lana lied and lied. She said we had talked it all out and were just going to spend some family time at home. No camp, no gatherings, and no, please, don't come by.

As for Max, I didn't see him until the next morning when he once again entered my room, buzzing like a caffeinated bee.

"Well Dil, you did it!" he said, brightly. "*Fait accompli!*" Then he saw my face and his expression darkened.

"Maybe a little too *accompli,*" he said with a sigh. He came over and sat next to me on the bed, assessing my face.

"I knew something was up when I came home and the chain was on the door. I had to climb in a window and then I found *ta mère* in the kitchen, just about to tip another bottle. I knew she'd done something bad but I didn't know she'd gone this far. Are you all right?" he asked. "Is what I see the worst of it?"

I nodded. Lana had focused her blows on my head. The rest of my body she had left alone.

"Good," Max said, "that's one good thing. But this isn't the first time it's happened, is it?"

I looked away, not wanting to answer. He came over and lifted up my chin, forcing me to look him in the eye.

"Is it?" he repeated. I shook my head. He moved away and began pacing the room, cigarette in one hand, coffee cup in the other.

"Why does she hate me?" I asked. There was no self-pity in my question, just an honest desire for an answer from one who had known her longer than I. He stopped his pacing and looked at me. He took a big drag on his cigarette and then exhaled noisily.

"Oh, it's *them,*" he said.

Somehow I knew he meant my grandparents.

"It's not her; it's them. I know you can't see that, but it's true. They were worse than she'll ever be. Really fucked-up people. She just repeats what she saw, and what she got. I was lucky. I got out pretty young, and for a while before that I had her to protect me, but she wasn't so lucky. They did some damage. Much worse than this," he said, approaching and running a finger over my forehead. "Much worse. She doesn't know how to react. She gets her wires crossed and sometimes the spark causes an explosion."

This made little sense to me. I knew my grandparents were not nice, but to blame them for what Lana had done, for the way she was, I couldn't accept that. If it had been done to her why would she do it to me? I had no doubt she was a little crazy. I'd seen it in her eyes the night before, and many times before that. A look of rage that was almost always in excess of whatever had provoked it.

Max finished his cigarette and his mood brightened. He seemed to realize that pity and outrage would do no good, so he smiled.

"It's a drag," he said with a shrug, "but you're getting too big. She'll realize that. It won't go on forever, and in some ways this is actually quite good. Not the beating so much, but the effects of it," he said, again gently touching the bump on my head. "You really played your hand well! Just how well, you don't even know yet. Ouch! She really did a number on that eye! Of course you haven't iced it. Come, come, let's do it now."

He pulled me up, gently draped my robe over my shoulders, and I followed him down the stairs. We went into the kitchen and I sat down on one of the bar stools. Max brought me some ice wrapped in a towel and had me hold it on my swollen eye.

"There," he said. "The swelling's bad but this will make it go down."

He lit a cigarette and smiled at me.

"I'm not going to camp, am I?" I asked, fairly certain of his response.

"Oh no, you certainly made sure of that! In fact I feel like you deserve a round of applause for how well you managed, well, everything."

And he began counting my accomplishments on his fingers.

"You got yourself out of camp. You got rid of Wayne. You've pretty much scared your mother away so she'll leave us alone, and last but not least, you convinced her—and let me say that the irony of this is not lost on me—you convinced her that I am the only hope of salvaging your heterosexual boyhood. 'I'll leave him home with his butch, prison uncle . . .'" Max said, doing a high pitched imitation of Lana's voice. "'. . . to do construction on the house, that'll make a man out of him! That'll straighten him out!' Oh, what a hoot this all is!" And he fell back on the sofa, laughing and kicking his feet in the air.

"But you know what the best part is, Dil?" he said, sitting up again and peering at me over the overstuffed back.

I shook my head.

"She gave me some money! She gave me the money she was going to use to pay for camp so that I'll look after you. I'm the baby sitter! The lunatic has been given the key to the asylum! She even gave me a credit card to buy paint and supplies for the house, and a gas card for the car! And it's all thanks to you, Dil! I don't think Vautrin could have done it better himself. I can't tell you how proud I am." He gave me a kiss on each cheek and then went about making breakfast.

As I sat holding the ice on my eye I reflected on the situation. The night before, I'd gone to bed feeling afraid and ashamed, only to be awakened the next morning with praise and congratulations on a job well done. Granted, most of my success had been accidental, and I had no desire to again travel the road that had gotten me there, but I had succeeded. Max was proud of me and I basked in the glory of that all the rest of that day, running to the mirror several times to admire my black eye and the cuts on my face. To me they had become like medals, badges given for an operation successfully completed. And yet I knew that the only thing that gave them significance at all was that Max admired them, was proud of the lengths to which I'd gone to do what needed to be done, and to me that was better than any medal.

Chapter Twelve

The morning after my beating, after we had eaten breakfast, Max and I drove to Boulder. We were to meet Serge at his shop, load up some equipment, and then do my first "real" climb at Eldorado.

Eldorado Canyon is about three miles south of Boulder. It was once a somewhat fashionable resort, drawing visitors to the mineral-rich hot springs that bubble beneath the surface. Today the resort has essentially been abandoned—an old hotel is all that remains—but the natural beauty of the place is still there, and the steep sandstone walls of the canyon have become a big attraction to climbers. Such an attraction, in fact, that on summer weekends the walls are so crowded they look more like huge slabs of wood, crawling with colorful termites. For that reason it is best to go on a weekday, when the only people you'll run into are university students cutting class.

Serge's shop was on the east end of Pearl Street, about four blocks away from any other shops. It was an old, two-story building of rough gray stone with a storefront below and residential space above. Above the door was a large rectangular sign on which was printed "Rostand's Climbing Shop," and under that, a picture of

Serge's logo: a curly-horned sheep balancing on top of a pointed peak. The yard out front was overgrown, and the mailbox, the base of which was nearly hidden by weeds, tilted slightly forward and to the left.

Inside, the place looked like anything but a sporting goods store. In fact, it was so dark and dirty that it was more akin to the army surplus store Max and I had hit earlier that week. The big difference, however, was that the army surplus had been a random, chaotic mess, whereas Serge's shop, although dirty, was almost mathematically ordered. Behind the large oak-and-glass counter hung several of the brightly colored climbing ropes, and behind those, on a pegboard wall, were climbing tools he sold, some factory made, and some, more specialized pieces he had forged in his shop out back. All were meticulously arranged and sorted according to size, use, and strength.

Serge was behind the counter when we came in, busy looking over a topo map with two scruffy-looking students. He smiled and gave a wave when he saw us, but then he noticed my eye, and the gash on my head, and his smile disappeared. He quickly finished his business with the two, folded up the map, and when he had seen them out, came over to us.

"What happened!" he cried, kneeling in front of me. He took my head in both of his giant calloused hands and examined my face. I had not thought of how to explain it, so I said nothing. We both looked to Max, but his face was blank, and his eyes were hidden behind his sunglasses.

He shrugged and said: "The family curse."

Serge looked down at the floor. It was an awkward moment and I remember sensing something in the silence; something that was being communicated without words. When Serge spoke, it was to ask me if I was okay to climb.

"He's fine," Max said before I had a chance to answer. "Aren't you, Dil?"

Serge looked at my face again, and then, questioningly, at me.

"I'm okay," I said, with as much enthusiasm as I could summon. "Really. I want to climb."

"Look," Max said, his voice flat and weary, "we've got to get him on some real rock before he forgets everything he learned last week."

Serge was wary and kept looking at one, then the other of us. Then he shook his head and stood up, his knees cracking. "Maybe we try something easier today," he said, patting my shoulder. "A shorter climb, or maybe just some bouldering."

"No!" Max cried. "No. We need to do Bastille. He'll be fine! Let's just stick to the plan, okay."

We both stared at Max but said nothing. It was a strange outburst, but not out of sync with the surly mood he'd been in all morning. "He'll be fine," Max said. "Fine."

"Did you bring your shoes?" Serge asked me.

I nodded and pulled them out of my bag.

"Okay then," he said, putting an arm around my shoulder and guiding me over to the counter. "Okay then, let's get some gear together and we go."

Wordlessly we gathered up all of the things we needed and got into the cab of Serge's old red truck. As we drove toward Eldorado, Max's mood improved, and he and Serge got into a spirited conversation about past climbs and about the different places in the world Serge had been climbing in the two years Max had been in prison.

"I wish you could have gone with me the last trip, *petit*. You would have loved it," Serge said.

"Yeah, well," Max grumbled, "it's hard to climb out of a locked cell."

We drove on in silence for a while after that, but then Serge spoke up again.

"Why did you do it?" he asked. "I still don't know why."

"Why did I do what?" Max asked.

"You know what I mean," Serge said.

"Why did I steal? Sell drugs? Get caught? What?"

"No, you know what I mean," Serge repeated. "Why did only you take the blame? She was the boss. Everyone knew it. She was more guilty than you! But she stayed free and you went to jail. Why?"

"Ahhh, you mean why didn't I snitch on Doris?"

Serge looked confused.

"I don't know, what is . . . snitch?"

"A tattletale. A rat. A stool pigeon," Max said. Then he lowered his sunglasses and looked over at Serge. "A snitch is someone who talks when it's better to remain silent."

Serge said nothing. He returned his attention to the road and the muscles in his jaw contracted.

"You, of all people," Max said with a laugh, "should know that I do not talk."

Again, Serge was silent. He was looking straight down the road and I could tell he was angry.

"Why didn't I tell on Doris? Is that what you mean? Is that what you want to know?" Max said.

"Yes" Serge said, as calmly as he could. "That is what I want to know."

Max chuckled. He lit a cigarette.

"I don't really know why," he said, exhaling and then picking stray bits of tobacco from his tongue. "I don't know. Maybe I didn't tell because it didn't seem right. I don't know. Maybe there is some honor among thieves, as stupid as that sounds. I don't feel any affection for the woman. I know she's ruthless, and a bitch, and would never do the same for me. But I was caught, and I knew I was going to jail. I didn't see any use in pulling her down, too. Besides, this way she owes me. She owes me for my little favor, and she'll pay. Don't worry. She'll pay."

This did not put Serge's mind at ease. On the contrary, he became more agitated, and when that happened his accent became much more pronounced.

"What!" he cried. "What are you doing? What do you mean by

this, 'She'll pay'? You need to stay away from her and that trouble! She's dangerous, you know that. You need to stay away!"

Realizing he was yelling, Serge stopped himself and tried to regain his composure. He exhaled, ran his fingers through his hair and started again, this time in a softer tone.

"Look, you're smart," he said. "You could maybe go to school for something. Get a degree. Or I could give you work again. You were a great guide. The people loved you. I could have three climbing classes a day for you tomorrow, if you want. I could do it. Only say the word. You'd make lots doing that. Just don't mix with her again. Don't do it! No money is worth that. No money is worth all that time in prison."

Max laughed and shook his head, as if to say that Serge had it all wrong.

"Don't worry," he said. "I can handle Doris. I worked for her for three years, remember?"

"Just be careful," Serge said, and he reached over and ran his hand along Max's cheek. "Please."

When we got to the canyon, they were both much more at ease. We got out of the car, loaded ourselves with the equipment, and I prepared myself for a long hike. From the parking lot, we walked all of about seventy-five feet and then Serge and Max dropped their bags and looked up. I followed their gaze. Above us was nothing but a solid, almost vertical slab of rock, the top of which I could not see.

"This is it?" I asked.

"This is it!" Max said. "*La Bastille!* The Bastille Crack. Get your harness on; you'll go up after me."

"Yes, it's a good day. We're lucky today," Serge said, excitedly running the rope through his hands. "Usually there is a line for this route."

I looked at the wall before me. I could not even see anywhere to start!

"Are you sure I'm ready for this?" I asked, my palms growing sweaty.

"You'll do fine, Dil," Max said, smiling and nodding.

"You're a natural climber, just like your uncle," Serge said. "Just remember to lean back this time and to use the jams we talked about. Jams, and lateral moves, and you'll do fine. Climbing *la Bastille* is easy! Beautiful! You'll see."

When we had all the rope and protection together, they explained the route. It was to be a four-pitch climb. I would belay Max, and he would climb up several feet and place some "protection" (which is the name they used to describe all of the little metal clamps) in between the rocks. The rope would run through this protection, so that if one of us fell he would fall only until the protection stopped him and not all the way to the ground.

Since there were three of us, I would go in the middle. I was to follow Max's route with the rope threading through two carabiners attached to my harness. When I got to the protection, I would open one of the two carabiners, lift it over the protection, and then clip it back onto the rope. Then I'd repeat the move with the other carabiner. The idea being that I would never be free to fall, one of the pieces would always be attached to both my harness and the rope. It was a bit like having the eyes of two needles around my waist, one of which I needed to keep threaded the whole time.

When we were ready, Max approached the rock. He jumped up about a foot, grabbed a handhold, and wedged in one of his feet. He then made several spiderlike moves upward so I had to be quick about releasing more rope for him. He went on for about five minutes and then called down that he had anchored in and I could start.

"Okay, Dillon," Serge said. "Storm the Bastille!"

I stood staring dumbly at the rock. I could see nothing. I approached, tried to grab the handhold I'd seen Max use, and made a weak attempt to place my foot. Nothing. I looked back at Serge, who was clearly amused by my predicament, but offered no advice. I turned back to the rock. I saw one place to possibly put my hand, but it was at least a foot above my head. Seeing nothing else, I decided to go for it. I jumped up, pushed my hand into the crack, and pivoted it slightly, so that it locked in place. It worked! I was then suspended, rather painfully, by my wrist wedged in the stone, with my legs dangling below me. I managed to place the balls of my feet on the rock and take a few steps up until my chest was parallel with my wrist. I was barely breathing, and again I could feel the muscles in my calves spasming. I paused, and tried to gather confidence, tried to breathe normally and remembered to lean back.

"If it feels wrong, sometimes it's right," I mouthed. "If it feels wrong, sometimes it's right." I saw another hold up above, placed my free hand in it, and then released my wrist from the jam. Again, I found places to put my feet and again, I moved up.

I could hear Serge below, whispering encouragement, saying, "Go Dillon. Beautiful. That's it."

As I moved up, the crack in the rock became more evident. It was a fracture in the face of the stone, one side of which had been pushed slightly over the other. Once I realized how to climb it—using a sideways grasp with my hands and swinging laterally upwards—I moved quickly, stopping only when I arrived at a piece of protection. In a few minutes' time, I reached Max. He gave me a hand up and we both perched on a small ledge.

"Excellent, Dil! Excellent! I knew you'd do well." And he put an arm around me. He pulled me close and kissed the top of my head. I smiled and looked down at my bloody chalk-covered fingers. I felt like I'd just passed another round of some initiation, and my fingers were, like my black eye, the badges to prove it.

We belayed Serge up and he arrived a few minutes later, having stopped along the way to remove all the protection Max had placed. He handed the pieces back to Max, who reattached them to a strap on his harness and then began climbing up the second pitch.

"You watch your uncle," Serge said after Max had gone, "but don't be so crazy. He is sometimes not so safe, you know? Use your own judgment. Push yourself, but know your limit. You understand?"

"I think so."

"Good, you're doing very well; you have your own style. That's good."

The rest of the climb went smoothly, and I arrived at the top in about half an hour.

Reaching the top was an incredible experience. I looked down the three hundred feet I'd climbed and couldn't believe I'd actually done it! It gave me the same feeling of triumph and accomplishment I got from stealing: an adrenaline rush that made me feel alive and free and extremely capable. A feeling that somehow anything was possible.

Max set me up so I could belay Serge and then took a few steps back.

"I'm going to hike on up a little way," he said. "You'll be okay, right?"

I looked at him anxiously, but was so surprised I didn't know what to say. Nor could I really protest since Serge was on his way up and I had to pull in all the slack as he climbed. Max emptied out his backpack and put it over his shoulders.

"If I'm not back soon," he said, "don't wait around up here. I'll meet you at the bottom, okay?"

I nodded, started to protest, but before I could, he was gone. I kept my eyes on the rope, kept pulling it in, but my mind was off wondering what Max was up to.

When Serge reached the top, he immediately asked about Max and I told him just what Max had told me. He got angry. He said some words in French, spat, and then shook his head from side to side in disbelief. Wordlessly we reracked the protection and wound up the ropes.

Descending from the top of Bastille was much less interesting than going up, since there was no climbing or rappelling involved. Instead, we put on our packs and hiked down a long, winding trail. Serge could never stay angry for long, and before we were even a third of the way down the trail, he was whistling again.

As we walked, I decided to take the opportunity of being alone with Serge to grill him about Max.

"Did you meet Max through climbing?" I asked.

Serge was walking behind me and did not respond immediately. When he did, it was in an uncharacteristically quiet tone.

"No, I met him when I was a teacher. I was a teacher and he was my student."

"What did you teach?" I asked. I knew from Lana that Max had never been to college so thought they must have met at a climbing school.

"Gym," Serge said. "I was a gym teacher."

"Where?"

He did not respond. I thought maybe he hadn't heard me so I turned around to look at him. His head was hanging down.

"I taught at a school called Emerson. Max and his friend Jane. You have met her? They were both my students."

That was odd. I had heard the name Emerson, but I knew that it was a junior high school.

"Your uncle," Serge continued. "He was always in trouble, even back then, always sent to the principal and always having the detention after school."

"So that's where he met Jane?" I asked.

"Ah yes, she was a new student—very new. I think her family had just come from Vietnam maybe a month before she started. Her English wasn't very good and her clothes were different, and, well, you know how kids are, they pick on her. But your uncle Max, he wouldn't allow that! No, no! He was her protector. Like a big brother. Always getting in fights with the other kids over Jane. His eyes were more often black than normal then, you know what I mean?"

I laughed and ran my fingers over my own black eye, feeling even more proud of it.

"So I became a friend to both of them."

Once we reached the bottom of the trail, Serge directed me up the road a bit farther to where there were some large boulders. We set down our bags and the ropes, and for the next hour or so we practiced bouldering. Around noon, Max finally returned.

"Where did you run off?" Serge asked, eyeing him suspiciously.

"Oh, I just hiked up a ways," he said, climbing effortlessly up the boulder that I had been falling off for the past twenty minutes. "It's been so long since I've been free to roam outdoors," he said, his voice lighter than it had been all day. "I just couldn't pass it up."

I noticed that when he joined us he didn't take off the backpack he was wearing. He had emptied it at the top but from the way it hung on his back it was clear to me that it now contained something bulky and heavy.

We were all getting hungry, so we headed back to the truck and returned to Serge's house. We took a back stairway up from the shop, entered Serge's living room, and were greeted by a graying golden retriever, gently whining and wagging its tail.

"Stella!" Max cried, embracing the dog and pulling her down on the floor. She licked his face and whimpered. "I'm so glad you're still here," he said, "but look how old now!"

Serge beamed down at the two of them.

"She's missed you," he said, and then joined Max and Stella on the floor. "We've both missed Max, eh, Stella?"

Serge's place was comfortable, but it was clear that he lived alone and took little interest in his surroundings. The room we'd come into was large and sunny, and like the downstairs, terribly dusty. It appeared spacious, but that was probably because it was so sparsely furnished: an old sofa and a chair, a coffee table made out of bricks and a piece of lumber, and a TV.

Off of that room was the kitchen, which, it was clear, had last been remodeled sometime in the fifties. The handles and the pulls on all the cabinets were shaped like small silver boomerangs, a motif that was repeated in the pattern on the formica countertops and in the worn linoleum on the floor. There was a kitchen table and chairs of chrome and vinyl at which Max and I took a seat while Serge prepared us a lunch of truly ghastly bologna and ketchup sandwiches, most of which Max fed to Stella when Serge wasn't looking.

All through lunch we talked about the climb that day. Again and again they told me how well I'd done, and how proud of me they both were. It made me so happy I never wanted it to end, and especially not the way it did.

After we finished lunch, the conversation dropped off and we all got quiet. Max lit a cigarette, Serge poured himself another glass of whatever liquor he was drinking, and I sat on the floor in the sun, petting the dog.

"Dillon," Max said, "why don't you take Stella for a walk."

I was content where I was, and was just about to say so when Serge added: "Yes. There's a place up the street for you to get ice cream, would you like that? Here, I'll get you some money." And before I could say anything Serge returned with the dog's leash and a five dollar bill.

I did not go get ice cream. It seemed like such a childish thing to do. Instead, I walked the dog around the block, getting angrier and angrier. I wasn't stupid. I knew why I'd been pushed out and it bothered me. I was being treated like the annoying little sidekick, the pesky kid brother, the third wheel, and that was quite an abrupt switch from the camaraderie I'd felt all morning. I knew what was going to happen between them, and I knew that it was natural that I would be excluded from it but I still felt jealous and angry and couldn't quite figure out why. Whatever was going to happen during my absence was mysterious to me, and, instinctively, I wanted to find out about it. Again, I wanted to know what it was like: what it was like to lust after someone, the way that Serge lusted after Max, and what it felt like to have someone want you that much. I wondered who that someone else would be for me. Who that shadowy first person would be, and where he was. I remembered the way Max had described it in the coffee shop. The clinical mechanics of sex had been clear enough and of course I wanted to do them, but what I was really curious about was the more abstract part. The part Max had described as being like food, or an empty canvas. I wanted to know what people said during sex, how their faces looked, and what they felt. It was like a carnival ride I'd never be old enough or tall enough to ride so I just stood at the gate stamping my feet in frustration.

About forty-five minutes later, sensing movement in the kitchen, I crossed the street and went back inside. I tromped slowly and noisily up the back stairs to give them ample warning, and then emerged into the apartment. Except for the fact that Serge had bed-head, one would have thought that they had not moved from the kitchen table. Max sat smoking and Serge sat drinking, just as before, both talking and laughing.

Max smiled when he saw me. Then he looked down at his watch.

"We should go," he said, and got up and retrieved the backpack from the couch. "We can still make the four o'clock movie if we hurry."

We all walked downstairs together, said our good-byes to Serge and Stella on the street, and then Max and I drove away. We had gone about a block when Max realized he'd forgotten his cigarettes. He went up to the next block and made a U-turn.

"I'll be right back," he said. He shifted into park, left the car idling, and ran back inside.

The backpack was right next to me. Initially I only meant to look inside to see if maybe he had left his cigarettes in there, but then I remembered his disappearance up the hill and how the backpack was suddenly full when he returned. I probably shouldn't have, but I opened it and looked inside. It was full of money. Stacks and stacks of hundred-dollar bills, some of which appeared to have gotten wet at some point because they were stained and muddy. As soon as I realized what it was, I quickly zipped up the bag. I knew this must be the money he had mentioned to Jane and to Serge; the money he had stolen from Doris. I looked down at the bag and felt uneasy, like it wasn't safe to be near it. A moment later Max came bounding out to the car, a new carton of *Gitanes* in hand, and we drove back to Denver. We went straight to the Ogden, as planned, and saw another Hitchcock film. *Strangers on a Train.* I remember that Max stayed through to the end this time. The ending is sappy and neatly sewn up, and one he certainly should have walked out on in principle, but the out-of-control-carousel-climax that gets you there kept us both rooted to our seats until the credits started rolling. We were still talking about it as we walked outside and around the block to the car. We got in and Max was about to turn the key when there was a knock at the window. We looked over and saw the gun, pointed at Max's head. He rolled down the window and a man bent down and looked in. It was the same gap-toothed man that had been with Doris the morning of Max's arrival.

"You're to come with me," he said, his voice low and level. "Get out of the car and come with me."

Max had set the backpack on the seat between us, and as he got out I carefully pulled it on to the floor and covered it with my sweater.

"You too," he said, waving the pistol at me. "Out of the car"

I did as he said and walked over to where they were standing. He waved the gun, motioning us over to a van parked on the other side of the street. He opened the back doors and motioned for us to get in. Once inside, he slammed the doors and made sure they were locked.

It was a cargo van so there were no windows or seats in the back, just metal walls and a rubber mat on the floor. We were separated from the cab by a perforated metal screen, through which I saw the unmistakable outline of Doris's large, blond hairdo. She did not look back when we got in but continued smoking and examining her long fingernails. The man got in the driver's seat and we drove away.

"Why hello, Doris," Max said, moving up close to the screen. "I was wondering when you'd call again."

"Maxxx," she said, her voice was high and nasal. "How've you been?"

"Not bad, baby, not bad. Two years in the tank does wonders for your skin. No sun, damp climate, it's great. Maybe you should try it sometime. Does wonders for your soul, too. Provided you've got one"

"Uh huh. Look," Doris said, her voice impatient, "you know what this is about. Let's resolve it and we can both go on with our lives and never see each other again, how's that sound?"

"Okay, I guess."

There was silence as she waited for him to say more. He did not.

"Honey," she said, "I'll be blunt. Doris wants her drugs or her money. I've waited two years. That's a lot of interest I could have been making. Don't make me wait any longer. If you've spent some of it, that's okay. Understandable. Everybody has expenses, but the bulk of it I just can't let get away, now can I?"

"You can and you will," Max said. "Write it off, Doris. You're not getting the money." His voice was hard and angry, and I was alarmed by how much it resembled Lana's. "I took the rap for you, remember? Remember that day in court when I just couldn't remember anything? Well, that case of amnesia cost me a fuck of a lot, and now it's gonna cost you! Don't think of it as a payoff, think of it as still having me on your payroll for the past two years."

That said, Max leaned his back against the side of the van and crossed his arms over his chest.

"Look, I appreciate what you've done," Doris said, her voice that of a parent dealing a petulant child, "but no one's time is worth that much! We can definitely come to some compromise, but you're not keeping the bulk of it. Un-huh, sweetie. Doris needs her money back."

There was a long silence. We could not have gone out of the city but wherever we were, there were few streetlights and almost no traffic. I looked at Max but he was up next to the screen, his face close to Doris's.

"I'll ask once more," she said, her voice full of warning, but at the same time almost weary. "Are you going to give it back?"

"No, I'm not," Max replied, shaking his head.

Doris touched the driver's arm and then pointed to the right. He slowed the van, made a turn, and then drove on. A moment later he stopped and turned off the ignition and lights. He got out and shut his door. I heard his footsteps as he walked around and opened the back doors. He crawled in and tried to grab Max. There was a brief scuffle, but the man got hold of Max's ankles and dragged him out. Then he shut the door and locked it again. The sounds of the beating followed. I could tell that the man had Max up against the side of the van and was punching him. From the sound of it, he started with his face and then moved down to his stomach, each punch punctuated by the sound of Max's body slamming into the side of the van.

"Still drinkin', sweetie?" Doris asked me, and then gave a little chuckle. I didn't answer. I could hear that Max was on the ground and that the man was kicking him.

"You ever watch *Sesame Street?*" Doris asked. Again I did not answer.

"Used to watch it with my kids when they were growin' up. You can learn a lot from *Sesame Street.*"

She paused and I could hear the sound of her gum popping in her mouth.

"Cooperation," she said. "They're always goin' on and on about cooperation. Mister Hooper, Maria, Gordon, and Susan. Cooperation, cooperation, cooperation. Makes sense."

Again, she paused and popped her gum. Max's body hit the van so hard it shook.

"Now myself," Doris went on, "I don't like to get rough. Most people don't. This whole scene could have been avoided with a little cooperation from your uncle out there."

The doors opened suddenly and Max was hurled back in. He was covered in dirt and his face was a bloody mess. He lay down on his back, held his stomach, and tried to catch his breath. I crawled over to see if I could help him, but he held up a hand and shook his head. The man got back in the cab, started the van, and resumed driving.

"Feel like talkin' yet, Max?" Doris asked, after we'd driven a way. She lowered the sun visor and checked her makeup in the vanity mirror. Slowly, meticulously, she applied her lipstick. When she was satisfied, she looked back at Max.

"Ooooh, ouch!" she said, and then blew a bubble with her gum. "Looks like that might leave a mark."

We turned the corner and Max rolled into me. I grabbed him and tried to prop him up. His face was in bad shape and his breathing sounded soggy. His nose, which had first been broken years before, had been broken again.

"Any time you're ready," Doris said, flipping the mirror back up. "Any time."

"Fuck you, Doris!" Max spat, and then fell back, groaning from the effort. I tried to smooth his hair out of his face and clear away some of the blood, but there was nothing to mop it up with. I had left my sweater in the car and had on only a short-sleeve shirt. It was hot in the back of the van and I was sweating, but I was so afraid that my whole body was shaking. I looked to Max for some direction, but he had his eyes closed.

We drove around for about ten more minutes. We seemed to be going in a circle and eventually I saw enough out the windshield to realize that we were driving around City Park. This made sense because it was nearly always deserted, especially at night, and was never well lit.

"Max," Doris said, "don't be silly. Just give me back the money and we'll send you on your way."

"No!" he growled, and then turned to the side coughing. The

van halted abruptly and again the driver got out. Again, I heard his steps coming around to open the doors, and again he reached in and grabbed Max by the ankles. I held him under the arms and tried to keep him from being pulled out, but the man was strong and pulled us both out and onto the pavement. I skidded on my shoulder, tearing the sleeve off my shirt, and it took me a moment to realize what had happened. The night air felt cool after being in the stuffy van. I looked around, dazed. We were definitely in City Park and, from the smell of it, were on the north side by the zoo. That was all I had time to see before the man scooped me up and threw me back into the van, slamming the doors behind me. The sounds of beating resumed, although slower this time. He was having to pick Max up after each punch. I started crying. I panicked. I had to do something and I think if the same thing happened today I would do just what I did. I crept up next to the screen and looked at Doris. She was smoking now, calmly, seemingly oblivious to the sounds outside.

"Make him stop!" I cried. She ignored me and looked out the side window.

"Please! I'll get you the money," I whispered. "I know where it is."

She flipped down the visor and glared back at me in the mirror.

"Don't play games with me," she said, shaking her head. "I don't like to play games."

"I'm not," I sobbed. "I know where it is."

"Where?"

I hesitated. I knew Max would kill me, but at the time I thought that preferable to listening to him get killed.

"*Where?*" she yelled and turned around. I'm sure she saw the fear in my face. "He'll kill him out there if you don't tell me!"

I had no reason not to believe her.

"Take me back to the car," I sobbed. "Make him stop and take me back to the car. Let me out and keep Max here. I'll get the money, I promise."

"You *better* not be playing with me." she said, pointing the long nail of her index finger at me. "No fucking games, hear me!"

"Yes, no games, I promise. I'll get it, just don't let Max know."

She stared at me for a good ten seconds, trying to read my face, while outside the noise of the beating continued.

"You're a good kid," she said. "Smart."

She opened her door, stood up on the runner, and pounded on the roof of the van with her fist.

"Okay, that's enough," she said. "Put him back."

The doors opened and Max's limp body was tossed in. He looked worse and was barely conscious, mumbling things I couldn't understand and spitting out teeth. I held on to him, my body still shaking, as the driver got back in and drove us back to the Ogden. The car was parked behind the theater on a residential sidestreet. They parked the van a few spaces behind it and the man came around and opened the door. I hopped out. Max made a weak protest, but I assured him it was okay and that I'd be right back. Doris was waiting outside. The man, who had me by the arm, led me to her. She had her purse on her shoulder and I saw that it was shielding the small pistol she held in her hand.

"It's all right," she said to the man. "Get back in. I've got him."

He released my arm and Doris motioned me to the car. I opened the passenger door, reached down and got the bag from under my sweater.

"Lemme see," she said, waving the gun. I opened it. She peered inside and then snatched it away. She motioned for the van to pull up. The man drove alongside the car and got out. He came around back, opened the van doors, and then opened the back door of the car. Once again, he pulled Max out, more gently this time, and set him on the backseat. Then he closed the car door, closed the van doors, and returned to his seat behind the wheel. Doris climbed in the passenger side of the van. She was about to shut the door but then paused and beckoned me over. I approached, trembling. She reached in the bag and took out one of the stacks of money.

"I'm not going soft," she said, holding it out to me, "but you've been good and I don't think that oughta go without something. Here. Take it." I did so and she quickly shut her door and they drove off.

I stood there, holding the money and shaking, staring after them as they drove down the street and turned the corner onto Colfax. I went back to the car, not knowing what to do. Max was sitting up in the back, looking like some horror film monster, blinking his eyes, and trying to orient himself.

"You okay?" I asked. He looked over and it seemed to take him a minute to recognize me.

"Can you . . . drive?" he asked, and then laboriously reached in his pocket for the keys. I had never driven before, other than sitting on James's lap and steering, but I nodded, accepted the keys, and got in the driver's seat.

Given my mental state and my lack of ability, it was not a smooth ride. It took me a good five minutes to extricate us from the parking space we were wedged into and it was not without damage to the vehicles in front and in back of us. Once out, we had several jerky moments as I experimented with the gas and brake pedals, while Max lolled and moaned on the backseat. The steering wheel was much more responsive than I anticipated and the first turn onto Colfax took us up on the sidewalk and nearly into the lobby of the Ogden. Somehow, I got us straightened out, and in about fifteen minutes we had made it down Broadway to the on-ramp for the highway, at which point Max said he would take over. He mopped away the blood on his face with my cotton sweater and then managed to get us home, one hand on the wheel and the other clutching his stomach. I was nervous enough about our safety as we drove, but added to this was my dread of what Max would say once he realized I'd given up the money.

When we got home it was about ten o'clock. Lana's bedroom light was on. I knew there was probably no way we could avoid her seeing Max, and I was right. As soon as we entered the front door, she appeared at the top of the stairs.

"What happened!" she cried, and ran down to us, getting under one of Max's shoulders to support him.

"I had a little . . . climbing accident," Max said. "It's nothing."

We got him to the bathroom and then Lana took over. She pushed me outside, poking her head out from time to time with impatient commands for bandages, or antiseptic, or more towels, clearly relishing the chance to actually put into practice some of what she'd learned at nursing school. I brought everything she asked for, but for the second time that day I was nearly overwhelmed by feelings of jealousy and anger. I was the one who had saved Max! I had stopped the beating! I had gotten him home! Now Florence Nightingale was moving in to take all the credit! But worse than that I was angry that she had not even asked if I was okay. I was covered in blood, my own or Max's she could not have known, and yet she immediately rushed to comfort him, excluding me from any part of it, even going so far as to lock the bathroom door after I'd given her what she'd asked for!

I felt hot tears rolling down my cheeks and had to fight the urge to beat the door with my fists. I had been terrified that night, more scared than I think I'd ever been before, or have ever been since, but there was to be no comfort for me. I paced around. I tried to get control of myself, tried to remember what Max had told me about Lana growing up, about her having damage inside, but it was not much help. It did not explain why she doted on him and hated me. I thought she must really hate me to exclude me from the one small room of the house that had any comfort in it! I leaned my back against the wall and slid down to the floor, staring at the bathroom door. Lana's commands for more supplies had ceased and I knew they would probably emerge soon.

I didn't want her to see me crying, so I got up again and went upstairs to another bathroom. I took off my clothes, washed the blood off of myself, and then went to my own room and closed the door. I got the half-empty Sandeman's bottle from the closet, took several large swigs, and sat down on the edge of the bed. I stared at the wall, nervously picking at the label, waiting for the alcohol to take effect. I wanted the night to end, but I was dreading the next day, when I would have to tell Max that the money was gone. I drank more. I drank until the bottle was empty and I fell asleep.

The next morning it was Lana who woke me up. "I'm off to school," she said, poking her head into my room. "Max is still in pretty bad shape so I'll need you to take care of him, all right?"

I could tell Lana was nervous talking to me about injuries, having recently made my own face such a mess, and was eager to get away.

"Sure," I said, sitting up and hoping I'd remembered to roll the bottle under the bed. "I'll take care of him."

"Okay then," she said, backing out of the room, "I'll see you tonight."

After she'd closed the door, I lay back down and stared at the ceiling. I did not think any more about Lana. She was, after all, just being herself. No, my thoughts were on the missing money and what I would tell Max. I knew there had been no real choice. Doris would have killed him, and probably me, too—but that money was all Max had. It had been the foundation for all his future plans and in an instant it was gone. I had given it away. Of course he didn't know that. He didn't even know that I knew there had been money in the bag. I was off the hook, so to speak, but that didn't make me feel any better. I got up and went down to the cellar. Max wasn't there. I went back upstairs, thinking that maybe Lana had put him in one of the bedrooms, but he was not there either. I stood on the landing, trying to think where he could be when I heard his voice coming from the living room.

"Dil?" he called weakly. "That you?"

I went back downstairs and there he was, on the couch. He was propped up and he looked bad. Lana had wound an excessive amount of bandages around his head, making him look almost cartoonish. His face was bruised and swollen and he, too, had a black eye.

"Dil, come quick!" he said, and his head bobbed, like it was too heavy to hold up. "Lana gave me some pills . . . I didn't know it till after . . .Quick tell me," he said, fighting to keep his eyes open, "did Doris get it? Did she get the bag?"

I looked down, ashamed, and nodded.

"Shit," he sighed, and his voice was sad, almost defeated. "It had money in it. All that . . . money . . . gone." And he fell back and closed his eyes.

Lana had given him Rohypnol, the ridiculously powerful sleeping aid that James had prescribed for her, known today as "the Date Rape Drug." Even if she had given him just one, which wasn't likely given his condition, I knew that he would be out for several hours.

I looked down at him sleeping and realized I'd been right: he thought I didn't know anything about the money. He thought I'd just innocently given up the backpack. I wouldn't have to explain it at all. I would be lying, but it would not be such a bad lie; and being gay, I was naturally used to lying.

Lying, prevaricating, hiding the truth, whatever you want to call it, gay people do it better than any other segment of society, excluding politicians, of course. It is a Darwinian survival mechanism designed to protect us from persecution. The need to lie becomes obvious at a very early age. From the moment we realize that we are attracted to members of our own sex, and how reviled that attraction is, the lying starts. From the moment we hear our first snide queer joke, or a slur against fags or dykes, the lying starts. We realize then that we are, without choosing to be, in a society that is hostile to our very existence. We learn to lie, are encouraged to conceal our identities and deny our feelings. Lying is sanctioned. Expected almost.

And for me, lying was *very* easy. I lied at home; I lied at school; and I lied at church. It was what everybody wanted and what I had to do to protect myself. And once I had done that, once I was false on such a grand scale, the smaller lies seemed trivial by comparison. They came easily, naturally. What's more, I became an expert at hiding the evidence. No twitches or stutters to give me away. For years I had practiced making my stone face, and rarely, if ever, could anyone make it crack.

It would have been so easy to lie to Max about the money. It was a lie of omission, really. The easiest kind. And yet, for some reason, as I sat there watching him sleep, I knew I wouldn't. Not because the truth would hurt him less, because it certainly wouldn't do that. The money was gone either way, if I had given it away or if it had been taken without me knowing about it. No, I decided to tell the truth because I respected him. He was the only person who had shown any interest in me since, well, since Mr. Sullivan had given me the Carpenters' album back in band class.

Later that afternoon, when the drugs wore off and Max began to wake up, I brewed him a cup of strong, hot coffee and I told him the truth. I told him I had looked in the bag when he ran back into Serge's house and had seen the money; that I had told Doris where it was when he was outside being pummeled, and had then led her back and given it to her.

If he was mad he didn't show it, but I could tell he was sad, and that made me sad. He retreated back down to the basement, like a turtle returning to its shell, and sulked. All his dreams of escape to *La Belle France* had disappeared with the backpack, and he spent the subsequent days idly thumbing through back issues of *National Geographic*, sighing over the glossy, aerial shots of Paris and Marseilles and Nice. He played his guitar and sang, but only sad, slow songs, in French, of course, and wondered aloud if he was ever going to get out of the suburban hell he'd fallen into.

Since we couldn't go to the movies and since it was hard for Max to read aloud with his broken nose, I took over the nightly reading of Balzac. I thought for sure this would cheer him up, but I was wrong. My reading was rough and stilted, and when we finished *Père Goriot*, it was only to discover that Vautrin gets captured and sent back to jail.

During those days in the basement, I'll admit that in a perverse way I was glad the money was gone. Glad, because I saw how close Max had come to leaving and I realized how much I would have missed him if he'd gone. Still, I hated to see him sad, so I kept looking for anything that would pull him out of his funk. At the end of the week, when something did happen to lift his spirits, I was genuinely happy and relieved.

The phone rang one morning at about eleven and the man on the other end asked to speak to Mr. Sawyer.

"He's, uh, just stepped out. Can I take a message?"

This was the standard response I had been ordered to give by Lana, who was still hoping to find out more information before the divorce.

"Yeah," the man replied. "This is Steve, over at McConnel Imports, I was just calling to let him know we've got his Jaguar finished up and he can come pick it up anytime. We're open till seven."

"I'll be sure and tell him," I said. "Thanks."

It turned out that this was just the kick that Max needed. As soon as I told him, he smiled and there was a sparkle in his eye. He emerged from the cellar, removed the elaborate bandage, and took a shower. Half an hour later we were out the door.

Max seemed to want a new image to go with the car so before we picked it up we took the thousand dollars from Doris and spent most of it on ourselves. We went to a barber and both got very short haircuts. From there, we went to a department store and actually *bought* some clothes and, more important, some sunglasses to conceal our black eyes. After that, we finally drove to the body shop, where they drove the gleaming car out of the garage and parked it at an angle in front of us. It looked more sleek, and shiny, and powerful than ever. Without a moment's hesitation, Max forged the necessary paperwork, and when he had finished, the man gave him the keys. Five minutes later we were gunning down the freeway toward downtown.

Chapter Thirteen

When Sunday evening arrived, Max and I drove to the restaurant owned by Jane's father. Denver was, and still is to a certain extent, a segregated city, with each ethnic group occupying its own section of turf and not mixing much with the others. As we drove north on Federal Boulevard that evening, through several different neighborhoods, I remember being amazed as the signs on all the businesses changed from English, to Spanish, to Chinese, and eventually, to the odd Roman letters used by the Vietnamese.

The Vietnamese section was poor, a fact made obvious by the ubiquitous graffiti and the badly maintained road, and Nguyen's restaurant was located in the center of the squalor. It was housed in a building that had clearly once been something else: a Tastee Freeze or a Kentucky Fried Chicken perhaps, with a peaked roof of wooden shingles, long ago painted red. The paint was peeling, and the brick facade below had been repeatedly patched with a brick-colored paint, to hide the graffiti. From the outside, it looked dismal, but the parking lot was, nevertheless, full of rather expensive cars, alongside which the Jaguar fit quite nicely.

Inside, the restaurant was dark, fragrant, and noisy. Next to the hostess station, there was a large fish tank, in which two enormous eels circled slowly. Through this I saw the spacious dining room crammed with as many people as it could hold. I thought it a good omen that as we waited, we were serenaded by a nasally Vietnamese version of "Close to You" being piped in through a hidden sound system.

You made it!" a voice called out, and I looked up expecting to be greeted by the enchanting, elegant Jane I had seen on the two previous occasions. What I saw instead was a harried girl in a black polyester waiter's pantsuit, her hair spilling out of the weak bun she had twisted it into. On one arm she carried an impossible amount of dishes, while in the other she held menus and an order book.

She paused when she saw our battered faces.

"What happened?" she cried.

"Car accident," we both replied, having agreed that we would adopt that as the party line to explain our injuries. She gave us a dubious look. Max shrugged.

"Well, come on," she said, motioning us to come with her. "We'll talk about it later. There's a place for you over by the kitchen."

We followed as she wove through the tightly spaced tables to a small table near the back of the restaurant. We sat down and Jane disappeared through the kitchen door. When she emerged, both arms were loaded with steaming plates of food that she quickly delivered to a table by the aquarium. She then took another table's order, refilled some water glasses, and wove her way back toward us.

"It's busy tonight, but believe it or not the whole place will be deserted in an hour. Stick around."

She kissed us both on the head, gave a concerned look at the gash on my forehead, and then disappeared again through the kitchen door. At various times over the next hour she brought several plates of food to our table: softshell crabs that had been dipped in a spicy batter and fried; tightly wrapped spring rolls stuffed with white noodles, shrimp, and basil; steaming bowls of peppery soup with floating tentacles of octopus and squid; and finally, a strawberry chicken dish unlike anything I had ever tasted.

Jane had been right about the crowd, and over the next hour we watched it thin to no more than a few groups of people spaced far apart. By nine-thirty, the place was nearly empty, save for the waiters clearing and cleaning and chattering away. Jane approached, carrying a tray with three Vietnamese coffees. She set them on our table, pulled up a chair, and collapsed into it.

"God, what a night!" she sighed. We thanked her for the food.

"I wanted to bring you steaks for those eyes!" she said, sitting up and leaning forward to get a closer look. "What *really* happened?"

I looked over at Max.

"We have no comment at this time," he said, and lifted his sunglasses to reveal his own shiner.

"You better tell me," she said, "or I'm going to charge you for all that food."

"Doris happened," Max sighed. Jane shook her head and then wagged a scolding finger at Max.

"I warned you not to mess with her."

Just then the kitchen door swung open and a short, squat, powerfully built Asian man emerged. He was dressed in badly stained chef's pants, and a blue and orange Broncos T-shirt. On his enormous round head he wore an absurdly small triangular paper hat. He saw Max and his face broke into a grin.

"Maxey!" he cried, extending one chubby hand to Max and giving him a hearty pat on the back with the other. "She tell me you here," he said, gesturing at Jane. "So I make special food, just for you!"

"It was great, Jimmy, best food I've had in a long time!"

Jimmy pulled up another chair, set it down with the back facing us, and straddled it.

"You been to France, she tell me . . ."

Max looked questioningly across the table at Jane. She grinned and nodded.

"Uh, yes," Max replied. "I, uh, just got back last week."

"Food pretty good there?"

"Doesn't even come close to yours, Jimmy."

Jimmy smiled and turned to me. "He a smooth talker. How you say, bullshitter! Professional bullshitter, that one!"

I laughed nervously.

"You look like Vietnamese," he said, pointing at my swollen eye. "You . . . boxer?"

I blushed and shook my head. I made a mental note that the next thing I stole would be an eye patch.

"Oh, he shy, that one," Jimmy said, and extended his hand to me. "Jimmy my name."

I shook his hand and introduced myself.

"He's Max's nephew," Jane said.

"I thought he look too young to be the boyfriend!" Jimmy said, laughing heartily. "You have little boyfriend in France?" Jimmy asked. Max laughed.

"No, still single."

"Then why you not marry her?" he asked, gesturing at Jane. She rolled her eyes.

"She only want rich man," Jimmy continued. "She go out with old man, more older than me." He scrunched his face into a sour expression and thumped his chest. "More older than her own father. You believe that? I don't like it," he said, folding his arms across his chest and shaking his head.

"Dad—" Jane started to protest.

"She want her own work, her own business," he continued, ignoring her, looking only at Max and me. "'That okay,' I say, 'Don't have to work in restaurant all the time, but have to work. Have to work hard!' She work hard, but she work harder to find more old husband with big money! That wrong."

"Daddy, stop," Jane pleaded, but he did not.

"I wish she the faggot, like you." he said, giving Max another slap on the back. "Much, much easier! I rather have daughter with wife than daughter with grandfather!"

Mercifully for Jane, there was at this point the sound of breaking dishes in the kitchen followed by several loud exchanges of Vietnamese invective. Jimmy grumbled, excused himself, and returned to the kitchen to see what it was all about.

"He's going to drive me to drink!" Jane said, pulling at her hair with both hands. "Thank God he didn't get started on grandchildren. There's no stopping him then."

"So?" Max asked. Jane looked confused.

"So . . . What?" she asked.

"So how did it go with Percy's mother?"

To this Jane did not respond. Instead, she pounded the table repeatedly with her forehead.

"That bad, eh?"

"Oh it couldn't have been any worse," she mumbled. She sat up, removed the small stick from her hair, and let her black mane fall around her shoulders, which made her look very small and tired.

"Do tell," Max said, leaning forward and stirring the layer of black coffee into the layer of condensed milk beneath it. She looked at both of us and rolled her eyes again. She stirred her own coffee, poured it into the glass of ice, and took a drink before starting. She began slowly, almost reluctantly, to recount her tale, but as she went on she became more and more animated.

"Well," she said, "he picked me up, you saw that, right?"

We nodded.

"I got in the car and he assessed me. He approved of my outfit and my hair, so we drove straight over to his mother's house."

"Where is it?" Max asked.

"Oh, it's one of those big stucco houses over by the Country Club, you know, right off of Speer?"

"Big?"

"Enormous! Anyway, I was nervous enough, but as we're walking up to the front door Percy tells me that he didn't tell his mother I was Asian. Odd, I think, so I ask him why not. 'Well,' he tells me (and here Jane began to mimic Percy's deep, elderly voice), 'Mommy's kind of old-fashioned, you know how old people are, I wouldn't worry about it.' "

"He calls her Mommy?" Max asked.

"Yes, but believe me, that's not the worst of it. So, he tells me she's old-fashioned. And that would have been fine if 'old-fashioned' weren't a euphemism for 'fucking crazy bigot bitch on wheels'! Anyway, I'm getting ahead of the story. So we go in, and I keep thinking, should I leave my sunglasses on, maybe she won't notice, but then I think, no that's pretentious, so I take them off. I go in, and oh my God, if there wasn't the most gorgeous Empire console I have ever seen right there in the foyer! I went right over to it and examined it top to bottom. Just beautiful! and with the original finish and gilt work. Percy said it was a gift to Napoleon from some rich Jew or something, which I highly doubt, but there was no doubting it was from that period."

"What about the mother?" Max asked, leading her back to the original subject.

"Okay, yeah, sorry, but they had some fantastic stuff in that house! Anyway, so the first thing I notice is that everyone working there—the maid who answered the door, the cook, the gardener out back—all black. Not a good sign. I knew it was really bad when I ducked into the little powder room off the foyer to check my makeup and I saw that Mommy has one of those metal lawn jockeys in there as a toilet paper dispenser. You know, the kind with the big white eyes and the huge red lips that you don't see anywhere except in front of a few trailer homes in Alabama. So anyway, I come out of the bathroom just in time to see the black maid wheeling Mommy out in her wheelchair, which was silver plated and had a blue button-tufted cushion on it. Silk velvet, if I'm not wrong, and the tassels alone must have set her back a couple hundred. Did I mention that everything was blue? No? Well it was. Blue walls, lapis lazuli floors (I can only imagine what *that* cost), blue moiré drapes, everything! And Mommy was dressed in some hideous, blue lace getup, with a matching hankie and a high Edwardian collar fastened at the top with (what else?) a Wedgwood broach. Christ, even her hair had been given one of those ridiculous blue rinses!"

Jane paused to take a sip of her coffee, but then resumed her tale with even more vim and vigor.

"Well, at that point, in my little blue Jackie O outfit, with my Princess Diana–knockoff sapphire ring, (which, incidentally, went right back to the pawn shop after this disastrous outing), I'm feeling pret-ty darn sure of myself, in spite of the racial red flags. Percy introduces us, I extend my hand, remove my sunglasses, and I'll be damned if the old bag of bones didn't have a stroke right then and there! Oh, she didn't, of course, but she pulled back like she'd seen a ghost and one whole side of her face just fell. Her hand went limp as a dead fish, and she glared over at Percy with those ice-blue eyes of hers (which is probably how she got started on the whole blue theme in the first place. Stupid.) He looked down and I could tell he was going to catch hell for it later.

"Well, for a while she managed to be civil, if nothing else, but then she had her maid bring out a bottle of anisette and some dainty little cobalt glasses. Percy and I had a glass, and she had about twenty glasses, one right after the other. She actually snapped her fingers when she wanted her glass refilled, and I thought the poor maid was going to get carpal tunnel she was tipping the bottle so often to refill the old cow's glass.

"As you can imagine, the more she drank, the looser her tongue got, and somehow she got it into her head that I was Japanese (you know how we all look alike), and she went on and on about how 'Old MacArthur really gave you Japs a whipping!' and 'I never trusted the gooks myself. Shifty people, if you ask me.' At one point she actually sent the maid to fetch her shawl because, as she put it, 'there's a little nip in the room.'"

Max and I were laughing in spite of ourselves. Jane went on, trying not to smile.

"Lunch only got worse," she said. "She couldn't remember my name, so she kept calling me Suki. 'You been stateside long, Suki? You need some chopsticks, Suki, my dear.' It was awful. And Percy did nothing to defend me! Just sat there smiling, pushing the food around on his plate.

"Then she started telling me all about his charming ex-wife, and then all about his other charming ex-wife, and the children, and the grandchildren. Which, I have to admit, is something I hadn't really given much thought to, but I sure did then! The thought of a whole family of these bigots was more than I could bear. This was definitely not the klan I wanted to join. I also started doing the math: Mommy's old, and still going strong, if I do marry Percy, which hardly seems likely while she's around, I could conceivably be with him for thirty more years! Although the family has money, when I thought of it divided up among children and grandchildren and great grandchildren, I saw nothing more than a few pennies being tossed my way. Oh, it might be enough to get established in my little shop, but only just. Percy isn't wild about the idea in the first place and now I know why—he's still paying heaps of alimony to his two ex's and God knows how much in child support. I'm sure that if I do get an engagement ring it won't be before I sign a lengthy prenuptial agreement.

"I was almost in tears as I sat there in the dining room thinking about how stupid I'd been. I figured the possibility of getting my shop was even more remote, and I was mad that I'd wasted so much time and money on my fucking blue outfit! I had to get out of there and try to compose myself so I got up and went to the loo again. I sat on the pot, getting angrier and angrier, and actually thought of just getting up and leaving, but eventually I calmed down and resolved to just get through it. I resolved that when lunch was over, that would be the end of it. No more putting out for Percy. I headed back to the dining room, but on the way something caught my eye. A bauble. On one of the end tables in the sitting room, I saw a tiny little clock. It was a small bronze, a Venus standing on a blue enamel base surrounded by four whirling balls that ticked off the seconds. I knew it was a Breguet even before I picked it up and saw the name stamped on the bottom, but nevertheless, my heart skipped a beat when I saw that it was genuine and quite obviously nineteenth century. It was so small and delicate, and—"

"You took it!" Max cried, slapping his thigh with his hand.

"Yes, how did you know? It fit so easily into my purse," Jane said. "I looked around to see that no one was watching and made sure to slip a tissue under the chime so that if it went off during lunch no one would hear it. Then I returned to the dining room, just in time to catch the punch line of yet another one of Mommy's jokes about the Jew and the Chinaman."

"So what will you do with the clock?" Max asked.

"It's already sold," she said. "I would have loved to keep it, but I'm not in a position to start my own collection just yet."

"Aren't you worried it will be traced?"

"No."

"Well, why not?"

"The person who bought it doesn't care where it came from. He specializes in, how shall I say, creating a paper trail. He makes up invoices and sales receipts, and in the end makes it appear that the last owner has just died and that's why it's for sale. He then ships it elsewhere to be sold and gives me a chunk of money once it has. He's very clever."

"Who is it?" Max asked, leaning forward, suddenly very interested.

"My secret."

"A collector?"

"No."

"Oh come on, tell me!"

"No."

Max leaned back and scowled.

"I won't tell you because there's no reason that you *should* know. It's not that I don't trust you but this person trusts me and he's really all I've got right now."

"Ahhh," Max said, "the little clock isn't the first thing he's sold for you . . ."

"You always were perceptive," Jane said. She leaned in close and looked around to see that no one else was listening.

"It's like this: my dates with the Ogres have gotten me into a lot of the swank little palaces of Denver. At first, I was just in awe of all the things I saw, the odd pieces of porcelain, the Chinese snuff bottles, the eighteenth-century miniatures . . . I always knew more about them than the owner, and there were several occasions when I thought to myself, 'Jane, it would be so easy to just stick that in your purse. No one would be the wiser.' Well it was only a matter of time until thought became deed. The first time, I'll admit it, I was drunk. I doubt I'd have had the courage if I'd been sober. I found myself alone in a fantastic room at the Boatwright-Starks' house. There was a corner cabinet where they displayed some of their treasures and I sauntered over to it and looked in. There was huge collection of micro-mosaics, so tiny and delicate, but they were so small I couldn't really see them so I opened the case. I only wanted to get a better look. I know I shouldn't have, but I picked one up. A little scene of Venice, only about two inches wide, done in the tiniest pieces of granite and marble you've ever seen. Some no bigger than a hair! Then I heard someone coming so I quickly closed the cabinet, but I'd forgotten to replace the mosaic. I held it tightly, my hand sweating, and then eventually slipped it in my purse, telling myself that when the coast was clear I'd put it back. Well, of course that didn't happen."

I looked across the table at Max and he was beaming, proudly. I was smiling, too, because as Jane spoke it was as if something was connecting the three of us, as if we had secretly joined hands under the table.

"I'm afraid . . ." Jane said, and then trailed off. Her brow was furrowed.

"Of what?" Max asked.

"Of getting caught, of what I'm doing. I mean, I shouldn't really be doing it. I do feel bad."

"Remorse at this point—at any point—is foolish," Max said firmly. "You can't be afraid of what's already been done."

Jane looked up and directly over at Max.

"I'm more afraid . . ." she continued, "of what I'm thinking of doing."

"Don't be," Max said, shaking his head, very matter-of-factly. "There's no reason you should be. Look, you're trying to establish yourself, to get out of this greasy kitchen, and you're running up against a brick wall doing it the conventional way. You want your own business; then do what you have to do in order to get it. It's the means to an end. Keep your eyes on the end—not on the road that gets you there. You have to focus on getting to the end any way you can, and the means be damned!

"But!—"

"But nothing! Look, you don't want to spend your whole life as a tadpole stuck in the pond, do you? At some point you've got to evolve into a frog and hop out of the mire."

This sounded vaguely familiar to me but it wasn't until later that I realized Max had been paraphrasing Vautrin's advice to Eugene in *Père Goriot.*

Jane nodded, but it was clear from the brittle expression on her face that she still had some reservations.

"Listen," Max continued, "you said yourself that your Ogres and their friends don't appreciate half the stuff they've got, right? That they have more money than they can possibly ever use. Well, then stealing from them will not make any more difference than scooping a bucket of water from the ocean!"

Again this sounded more like Vautrin than Max.

"Despite what Grandpa Reagan tells us," Max went on, "trickle-down economics is a sham. It sounds good in theory, but it doesn't take into account the fact that the rich are usually reluctant to let any of the water flow out. For that reason you've got to reach up and twist open the tap yourself. Tell me what you're thinking."

Jane's head seemed to be swimming in these soggy comparisons, but it appeared that she was giving them real consideration. We sat in silence for what seemed like a long time, the clink of dishes being washed in the kitchen the only sound.

"I'd need some help," Jane said, leaning in close, gripping her glass with both hands.

"That's what we're here for," Max said, elbowing me and grinning broadly.

And so it began, the plot that would dominate the next three months of our lives. The plot that would affect each of us, for better and for worse, for a long time to come.

Chapter Fourteen

To commit a crime successfully, three elements must be present: desire, ability, and opportunity.

Desire: the reason, urging, or yen to do something.

Ability: the tools and the know-how to get the job done.

Opportunity: the window that has been carelessly left open (or, in some cases, been propped open), the door that is left unlocked.

All three of us had the desire. All three of us had some ability. Jane alone supplied the opportunity.

On the surface the plan was deceptively simple: Jane, on the social arm of one her Tottering Ogres, would, via parties, friendship, and so on, gain access to some of the wealthier homes in the area. While there, she would scope them out, using her knowledge of jewels and antiques to note the things of value and their location. If possible, she would duck into a bathroom and sketch diagrams of the layout, and record her impressions into a small tape recorder. She would also investigate the security system and possible ways to outsmart it. Through observation and subtle conversation she would discover if they had servants or a cleaning lady, and if so, on which day they usually came. The next morning she would present all of her information to us and with it Max and I would then plan our attack.

How to outsmart the alarm system took up most of this time, but Max was familiar with most systems and he had a special technique for rewiring them to a dummy box so that they appeared to remain armed after they'd been disabled. Usually, though, Jane had made our job much easier by disconnecting one of the windows from the alarm and unlatching the screen. Once inside, we would follow Jane's directions and steal the pieces she had deemed most valuable.

Later, usually the next day, we would rendezvous with Jane, either at Paris on the Platte or in the wine cellar at Lana's, and she would pick up the loot from the night before. She sold what she could to her mystery man and then, usually a week or so later, would return bearing cash.

The first job was almost too easy. It was a house that belonged to an elderly couple, the Stanovers, who, like most people their age, sometimes had difficulty remembering. For that reason, they rarely kept the alarm on, and when they did, they kept a cheat sheet tacked to the wall next to the box, on which the four-digit code was plainly written.

One evening, when they were out dining with Jane and one of her Ogres, Max and I went over and jimmied open the back door. Once inside, we had a full sixty seconds to find the box and enter the code before the alarm started whooping. When that was done, we made our way up to the bedroom and stole what jewelry they had (which was, unfortunately, not all that much since they, like most people, kept the really valuable pieces in a safe deposit box at the bank). From there, we went back downstairs, took their silver candlesticks and their entire collection of Meissen porcelain figurines, which were in the exact spot Jane had said they would be, and then snuck back out the same way we'd come in.

There were only two little snags in an otherwise seamless job: schnauzers and Vautrin.

Snag number one: Jane had neglected to mention (and continued to neglect to mention over the entire summer) the fact that the couple had dogs, an aged pair of schnauzers that came charging and snarling out of the bedroom as soon as we opened the door. We both panicked. I ran as fast as I could down the stairs and jumped up on the dining-room table. Max veered off into the kitchen and, luckily, the dogs followed him, barking all the way. A moment later all was quiet and Max emerged wiping his hands on his pants. I looked up at him, wide-eyed, afraid to hear what he'd done.

"Schnauzers like ham," he said.

Snag number two was, as I said, Vautrin, although it would probably be more accurate to say it was Max's ego. We were finished with the job, our little velvet bags loaded with jewelry, and porcelain, but Max was lingering. The schnauzers had finished the ham and were clawing at the kitchen door. I was over by the back door, ready to go but Max was looking in the desk for a piece of paper and a pen.

"What are you doing?" I whispered, exasperated by the delay. "Come on!"

"Just adding a little style," he said, and started writing. I came up behind him and looked over his shoulder. In elegant cursive he had written, "This house has been burglarized this evening as a courtesy of the disciples of J. C." He then folded the paper in thirds, put it in an envelope, and propped it neatly next to the lamp. "J. C." was of course, Jacques Collin, the real name of Vautrin, but no one other than Max and myself would ever have made the connection from those initials. In fact, when the burglary was reported in the paper a few days later, it was hinted that it may have been carried out by members of some bizarre religious cult.

The following Monday, Jane came to the house and we had a rendezvous in the cellar.

"Oh, this is lovely!" she exclaimed, examining the Meissen figures. "Just absolutely lovely. I hate to have to part with them. I can't believe you got the whole collection, and without a single chip."

"We are professionals," Max said. "How long until you get the money?"

"My my, but you're greedy. Relax, my man knows what's coming so he should be able to pay me C.O.D. I don't see why I shouldn't have the money by the end of the week."

"What's next?" Max asked. Jane grinned devilishly and wrapped up the figure she'd been holding.

"Well," she said, digging excitedly in her purse and removing some crumpled sheets of paper on which she had written her information.

"It looks like Ned and Jocelyn Wilson will be next. Percy and I went to a cocktail party at their house the other night and there were a few things that caught my eye."

"Do tell," Max said

"Well, over the years they've amassed an incredible collection of Southwest pottery and baskets. Unfortunately, Mrs. Wilson has taken that theme and run with it. Their whole house is really a hideous mistake. I mean, when did the colors teal and pink, and the image of little howling coyotes with bandanas around their necks come to represent the Southwest? Never, that's when! Anyway, the baskets are great. Truly great! Museum-quality stuff. In fact, some of it I've never seen outside of museums and I'd be willing to bet they were bought on the black market. If we could get those pieces, I think they'd have a hard time reporting them stolen."

"Where are they?" Max asked, examining the floor plan she'd sketched out.

"They're all in two pine display cases in the living room. They look like they'd open from the front but that's the trick, they don't, they open from the top. No lock, no latch, just lift up. But they look quite rustic and heavy so be careful. One of you will have to hold up the lid while the other reaches inside.

"The one on the right contains the baskets, but don't take any that look too fragile or any that are fragments! These things have a way of turning to dust if they're handled incorrectly so take only the ones that look fairly solid. What you'll really want to concentrate on is the pottery in the case on the left: the black and white pots and the brown and white pots. Again, be very careful. If you can get them, they'll be worth a lot of money—but they must remain intact. Take some of that egg-crate foam and line the bags with it. Take extra pieces for padding in between."

"When could we do it?" I asked.

"Soon. Very soon. Like, this weekend. They'll be going to their son's wedding in Arizona. They leave on Friday afternoon at three and from then on the house will be empty until Monday. No servants, no cleaning lady, no—"

"Dogs?" I asked.

"Oh, as a matter of fact, yes," Jane said, smiling as she remembered them. "Three cute little Chihuahuas, but I'm pretty sure they'll be going to a kennel."

Max and I exchanged weary looks.

"Now, listen up," Jane said, "because here is the downside. There's a doorman on duty twenty-four/seven, who buzzes everyone in. A real ex-military, Soldier of Fortune weirdo. There's no way to get around him and I noticed that he keeps a loaded thirty-eight behind the desk. I thought maybe you could go in the back, through the delivery dock, but there's a camera and it's just too risky. The upside of the downside is that since there's so much security downstairs, they don't have an alarm system in the residence; so once you're in, you're safe. Getting in, however, may be the difficult part."

"How so?" Max asked.

"Well if you're going to do it, you'll have to go in the sliding glass door off the balcony, which is locked, and has a broom handle stuck in the track as an extra precaution."

"No problem," Max said, confidently.

"But . . ." Jane paused here and looked at both of us.

"But what?" Max asked.

"It's a high-rise. The balcony door you need to enter is eight floors up."

"Jane, Jane, Jane," Max scolded. "Not to worry. Not to worry."

"We like a challenge!" I added.

The rest of that week fell into a steady routine. Each morning as soon as Lana left for school, Max and I got in the Jaguar and drove to Boulder. We'd have breakfast with Serge, and then go climbing in Eldorado, where Max introduced me to the practice of free climbing (climbing without a rope) in order to prepare me for the upcoming heist. It was scary at first, but as the week went on and I got more experience, that fear turned into excitement. Soon, I was scrambling up rock faces right behind Max, almost without a thought.

Around noon, we returned to Denver. We'd buy sandwiches at a deli and take them to Cheesman Park to eat, staring up at the building we were soon to attack, discussing different angles and strategies. After that we usually went shoplifting, or to a matinee at the Ogden, and returned home in the evening to eat dinner with Lana. When she was asleep, I'd come down to the cellar and Max would again read from the Balzac. He had gotten over his depression about Vautrin's imprisonment in *Père Goriot*, ever since the little pipe-smoking bookseller at Paris, a fellow Balzac fanatic, had given Max three new books from his own collection, in which Vautrin was alleged to reappear.

But it wasn't just Vautrin that Max became fascinated with. He grew to relish Balzac's detailed and realistic depiction of French society—into which he, Max, felt sure he would soon be venturing himself. He read the novels as a sort of primer for his upcoming voyage, almost like a Michelin guide. Never mind that it was nineteenth-century society Balzac was describing. In Max's mind, I think he truly imagined he'd be running into all these well-dressed

Mesdames and Messieurs, trotting along cobblestone streets in horse-drawn carriages emblazoned with their coat of arms. I suppose it was the equivalent of some French person sitting in a Paris tenement reading the *Little House on the Prairie* books and imagining life in the United States as some pastoral, uncharted paradise.

As Max read on, night after night, filling a notebook with sights to see, and places to eat (most of which, I'm sure, no longer exist, if indeed they ever did), I remembered back to that first morning we met Jane at Paris on the Platte, and how her face had suddenly taken on a look of sad compassion when Max started spouting off about France. For an instant I wondered if maybe he might be a little bit crazy. The look Jane had given him was the same look you give a bride-to-be on the eve of her disastrous marriage. You know the groom's a loser and her life with him will not be what she imagines, but she's so upbeat and excited about it you really don't have the heart to tell her she's making a mistake, and even if you did she wouldn't listen. No, Max had his own vision of France and it was of such density that truth could not penetrate it.

When Friday arrived, we met with Jane at Paris and finalized our plans for the next "opportunity."

"As far as I know," she said, "they're gone for the whole weekend. I called once about three o'clock, and there was no answer. Here's their number," and she handed Max a piece of paper. "Call again right before you go in."

We reviewed the plans one last time, and then Max and I returned home and ate dinner with Lana. When she went upstairs to study, we went downstairs and got ready. Earlier in the week we had each bought a pair of black running tights, two black cotton sweaters, and some black knit hats. We put them on and then waited for Lana to go to bed. After her light went out, we waited another half hour just to make sure she was asleep. Then we snuck out of the house to the driveway where the Jaguar was parked. I got in the driver's seat and shifted it into neutral. Max stood in front and pushed the car as hard as he could down the driveway and back into the street. I then jumped over to the passenger side, Max ran and jumped in the driver's seat, and gravity pulled us down the hill. Once at the bottom, out of earshot of Lana, he turned the key, started the throaty engine, and we were on our way.

Twenty minutes later we were parked on Race Street about a block away from the building. It was after midnight and all was quiet. Before we got out, we reviewed strategy.

"Okay Dil," Max said, "once we're out of here, no talking, so if you've got anything to say, any questions to ask, you do it now."

"I think I'm ready," I said, trying to exude a confidence I didn't really feel.

"Good. Good, then let's go."

We got out and walked quickly along the sidewalk. We were both wearing the pointy toed climbing shoes with smooth rubber soles and had our velvet bags, stuffed with the foam egg crates, on our backs. Max had a rope draped over his shoulder, which we would use to rappel down once the job was done.

We went around the front of the building and saw the doorman sitting at his desk, smoking. Behind him was a wall of TV monitors, showing various shots around the building, but the set that held his attention was a small portable on the desk in front of him. We watched him a moment and from the way he was chuckling, I gathered he was not watching a picture of the loading dock. We moved on around to the west side, the side facing Cheesman Park, and looked up. The first balcony was at least fifteen feet above us. We would have to climb along the side of it, resting only when we reached each railing.

Max went first, moving steadily up the aggregate blocks. He made about five moves before he reached the first balcony. He then grabbed on to the railing, turned, and looked back down, nodding for me to start. I rubbed my hands together and approached. We had been planning this for days so I knew I was ready, but my heart was pounding nevertheless. I got my fingers in between the blocks, pulled myself up, and set my feet. The shoes stuck nicely and made it fairly easy to move. Once I started, Max moved up to the second balcony, stopping when he'd reached it to check on me. We continued this way until Max reached the eighth floor, at which point he disappeared over the railing. I looked down and could see only a few streetlights in the park, and the orange koi swimming slowly in the illuminated ponds in the Botanic Gardens. I turned back to the wall, climbed the last stretch to the eighth balcony, and Max grabbed my arm and pulled me over.

Without a word, we removed our bags and set to work. Max had a glass cutter that was attached to an engineering compass. He put it up against the glass door, about three inches away from the handle, and etched a perfect circle. It made a slight grating noise the first time around but once it had etched a groove, it was almost silent. When that circle was complete, Max moved down to the lower corner of the door and etched a similar circle. That done, he gave me the compass and I handed him a large suction cup—the kind designed to hold a ski rack onto the roof of a car. He spit on it, rubbed the saliva around to moisten the rubber, and then gently placed it over the fist etched circle. He pushed it into place and pulled back on the small lever on the side. Doing this made the rubber concave and created suction, thus enabling Max to pull out a perfectly cut glass disk. He removed the disk from the suction cup, handed it to me, and went to work on the lower circle. While he did that, I slid my hand in the new hole and unlocked the door. Once he had the second disk removed, I moved down, slid my hand through that hole, and plucked the broom handle from the door track. Then I pulled my hand back out and we both stood up. Max had replaced all of the tools in his bag and the two disks were moved far off to the side so we wouldn't step on them when we left. Max looked at me, took a deep breath, and slid the door open.

It was always hard, that first step into a dark house or apartment. Almost like stepping out onto the moon. We had called beforehand from a pay phone down the street, so we were sure the house was empty; and yet, the first minute was always the most frightening. If anything really bad was going to happen, it invariably occurred in the first minute. If the alarm was going to go off, or if the dogs were to come charging, it would happen in the first minute. If someone was home, or if we were in the wrong house, we would discover it within the first minute. But once that minute passed, the rest of the time was incredibly satisfying. Like the feeling you get when you painstakingly put something together, plug it in, and find that it actually works. A sense of pride and amazement bordering on disbelief. It is incredibly satisfying to be given directions and have them lead you to your goal; pleasing to have something described to you and then find it exactly as it is supposed to be. Of course the places were never quite as I'd imagined from Jane's description, but they were close enough to give me an odd sense of déjà vu. And whenever I got that feeling, I knew it would go well. It was comforting, a feeling like someone was watching out for me.

Once inside, we turned on our flashlights and moved through the house. Max had said we should try and get any jewelry first, so I followed him down the hall to the master bedroom.

He always took the women's dressers and left me to go through the men's, which I hated. The men's dressers were never very exciting, always much more utilitarian and sparse than the women's and that is probably why Max never let me near the women's. He saw the sentimental streak in me and knew that I'd be less likely to take something that I thought might mean something to the homeowner. The men's dressers were safer. There were rarely any baubles, or sentimental remembrances. I never found anything more than small change, cufflinks, perhaps a watch, but that was about it.

Max finished about the same time I did, and we moved back to the living room. There was probably silver we could take in the dining room, and there were certainly other valuables throughout the house but we were limited by the space in our bags so we moved on to what Jane had deemed most valuable.

We found the pine display cases and shone our lights inside. The pots and baskets were there but difficult to see with the light. Max felt around the front and sides of the case and found a switch. When they were lit up, it was evident that much thought and planning had gone into their arrangement, and it was clear that the most valuable pieces, those they were most proud of, were in the front.

I lifted the lid of the case and held it while Max carefully removed the pots, setting them carefully on the floor behind us. When he finished, I lowered the lid and we began wrapping the loot in the egg crates. Once that was done, we put our bags back on and went to the door. I stepped on to the balcony and then turned to get direction from Max, but he was not there. I shone my light back in the living room and saw him walking back down the hall to the bedroom. In a moment he returned and stood before the cases. He had a small lipstick in his hand, one he had evidently taken from the master bath. He twisted it up and then wrote something on the glass. Curious, I returned inside and saw that he had written, again in rather ornate cursive, "This burglary brought to you by the disciples of J. C." And then, just as a further hint, he drew a little Eiffel Tower beneath. He then took a step back and assessed his work, cocking his head from side to side. When he was satisfied, he recapped the lipstick, put it into his pants pocket and went out to the balcony.

I rappelled first, and Max followed. We could only make it to the fourth floor before the rope ran out so we paused there and rerigged the pulley. Then we rappelled down the remaining distance to the ground, gathered up our belongings, and quickly coiled up the rope. When that was done, we walked slowly back around the building to the car and drove home. We usually arrived home from these outings at about four or five—always at least an hour before Lana woke up.

I suppose I should elaborate here on "Max's calling cards," which is how Jane and I referred to the messages Max left for the homeowners. Jane laughed at the cult reference in the newspaper after the first burglary, clearly thinking it had something to do with the ham we had fed to the schnauzers. It was only later, when she was at an opera fundraiser with both the Stanovers and the Wilsons, and heard them each talk about the mysterious messages from the disciples of J. C., that she got angry.

"What are you doing?" she demanded when she came by the next day to retrieve the haul from the night before. "What does that mean?"

"Relax," Max soothed. "It's just to add a little spice to the recipe."

"It's going to add our little asses to the prison dock if you don't cut it out," she said, grabbing him by the shoulders and giving him a shake. "We're doing something illegal, remember? This is one time in our lives (maybe the only time, so far) when we don't want to draw attention to ourselves. The police never would have known the two jobs were connected if it weren't for your dumb little egotistical messages!"

"Don't worry," Max said, petting her arm. "We're not going to get caught."

"No, I bet *you* won't, but *I* might!" she screeched. "You've made a little link between these two jobs, well great. Fine. But you know what else they have in common? *Me!*

"Dillon," she said, turning and pleading with me. "Can't you do something about him?"

"I'll try," I said, but I think we both knew it was useless.

Chapter Fifteen

All through the month of July we worked hard. The rationale behind this was not, as you might assume, to speed things along for Max's departure or Jane's acquiring her shop. No, the reason for our frantic pace was the fear that there was only a limited amount of time before the publicity surrounding the heists became too big and the police really started taking an active role in the investigation. Very rarely is stolen property recovered from a burglary, so the police don't put much effort into it, preferring to focus instead on prevention. But when a group like ours pops up, one that systematically and successfully knocks off house after house after house in an organized and efficient manner, it is only a matter of time before they zero in on it.

The fact that Max's calling cards had indicated a connection between all of the robberies didn't help. Once the jobs were connected, we should, arguably, have laid low for a while, but we did not. Despite what Jane had said about not wanting to draw attention to ourselves, both she and Max were narcissistic and loved that their deeds had been noticed. They loved to see their work referred to in the paper, especially when it was accompanied by phrases like "well planned" and "flawlessly executed." If anything, it just made them more cocky.

Toward the middle of July, Jane's tactics became bold, bordering on reckless, and more often than not she was blinded by her desire and greed, placing all three of us in difficult situations. Usually, she was meticulous about planning our jobs, making detailed notes and floor plans, discreetly discovering when would be the safest time for us to strike. Usually, she would discover when the homeowners would be out of town, or out for the evening, when the servants were off, and so on—usually. But as June turned to July, Jane got impatient, and it was then—when she saw something she lusted after and just had to have; some silver bowl made by Paul Revere, or a piece of export porcelain with a *doré* mount—that she got reckless and would do whatever it took to get them out. Usually, she would hurry and call us from the house itself, give us hasty, improvised directions over the phone on how to get in and what to steal, and then assure us that it was "perfectly safe. A sure thing." Any time I heard her say that, I knew to be wary.

These hurried jobs, which Max and I came to call the "haphazard night raids" went beyond exciting to frightening, for the obvious reason that the victims were usually still in the house. But what really bothered me was how Jane's obsession with antiques could smother her usual practicality! She was sometimes so blinded by her desire for baubles that she was less than thorough when it came to getting information on the alarm system or the layout of the house, or the comings and goings of the help. Things were always sloppy on these jobs, and we never quite got all of what we were after, never quite got away without leaving any clues for the police. There was always some dropped glove or something that we tipped over and shattered.

Max was no better. The more notoriety we got in the paper, the more outrageous his calling cards became. They went from being vague literary allusions scribbled on paper and left propped on a desk to grand murals, executed in spray paint and glitter, proclaiming that "Vautrin was here," or that "Father Carlos Herrera has given you his blessing," leaving the police to puzzle over just what the hell it was all about. Finally a professor of French literature made the connection, and from then on we were dubbed the Balzac Bunch.

I remember sitting at Paris one day with Jane and Max going over the plans for the next heist when the little beret-wearing bookseller came rushing over to show Max the paper detailing one of our crimes.

"Isn't it funny?" he said, puffing excitedly on his pipe. "I mean, we were just talking about Vautrin, when? Last month, was it?"

Jane and I froze, our eyes wide.

"Yes," Max said, calmly tapping the ashes from the end of his cigarette. "I've been meaning to get those books back to you. I've been so busy I never did get a chance to read them. Are all of these names here in the paper, this . . . Carlos Herrera, and J. C.," he said, pointing to the article, "are they all referring to that character, Vootrim, was it?"

"Vautrin," he corrected. "Yes, yes! The very same. It's so exciting! I can't believe this is happening right here!"

"Imagine that," Max said, cocking his head and grinning at Jane. "Right here in Denver. Of all places!"

"Who'd have thought," Jane said, tentatively entering the deception, "that such, uh, literate criminals existed, hee, hee."

On the home front the situation was not much easier on my nerves since Lana began to wonder what, if anything, was happening to the house. It had been over a month since she gave Max money to get started on the exterior painting, and she still had not seen any progress.

"It's the prep," Max said one night, in answer to her question about it. We were all seated at the kitchen table eating dinner. "Of course you can't actually see it," he went on, "but it's all the important work that has to be done before you can paint. Isn't that right Dil?"

"Uh, yes. Why yes, all the prep work like . . ."

"Like caulking the gaps in the siding and, uh, priming."

"Ohh," Lana said, nodding. Max was very good with Lana. Rarely did she question him.

"Yes," he said, warming to the story, his voice becoming more authoritative. "The painting itself is a breeze. It goes on in no time. It's the priming that takes a long time since it's the foundation of any good paint job. And you know, you never want to skimp on the foundation."

"Hey, wait a minute," Lana said, her voice full of suspicion again. "Isn't primer usually white?"

Max was not prepared for this, and I saw him struggling to think up a response.

"There's no primer on this house!" Lana exclaimed, placing both hands on her hips.

"This is clear primer," I said, jumping in with my own quick lie. My tone was knowing and a little condescending. "It's much better than the white. That contractor started using it before—well, you know, before he left town. We found a few cans of it in the basement, so we've been using that."

Max gave me a visual high five.

"Oh," Lana said, somewhat appeased. "Well. But when do I get to see some colors? This is taking forever!"

"Sometime next week," Max said. "Or the week after. They left a lot unfinished, those damn contractors. As soon as we fix their mistakes, we'll sit down together and pick out colors."

The conversation then veered off onto safer subjects and Max and I were free—at least for another two weeks. At least from Lana.

Unfortunately, at about this same time Max's parole officer, Meredith, resurfaced. She appeared one morning at 9 A.M. looking less bright and spunky, and more businesslike and serious. Gone was the colorful dress and the clownish makeup replaced by a black pantsuit and a light application of mascara. When I opened the door, she was several feet down the walkway, looking up at the house and making notes on her clipboard.

"Oh hello," she said when I opened the door. "Remember me?"

Yes, I thought, picturing her necklace of hickeys. You made quite an impression the last time.

"I'm here to see Max," she said. "Is he around?" I stood back and made way for her to enter, closing the door behind her.

"Did I wake you up?" she asked, looking at my robe and my messy hair. I nodded.

"I don't know if Max is up yet," I said, rubbing the sleep out of my eyes. "Come in and sit down. I'll go check."

I led her into the living room, and she perched rigidly on edge of the couch. I went down to the cellar and knocked on the door. Max grumbled a reply, so I went in.

Waking Max was never pleasant, and it was rare that I had to do it. Usually he was the one who arose first; by the time I got up, he had consumed enough coffee to reanimate a corpse. Before coffee was another story, and I dreaded having to wake him before I had a cup of the stuff to hand to him. We had been out late the night before and had not made it back until almost five that morning. It had been a stressful, difficult job, another one of Jane's hastily thrown together plans, and when we were safely back home, we had each retired to our beds without even saying good night or brushing our teeth. Being awakened after less than four short hours of repose did not put either one of us in the best humor.

I entered the dark cellar and shook the sleeping lump on top of the rack.

"Meredith's here," I said. "She's waiting upstairs."

This took a moment to register, but when it did he rolled over on his back and groaned.

"What time is it?" he asked.

"Early. A little after eight."

"Is Lana gone?"

"Yes. I'll go make some coffee."

When I emerged once again into the morning sun, Meredith was up and walking around the living room, looking with disapproval at the unpainted walls and plywood floor of the living room.

"He'll be right up," I said, and made my way over towards the kitchen. "Coffee?"

"No, thanks," she replied, still looking around and shaking her head. A few minutes later Max came up from the cellar, dressed only in boxer shorts and dragging his blanket behind him. Meredith looked at his eye and his nose, which still bore traces of the beating.

"Meredith," Max said, his voice froggy. "How nice of you to call . . . and so early."

He shuffled over to the couch, wrapped himself in the blanket and sat down. He stared straight ahead, a glazed expression on his face.

"Yes, well," Meredith said, bubbling and cheerful. "I've got a really big caseload today, and you were at the top of my list!"

"Lucky me," Max said, and then made a series of loud, snorting noises as he cleared his sinuses.

"What happened to your face?" Meredith asked, "and, uh, his face?" she said gesturing at me in the kitchen. Max said nothing for a moment, clearly annoyed with a question requiring a pat response this early in the day.

"On-the-job accident," he said wearily. "Yeah, an accident that happened on the job."

"Golly, what happened?"

Max's head wobbled as he looked her direction, one eye more open than the other. I reentered the living room and handed Max his coffee. His hands came out of the blanket and he took the cup without even looking at me. "Why don't *you* tell her, Dil. About the accident."

I was not much more alive than Max, but I turned, faced

Meredith, and said: "Um, it was pretty bad, you know. Like, we got really hurt."

Meredith's face registered her confusion, "Did you fall?" she asked.

"Yeah," I continued, "a pretty bad fall, like, on my face. And, um, there was this rock down there where I fell and it, like, hit me in the eye. And, well, Max tried to catch me, but then, you know, like, he fell, too."

"On his face?" she asked. Her tone and expression skeptical.

"Uh-huh."

"On the same rock?"

"Uh-huh. I mean, no, a different one."

Max groaned into his coffee and rolled his eyes.

"What on earth were you doing?" Meredith asked.

"Um, we were, like, putting up this ladder. You know, outside. For the painting.

"Yes."

"And it was really muddy. Yeah, really, really muddy," I said, push-starting my brain. "And the ladder sunk way down and sort of tilted to the side and I fell off. Max was on the roof and he reached over to try and grab me—before I fell, you know?—and then, like, he fell too. It was pretty bad," I concluded, fingering my eye and the scab on my forehead.

"Well," Meredith said, again placing her hands on her hips. "Sounds terrible. Now, about the house . . ."

Max looked up at her.

"Now I'm no expert," she chuckled, "but it doesn't look to me like all that much has been done since the last time I was here. What exactly have you been working on?" she asked, pen poised above clipboard, ready to take notes.

"The prep," Max and I said in unison.

"The prep?"

"Yes, Meredith," Max said, his voice tinged with impatience.

"The prep. The preparation. All the unseen work that has to be done before the actual visual work can begin." He held out his empty cup, dangling it from his pinky by the handle, which was my cue to refill it. I took it and returned to the kitchen, glad that Max was finally taking over. "Maybe you better have some, too, Sport," he called after me. "Your wits are, like, a bit slow this morning."

Meredith began tapping the clipboard impatiently with her pen. "You need to show me *something*," she said. "Because to me, it doesn't look like anything at all has been done in here and I did tell you last time that I would have to see some progress, remember?"

"Oh, now of course I do," Max purred, rising and taking one of Meredith's hands in his. The blanket fell away and he stood before her in his boxers. "And there has been progress, plenty of it, hasn't there, Dil?"

I set his coffee on the table and scowled. I did not particularly like being pulled into this lie again, but I nodded and gave a non-committal, "Sure."

Meredith made a noise like *tshk* and rolled her eyes. She shook Max's hand away and crossed her arms on her chest.

"Yeah, right. Like what? I'm not blind and I'm not stupid. You haven't done *anything*."

Max's own eyes narrowed and again I was alarmed at how much he could resemble Lana when he was angry. His stab was quick and efficient.

"Meredith," he said, his tone low and precise. "Progress has been made. Trust me. Perhaps you were a little . . . preoccupied on your last visit so you didn't notice what a shambles the house was. Maybe you weren't seeing things as a professional. You certainly weren't acting like one."

He paused here for effect. "Progress has been made, Meredith. You'll just have to take my word for it."

She said nothing but swayed slowly back and forth, enraged at what he was doing and that she was powerless to do anything about it.

"Look," she said. "I'm only saying all this for your own good. Next time it might not be me who comes to check on you, so—"

"It had *better* be you who comes the next time," Max said sternly. "You make sure of that, Meredith. For both our sakes. Neither one of us wants trouble, do we now? Let's work together to make sure there won't be any."

She was too angry and bewildered to speak so she just took her clipboard and marched out of the house.

"She got the message this time," Max said, after she'd left, "but next time, if there is a next time, we might have to play hardball. We might have to tell it to her straight, that she'd lose her job if they find out she's slept with one of her clients. Especially when I have you to back up the story, Dil."

I said nothing in response, but my thoughts about it were uneasy. Lying to Meredith was one thing, but blackmailing her into silence was something new, and I wasn't quite sure what to make of it. On the surface it didn't seem all that bad: just something that needed to be done. But underneath, it seemed an awful lot like bullying to me, and was the kind of cruel manipulation I would have associated with Aaron, or Lana, or my grandmother, but never, until then, with Max.

Another problem that arose that month involved the car. James's lawyer, going over the financial paperwork for the upcoming divorce, had red-flagged the insurance bill on the Jaguar, noting that a two-hundred-dollar deductible was due for repairs on a car that was not even in his client's possession. When that was brought to James's attention, he immediately called Lana, and the call came while she and Max and I were eating dinner.

"It's James!" she hissed, covering the receiver with her hand. "He got the bill for the car and he wants to know what happened. What should I tell him?"

Max lit a cigarette and puzzled over this for a moment.

"Tell him the truth, so to speak, that the car was in the driveway during the hailstorm and it got pummeled."

She nodded, took a minute to formulate her speech and then put the phone back to her ear.

"Yeah, James? You still there? Yeah. The car. Well, you remember the storm we had a couple weeks ago? Uh-huh. Well the car was in the driveway during that stor—"

Lana abruptly stopped speaking and held the phone away from her ear, wincing. We could hear James screaming on the other end.

"James, listen," she said. "LISTEN! If you're going to yell, I'm not going to talk to you." She hung up.

"He's mad," she said, looking dumbly at the two of us. "He loves that car."

I knew the repair job was great, but the fact that the car had been damaged at all is what made James crazy. It was bad enough that Lana was holding it hostage.

"He'll call right back," she said, the terror evident on her face. She could stand up to James on any topic except the car. "What should I tell him?"

The phone rang. We all looked at it and then Lana and I turned our attention to Max.

"Tell him . . ." Max said, and paused to take a drag from his cigarette. He closed his eyes and drummed his fingers on the side of his head. "Tell him . . . that it was out of the garage because you were, uh, uh, you were having some lumber delivered, for . . . for the . . . crown molding. Some lumber for the crown molding that you're having put all through the house and you had to make space for it in the garage so that it wouldn't get wet and warp."

Lana made a brief mental review of all this information. She then answered the phone and quickly regurgitated what Max had said, almost verbatim.

"So that's what happened," she said, pausing to take a breath at the end. "But it's fixed now, so don't worry. It's nothing really, it looks brand-new . . . What? . . . No . . . No, no, no, no, no! Possession is nine-tenths of the law! I'll keep it until my lawyer says I should give it back, thank you very much! . . . Look you prick, you're the one who walked out on me, remember?" And again, she slammed down the phone.

So we got to keep the car a while longer. The court date for the divorce was not until October, and it appeared that as long as we were careful Max and I would have transportation at least until then. The issue seemed to be settled; but of course, it was not. James's lawyer communicated with the insurance people who said that Mr. Sawyer himself had requested and signed the approval for the repairs and had picked up the car himself when they were completed. The lawyer asked James about this and James asked Lana and Lana asked Max who had no good answer. Soon, men began to call and appear on the doorstep. Strange men dressed in suits wanting to speak to Lana or Max. For that reason, Max again went into hiding. If he were to get caught for forgery, on top of violating his parole, he would be sent straight back to jail. He retreated to the cellar, but this time around both Lana and I had to screen the people at the door and never let on to anyone that Max was even living there.

Oddly enough, it was in our concern for Max that Lana and I found some common ground. We were both afraid of him getting caught and having to go away so we cooperated, without question, when it came to keeping him safe.

My own reasons for wanting to protect Max were clear: he was a friend to me when I had none, and I didn't want to lose that. Lana's reasons for doing so were more enigmatic to me. I knew that she and Max had endured a difficult childhood together, but, as an only child, I don't think I was capable of understanding that bond between them. At the time, it hardly seemed reason enough for her to endanger herself by protecting him, but I suppose it probably was. Looking back, I think she must have felt guilty for leaving the house when he was still young, leaving him alone with my grandparents, and that maybe she saw protecting him from the police, from the insurance investigators, from Doris, and Meredith, and whomever else was after him, as a way to make up for that.

As if things were not chaotic enough right then, Wayne also resurfaced. I had contacted him on my own, the day after my beating, since I knew he would be worried and, well, I guess because I wanted to reassure him that I was all right. Even though he was hokey and annoying, there was something honest about him that I always sort of respected. He was so earnest in his desire to help, to make situations better. I didn't necessarily agree with the way he went about it, but I guess I did respect him. Little did I know then, but Lana had also been in contact with him. They had been actively conferring behind my back on the subject of my future. A fact I discovered one day when he showed up on our doorstep with a thick envelope for Lana.

"Hello, Sport," he said, smiling his thick smile. "Got some paperwork for your mother. Will you be a good kid and make sure she gets it?"

"Sure," I said, and as soon as he left I went straight over to the stove and steamed it open. Thank God I did because inside there were several different brochures and information packets on various military academies! I was stunned. The summer was going along so well, and I was so happy that the thought of returning to school at all, let alone a military academy, seemed just awful. I'd felt sure that idea of military school had been tossed out with the idea of Bible Camp, but as I thumbed through the brochures with their pictures of neat, orderly youth, all uniformed and marching around, I realized I had been mistaken. I was worried, yes, but at the same time I really thought that Max would devise some way to keep me at home. I had faith in him. He would not allow me to be sent off when I was now such a vital, integral part of the thieving organization. He would run interference for me the same way I was doing for him with Meredith and the insurance companies, I felt sure. No way he would let me be sent off to one of these jarhead schools, no way.

I replaced the brochures in their envelope, threw them in the trash, and hardly gave it another thought.

Chapter Sixteen

It is probably appropriate that the book we were reading when I began to doubt Max's infallibility was titled *Lost Illusions*. It was, of course, another Balzac book, and one in which Vautrin reappears, although not until the very end.

Like the previous book we'd read, the main character in *Lost Illusions*, Lucien, is yet another ambitious young man who leaves the dull and dreary provinces for the bright lights of Paris, with dreams of entering high society. Throughout the book his success goes up and down, but in the end he is a failure, his progress hampered by society's prejudice and his own lazy decadence. He has soured his friendships, plunged himself and his relations into poverty, and is just about to drown himself in a deep lake on a lonely country road when who should come along but old Vautrin.

Vautrin, older now, more cynical and less jovial, is disguised as a Spanish priest, Father Carlos Herrera. Of course he takes a fancy to the youthful, handsome Lucien and, after hearing his troubles and his plan to solve them all through suicide, Vautrin offers him a deal. He will pay the money Lucien owes and in exchange Lucien will return to Paris with him and Vautrin will employ him as a front for his dirty work and keep him as a sort of sexual concubine.

Max loved it all and eagerly thumbed through page after page of the book. I enjoyed it too, but less so than before, due in part to my sentimental nature. I had grown fond of Lucien. There was something about his bumbled attempts at legitimacy, and the way he was savagely teased and taken advantage of by the snobs, who made fun of his clothes and his manners, that struck a sympathetic chord with me. Oh I knew that he was foolish and had squandered his opportunities, but beneath all that I saw that Lucien was not a bad person. He had been seduced by the flash and glamour of the big city into pretending he was something he was not. In short, he was all too human, and when he made up his mind to commit suicide in the end, I felt terribly sad.

Max, on the other hand, was so sick of him that I could easily imagine the two on the country road, Max filling the pockets of Lucien's waistcoat with stones and giving him a firm shove into the water.

When Vautrin reappeared at the end of the book, I suppose I should have been thrilled, like Max was, that the scamp had returned, but I was not. Don't get me wrong, I liked Vautrin. I respected him as a fellow thief and homosexual, and I was glad that he was able to prevent Lucien's suicide, but I couldn't help feeling uneasy about it.

As for my illusions about Max and Jane, they were not quite lost. I still idolized them both, but lately some of their gilt had begun to chip off and I was beginning to suspect that underneath it all I might find they were made of nothing more than common plaster. Their selfish motives were becoming more and more obvious and that was disappointing. Oh, it was admirable that they were so intent and focused on their goals, but that focus often had the added effect of making the jobs we did almost joyless.

I had never minded the fact that I did not really get any material things or any money out of the racket. When you are fourteen years old, there is only so much you need that is not already provided for, and any material thing I wanted (usually nothing more than books or records or clothes) was so trivially inexpensive that Max or Jane would not hesitate to buy it for me. No, what I really wanted, more than anything else, was for the stealing to be fun again—to be as exciting and thrilling and taboo as it had been in the beginning, in the days before Jane and Max had become so greedy. As the summer progressed, our outings were less fun and more like work. Work in which it was assumed I would participate whether I wanted to or not.

Another thing that bothered me was the day Max bought us both guns. We were down at one of the pawnshops on Larimer Street, trying to unload some of the lesser items we had stolen that Jane couldn't use, when Max's attention was drawn to a display case containing several antique guns. There were pearl-handled pistols, Saturday Night Specials, .22s, and .38s. He asked to see one of the pearl-handled pistols and listened as the salesman explained all about it.

"Used to belong to Merle the Pearl," he said, handing the gun to Max. "He was called 'the Pearl' on account of his shiny bald head. In fact that's what did him in."

"How so?" Max asked.

"Well, he was running away, after doing a safecracking job over at the Wells Fargo, and the police were on his tail. He tried hiding, but there was a full moon out and it reflected offa that bald head like a mirror. They got him in one shot."

Of course Max bought the gun on the basis of that story, which was as good a reason as any to buy a gun, I guess.

So he's got a gun, I thought at the time. *No big deal.* But a few days later it became quite a big deal when he came into my room one morning and gave me a gun of my own. A small black pistol that he twirled around on his finger. Initially, I was excited by the whole thing; we went out into the field behind the house and practiced shooting at cans. I loved the way Max used to stand behind me and encircle me with his arms, his head close to mine, our hands both clasping the gun as he showed me how to aim and fire. It was only later, when he insisted I carry the gun on all of our jobs, that I began to get nervous. It seemed like an unnecessary precaution, something that could make a simple situation suddenly very complex. It just didn't feel right somehow, in my gut, but then I remembered how at first the climbing had not felt right either. How the idea of leaning back had felt so absolutely wrong. Max's words echoed in my ears: "If it feels wrong, sometimes it's right. Trust me." So I did.

At that point it was easy to do since I was in love with him and would have done just about anything he asked, even if I had misgivings. It might sound strange to say I was in love with him, since he was my uncle; but when you think about it, it makes perfect sense. Max was sexy and witty and smart—the most exciting adult, and the only other gay man I'd ever met. How could I help but fall in love? I knew he was my uncle and I knew that was wrong. But I couldn't deny the way I felt, and Max did little to discourage my crush. On the contrary, at times he even seemed to encourage it, subtly fanning the flames of my teenage lust, always with just enough subtlety to make me wonder if maybe I wasn't imagining it. He did this in the mornings when he emerged from the cellar, his morning wood tenting his boxers, and in the evenings, when he sat behind me teaching me chords to a Bachrach song on the guitar, his chest pressed against my back and his hands on mine. He did it at the Ogden, when he casually draped his arm over the back of my seat and repeatedly brushed my arm with his fingers. It was maddening! It was frustrating! It was confusing! But above all, it was terribly, terribly wonderful.

And yet, why, I wondered, was he doing it? If I was right, and he *was* sending out signals, why didn't he act on them? At the time I thought it was because he knew it was wrong, knew it was taboo, but that wasn't it at all. No, the reason was far more calculated. He didn't take action because that was his ace in the hole, the card he would pull out and use if and when he needed it. It was the same thing he had done with Meredith but instead of veiled threats, he offered me veiled promises. Promises in the form of back rubs, or views of his body as he changed clothes, or meaningful winks over the top of the book as he read to me, until he had whipped me up into such a frenzy that I got a hard-on every time he brushed against me, or if I even caught a whiff of his cigarette smoke. Of course I didn't realize any of that then. Lust makes you blind, and teenage lust makes you blind, deaf, and dumb; so I went on, eagerly doing whatever he told me, pausing every now and then to reposition my hard-on in my pants.

Chapter Seventeen

The card game.

Like all the other jobs, it started out simply. And, like all the other jobs, it did not stay that way. Max, Jane, and I were sitting at Paris one Sunday morning, each reading a section of the paper, when an article caught Max's attention.

"Listen to this," he said. "'Society mavens Lloyd and Beverly Boatwright-Stark were the hosts Friday evening for the wedding reception of their eldest daughter, Donna Anne, as she became the new Mrs. Jarvis Q. Pittredge III.

"'The seven hundred plus guests were treated to a never-empty fountain of Veuve Cliquot and a five-course meal prepared by Chef David Yzek of Raquin's Bistro, who was also responsible for the twelve-tiered, spun-sugar cake, the frosting on which echoed the lace pattern on the bride's Vera Wang dress. Music for the evening was provided by a string quartet that kept the crowd dancing well past midnight, long after the bride and groom had jetted off for their honeymoon on the private Caribbean island belonging to the bride's parents.'"

"Their own private island!" I cried. "Could you imagine having that kind of money?"

"Oh, I could imagine," Jane said wistfully, "but that's about as close as I'll come, I'm afraid. Percy was there. At the wedding. But of course whenever there's a really important function, I take a backseat to Mommy."

"Have you ever been to their house?" Max asked.

"The Boatwright-Starks'? Once, yes, no twice actually, both times this past spring. They had a silly polo party last May. That was the first time, although I never really met either of them then because there were so many people."

"What was silly about it?" I asked.

"Oh God, what *wasn't* silly about it! They'd converted their whole front lawn into a polo ground, which was a bit of a waste since none of the people attending knew how to play polo. The whole day degenerated into a sort of equine petting zoo/croquet game. If nothing else, it gave everyone a chance to wear their best Ralph Lauren outfits and practice acting blue bloodier than thou. Stupid, really. I got drunk and puked in the bushes.

"But their house!" she continued. "Oh my God! Or perhaps I should say, oh my gaudy! It is absolutely nouveau riche, overdone trash, but it is huge! And they are huge collectors. I'd be thrilled to have even a few of their things to call my own. In fact . . ." she said, leaning in close to the table and lowering her voice, "it was from their house that I pinched the little micro-mosaic I told you about. You remember, the one with the tiny scene of Venice. They probably haven't even noticed it's gone. They have a whole collection of them—all the different cities in Italy. Can you imagine what that would be worth? It's even been rumored, although I don't know that I believe it, that they have a Fabergé egg!"

"You stole the mosaic at the polo party?" Max asked.

"Oh, God no. I didn't even get to go inside then. I stole it on bridge night."

"Bridge night?" I asked.

"Yes, they are card-playing fanatics. Percy and I were on our way to dinner one night and made the mistake of dropping by for cocktails on their bridge night. They were short one person, so he joined in."

"Did you play?" Max asked.

"Me? Please! I don't even know how to . . . oh, what's it called when they mix the cards up."

"Shuffling?" Max asked.

"Yes, that's it. I don't even know how to shuffling the cards, let alone play bridge, or canasta, or euchre, or whatever! I sat in the corner, drank several martinis, and then got up and wandered around. Percy swore he'd only play a few hands and then we'd go to dinner. Well, of course Percy's 'few hands' were more like twenty, and they take it all so seriously. No one even knew I was there."

"Could we hit that house?" I asked eagerly, images of polo parties and Fabergé eggs whirling in my head.

Jane shook her head.

"Why not?" Max asked.

"Well, because it's guarded like, well, like, *really* well guarded!" she said, unable to find a suitable comparison. "It's in a gated community with a guardhouse at the entrance. Once you're through that then there's another gate and another guard house at the entrance to their driveway. From there you have to go up the drive a quarter mile to get to the actual house, which is always full of servants. It would be impossible."

"It would be a challenge!" Max said, rubbing his hands together, a demonic look in his eyes.

"Oh, no," Jane said, shaking her head and waving her finger. "No, no, no. These people live in a higher strata of wealth. Nothing like the people we've been picking off. They have some big league security. "

"Big league, shmig league," Max said, waving his hand from side to side. "That's all the more reason. When do we do it?"

And so it began. The card game plan. Again, it sounds simple enough on paper, but lift the veil . . . Well, you know. Here, then, is a synopsis:

Jane and Percy would get themselves invited to play cards. Once there, Jane would carefully case the house, making sure to find out how many servants were on duty, what type of alarm system, the what and where of the valuables, and so on. With any luck, she and Percy would be invited back the following Wednesday to play again. She would volunteer to mix the first round of cocktails and would spike them with Rohypnol. That done, she would excuse herself to go to the ladies' room and on her way would make a detour along the gallery and unlock the large French doors leading out to the back lawn. Max and I, dressed in our black outfits and black ski masks, would enter through these doors and overpower whatever servants happened to be on duty that night. Once they were secured, and once all of the guests had passed out, Max and I would rendezvous with Jane in the game room and the three of us would go on a looting tour of the giant house, loading our velvet sacks with as much jewelry and as many collectibles as we could carry. When that was done, we would return downstairs. Max and I would exit once again through the French doors and Jane would consume her own Rohypnol martini, so that when the police arrived, she could claim to be as bewildered and clueless as the rest of the party.

As for the difficult task of getting in and getting out, Max and I had, of course, thought of a way to do that without going through the many guard stations leading up to the house. Instead of coming through the front, we would come in across the back lawn. This we would be able to do because the back lawn of the Boatwright-Starks' house butts up against the country club golf course. The same country club, conveniently enough, to which James, my ex-step father, belongs, and the entrance pass for which was still in the glove compartment of the Jaguar. We would show up, Max and I, golf clubs in tow, and play the course, as usual, until we got to the sixteenth hole. At that point we would cache our clubs in the pines, change into our black outfits, and scale the brick wall separating the golf course from the booty-stuffed Boatwright-Stark mansion.

Sounds simple enough, right? But lift the veil . . .

The first problem to arise was the rather glaring fact that Jane had no idea how many cards were in a deck, yet she needed to become a competent bridge player in less than two weeks. Fortunately, we found someone who knew all the ins-and-outs of bridge and who was willing to teach her. Unfortunately (for Jane, anyway), that person was none other than her own father, who had perfected his game over many tedious months in a Lao refugee camp. Of course this meant Jane would have to spend hours of time with her father, which was probably the thing she least wanted to do, made worse by the fact that every time she lost a hand he made her pay for her losses with promises to go out with a cousin or to work additional nights in the restaurant. They played at night, after the restaurant had closed, and several times Max and I stopped by to see them on our way to a job.

"I don't know why she no open nail salon like her sister," Jimmy said one night, as he examined and sorted his cards.

He and Jane were alone, sitting at a small table in the middle of the darkened restaurant, drinking strong Vietnamese coffee and playing hand after hand of bridge.

"Good money in nails!" he continued. "She alway want more money, but she alway try tricky. Now she learn bridge to impress more older man. That not right," he grumbled, shaking his head. "But I make her pay to learn. She have to pay!" he chuckled and threw down his trump.

In the meantime Max and I kept up on our evening work. Before Jane went into her bridge hibernation, she had managed to give us the plans for three more jobs, which we executed on the nights she had prearranged. They all went off without a hitch. No problems whatsoever. The problem came when we had finished and had time on our hands. Max began to get antsy. He feared not having enough money, and he couldn't bear the fact that there were all of those houses out there, just ripe for the picking, and there we were sitting on our hands. Instead of simply biding our time, waiting patiently until after the card game heist when Jane could again supply us with more prescreened houses, Max started us doing something really scary—even scarier than Jane's "haphazard night raids." We started hitting houses with no advance planning whatsoever.

On these "shot-in-the-dark-suicidal-night-raids," as I called them, we would drive around late at night in rich neighborhoods scoping out houses (which is easy to do without arousing suspicions when you do it as we did, in an expensive car) until we saw a house that looked empty. We would watch it for a few minutes, take a few minutes to develop a plan, and then attack.

I realize this is the random way that many burglars execute every job they do, but I did not like it. It seemed unnecessarily dangerous to me, and worst of all, somewhat amateurish. Max thought otherwise and was, as usual, very persuasive.

Anytime I was reluctant to do something, he would pull out his ace. "Look, Dil," he'd whisper, as we sat in the car, looking up at some dark ivy-covered mansion. "I've done a lot for you this summer, remember?" And he would then proceed to list it all: how he'd kept me out of camp and got me new clothes, how he'd taught me to climb and play guitar, how he'd bought me some sheet music and essentially gave me money for anything I really wanted; and if I wanted his benevolent largesse to continue then I'd better help! And why wouldn't I? Was I that selfish?

It was the seesaw of favors again. I had been riding high because of what he'd done and now, he told me, it was his turn. Usually that rationale was enough, and I would give in. If not, he'd push things a little further and take my hands in his, or gently massage my thigh and look into my eyes, his own eyes full of suggestion and possibility. That always did it. Yes, I was grateful for all he'd done, of course, but I would have moved mountains to sleep with him, and even the hint that there was a possibility of that was the only kick I needed.

Nevertheless, I was naturally afraid of going into these jobs without any prior information. I was afraid of the alarm system we weren't familiar with and that often went off the second we opened a window, or of the dogs that came running as soon as we entered. But most of all, I was afraid of getting shot. Afraid of some homeowner coming round the corner and surprising us with a gun. Thankfully, this never happened, but it was always in the back of my mind, especially since, on these random jobs, Max insisted that I carry my gun.

It felt like the devil in my pocket. It was such fun to shoot when we were out on the prairie behind the house harmlessly toppling cans, but I could not even imagine using it to shoot a sparrow, let alone another human being! For that reason I always made sure to trail a few steps behind Max as we crept across the lawn toward the unknown house, emptying the chamber of bullets as I went. I could use the gun as a threatening prop, I thought, but never for anything more than that.

Finally, after a week of card practice with her father, Jane was ready to put her playing skills to the test. She convinced Percy to get them invited to the Wednesday night bridge match, and as it turned out, Lloyd and Beverly were thrilled to have some new blood injected into their tired old game since they'd been playing with the same couple for the last eight years. They were charmed that a young person like Jane was taking an interest in the game since their own children made it plain that they had absolutely no interest in it.

We met up with Jane the Thursday after her first big game, when she came to the house to pick up the paltry goods we'd gotten the night before and to get us started devising the plan for the following Wednesday.

"How did it go?" I asked eagerly. For my own sake I hoped it went well as it would mean an end to the unplanned jobs.

She sighed, dropped her purse on the floor and collapsed into the sofa.

"It was really hard," she said, rubbing her temples. "I don't know if I can do it."

"Of course you can," Max said, bringing her a cup of coffee and some toast. "Tell us all about it."

Max and I sat down opposite her and listened eagerly. Jane did not sit up, but remained slumped into the cushions.

"Oh, they were all patient with me," she said, taking a sip of her coffee, "but there is just so much to remember! Beverly and her friend, Mrs. Gouldstein, they get so competitive sometimes, almost as if their husbands' fortunes were at stake. I don't think either one of them is very fond of me and I sensed the green-eyed monster as the motivation for their glee whenever I folded my hand."

"How did the house look?" I asked, rubbing my hands together. "Is there lots of treasure?"

"Oh, Dillon," she said nervously, "I wish I knew! I was concentrating so hard on my game that I barely had a chance to look around."

That was not what I wanted to hear. After a week of shot-in-the-dark-suicidal-night-raids I dreaded another job for which we were not prepared.

"Can we still do it?" I asked.

"Of course, we can!" Max snapped.

"Yes," Jane sighed. "I suppose we can, but it won't be easy. I got enough information to get us in, and I did find out about the servants, but I don't really know what we're going after. I mean, I didn't get a chance to see the upstairs at all! I only really saw the foyer, the dining room, and the game room, so we'll have to do a room-by-room search once everyone is knocked out. It would be better if I knew what they had first, because then I could ask my man what he'd take and we could avoid taking a bunch of stuff we can't unload."

"We'll just have to make the best of it," Max said. "Now let's go over the layout."

* * *

When Wednesday rolled around again, the three of us met once more at Paris to go over the final plans. Max gave Jane another packet of Rohypnol and told her to make sure and grind it up well.

"I'm a little worried about one thing," she said. Max and I looked at her, questioningly.

"Well, Mrs. Gouldstein doesn't drink, and she's got a bladder condition so she doesn't even drink water or anything! How am I going to get her drugged!"

Max didn't conceal his annoyance at such a large oversight on Jane's part. He scowled at her and shook his head, but then looked away and puzzled over the the problem.

"What if . . ." he said, still formulating the plan as he spoke. "What if you brought a box of chocolates? Something fancy. Truffles maybe, with a coating of powdered sugar. Do you think she'd go for that?"

Jane nodded eagerly.

"Good. Excellent. Here's what to do: grind up the pills very fine, like powdered sugar, and roll the truffles in the dust. Mix some sugar in with them, of course, to hide the bitterness."

"Yes, yes!" Jane cried, clapping her hands. Then something else occurred to her and her expression fell.

"What about the truffles when it's all over?" she asked. "I mean, we can't just leave them for the police to analyze if everyone knows I'm the one who brought them with me."

"Good point," Max said, gesturing with his cigarette. "Excellent point. I'm glad you're thinking. Get two boxes and dose only one of them. When Dil and I leave, we'll take the dosed box with us. No one will be the wiser."

The rest of the day, Max and I prepared our end of the plan. We got all of James's golf accessories together and outfitted ourselves in what Max imagined was typical golf clothing: Kelly green, plaid slacks, white polo shirts, and two ridiculous tweed caps. I tried to tell him that was not really the way people at the country club dressed, but he wouldn't hear it.

"Nonsense," he said. "We look perfect! Just like the golfers on TV!"

"Maybe so," I groaned, "but matching outfits?"

He gave me a dismissive wave and went back to admiring himself in the mirror as he practiced miming his golf swing. I knew it was useless to protest once his mind was made up, so I put on the ridiculous outfit and loaded the clubs in the back of the car.

Around four o'clock, we left and drove to the country club. It had rained earlier that afternoon, but the sky had cleared by the time we arrived. I took that as a good omen. Our plan involved hiding out in the bushes for several hours until the bridge game started, so I was glad we would not have to wait in the rain.

As we arrived at the country club, we encountered the first hurdle. We drove up to the guard station and I handed Max the entrance pass. He flashed it at the guard, the guard glanced at it, and then waved us by. We were just through the gate when we heard him call out.

"Wait! Stop!"

Max stopped and looked back impatiently. He leaned out the window.

"Yes, what is it?"

"I'm sorry, sir, could I see your pass once more?"

Max handed it to the guard who took it and returned to the booth. I felt sweat break out on my forehead. Max sensed my anxiety and gave my thigh a reassuring pat. A moment later the guard returned.

"Mr. Sawyer?" he asked.

"Yes," Max replied.

"I'm sorry to hold you up, sir, but I'm showing that this pass has been replaced. You don't happen to have the replacement pass with you?"

There was a momentary pause.

"Oh, that woman!" Max cried, slapping the steering wheel with his fist. "Listen," he said, turning to the guard, "my goddamned wife lost *her* pass. I never lost mine. I told her to replace *hers*, not mine!" His tone was so impatient and angry that the guard became a bit intimidated.

"Oh," he said. "Your *wife's* was lost."

"Yes," Max said. "That's what I told you. Listen, we've got a four o'clock tee time and I have some very important clients waiting for me inside. I really don't have the time right now to argue with you."

"Yes, Mr. Sawyer, let me just call up to the clubhouse and have them check it out."

"Oh, give me that!" Max said, grabbing the pass out of the guard's hand. "I told you I'm late!"

Max's face was red and veins were popping out of his neck. It was a convincing performance.

"I'll give them an earful at the clubhouse myself! *After* my game! I pay a shitload of money to come to this place; now open the goddamned gate!"

The guard peered in at us for a few seconds more and then looked again at the car. I think it was the car that did it, because without another word he went back to his station and opened the gate.

"The insolence of these people!" Max said as we drove away, his face still red. It always took him awhile to get out of character when he'd just pulled off such a big lie so I knew better than to offer any commentary. In fact, I hoped he could keep up the charade at least until we were safely out on the course. I gave him a few directions on where to park, which he followed wordlessly until we found a space. Then we got out of the car, set up our golf bags, checked in with the starter and walked toward the first hole, quietly reviewing the plan.

Out on the course we ran into yet another obstacle. Something neither of us had foreseen. While Jane had spent hours and hours perfecting her bridge game, Max and I had not played even one round of golf and neither one of us had the slightest idea what we were doing. We stood at the first hole wondering which club to use and even which direction to hit the ball. Once that was determined, there followed another ten minutes of useless swinging before we actually made contact with the ball, having dug a large, brown trench in the grass with all of our initial efforts. This did not amuse the group that was set to tee off behind us. Needless to say, before we finished the first hole (having taken about fifty strokes each), we allowed that group to play through rather than wait on us. By the seventh hole, we had allowed two more groups of people to play through, and I was exhausted! My shoulders ached and I'd twisted my back. Max was swinging away in a sand trap, cursing loudly, while I stood watching, trying not to laugh. By the eleventh hole, we were out of balls, having lost all twenty-four that we'd brought with us. This was disappointing in a way. In desperation, we had resorted to using the bent club Lana had used to whack the Jaguar and found that it worked quite well, meaning that we could actually hit the ball with it as opposed to the swing, miss, swing, miss pattern we had both fallen into. It's probably good that we did run out of balls since we were losing daylight and were in danger of running behind schedule. Bridge was scheduled for nine o'clock and it was already eight-thirty! Realizing this, we decided to mime our way to the sixteenth hole, and our game improved markedly after that.

The sixteenth hole was deep in a grove of tall pines. We waited for the group ahead of us to finish up and then ducked to the right under the boughs and over toward the tall brick wall. We took all the clubs out of the golf bag and removed the black outfits. Once dressed, we looked a little frightening, our faces concealed with the ski masks, but then I guess that was the idea. We double-checked that we had everything we'd need and then Max started climbing. The wall was covered in ivy and looked like it would be an easy climb, but the thick vegetation was home to several small birds that darted out suddenly, flapping their wings and squawking the second we got too close to their nest, causing me to fall several times from the surprise.

When we reached the top we saw the Boatwright-Stark mansion about a hundred yards off. It was a mammoth house, with French windows stretching up three floors on the main part of the house and two lower wings shooting off to the sides. It was just getting dark and we could see lights in the room to the left, which we knew, from Jane's directions, was the game room. We were to enter from a door on the right wing and then go to the kitchen and overpower the cook and the butler. By then, with any luck, the Rohypnol would have taken effect and most of the card players would be falling asleep.

Max gave me a nod and we climbed down the wall into the Boatwright-Starks' property. It was nine o'clock. By about nine-fifteen, it was dark enough that we could make our way across the lawn and up on to the stone porch without being seen. We did so, as quickly and quietly as possible, and then peered in the large French window of the right wing. The game room was enormous, with a high ceiling and massive plaster columns in each corner. On the wall opposite us there was a cavernous fireplace in which, although it was July, a fire raged, and above which were mounted the trophy heads of several dead animals. In the middle of the room was the large rectangular game table. It had legs of dark carved wood, and a green felt top like you'd find on a pool table. The decks of cards sat ready and waiting. Two women, both with tight leathery faces and overly bleached and back-combed hair, sat talking to Percy on the sofa and eating from the truffle box. Over by the bar, Jane was mixing drinks and telling jokes to the two older men, who laughed and smiled at her, much to the chagrin of their jealous wives. We were so busy watching the scene that we almost didn't notice when one of the men broke away from the bar and stepped out on the porch to smoke a cigar. Luckily, we were able to conceal ourselves behind one of the decorative urns and, by pinching each other, kept from laughing as we listened to him fart.

Eventually, the man went back inside, and we crept back up to the window. All were enjoying their cocktails, and Jane had slipped away from the crowd to go to the ladies room. That was our cue, so we crept across the porch, along the gallery, to the other set of French doors off the dining room, just in time to hear Jane disengage the lock. She didn't see us, which I hoped meant that we were, indeed, well camouflaged. We put on our black cotton gloves, and Max slowly turned the handle. He pushed the door open, and we both crept in. Once inside, we set down our bags and removed the supplies we'd need. Max put a large roll of duct tape on his wrist, like a bracelet, and put the small packet of ground-up Rohypnol in the pocket of his pants. He then took out his gun and stuck it in the leather holster running across his chest and motioned for me to do the same. When he wasn't looking, I again made sure to empty out all of the bullets and slip them in my pocket. That done, we stashed our bags behind the drapes and crept quietly in the direction of the kitchen. Or, at least, in the direction Jane had assumed the kitchen to be, since she hadn't really discovered its location the week before.

The cook and the butler were supposed to be the only two on duty, so we did not anticipate any difficulties in overpowering them, especially since we had the guns. After several wrong turns, we found the kitchen and there, watching a small TV and smoking a cigarette, was the cook. She was a short woman, with her hair pulled back in a large bun. Her back was to us, so Max slowly removed his gun from the holster and stepped up behind her. He placed the barrel of the gun against her temple, and she jumped and gave a startled cry. Max covered her mouth with his hand. He moved around in front of her and put his index finger to his lips. He nodded for me to come over and then handed me his gun. I held it against her head and she stared up at me, wide-eyed with terror. I was just as terrified, knowing that there were actual bullets in this gun, and my hand trembled. Max ripped off a piece of duct tape and placed it over her mouth. He then bent down and taped her ankles together, going around them several times with the roll of tape. He stood her up, turned her around, and similarly bound her hands behind her back. She would probably not be able to escape, but, just to be sure, Max wrapped more tape around her whole body several times and then led her, hopping pathetically, to a pantry closet. He pushed her inside, closed the door, and then put a chair up under the handle.

I gave him his gun back. I didn't even like to touch the thing, and it made my heart pound like a kettle drum in my head. I was getting nervous again, just as I'd done in the dressing room at Fashion Bar on my first day of shoplifting. My breathing was erratic and my clothes were drenched in sweat. We had done so many jobs that summer, but this was the first time we'd had to catch and contain people. I didn't like it and we still had one more to go.

Finding Hamilton, the butler, was not difficult. We figured he would probably be somewhere near the game room in order to respond promptly to any calls from his employers. We made our way across the foyer, where, as luck would have it, Hamilton found us. We were slinking around the stairway, guns drawn, trying to find him, when suddenly I heard a voice behind me.

"Dear me," he said, his reedy voice almost deadpan. "Thieves."

I spun around and saw a man in a dark suit carrying a tray full of empty drink glasses. He did not try to run, did not even appear very alarmed. He was an old man, hunched over from osteoporosis. His nose was a large hook, like the beak of a toucan, and he squinted at me from tiny eyes.

"Madam will not be pleased," he said, shaking his head, as if he'd just discovered that one of the parlour maids had broken a vase.

"Come on," Max hissed. "Let's get him in the kitchen!"

I got behind the old man and prodded him along with my gun.

"Young man," he said, halting and turning his turtle-like body around, to face me. "I'm afraid the kitchen is *this* way."

In the kitchen he set down his tray and called out to the cook.

"Miss Brooks, I'm afraid these men have come to burgle the house. Miss Brooks," he called. "*Miss Brooks!*"

"Miss Brooks is busy," Max said, and opened the pantry door to reveal the bound and wide-eyed cook. Max tried to bind the man's hands behind his back, but because of his advanced age and his poor posture the hands would not come together. Nor could we imagine him standing for hours until the police arrived. We puzzled for a moment but then decided to seat him in a chair and duct-tape his hands in his lap and his legs to the legs of the chair. When that was done, Max wound the tape all around him and covered his mouth. We then hurried off to see how things were going in the game room.

The game room was, as I've said, enormous, with one side facing out on the back lawn, and the opposing side containing the large fireplace. The two other sides had tall pocket doorways leading to other rooms. The doors to the foyer were open a crack, so we crept up next to them and peered in.

All the guests were seated at the table studying the cards they held in their hands. Jane was trying to focus on her hand, but was obviously distracted and kept glancing around the room.

"It's your turn, dear," Mrs. Gouldstein said, patting Jane on the wrist.

"Oh, I am sorry," Jane said, again turning her focus to her cards. Mrs. Gouldstein took another truffle from the box and popped the whole thing in her mouth. The others sipped at their drinks and exchanged weary glances, wondering if maybe it had not been such a good idea to invite this newcomer. Percy was embarrassed by Jane's delay, and he drank nervously as he waited for her to make her move. When she finally did so, they all gave an audible sigh of relief. The play went on quickly after that, and as the round finished out, the yawning began. It started with Mrs. Gouldstein and Percy, of course, since they had each consumed the largest quantity of the drug, but soon everyone around the table was doing it.

"Maybe I should ring for Hamilton," Mrs. Boatwright-Stark said, "and have him bring us some coffee."

"No!" Jane cried, and then quickly realized her mistake. "No, I mean, none for me, thanks, hee hee. Coffee at this hour? Hee hee, why, you'd be up all night. Have a truffle," she said, snatching the box from the greedy Mrs. Gouldstein and thrusting it toward the other players. "There's plenty of caffeine in these! At least enough to keep you all awake through another one of my turns!" she joked.

They did not laugh.

"No, Percy," Jane said, smacking Percy's hand as he reached for another truffle. "You've had enough! Remember your glucose levels. Please, the rest of you, eat as many as you'd like, I sampled no less than ten of them in the shop this morning, and if I eat even one more I'm surely not going to fit in the car on the way home."

The men laughed politely at this little joke, but Percy and Mrs. Gouldstein were quickly fading, much faster than the others. Mrs. Gouldstein's eyes were getting droopy and her head lolled about. She pushed herself up from the table and wearily exclaimed that she would sit this hand out. She sidled over to the sofa in front of the fire and collapsed onto it, her heavy head wobbling onto one of the pillows. Percy said he thought he might keep her company, and stumbled over to a chair next to her. He similarly collapsed and that left four players: the Boatwright-Starks, Mr. Gouldstein, and Jane.

"What shall we play next?" Beverly asked, deftly shuffling the cards. "Canasta? Euchre? Whist?"

"Oh I don't care, sweet pea," Lloyd said, "Dealer's choice."

"Yes," Mr. Gouldstein chimed in. "But let's make it something easy, for our new guest." He smiled over at Jane and slid his leg up next to hers under the table. She was used to such treatment from men and so didn't even flinch. She smiled over at him and carefully refilled his glass from the shaker.

"A toast," Jane said, raising her glass. They all raised theirs and looked at her expectantly. In her eagerness to get them all guzzling, she hadn't really thought of anything and stared ahead blankly.

"To what, my dear?" Beverly asked, wearily.

"To . . . Uh, many more nights like this!" Jane said.

"Here, here," said Mr. Gouldstein. "I'll drink to that."

"I'll *need* to drink for that," Beverly muttered, taking a large sip of her drink and lighting a cigarette.

"You've all been so kind and patient." Jane gushed, still holding her glass aloft. "It means so much to me. More than you can ever know."

The men, of course were enchanted, and Mr. Gouldstein was so bold as to move one of his meaty hands up onto Jane's thigh. Again, she replenished his drink.

Beverly was shuffling furiously now, a burning cigarette dangling from the corner of her mouth. She looked disgustedly at her husband and Mr. Gouldstein, each smiling like giddy schoolboys at Jane, and then rapped the deck on the table.

"Jane, dear," she said, passing the cards across the table. "Why don't *you* teach us a game. Something from Vietnam, maybe. Something you learned as a child, although for heaven's sake, that was just yesterday!"

The two women exchanged frosty glances and artificial chuckles. Jane seized the deck and scooted her chair closer to the table. She tapped the cards, cut them, and gave them a clumsy shuffle.

"Okay," she said. "We'll play a game I know, one I learned in college, but everyone fill up your glasses because it's a drinking game."

Mr. Gouldstein and Lloyd both nodded their assent and refilled their glasses from the shaker. Beverly shrugged, rolled her eyes, and pushed hers forward to be filled.

"Here's how it works," Jane said, holding the deck. "I flip the cards down, one by one, and anytime a Jack appears you slap it with your hand. The one who hits the Jack first gets the pile of cards and the three who miss it have to take sips of their drinks. Whoever has the smallest pile of cards at the end has to chug the whole thing. Get it?"

"Oh good Lord!" Beverly sighed, raising her heavily bejeweled hand so it was ready to slap the Jack.

Jane dealt quickly and the men lost quickly. After three rounds, Lloyd slumped forward and rested his head on the table. Soon after that, Mr. Gouldstein gave up and went out to smoke a cigar. He did not return. Then it was just Jane and Beverly, facing each other and angrily slapping at cards, each drinking more and more.

Max and I were worried. Jane was not supposed to be drinking at all. At least not yet. Not until after she had taken us through the house and pointed out what we should steal. We sat watching helplessly as the two women went on, hand after hand, until suddenly, Jane stopped the game.

"Hey, Bev," she said, her head swaying. "You gotta quarter?"

"Eh?" the woman asked. "I don' carry money, dear."

"Wait, wait, I think I got one," Jane said, reaching over and digging in Lloyd's pants pocket.

She obtained a coin and held it up to the light.

"A dime? Guess it'll work. Even though the game's called quarters ye' jus' need any coin, or somethin' round, like zish."

Beverly began laughing and lit the wrong end of her cigarette. She scowled when she tasted it and both of them laughed. When the hilarity subsided, Jane tried to explain the fundamentals of quarters. She pushed a martini glass to the middle of the table and filled it to the brim. She then filled each of their glasses.

"Okay, Bev, lishen up, heres's a rules. I bounce a quarter off a the table and try an' get it in the middle glass. If I miss, I take a li'l sip of my drink. Wait. No. Yeah, tha's right. Okay, tha's right, an' if I miss, I take a sip of my drink. Yeah. If I make it—in the glass, I mean—you have to drink your glass *and* thish glass in the middle. Unnerstan?"

Beverly gave a whooping laugh that turned into a fit of coughing.

Jane bounced the quarter once and then we saw it rolling on the floor. She took a sip and then leaned over and dug in Lloyd's pocket for another coin which she tossed over to Beverly.

"Go for it, sishter."

Beverly held the coin in her hand, shook it, blew on it, pretended to spit on it and then bounced it off the table. It landed with a plop in the middle glass.

"Goddamnit!" Max whispered. "What the fuck is she doing?"

Beverly gave an excited shriek and then got up and did a little victory dance around her chair. Jane eyed the glass in disbelief.

"No, wait," she tried to protest. "Wait. I wasn' ready. Wait."

"Wasn' ready!" Beverly cried. "Wasn' ready! Whassat mean? There's no *ready* or *not ready!* Bottoms up, Janey dear!"

Jane lifted her glass with both hands and sipped, making mournful faces as she did so, looking almost as if she might cry. She glanced around, clearly wishing we'd pop out and save her. Finally, a frustrated Beverly reached across and picked up the glass from the middle. She raised it, sloshing some onto the green felt.

"Oh come on, you big baby," she chided Jane. "Drink it like you got a pair! You girls! You haven't won out over us broads yet!" And with that she tilted her head back and downed the cocktail in one gulp. She looked at Jane, her eyes spinning, gave out an enormous belch, and then her knees gave out and she toppled to the floor.

Max burst into the room and Jane stood, unsteadily.

"You're drunk!" he cried, grabbing her by the arm and giving her rubbery body a shake.

"I couldn' help it!" she whined. "I kept feeding her truffeses and drinks but she jes wouldn' go down!"

"Oh, come on," Max said, exasperated. "We better hurry before *you* pass out, too. Dil, go get the bags!"

I ran to the dining room and retrieved the velvet bags from behind the drapes. When I returned, Max was holding Jane up with one hand and lightly slapping her cheeks with the other.

"Where do we start?" Max asked, his tone almost pleading. Jane's head was getting too heavy for her to support.

"Uhsstairs," she said. "Jew'ry's uhsstairs."

I came over, took hold of her other arm, and together Max and I managed to drag her across the floor, out into the foyer and to the foot of the staircase. Then she started giggling and her knees buck-led.

"Shit!" Max cried. "Shit, shit, shit!" He tried slapping her, harder this time, but she was almost gone. Even if we did manage to get her up the thirty or so steps, we realized, she would hardly be able to see, let alone determine what was worth stealing.

"Oh, let's just take her back," Max said, his voice full of disgust.

We made a loop and dragged Jane, head drooping forward, back to the game room. We sat her back in her chair, leaned her forward, and rested her head on the game table.

I remembered the truffles and took the new box out of my bag. I picked up the old box, collected the few uneaten pieces that were lying around, and emptied about half of the new box into the old, and placed the new one back on the table. When I'd finished, I looked up and saw Max prying the rings off of Beverly's bony knuckles. I went over to the sofa and did the same to Mrs. Gouldstein, and then to Jane, figuring that it would look suspicious if she remained untouched. We stole the watches from both of the men, and the cash from their wallets, and then quickly went to the next room.

"Stick close," Max whispered. "There's probably not anyone else here, but we can't be too careful."

We were in a formal living room then. Another huge marble fireplace dominated one wall and facing it were two long sofas. In the corner, Max found the cabinet housing the micro-mosaics and quickly began emptying it. There were about twenty of them alto-gether and they were just as Jane had described them: tiny stone portraits of Italian cities. He removed them one by one from the case and handed them to me to put in my bag.

We went from room to room on the lower level and looted sim-ilar cabinets, taking Murrano glass animals, Russian icons, ivory figurines, and whatever else we could find during our frantic search. Then we went upstairs.

The staircase was wide, with a stone balustrade on either side. It went straight up about twenty steps to a landing and then divided in two. The two sides turned at right angles and continued up to the second floor. We made our way up to the next level where we saw more display cases packed with silver trinkets. These were quickly bagged by me while Max ran off in search of the master bedroom. Our bags were nearly full at that point so we figured we had better find the valuable jewelry and avoid any more potentially worthless baubles.

The upstairs hallway was almost surreal: a long corridor punctuated every twenty feet or so by a doorway. We stood for a moment while Max debated whether we should go to the right or to the left. He went right, and I followed, trying the doors on one side while Max took the other. We opened every door along the way, finding guest room after guest room, until finally we reached a set of double doors. I turned the handle, pushed them both open, and gasped. Inside, the whole room was pink—pink walls, pink fireplace, pink carpeting, even elaborately painted pink furniture. Max came up behind me and we both stared for a minute at the odd beauty of it all. It was not an inviting room, and it didn't suit my taste, but I couldn't help but admire the incredible singularity of purpose that must have gone into orchestrating so many different pink things in a single room.

As usual, Max took the woman's dresser and I went through the man's. We rooted through them thoroughly but it didn't take long for us to realize that they contained nothing of real value. If the Boatwright-Starks had jewelry in the house, it certainly wasn't kept in the dressers.

It was as we were turning to leave, giving up on the bedroom, that we saw it. We had been so focused on the dressers that we'd not noticed it. It was lit from above by a spotlight and it shone in its gilt and glass cabinet, like a tiny, shimmering, pink sun.

It was, of course, the rumored Fabergé egg.

We both stopped and stared, unable to speak, unable to believe what we were seeing. It was a large egg, probably about the size of a grapefruit, resting on an elaborately carved base of onyx, platinum, and diamonds. The egg itself was a translucent pink enamel, encircled by three bands of intertwined silver and black garland. It was cracked in half, so to speak, and the top half was tilted back on tiny hinges revealing small black silhouettes of Nicholas and Alexandra, and all of their doomed offspring, each dark face set in its own pearl-and-diamond-encrusted frame.

It was the kind of thing words like "exquisite," "meticulous," and "extraordinary" were designed to describe. It was a hyperbole of beauty and excess, and for that reason any exaggerated descriptions could hardly do it justice. How could we even touch it, I thought, let alone take such a thing?

Max approached the case. He bent down and gazed in, wide-eyed, at the egg. Then he leaned back and examined the display case. The front panel was hinged on the left side and was held shut on the right by a simple gold clasp—the kind you might see on the diary of a teenage girl—useless to keep anyone from invading the space, but there all the same as a reminder that you shouldn't. I held my breath as I watched Max's hand undo the clasp. He slowly pulled open the front panel and as he did so I had the feeling an archaeologist must have when he opens a tomb that has been sealed for centuries: a feeling of rare air escaping.

Max's hand moved toward the egg. When he was inches away, he hesitated a moment, his hand hovering, but then moved forward and touched it, lowering the top portion of the egg and concealing the silhouettes. The two halves came together with an audible click. Max reached his other hand in the case and grasped the egg carefully in both hands. As he lifted it, the alarm went off.

Suddenly sirens blared throughout the house. In the hallway, lights were flashing on and off. It startled Max so much that he jumped back and dropped the egg. I picked it up and handed it back to him quickly like a hot potato. He gazed at it a moment and then took off running. I grabbed both bags and followed after him, running out of the bedroom and down the hall. We reached the stairs and took them three at a time. As I turned on the landing, I missed a step and tumbled down the remaining steps. I landed on my back at the bottom, still clutching both bags. I barely had time to sit up and orient myself before Max had me by the arm and was dragging me back through the foyer. The noise had been loud upstairs, but it was ear-splitting on the lower level. We ran back through the living room and through the game room, in which all the players were still snoozing soundly, and headed out along the gallery. Max was ahead of me. As we reached the dining room, he pulled back the curtain, whipped open the French door and went out. I paused for a moment. I heard pounding on the front door. My heart leapt and I jumped out onto the porch and closed the door behind me.

Outside, the house and lawn were illuminated like a prison. Mr. Gouldstein was passed out in one of the lawn chairs, his cigar dangling from his mouth. Max grabbed my shoulder and pulled me close.

"Run, Dil!" he yelled. "As hard and as fast as you can! Don't stop until you're back over that wall!"

He vaulted off the steps and took off sprinting across the lawn. I followed, the heavy bag on my shoulder bouncing with each step. The distance between the wall and the house seemed much longer this time, and the only way I could tell I was making any progress was by the slowly receding sound of the alarm and the dimming light. Max was several yards ahead of me, and I saw him disappear into the trees. A moment later I was in the trees too, branches slapping me in the face as I went. The vegetation was thick and the ground was uneven with exposed roots and rocks but I went on, resolved not to stop until I got to the wall.

Well, I got to it all right. It was so dark I didn't even see it until I slammed into it head-on. I bounced back and fell on my ass. I sat dazed for a minute, but quickly shook it off and got back up. I could hear Max rustling in the vines above me, so I grabbed on and tried to go up.

Trying to climb in a panic is like trying to swim against an undertow: dangerous, exhausting, and useless. I couldn't find any place to put my feet and tried instead to pull myself up the vines. They would support my weight for about two steps, maybe three, but then they too, would lose their grasp on the wall and I'd come tumbling to the ground. After the third fall, I stopped. I was almost hyperventilating. I was afraid, but I knew that if I was ever going to get out I had to calm down. I took several deep breaths, shook out my hands and feet and approached the wall again. My eyes were beginning to adjust to the darkness. I started climbing. I got up several feet, panicked, pulled my body in close to the wall, and fell. Again, I got up. Again, I tried the deep breaths, but they turned into hysterical sobs. I fell back down on the ground, exhausted from my efforts, my mind going in all different directions. I was losing it. I was going to get caught because I could not get up this stupid, fucking, vine-covered wall—the easiest thing I'd climbed all summer!

Then I heard something hit the ground a few feet away. A moment later I was lifted up.

"Come on, buddy. Come on. It's all right. You're all right. We're almost out. Get on my back."

I climbed on Max's back, wrapping my legs tightly around his waist. I got one arm under his arm and the other around his neck. I could feel the sweat on his head and feel his chest heaving from exertion. He placed his hands and feet and slowly started moving up. Sirens now joined the wailing of the alarm in the distance. I tried to make myself as light as possible, tried not to cling too tightly to him, but I could tell he was straining under the added weight. He would make a few moves and then stop, leaning back on his feet, giving his arms a rest. After several of these starts and stops, we made it to the top. I got off and we rested for a moment. He grabbed me by the shoulders and looked me in the face.

"Be careful on the way down!" he said sternly. "Do not jump until you're sure you're near the bottom. Got it? The last thing we need is for you to break your ankle."

I repositioned my bag and slowly lowered my feet. I clung to the top of the wall with my hands, reluctant to let go, but remembered to lean back and then felt my feet lock in.

Down, step, down, step, slowly, methodically. I got a rhythm going and was soon close enough to see the ground. I let go and dropped down. The sirens were muffled on this side of the wall and that made me feel much safer. I'd stopped crying, but I was drenched in sweat and my breathing was still erratic. Max emerged from the bushes with the golf bags and was quickly stripping out of his black clothing. I did the same, but I was sweating so much that my clothes clung to me like a skin. Eventually, I got them off and Max tossed me my ridiculous plaid slacks and polo shirt. I put them on, stuffed the bag of loot in the bottom of the golf bag, put the black clothes on top of it, and then wedged the clubs in as best I could. Max was already waiting at the edge of the trees when I'd finished. I grabbed the handle of the bag and pulled it over the uneven ground, the wheels squeaking as I went.

The course was dark and empty. We could see the lights of the clubhouse off in the distance and made our way silently across the grass toward it. Just as we were leaving the course, we heard the sprinklers come on behind us. I turned and watched as the streams of water rose and pulsed in the air, and wondered if they were supposed to come on just then, or if someone had been watching us, waiting until we'd left the course. It was another thing to worry about, but I was too tired.

We were silent as we loaded the bags back into the Jaguar and drove out of the country club. Usually, when we finished a job, we both had an adrenaline rush and would talk a mile a minute as we recounted the highlights and discussed what we'd got. This time, however, even though we had something much more valuable than anything else we'd stolen that summer, there was no exuberance, no adrenaline. We were exhausted. Spent. Worn out. The stress level, from the time we entered the country club that afternoon, until we drove back out the gate late that night, had been so consistently high that once it finally lowered, we could do nothing but exist until such time as we could collapse, which we did as soon as we got back home. We parked the car in the driveway, took the bags inside, and without a word retired to our respective rooms, not waking until late the next morning.

Chapter Eighteen

The next morning Max and I slept late, which was easy to do as the sky was overcast and a steady, rhythmic rain was falling. When I got up, I found Max already seated at the kitchen table drinking coffee, the newspaper spread out before him.

"Anything about last night?" I asked. He looked up and smiled at me.

"No, I expect it all happened too late to make it into today's paper."

"Any word from Jane?" I asked, pouring myself some coffee (a habit I had recently acquired).

"No," he said, lifting up his own cup to be refilled, but still staring down at the paper, "and I'm a little worried. They'll hit her with lots of questions and I keep imagining her waking up and saying things she shouldn't. She's a smart girl though, knows when to keep quiet, even in a pinch like that, so she'll probably do all right."

I took a section of the paper and began to thumb through it.

"What would you like for breakfast today, Dil?" Max asked, getting up and moving toward the refrigerator.

"I don't care," I shrugged. "Cereal, maybe. Whatever."

"Cereal? Cereal!" he cried, in mock outrage, his back to me. "Why on earth would you want cereal?" he turned around and in his hand he held something concealed by a napkin. "Why on earth would you want cereal," he repeated, a sour expression on his face. "Or toast, or even waffles . . . when you can have . . . an egg!" And like a magician, he whipped off the napkin to reveal the jewel-encrusted wonder, setting it gently on the table before me. I had not seen it since the night before and in the grim light of morning, and in a suburban setting it looked even more spectacular. I picked it up, surprised by its weight and solidity, and gazed at it.

"The czar once held that," Max said, as proudly as if he'd laid the egg himself.

I undid the clasp and pushed back the top half. As I did so, the framed silhouettes, which were each mounted on tiny gold accordion brackets, blossomed into view.

"What do you think it's worth?" I asked, awestruck.

"I really don't know," Max said, bending down to examine it more closely. "Jane will have to say for sure, but I think this will push us over the top of the fund-raising goal. It should be more than enough to finance *ma vie française*, and enable Jane to stock the shelves of the little space she found last week."

Since the weather was so bad, we decided to stay at the house that morning. Usually we would have gone climbing, or shoplifting downtown, but that day, I remember, we were content to sit on the sofa and read, and glance proudly every now and then at the egg.

Again, Max read and I listened, and again, he read from Balzac, pausing now and then to have me enter something in the notebook he was assembling on France.

"Write down *Flicoteaux's*," he'd say, and then slowly spell it out for me. "From the description here it sounds like an inexpensive place to eat, and a place where I could meet some of the more roguish people of Paris. *Flicoteaux's* and the *Rocher de Cancale;* write that down, too."

Dutifully, I wrote, and Max resumed reading until something else caught his fancy and he'd look up from the book and muse out loud.

"I wonder how much a box at the *Italiens* will cost me?" or, "Do you think it will be difficult to find suitable apartments in the *Faubourg Saint Germain?* I suppose I'll have to start out humbly in the Latin Quarter. Probably wouldn't do to draw attention to myself as soon as I arrive."

We were reading from *Splendors and Miseries of a Courtesan*, the plot of which picks up where the last book, *Lost Illusions*, left off. In this new book, Lucien, now rescued from suicide, and Vautrin (still disguised as a Spanish priest) have arrived in Paris and started their scheme to elevate Lucien to a position of wealth and power. Soon after their arrival, Lucien meets and falls in love with a beautiful young prostitute named Esther. Their love is mutual and Esther decides to abandon her trade, mend her ways and try to become a woman worthy of Lucien. This love affair was not in Vautrin's original plan, but he manages to use it to his advantage, dangling the prospect of their future happiness before them as an enticement to get them to do whatever he wants. Having little choice but to put their trust in him, Lucien and Esther allow him to pull all of the strings, and they dance and strut as he directs. They become nothing more than pawns in his nasty game to acquire wealth and power.

Of course, Max relished the tale. He loved all the disguises that Vautrin could assume and the way he could manipulate others, like an evil puppeteer, coercing them into whichever position he desired. But while Max's admiration of the master criminal rose with each new revelation of treachery, my own regard for Vautrin sank. I was secretly rooting for the star-crossed couple, and I hated the cruel way Vautrin was using them. Worse than that, as the story went on, I began to catch glimpses of my own situation. Although Max was not forcing me to sleep with an ugly Alsatian banker, like Vautrin did to Esther, or making me woo the homely young daughter of a millionaire, as he did to Lucien, I was, nevertheless, aware that both Max and Jane were using me. They were using my efforts and abilities to help finance their own ventures, and, like Lucien and Esther, I was getting very little in return. Oh, Jane and Max gave me money, and any "thing" I desired, but that wasn't what I wanted. No, what I wanted was the same intangible thing that they wanted: freedom. Freedom from my horrible school life. Freedom from Lana. Freedom from my lonely existence. Freedom, and the chance to exist in the universe of Max and Jane, to bask in their sun, to be recognized by them as one of them. But, I was beginning to realize, those were things that not even the profit from the egg would enable me to have. So I did my best to content myself with the tangible things they gave me: a watch, an autographed photo of the Carpenters, clothing, a new clarinet, and some of the stolen trinkets that Jane could not sell, knowing all the while in the back of my mind that the days were getting shorter and that the fantasy life I was living would most likely end with the summer. With a tinge of sadness, I saw that once Jane had her shop I would rarely, if ever, see her anymore. And once Max was gone, he would not, indeed he could not, come back. Ever. And for the first time, I began to wonder what would happen to me. When they had both moved on, what would I do?

I continued staring at the egg and I realized that although for them it represented a new beginning, for me it symbolized the end. The end of summer, the end of my adventures with Max and Jane and Serge. The end of my happiness, really. When they were gone, my life would return to the way it had been, and that thought was more dismal to me than the gray sky overhead. It was the kind of thought that made me want to start drinking again, to just retire to my bed and numb myself with port. I tried to shake it, tried my best to hide the depression I felt creeping into my life that morning; but as the day went on, it just got worse.

Later that afternoon, Max and I went downtown to go shopping at the gourmet grocery store on Capitol Hill. He had found an old copy of *Larousse Gastronomique* on the bookshelf at Paris a few weeks earlier and decided that he wanted to make a huge French meal for Lana and me that night, as a sort of celebration.

At the store, I trailed morosely behind Max as he wandered the produce section, humming and gathering up all the exotic ingredients he needed. Without warning, I felt myself starting to cry. I tried to stop it, but I couldn't. My grief had been quietly inflating inside of me all morning and, quite suddenly, it popped.

Max was bagging up some shallots, turned, and caught sight of me.

"Dil, what is it?" he asked, a grave look on his face.

Again, I tried to stop myself, but I couldn't. The tears fell fast and heavy. Max looked alarmed, like he thought maybe I was physically hurt. He dropped the plastic bag he was holding, took me by the arm, and led me outside. He sat me down on one of the planters and knelt in front of me, both hands on my arms, his eyes scanning my face.

"Dil, what's happened?"

People were beginning to stare as they passed. I wiped my eyes and nose on my shoulder and looked down at my feet. My body heaved and shook. I didn't know what to say, where to look. He kept holding on to my arms, waiting for me to say something.

"I'm . . . I'm going . . . to miss you," I managed to say.

I didn't look at him, but I felt him let go of my arms. He ran his hand through his hair and then rubbed his eyes, as if he had a headache. I was aware, even before I had opened my mouth to speak, of the danger of what I was about to say. In saying it, I had opened up a landscape Max rarely, if ever, entered and beckoned him in. I knew how he hated gushing of any sort, knew it was just like the sappy climax of the movies he walked out of, knew that it was the reason he never let me go through the women's dressers. I knew, yet again, I was being sentimental, but I couldn't help it, and that disappointed us both. I wanted so much to be like him, so cool, and dispassionate, and detached, but I just couldn't. I couldn't play stone face anymore. Not then. Not with him. I knew he was going to leave and the sadness affected my body like some strange pollen, making me cry instead of sneeze.

Max stood up and looked blankly across the parking lot into the distance. I knew he didn't know what to say. I think he was honestly surprised that I was so upset. A few moments later, he looked back down at me and smiled uneasily. He rubbed my head, put his arm around my shoulder, and led me back to the car. Nothing more was said about it. Not that day, not ever. We abandoned the plans for dinner and drove silently to the Ogden where we bought tickets for the three o'clock show.

We were early, so we sat in silence in the balcony waiting for the film to start, Max smoking next to me. I sensed that he felt bad, and I suppose that was some consolation, although I still wished he would say something to me.

Like most of the movies that summer, we did not see the end of this one. I don't think we even saw half of it. But this time it wasn't Max's doing. No, this time our viewing pleasure was interrupted by Jane, who came stomping noisily up the balcony stairs.

"Max!" she whispered, peering into the darkness. "Dillon!"

She was scanning the seats trying to find us. The theater was nearly empty but there were still some "shhhs" that came out of the darkness. We got up and went to where she was standing.

"I knew I'd find you here!" she hissed and smacked Max in the arm with her purse.

"Shhh!" said the voices, more emphatically this time.

"We can't talk here," she said. "Meet me at Paris. Don't follow me out for about five or ten minutes. I'll be waiting."

She then disappeared down the balcony steps. Max and I waited, as she'd instructed, and then made our way outside.

When we arrived at Paris, we found Jane seated in a corner, away from the window, hiding behind a copy of the *Denver Post.*

"Anything about us?" Max asked, pulling back an edge of the paper. She folded it angrily and glared at us from behind her large sunglasses. With her hair pulled back and her lips tightly pursed, she looked like some angry wasp about to move in and deliver the sting. Max and I backed away.

"We'll, uh, get coffee," he said. "Anything for you?"

She scowled.

When we returned, she continued glaring at us, not saying a word. Max sipped his coffee as casually as he could and smiled.

"We thought maybe we'd hear from you sooner," he said cheerfully, "but I suppose you were tied up for a while."

Still nothing. It was obvious that she was barely containing her anger.

"So, what happened?" Max asked. "There was the hospital, I suppose, then the police, and . . ."

Silence.

Max and I glanced at each other uneasily and then back at Jane. When she spoke, her voice was low and level, almost like a robot.

"You took the egg," she said.

"Yes, we certainly did!" Max exclaimed reaching out to take one of Jane's hands in his. She snatched it back into her lap and shook her head in disbelief.

"Stupid!" she said, still shaking her head. "Stupid! How could you be so stupid?"

Max's surprise was evident on his face. We had both thought she'd be pleased we'd gotten the egg. It was, we felt sure, the most valuable thing in the entire house and we had gotten away with it.

"What's the matter?" Max asked, confused. "It's not fake, is it?"

"No, it's not fake," she said, pounding her fist on the table. "But it would probably be worth more if it was!"

Now I was really confused. She gave a tired sigh and began her explanation.

"That's a real Fabergé egg, dummy. There are only fifty-six of them in the whole world. Twelve of them are unaccounted for. That leaves forty-four that *are* accounted for. Their locations and their owners are all very well known! Are you getting it? The one you took is one of the forty-four. Our trying to sell it would be like trying to sell the Lindbergh baby or, or, or the fucking crown jewels!"

"What about your man?" Max asked. "He must be willing to take it for something. Granted, we'll have to take a deep cut in price but surely—"

She shook her head.

"He even called me when he heard about it," she said.

Max and I were a bit surprised he had already heard anything about it, since it had happened less than twenty-four hours ago. "We joked about it," Jane continued. "He said he was glad that I was not so stupid as to steal something like that!"

Max massaged his forehead with his fingers.

"How did he know about it?" I asked.

"Oh, word travels fast when something like that is stolen. Believe me! Anyone who's important in the jewelry and antique circle has heard about it. If they ever hear I'm connected to it, I'm screwed. There goes my reputation!"

"There must be someone," Max said, his mind still on selling the thing.

Jane shook her head.

"I mean it can't be . . . worthless."

Jane nodded.

Max's shoulders fell and I saw that his hands shook when he tried to light a cigarette. I knew he was upset, but he was trying to hide it. He had spent the entire time since we'd acquired the egg building paper castles in France and now he was abruptly back where he'd been two days earlier. It was almost as if all of my anxiety from that morning had suddenly transferred over to him.

"What about . . . what about this?" Max said, his voice eager and shaky. "What if we ransomed the egg back to them? The Boatwright-Starks, I mean. Like it's been kidnapped or something."

"Like the Lindbergh baby?" Jane added tartly.

"No? You don't think we cou—"

"No. In fact when I spoke to Beverly this morning at the hospital she said she was almost relieved the egg was gone as she'd always been afraid of having it stolen. She's more than a little thrilled with the insurance settlement they'll get. Face it, we've got a worthless piece of priceless art. I still can't believe you could have been so stupid!" Jane repeated, addressing us both this time. "What were you thinking? I just can't believe it."

"Oh you can't?" Max said. His tone had shifted and I could hear that he was about to vent his own anger. "Well you know what I can't believe? I can't believe you got so goddamned sloppy drunk that you couldn't even fulfill your end of the bargain! You do remember, *chère* Jane, that you were to be the one determining what we should steal? If someone hadn't lost her head and resorted to sorority girl drinking games, maybe we'd have fucking known what the fuck we were supposed to fucking take!"

This last sentence was shouted and caught the attention of the other patrons. They all stared over at us and the café went silent. Jane slumped down in her chair and put her hand on her forehead to conceal her eyes.

"Will you please lower your voice?" she said, a false smile animating her face. "We really can't draw attention to ourselves. We're taking a great risk even being seen with each other. The insurance guys are already all over this case, not to mention the police."

This quieted Max. He looked around, suddenly aware of all the other people. We were all silent for a moment.

"Tell me about it," Max said, his voice somber. "What happened after we left?"

Jane leaned forward, both elbows resting on the table. She seemed both nervous and confused.

"I wish I knew," she said. "I mean, what *did* happen after you left? The first thing I remember is waking up in the hospital. It took them a while to figure out what we'd been poisoned with, but once they did, they just let us sleep it off. By this morning, we were all fine. A little hungover, but fine. You did remember to take the box of truffles with you, didn't you?" she asked, an urgent, pleading expression on her face. "*Please* say you did!"

"We got it," I said.

"Oh bless you, Dillon. That was the one thing I was most worried about! Of course I was afraid that maybe you'd been caught, too, but oh, thank God!"

"So who do they suspect?" Max asked, his hand still trembling as he smoked.

"It's hard to say," Jane said, pensively. She then reached for the package of cigarettes and lit one for herself. This was the first time I had seen Jane smoke and even though I could not see her eyes, I knew she was as scared as Max.

"The police came into my room this morning, right after the nurse brought in my breakfast tray. I was a little nervous, but I think I did quite well, considering. I mean, it's almost better that I did pass out early, because I had even less to hide. I was almost as much in the dark about it as the others, so there wasn't very much I could tell them. They asked if I'd seen anything or anyone acting strangely at the party; and I said no, but that some of the events of the evening were all a bit sketchy. That's because of the drugs, they told me. I played dumb then, which, as you can imagine, is not easy for me. "Drugs!" I said. "I can't speak for the others, but *I* certainly hadn't been doing any drugs!" Well, they had a good chuckle over that one and explained that two men had broken in, drugged us somehow, and then burglarized the house.

"Do they suspect us?" Max asked.

"No," Jane replied. "I even asked specifically if it had been the Balzac Bunch and they said no. They said they didn't find any of the usual clues, which I'm assuming meant your little calling card, and let me just state here how proud and thankful I am that you didn't leave one this time. I don't think my poor, weak nerves could take it."

"There wasn't time," Max said. "As soon as we lifted the egg, the alarm system went whooping wild! Didn't it, Dil?"

"Well, thank God for that," Jane said. "Anyway, the detective said that the Balzac Bunch only strikes when the homeowners are out or have gone to bed. Never when they're awake and at home, like on this job. They said the cook and the butler each gave descriptions of the burglars but that they were wearing ski masks and so the descriptions can only tell so much. Then the whole thing got a little odd . . ."

"How so?" Max asked.

"Well, the cop started asking me if I noticed anyone acting strangely during the bridge game. I said no, not really. I said Mr. Gouldstein had gotten a little friendly once his wife dropped off, but that was all. They perked up when I mentioned his name and asked if I had noticed when exactly he had passed out. I said no. I said he kept getting up to go outside and smoke his cigars, but that was all. Then they asked if I had any knowledge of his business troubles. . ."

"Now that is odd," Max said, leaning forward and emphasizing the point with his cigarette. "He must be in some sort of money trouble."

"That's exactly what I thought."

"So the heat's off us."

"It would appear so, for now at least."

And it probably would have stayed off of us had not Max and I done two very stupid things. That's not entirely true. Wayne is the one who truly complicated the situation, but not until after Max and I had done our damage. Since I am the one telling the story, and you, the reader, are therefore subjected to my biased point of view, I suppose I ought to be brave and tell you my part first. But I'm afraid that would upset the chronology of the story. Besides, it was

Max's part that made me think my part might be okay to do in the first place, so I'll tell you what he did first. Confused? Buckle up and hang on.

In the days after our meeting with Jane, the "Bridge Game Burglary" was big news. It was the lead story on all the local newscasts and made the front page of both newspapers. There were tearful accounts of the things lost and colorful photos and descriptions of the egg. Mrs. Boatwright-Stark was particularly upset at the loss of her engagement ring, which was, ironically, worth nothing. A stainless steel band from a gumball machine that her husband had given her long before he'd amassed his fortune, but to which she had attached great sentimental value over the years. There were said to be no suspects, but it was not, as Jane said, believed to have been done by the Balzac Bunch, because, to quote one of the detectives, "This was a real professional job."

The implication in that was, of course, that all of the jobs done by the Balzac Bunch were petty, sloppy, unprofessional little heists. When Max read that quote, his hubris took over. He threw down the paper and immediately drove to Woolworth's where he stole a Polaroid camera and several packages of film. He bought a newspaper from one of the boxes on the street and then returned home and took all of these things down to the cellar. He positioned the egg on the floor, had me hold the newspaper behind it so that the date could be seen, and then snapped several pictures. While they were developing, he put on a pair of white cotton gloves and composed the following letter on Lana's typewriter:

To Whom It May Concern:

We, the Disciples of Jacques Collin (AKA The Balzac Bunch), were most gratified to hear that the recent burglary at the Boatwright-Stark mansion was executed by "professionals." We had been terribly afraid of never losing our amateur status and are relieved that we have now, according to the Denver Police Department, entered the big leagues.

Sincerely,
The D. of J. C.

He then pulled the letter from the typewriter, placed it and the best of the photos in a plain white envelope, and addressed the envelope by hand, using his left hand to write. It was to go to the newspaper that had run the "professional" quote from the officer. Later that day, on the way to the movies, he dropped it in a mailbox near the Ogden. In the meantime, I did a little letter writing of my own.

I am, as Max had discovered, a somewhat sentimental person and the story of Beverly being grief-stricken by the loss of her cheap ring touched me for some reason. Maybe it was because my own mother had eagerly pawned both of her engagement rings even before her divorces were finalized. Maybe it was because Beverly's story reminded me of that story in which a woman cuts off all her hair to buy her husband a watch chain but her husband has sold his watch to buy her some combs for her hair. I don't know. But whatever the reason, without telling Max, I plucked the tin ring from the pile of stolen lucre in the cellar and, as Max had done, I placed it in a plain white envelope. I was careful to wear gloves, just as he had done, and to address the envelope with my left hand, so that the handwriting looked blocky and childlike. I then mailed the ring from the same box near the Ogden and felt warm and happy for the rest of the day, imagining Beverly's glee when she cut open the envelope and tapped out the contents.

When Max's letter became public, Jane was livid. She no longer came to our house, out of fear that the police might be watching her, but the ear-lashing she gave Max over the telephone was clearly audible in the next room. Max listened, recited penitent apologies to her, and grave promises not to do anything else so foolish in the future, but all the while he was smiling, and smoking, and gleefully opening and closing the egg, watching the Romanov silhouettes appear and disappear. Appear and disappear.

Some days later, when the story of the returned ring came out, Jane's outrage, like a virus, infected Max. Gone was all his puckish playful humor, replaced instead by a stern angry disbelief.

"Honestly, Dil!" he yelled, after we'd seen a news report on the ring and after I had confessed that I'd been the one who sent it. "I don't know how you could justify taking a risk like that. Stupid! Just plain, unnecessarily stupid! Never, Dil! Never give in to sentiment! How many times have I told you that?"

That he said all that with a straight face is a testament to Max's unique method of hypocrisy. His vain acts of whimsy were justifiable, whereas my sentimental gesture was just plain dangerous! Instead of yelling he really should have thanked me because returning the ring was the best PR we could ever have had. In the eyes of society the Disciples of Jacques Collin were still dangerous criminals, but I think people were glad to discover that if we were dangerous criminals at least we were dangerous criminals with a soft spot.

Max, however, did not soften. In fact, if anything, he became harder and more unyielding than ever. It was now mid-August and despite a summer of profitable thefts, he still did not have enough money to get himself out of the United States and legitimately established in France. The reality of this economic shortfall was only made worse by the fact that Jane was herself doing quite well. The last load of micro-mosaics from the Boatwright-Starks had pushed her over the top and brought her enough money to finally open her own shop. She was rapidly using her knowledge, now backed up with cash, to acquire stock from various estate sales and dealers around the world, and was selling her goods almost as fast as they came in.

Ironically, she had the most business from the people whose

houses we had burglarized. Day after day the society matrons marched into her shop, insurance checks in hand, eager to replenish what had been stolen. Max's envy was palpable, and it got even worse when Jane, still furious about our letter writing, informed us that she would no longer participate in or supply information for any more burglaries.

"Besides," she said, with a toss of her hair, "I am far too busy now."

This made both Max and me uneasy. Me because I did not wish to do anymore of Max's shot-in-the-dark-haphazard-night-raids, and Max because he knew that even if we did them, he did not have the knowledge of what to steal or where to sell it.

Despair took up residence in the house after that, and Max's spirits sunk so low that he actually considered doing some of the work he'd promised Lana we would do that summer. We even went out one morning and half-heartedly stole some painting clothes and some brushes, and bought a few gallons of paint, but that's about as far as it went. By the time we returned home, it was raining again so we parked all of the supplies in the garage where they remained, undisturbed.

The next day Max was even more depressed and listless. He lay around all afternoon smoking, and drinking coffee, and mooning, yet again, over the glossy pictures of France in the dog-eared *National Geographics.*

I knew it was bad when the *National Geographics* and the Berlitz tapes came back out. They had both come with him from prison where, I suspect, they had given hope to his caged soul like a crack of sunshine and the view of distant hills. And yet, shortly after he arrived at our house and started making real progress toward realizing his dream, they were stuffed away in one of the empty wine racks and pulled out only when he wanted to cross reference something we'd read in Balzac, or to check on pronunciation.

When I'd first heard the tapes at the beginning of the summer, it was almost as if the house had been turned into a French echo chamber. The bland nasally voice on the cassette would call out from the tape player, and Max would dutifully answer.

"Bonjour, comment ca va?"

"Bonjour, comment ca va?"

"Très bien, merci, et vous?"

"Très bien, merci, et vous?"

And yet, when Max pulled the tapes out this time, the conversations were mournfully one-sided. I sat alone in my room, practicing my clarinet, and all I could hear was the tape-recorded voice coming up from the cellar through the heating vent, followed by a heavy silence.

"Allez-vous au marche?"

"   "

"A quel heur?"

"   "

The house resonated with Max's silence. It was a testament to his misery and resignation.

When he pulled the tapes and magazines out that morning, I knew it was not to practice or plan. It was because at that point his French dream seemed further away than ever from becoming reality. The pictures and voices did not give him hope, as they had in prison, but rather, augmented his despair, making the pain of impossibility all the more bittersweet. It was as if he were slowly resigning himself to the fact that they were all he was going to get: pictures and a recorded voice, other people's impressions, other people's conversations.

At first, I'll admit, I took a perverse pleasure in his misery because I felt sure he'd stay on at the house, at least a little while longer. But later, after three days of watching the one I idolized pine away, I decided to do something about it. I put down my clarinet and went down to the cellar. The door was closed so I knocked before I went in. It was dark, but the air was thick with smoke and I saw the burning ember of Max's cigarette, so I knew he was there. I pulled on the light. Max was lying on his back on the top of the wine rack, staring up at the ceiling. I went over to the tape recorder and stopped the tape.

"I know I'm not a very good reader," I said, searching in the rack for the book we'd been reading, "but I could try and read to you if you'd like. From the Balzac."

He shrugged his shoulders, gave an indifferent grunt and turned over to face the wall.

"I'd like to know how it turns out," I lied, trying to sound as cheerful and enthusiastic as I could. In truth I hated Balzac. I was so tired of the convoluted plots and difficult names that I would almost rather have read from the hokey *Teen Bible* Wayne had given me for my disastrous confirmation. And yet I suspected that if anything would please Max it would be listening to the naughty exploits of his alter ego, Vautrin.

I found the book and opened it to where we had left off and started to read.

Lucien and Esther were both miserable in their enslaved servitude. Vautrin was pimping Esther out to the Alsatian banker and then using the money she obtained to prop up Lucien's position in society. The goal of this plan was to make Lucien appear wealthy so that the father of the rich young heiress he was pursuing would not think him a gold digger and would allow him to marry his daughter. Once Lucien had married and taken control of his wife's money, Vautrin's idea was that the three—Lucien, Esther, and Vautrin—would all take a share. If all went according to plan, Lucien would be rich and his position in society secure. He would then be able to keep Esther as his mistress. As for Vautrin, he would presumably have enough money to move to America and buy the plantation he had always dreamed of.

As I read on, it became clear that Vautrin's plan was not going smoothly. The actors were revolting against the director. Esther realized that she could not give herself, for any amount, to the despicable Alsatian and decided to commit suicide rather than sully her love for Lucien. Unaware of her plan, but himself tired of being under Vautrin's evil spell, Lucien decides to write a letter and tip off the police that Father Carlos Herrera is really none other than the master criminal Jacques Collin.

As I read we both became increasingly interested in the direction the plot was going. It was an exciting turn of events and I mentioned to Max that I was pleased to see that Lucien was finally fighting back. Max however, was unimpressed.

"It's like mice setting a trap for a tiger," he said, referring to Esther and Lucien's moves to block Vautrin's plan. "Foolish. The tiger is smarter and more powerful. He'll stop them. You watch, Dil."

He then seized the book from me and began reading on with renewed vigor. The reading had, as I thought it would, reignited his spark, given him the jump-start start he needed to pull himself out of his funk. As I practiced my clarinet in my room later that evening I was relieved to hear, once again, both sides of the Berlitz echo. By the next morning Max was back to his usual self and burst into my room again, heavily caffeinated and ready to go.

"Dil," he said, holding his index finger up in the air, "I have a plan!"

And what a plan. A miserable plan. A plan I wanted absolutely no part of. A plan more reckless and stupid than any Lucien and Esther (or Lucy and Ethel, for that matter) could have devised. A plan to get his money back from Doris.

Doris. The woman who surrounded herself with no-neck henchman and always carried a loaded pistol. The woman who would, without a second thought, have killed Max (and probably me as well). The woman who had made me afraid every time I even caught a glimpse of a back-combed hairdo.

"You're . . . kidding?" I said, and grinned tentatively. "You are kidding . . . Aren't you?"

He said nothing but went over to my closet and retrieved the pistol he had bought me. He held it up to the light and examined the chambers.

He wasn't kidding. The mouse was going to set a trap for the tiger.

"It'll be easy," he said, snapping the chamber shut and aiming the gun out the window. "You'll see."

"I won't do it," I said.

"But it'll be easy."

"No."

"Now come on, Dil, don't be difficult," he said, moving over to where I was sitting on the bed and caressing my calf. "I neeeeed your help."

"No," I said, and tried my best to look hard and unyielding, all the while conscious of his hand on my leg. We stayed like that for several moments, each staring at the other, my erection stirring under the sheets. Finally, he spoke.

"I guess it is a lot to ask," he said. He removed his hand from my thigh, stood up and walked to the door, pausing when he reached it. "Never mind. Forget I mentioned it." And he walked out.

He ignored me most of that day, sitting at the kitchen table with a pencil and a yellow legal pad making detailed notes on his plan of attack, but I would not be ignored. I could not let him do something so foolish and potentially deadly. Trying to be optimistic, I suggested various alternatives: shoplifting outings that might bring in bigger money, more shot-in-the-dark-night-raids, a jewelry store heist, but to no avail.

He rarely looked up from his legal pad while I spoke and when he did it was only to say, "Don't worry, Dil. If you're not with me, I'll do it myself. It's no big deal."

"Look," I said again and again, "I'll do anything to help you. Anything but the Doris job. I'll do the suicide-night-raids, I'll rob a bank, I'll mug old ladies at the mall, whatever you want! But not the Doris job."

"Thanks, Dil," he said, giving me a plastic smile. He was at the top of the stairs about to descend into the cellar, his coffee cup and legal pad in hand. "But they would hardly be worth it. I need money, not more stuff to unload. We're already stuck with the world's most expensive paperweight." And he descended once again to the cellar, closing the door behind him.

For the next few days, we avoided each other. I stuck to my room and pouted. Max spent most of his days plotting out his plan at the kitchen table, or target shooting out behind the house. Several times I asked if he wanted to go climbing, or to the movies, or out shoplifting, but he'd just look up at me with that same plastic smile and say, "I'd really like to, Dil, but I'm busy right now." Then he'd retreat back into the cellar and close the door behind him. When he emerged, I asked him what he was planning; but he just shook his head, gave me a condescending look, and said, "Since you're not in on it, Dil, it's probably safer if you don't know too much about it."

In the end, curiosity and loneliness got the best of me. I was tired of being left out, so I gave in. I stomped downstairs one afternoon, after having played every song in the Carpenters' songbook several times over on my clarinet and found Max, as usual, seated at the kitchen table, smoking, his mysterious legal pad on the table in front of him. I stood there, but he would not look up at me. I cleared my throat.

"Yes, Dil," he said with a sigh, "What is it?"

I said nothing, hoping that my silence would make him curious enough to look up. I wanted to see the expression on his face when I made my dramatic declaration. He would not oblige.

"All right!" I exclaimed, frustrated with his obstinance. "I'll do it."

Max did not respond, did not even look up. He just raised his hand in the air for me to give him a high five.

Chapter Nineteen

Max did not tell Jane about the Doris plan. In fact, Max and Jane did not really communicate at all for almost two weeks after the letter-writing scandal. They talked on the phone a few times, but these were mostly heated exchanges about money; and after hanging up on each other numerous times, the phone calls stopped, too. Jane did call again, but at about that time we stopped answering the phone. It was almost invariably James trying to persuade me to let him come by and get the Jaguar, or the insurance inspector wanting to know who exactly had signed the authorization for the repairs, or the police, who were now looking for Max either because of the insurance people or because of Meredith.

It was not a complete surprise then, to be sitting in my room one morning playing the clarinet and hear the front doorbell ring. I crept out into the hall and peered through the octagonal window, but there was no car in the driveway. That roused my suspicions. I stood there, not knowing what to do. I knew Max would never answer it. If he had heard it at all, he was probably busy hiding.

The doorbell became more insistent and was accompanied by loud knocking. I made my way down the stairs, set my clarinet on the floor and peered through the peephole. It was Jane. I unlocked the door, and it was immediately pushed open with such force that it made an arc on its hinges, hit the wall, and then slammed shut.

"Damnit!" she yelled, and pushed it open again. She sailed past me into the foyer.

"Where's Max?" she insisted. "And why haven't you been answering the phone? I've been calling for days!" She was out of breath.

"There are some people after Max," I said, "so we've been ignoring the phone."

She groaned and narrowed her eyes.

"People are *always* after Max. Who is it this time?"

"An insurance guy."

"What!" Jane shrieked. She staggered backward if she'd been struck.

"About the *car*," I said as reassuringly as I could. "The car. The Jaguar. My stepfather's car."

She let her shouders relax and released her breath. Max must have heard her voice because he emerged from the cellar.

"Miss Nguyen!" he said, his voice full of sarcasm. "To what do we owe the pleasure?"

"It's hardly a pleasure, I'm sad to say."

She sidled up to Max and plucked the box of cigarettes from his shirt pocket, removed one, and Max lit it for her. She stood for a moment inhaling deeply and then sat on the arm of the sofa.

"There's trouble," she said, eyeing us both.

This was hardly news.

"Does anyone know you're here?" Max asked, seating himself in the chair opposite her and lighting a cigarette for himself.

"No, no. I took a cab and had him drop me on some street in the subdivision down below. I ran up here from there."

"Good. Fine," said Max. "Now tell us what's happened."

"It's the police."

"Yes."

"They're on to us."

"How do you know?" Max asked, still more curious than concerned.

"They came to the shop yesterday evening and brought something with them. It was a tool. A climbing tool, I think. Silver, shaped like a figure eight. They said they'd found it at the base of one of the buildings in Cheesman Park and they're sure it was used in the robbery."

I remembered the job immediately. It had been the one with the southwestern pottery. Eighth floor. We had rappelled down and used the figure-eight tool as a pulley. It must have fallen out of the bag when we were putting things away.

"Fingerprints?" Max asked coolly.

"No," Jane said. "I asked about that. One of the gardeners found it and he messed it up. 'Contaminated it,' they said."

"Wait a minute," Max said, taking a drag on his cigarette, his brow firmly set. "Why did they ask you about it? They can't connect you to that job!"

"No, no," Jane cried. "They showed it to me after they showed me the picture of Serge!"

"Serge!"

"Yes! That's what I came to tell you. They think he's behind it all!"

"But . . ."

"They said the tool was definitely his because it's stamped with his own personal logo."

I remembered the little sheep teetering on the mountaintop that he put on all the climbing tools he forged.

"But he sells some of those!" Max cried. "And he gives them away. Anyone who climbs in Boulder could have one. There's no reason for them to think he did it."

"True, but think about it in relation to the other clues," Jane said. "He's a climber; his business is not doing well; he's French."

"He's not French!" Max interrupted. "He's Canadian!"

"Oh, God! Whatever!" Jane shouted. "The point is French is his native tongue! Look, the reason they showed me the picture was to ask if I'd ever seen him before. Of course I said no, but I don't think I hid my surprise very well. It's only a matter of time before they realize I know him; and when they do, it's only a matter of time before they connect me to you, and then, oohhhh, what should we do?"

Max had no answer to this. Lots of silent smoking followed as we all considered the situation. I wanted a drink.

"Listen," Max said. "Maybe it's not such a bad thing."

Jane and I eyed him, confused. Max went on: "I mean, he obviously didn't do it, right? So the less he knows about it the better. He's got an alibi for the nights of the robberies. We better not say a thing—to him or to anyone else. If he's in the dark about it then he can't really sound guilty."

There was a certain logic to what Max was saying and yet I felt uneasy about it. I thought of Serge, alone in his sparsely furnished apartment, and how I knew he spent most nights watching TV and drinking by himself. What alibi could he possibly have other than that of his dog, Stella?

"So we don't tell him anything?" Jane asked. "We really should tell him something, don't you think?"

Max shook his head.

"We have to help him!" I cried.

"No." Max's voice was firm and his expression severe. "No. Now listen. We're not going to tell him anything! Any of us! They're on the wrong track now; let's take advantage of that."

We hashed it over for a while, but in the end Jane and I reluctantly agreed to keep quiet. At least until we could formulate a plan for Max to escape. We drove Jane back to her shop and then Max and I went on, as best we could, planning our robbery of Doris.

The next day, two days before we were to pull off the robbery, Serge was arrested. Jane had been calling to tell us about it, but, as usual, we hadn't answered. We didn't hear about it until the paper arrived the next morning with a headline proclaiming that at last a suspect in the Balzac Burglaries had been caught. I picked up the paper from the driveway that morning and quickly took it in to Max who was seated at the table, about to have his first cup of coffee and cigarette of the day. I marched over and slapped it on the table in front of him. He gave me an annoyed look and then turned his attention to the paper. He read the entire article without a single comment. When he'd finished, he pushed it away, took a sip of his coffee, and asked for an ashtray.

"Thanks. Don't let me forget we need to check your gun before we do the job. I didn't like the way it was firing yesterday, it probably just needs to be cleaned. We'll need more bullets, too, so let's go downtown. I've got to get some passport photos taken and maybe find some smart little piece of luggage. You know, one bag that will hold everything. Then there's a three o'clock showing of *Gilda* at the Ogden today. You up for it?"

For several moments I was too shocked to even speak. I stood there not believing I had heard all he'd just said. "What about Serge?" I demanded, pounding with my fist on the newspaper.

"What *about* Serge?" he shrugged.

"*What!* Don't you even care? He's your friend. We can't just leave him like that. He didn't do anything!"

"Precisely!" Max said, pointing at me with his cigarette. "That's exactly my point. And if he's smart he'll play dumb and that will keep him out of trouble. It's best if we do the same and just pretend we haven't even heard about it."

He picked up the paper and put it in the garbage.

"But he's your friend!" I protested. "We have to do something!"

"Oh, Dil," Max said, flicking his ash, a condescending tone in his voice. "Sentimental little Dil. That will be your downfall, *mon enfant*, if you're not careful. It's your Achilles' heel, the albatross around your neck. You really need to try and give it up. Serge is a big boy, perfectly able to take care of himself. He's been in scrapes before."

I turned and left the room. I stomped angrily up the stairs and slammed the door to my bedroom. It was too much, I thought falling back on my bed. Too much. All Max wanted was his money, and his France, and it didn't matter who he had to sacrifice along the way. Focus on the end and ignore the means, just like his hero Vautrin. And yet, I could not believe that even wicked Vautrin would abandon a friend the way Max was abandoning Serge. But Serge was even more than a friend! Serge was a boyfriend, a lover. How could Max just turn away? If Serge had been my boyfriend, I knew I would have ripped through stone walls, swam across oceans, done whatever I needed to do to help him. Max, however, was not going to do anything. He was genuinely unfazed by the arrest. All the rest of the day he continued along his path, parroting his Berlitz tapes, planning the Doris job, and worrying about where to find the perfect bag.

The rest of the morning we spent in testy silence. Max tried to break it by offering to read some Balzac or suggesting that we go out and do some target practice, but I resolutely refused to do anything with him. Later that morning he came into my room again, pen and legal pad in hand, wanting to review the scenario for the Doris job.

"I won't do it now," I said, crossing my arms on my chest and shaking my head.

"Won't do what?" Max asked.

"The Doris job. I won't do it. Not after this morning."

"Ahh, Dil, not again! Come on, don't be that way. I *need* your help. It's a two person job."

"Well, Serge needs your help," I countered, my voice full of righteous indignation. "And you're not doing anything about that! All you're worried about is your own self! You and Jane both! Your dumb France and her dumb shop. Well what about the rest of us? What happens to Serge? Does he just go to prison? What happens to me? At the end of the summer you just leave!" I yelled, pounding the bed with my fists. "Well, what do I do? I can't leave! I'm stuck right here. I have to stay right here!"

Hot frustrated tears ran down my cheeks, but I quickly wiped them away. I was mad, and I got even madder at my body for betraying me by producing tears.

Max said nothing. He sat next to me on my bed and put his arm around my shoulder. I could smell his musky, smoky odor.

"Serge is going to be all right," he said, stroking my hair, his voice low and calm. He reached over and placed his other hand on my chest, which was heaving as I tried to control my crying.

"We're not going to let anything bad happen to Serge. Trust me. And as for you, well, we'll work on that, too. I'm not going to forget about all that you've done for me. We make a pretty good team, don't you think?"

I nodded and began crying even harder. He pulled my head into his shoulder and kissed the top of my head.

"Don't worry, Dil. It'll all work out."

"What can we do?" I pleaded. "We have to do something, at least about Serge."

"We will," he said. "We will. Of course we'll figure something out, we'll get some plan going. Trust me . . . Just as soon as we finish the Doris job."

I jumped off the bed as if I'd been shot up by a rocket. I was so mad I wanted to hit him.

"We're not going to do the Doris job!" I screamed. "At least I'm not. And if you don't help me think of something we can do to help Serge right now, then, then . . . then I'm going to the police!"

That was an empty threat I had no intention of following through on and it was obvious from Max's calm expression that he knew it. He got up, stood very close to me, and gently rubbed his hand across my cheek. I turned away from him.

"I love Serge," he said. "I know you know that. I wouldn't let anything really bad happen to him. We'll figure something out. I love both of you."

He was standing behind me. He encircled me with his arms and pulled me back close to him.

"It's all right," he said, running his hands up and down my chest and stomach. "It's going to be okay."

We stood like that for several moments, no noise other than the sound of our breathing. I could feel Max's heart beating against my back. Max's hand lowered briefly and then came up again but this time under my shirt. I froze, my arms rigid by my sides. I felt his rough calloused hand as he slowly traced light circles on my flesh. He lifted my chin up with his free hand, turned my head back toward his and kissed me, briefly at first, light kisses, again and again, and then slowly his lips began to part. I kissed him back tentatively, clumsily, but then my adolescent lust took over and I turned around to face him. It was as if the sexual tension that I'd kept hidden all summer was suddenly released, and I reached my arms around and pulled him closer to me. The pace accelerated. He pulled my shirt over my head and then began kissing my ears and my neck and my chest. He undid the button on my shorts and lowered them and my underwear to my ankles. His hands roamed my chest, and stomach, and ass. He put both arms around me, lifted me up off the floor and dropped me on my back on the bed. When I was down, he pulled my shorts and underwear off my feet and then stood and removed his own clothes.

I had seen his lean, taut body before, but never as it was then. The funny thing was that I felt I should have been looking at his body, but I wasn't. I kept looking at his eyes, trying to make contact with them, but he wouldn't do it. He kept them downcast, and I knew he was avoiding mine. I guess that was my first indication that something was not right. A small misgiving, but one that I quickly shelved when I felt the pressure of his body on mine, felt his arms wrap around my shoulders, felt his lips on mine. I had imagined this moment hundreds of times over the summer and finally here it was. And yet, when he straddled me and put me inside of him, again I had the nagging sense that something was not right. It was the same feeling I'd had when we were first climbing and he told me to lean back. Leaning back felt wrong, but it was really the only way to keep from sliding off the mountain. It felt wrong but it was right. What he was doing to me then, as he slowly rocked above me, felt so warm, so good, but again, something was not right. This was probably because it was so different, I told myself. So new and foreign. It was bound to feel strange. He was my uncle, after all, and considerably older than me. But no, that wasn't it. That wasn't it at all. Those things didn't really bother me. Even today I do not think what we did then was wrong for that reason. No, the reason it felt wrong was much less complicated. It felt wrong because at the last moment I realized that it *was* wrong. He didn't want me. He wanted me to do something for him and this was the way he got it. He was indulging me, bribing me, appeasing me. Doing what had to be done to keep me cooperative.

Like ghosts, the images of Serge and then Meredith appeared to me and I shuddered. I pushed Max off with all the force I had and he landed hard on the floor. I sat up on the bed and looked down at him angrily. He knew he'd been found out and he did not insult me further by looking up at me with a false expression of bewildered shock. He didn't look at me at all but just sat there for a moment staring off into space. Then he calmly reached into the pile of clothes on the floor and retrieved his cigarettes. He lit one and inhaled, staring out the window. I took my clothes and went into the bathroom. When I came back, he was gone.

I didn't know what to do with everything I was feeling then, or even what I was feeling. I got the port bottle from my closet and took several large swigs, revelling in the familiar warmth as it went down my throat and into my stomach. Soon that warmth had spread all through my body. My thoughts stopped racing around in circles and my shoulders relaxed. I picked absently at the label on the bottle. The cloaked and masked caballero stared back at me. A silhouette, just like the portraits in the egg, just like the gypsy on Max's cigarette box. They all seemed emblematic to me then, half-realized ideals of people I could look up to, representatives of all the shadowy, dimly remembered men in my life—of my father, and

James, and somehow, I knew, of Max, too. I knew that he would be leaving and once he'd gone the mental picture I had of him would start to fade, his features becoming more and more indistinct as time passed. I felt I'd always be stuck with poor substitutes, like Wayne.

Then I heard gunshots. Terrified, I got up and ran to my bedroom window. Max was dressed and out behind the house, shooting at the bottles and targets we had set up earlier that summer. He was just testing my gun. No reason to fear he might do himself harm. Max would never do that. I realized that he had probably wanted to make me think that he might, and I felt stupid for even having considered it. In his scenario I would run out into the yard, crying "No, stop!" We would have an emotional struggle as I wrestled the gun away from him, and then, slowly, he would begin to weasel back into my favor. I could see it clearly. I could see what he was doing and it made me mad. But what made me even madder was that I knew if I stuck around much longer that day he would succeed. I would give in and we'd go back to preparing the Doris job.

I turned away from the window and paced the room, wondering what I should do. I was still worried about Serge and decided that if Max wasn't going to do anything to help him then I would do it myself. I got dressed quickly, went downstairs, and got the newspaper and the Yellow Pages. After making a few phone calls, I found out where Serge was being held. I threw a few things in my backpack and without a word to Max went out the front door. I walked quickly down the muddy street into the lower subdivision. As soon as I got to a busy street, I started hitchhiking. It took quite awhile to get a ride, but I was so angry and so resolved to my task that I didn't mind the wait. After about fifteen minutes, a truck driver picked me up and took me to the outskirts of downtown where I caught a bus up Lincoln to Fourteenth Avenue. A little less than an hour after my departure from home, I arrived in front of the city jail.

The woman behind the Plexiglas at the information desk informed me that visiting hours were not until afternoon, so I put my name on a list and then took off walking downtown. It was hot, the last week in August, and the sun seemed to be challenging the leaves on the trees to stay green. I walked between the art museum and the library and then across Civic Center Park over to Sixteenth Street. I had about an hour to spare so I walked slowly, up and down the streets, looking absently in shop windows, remembering all the times I'd looted them with Max. I walked all the way down the street, past the post office and the railroad station, and went under the tracks and then over the river. Eventually, I arrived at Paris. I ordered a coffee and sat out at one of the tables on the sidewalk.

Max was surely going to leave soon, I thought as I sipped the hot bitter liquid and stared down at the street. I could not entertain any more romantic notions to the contrary. I wondered if he would, as he'd said, really give any thought to what would happen to me or if he had just said that to appease me. If he said nothing to Lana, I would certainly be sent off to military school, and the thought of that made me shudder. I was pretty sure he would do nothing to stop it. He and Jane both had a list of priorities and "Dillon's Fate" was somewhere at the bottom of the page, a footnote, if it was there at all. The thought of their selfishness made me angry again. It was always Max, Max, Max and Jane, Jane, Jane. Well, what about Dillon? What about me when all the jobs were done, when all the money was counted, when Jane had her shop, and Max was off counting his francs on some beach in St. Tropez? What would happen to me then?

It hit me like a slap. The realization that I was no better. Serge was rotting away in jail and there I sat, mewling and puking about my own wants just like Max and Jane, more concerned with my own future than anything else. I stood up, took my cup and saucer back into the café, and started walking back downtown. I told myself I would not be like that, if for no other reason than to outrage them. I would not be that selfish and greedy. Serge was a good friend to me, always offering his time and his patient instruction. He was a true friend, and I owed it to him to tell him what was going on. That was the least I could do. I would tell him what we'd done and then leave it up to him to decide what he would do with the information.

As I headed back downtown, I found myself hoping that maybe Max would have had the same idea. Maybe he was going to see Serge as well. As I walked, I imagined running into him in the lobby of the jail, or being told by the woman behind the Plexiglas that Serge was busy talking to someone else. But that was just me being sentimental again. When I arrived, Max was not there. I was given a sign-in sheet and told to wait. About ten minutes later my name was called and I was led through a door to a room filled with several cubicles; each cubicle cut in half by another thick Plexiglas wall. In each cubicle, on either side of the wall, there were telephone receivers—one for the visitor and one for the prisoner. I was instructed to take a seat at cubicle number three and wait, while they went and got Serge.

When he arrived, dressed in the usual orange prison garb, he smiled when he saw it was me. Then he looked around and his smile faded. I knew he had been hoping for Max. He came over and picked up the phone on his side.

"Dillon, what are you doing here? Is Max with you?"

I shook my head. "No, I came alone. I saw the story in the paper and I . . . I wanted to tell you. I wanted, I mean, I know you didn't do it."

He silenced me with his hand and gave me a look that said I should say no more. He looked nervously over my head to the guard who was standing a few yards behind me.

I ignored him and continued. "I know you didn't do it," I whispered, "because Max and I and Jane are the ones who did it. *We* did it, not you."

Again, he tried to silence me. He shook his head quickly and held his finger to his lips.

"It's all right," he whispered. "I know."

"No, you don't," I protested. "You don't know anything, we did it all! Max and Jane and me, we were the Balzacs, we took the egg and—"

"Dillon, shhh. Stop it! I know. I knew all along. Please, don't say any more. Please!"

"How do you know?" I insisted, not believing him. "How?"

He looked at me and his expression softened. He smiled and gave a little laugh. "I knew when I first read it in the paper. I knew it was Max. Who else could it be?"

"But why—"

"Dillon, don't. Don't say anything. Shhh. I know Max very well. It's okay."

"But you're in jail! You didn't do anything! We did it! Why are you doing this? We should be the ones in jail, not you!"

"Dillon! It's okay. Max will leave soon and then everything will be clear. He hasn't left already, has he?" Serge asked, suddenly anxious.

I shook my head.

"I probably won't see him before he goes . . ." he said, and his words trailed off wistfully. For the next few moments, he seemed to forget I was there, seemed to forget where he was. Then his eyes focused on me again, and he smiled. I did not return the smile. I was angry. Here again was someone over whom Max held sway, another victim of his charms. I was angry that Serge was willing to take the fall for him and because I knew that if I'd been in Serge's shoes I would have done the same thing! Of course I was still smarting from Max's attempt to sexually manipulate me, but I was alarmed to realize that the anger was slowly being replaced by regret! Regret that I had stopped it, regret that soon Max would be gone and with him would go the opportunity for it to happen again under different circumstances.

I looked at Serge then and knew that he felt the same way. He, too, was a victim, but it was an odd victimization. It was like Max was a vampire, and we were two willing victims, offering up our necks, hoping that his bite would somehow bind us to him, make us like him. I was still angry, but worse than that I was becoming jealous. Jealous of Serge's love for Max but also jealous of Max and his ability to make everyone fall in love with him, jealous of his charisma and charm, his fearlessness and audacity, his lack of sentiment. Jealous that when I looked in the mirror it was myself that I saw and not him.

I did not know what to say then. My head was swimming. Suddenly I was not sure why I had come. Serge looked at me and I could tell by his expression that he understood my confusion. "Dillon," he said, "do you remember that day climbing when you asked how I met Max?"

I nodded.

"I told you I was his teacher, yes? But there is more to the story than that."

I waited for him to continue. He stared at me but his expression was vacant.

"You see," he said, and looked down at his hands, "Max was more than a student to me. It was maybe not so healthy to do, a thirteen-year-old and me, a much older teacher. I had never done it before. I'm not like that. And I have not done it since, but I did it then even though I knew it was not right. Maybe you won't understand . . ."

I swallowed hard and felt my pulse quicken.

"I think we both needed each other then," he continued. "We both needed to—oh, I don't know, I was still married, but not happy, and Max, well, he was alone, as most boys like that are alone."

He looked directly at me and held my gaze. "You know how it is, Dillon, you imagine you are the only one in the world." He paused then, waiting to see if I had any response. I did not, but I felt a lump in my throat and found it difficult to swallow.

"Maybe it was wrong," Serge continued. "What we did. I still wonder about that. The wrong is more society's problem, I think.

Not mine. Not Max's. No, it was not wrong," he said, more to himself than to me. "It was not dirty. I would do it again. We were both alone. We were different, which is also the reason he was friends with Jane; she was foreign, and different, and always teased by the other students, just like Max. Children can be not so nice, you know?"

I thought of Aaron and my own miserable experiences at school. Yes, I knew all too well.

"Max helped Jane, and he helped me, too." Serge paused here, searching for the right way to say what he wanted to say. "I . . . I had never been with a boy," he said. "I did not understand. I liked Max, but I never would have done that. Never would I go after a child. It was not like that. I gave him a ride home from school one day and it just happened. He knew what he was doing, more than I did. Of course I wanted to do it once we were started and I did nothing to stop him . . ."

At this point he paused again. He seemed to be staring at the glass partition between us, not seeing me at all.

"But of course we got caught," he continued. "It was one day, during the summer, when we thought Max's parents would be away. They came home and caught us together."

I remembered my grandparents then, and how they had both recoiled when I even mentioned the photo of Max.

"I was a coward," Serge said. "I ran away as soon as we were caught and left Max behind."

He paused here and his regret hung in the air. It was difficult for him to go on and he started and stopped several times.

"The odd thing about it," he said, "was the way your grandparents reacted. They didn't call the police. They didn't call the school. They didn't even call me. I guess they thought the whole thing would be too embarrassing. So instead, they beat Max."

Again Serge paused, still staring at the glass. He did not cry, but a profound sadness seemed to settle on him.

"They beat him badly," he said, "and they beat him often. It was a difficult time for all three of us. You see, Jane was around then, too, and she knew about it all. We didn't know what to do. I tried to talk to the parents, but they refused. Then I was going to turn myself in, but Max wouldn't let me. He got very angry, said he would say it was not true, said he would kill himself if I did. Jane, too, was going to report the beatings, but again, Max got very angry and made the same threats, to do himself harm, if she told. So," he said, his clear, blue eyes welling up, "we did nothing. We suffered with him.

"We always knew when the beatings had occurred because for days after, they would keep him home from school. We used to go over to his house on those nights, Jane and I, and try to talk to him at his bedroom window. Usually we couldn't get that close because the dog would bark, but when we got close enough we would flash a light at his window. Max would get up and turn on his own flashlight and send us signals. I remember he used to make the little animals, you know? with his fingers and the light on the window shade, and in that way we knew he was all right."

The tears ran slowly down Serge's tan cheeks and he made no attempt to wipe them away. I don't think he even knew they were there.

"But what about Lana?" I asked, wondering how she could possibly have sat by and done nothing. She loved Max, much more than she loved my grandparents, more than she loved me. That much I knew.

"Lana?" Serge asked. "You mean Max's sister? Oh, she was not there. She was done with school then. Done with them. Graduated. She didn't live there anymore. She had her problems with them, too, you know. Maybe worse than Max's. Your grandparents are not such good people. As soon as she was old enough, she left and took a job in the mountains. When Max did leave, he stayed with her for a while. She helped him, gave him money."

We were silent then, each holding our phones. I did not know what to say. Suddenly I saw Max differently. Another facet had been added to him and to my mother. One that I never would have imagined either of them having.

"So maybe this is all right," Serge said, giving a wave of his hand to indicate the prison. "Maybe if I stay here for a while I can do something for *him.*"

When Serge said that, I suddenly remembered the night in the cellar with Max. The night he told me he would try and dissuade Lana from sending me to camp if I promised to help him steal. "Life is like a seesaw of favors," he'd said. I saw that Serge's taking the blame for the burglaries was an odd way of bringing their relationship back into balance.

There seemed to be nothing else to say after that, so we said good-bye. Serge told me not to worry and to tell Max not to worry. I left the building in a daze and when I stepped outside it was like stepping into an oven. It was a little after two o'clock and the heat of the day was at its peak. As I walked back through Civic Center I thought of hitchhiking back home, but I felt I didn't really want to go home yet. I went a block over and started walking up Colfax. Eventually, perhaps inevitably, I found myself at the Ogden.

The movie was not scheduled to start for another twenty minutes, so I bought a ticket and went up to the balcony to wait. I sat in the back, right up against the wall by the projector, and watched as the small, matinee audience arrived and took their seats. Most people who go to movies in the middle of the day usually do so alone, so there was no conversation, just silent waiting, staring ahead at the darkened screen. Eventually the lights faded and the film began. It was, as Max had said, *Gilda.* The film was almost over before I noticed Max, seated a few rows ahead of me. He was slumped down in the seat, so all I really could see was the outline of his hand holding his cigarette, always between the third and fourth fingers. I had been so lost in my own thoughts and the film that I'd not seen him come in. I wondered if he had noticed me.

The film rolled on, slowly unraveling its dark, somewhat sinister plot until it neared the end. At that point, the two characters who "really" love each other are pushed together and the violins begin to soar in anticipation of the happy ending.

I saw Max exhale a billowing cloud of smoke and mutter something to himself. He shook his head, got up, and walked out.

I didn't get home that night until almost eight o'clock, which somehow did not surprise Lana. She gave me a wave from the sofa, where she was watching TV, but did not say anything to me, did not seem curious where I had been.

"Is Max home?" I asked.

"What?" she asked, her eyes still glued to the TV. "Max? No, no."

I knew it was useless to pump her for information so I went into the kitchen. I made myself something to eat and then went up to my room. I must have fallen asleep because when I woke up, hours later, it was dark and the house was silent. I was curious to see if Max had returned so I got up and tiptoed downstairs. The cellar door was open, so I was pretty sure he wasn't down there. I went out to the garage and flipped on the light. The Jaguar was parked next to Lana's car. I went back inside and stood at the top of the stairs to the cellar, debating whether I should go down or not. Then I heard a cough. It had come from the back deck. I went into the living room and looked at the sliding glass door. It was open, but I could see nothing outside. Then I saw it, just as I had the first day he arrived: the burning ember of his cigarette as it got brighter and then darkened. I walked silently across the living room floor and went out onto the deck. Max was standing against the railing, looking off into the empty distance. He turned when he heard me but, seeing it was me, he said nothing and turned back. I approached and stood next to him, leaning my elbows on the railing.

"Evening, Dil," he said, his voice just above a whisper. When he spoke I caught the usual smell of smoke I'd come to associate with him, but under that there was something else, something I knew all too well: alcohol. I turned and looked at him but was too shocked to say anything. I saw the glass in his hand and then, farther down along the railing, I saw the bottle.

Approaching someone who has been drinking, especially when you don't know the quantity they've consumed or the amount of time they've been consuming it, is a lot like approaching a wounded animal. It may be grateful for your help, but it's just as likely to turn and bite you. From my experience with Lana, I knew to proceed with caution.

"And how was your afternoon?" he asked. I heard the thick laziness in his speech.

"It was okay," I said. "I went to the movies."

"Oh? Were you there?" he asked.

"Yes."

There was a long silence. He continued to smoke and we both stared out at the prairie and the stars and the darkness.

"I'll do the Doris job," I said, but did not turn to look at him. "Whenever you want, I'll do it."

He did not respond, but drank the remainder of the alcohol in his glass and then set it on the railing.

"Ahh, Dil, you really don't have to do tha—"

"I know," I said. "I know." And I turned and went back into the house.

Chapter Twenty

The next morning, nothing from the day before was even mentioned. No mention of our aborted sexual encounter, no mention of Serge, and certainly no mention of the fact that I'd seen Max drinking, although I could tell by his bloodshot eyes and by the way he rubbed his forehead that he was hungover. We ate a quiet breakfast together, chitchatting over trivial items in the newspaper; and when we had finished eating and had put the dishes in the dishwasher, we set to work, once again, refining the plan to get Max's money back from Doris.

The plan was to burglarize Doris's private residence. Max had been to her condominium many times in the past (although the last time had been before he went to prison), and he knew she kept most of her yet unlaundered money in a large safe in her bedroom. He felt certain, although I was never able to ascertain why, that the money she had taken from him would be in that safe and so all we would need to do was go in and pluck it out.

The plan was more complex than that, but not much more. We were to break into her apartment (which was on the seventeenth floor of a Cherry Creek high-rise), subdue her (which is what frightened me most), and then set to work cracking the safe. That done, we would simply rappel down the building, just as we had on the Cheesman Park job, and Max would finally have enough money to get away.

The job was to be done the next day, so we had a lot to review before then. Max had broken our day down into various activities, and before we began, he handed me a small itinerary he had written up on one of the pages of the yellow legal pad. The first half of the morning we would spend working with James's stethoscope and the safe in his study, trying to decipher the combination. Later, we would do target practice in the backyard, and then, after a short break for lunch and a siesta, we would head to Eldorado canyon and practice some climbing.

We made it successfully through the first activity and were well into the second, doing our target practice out back, when the peaceful orderliness of the day was shattered by the arrival of Jane.

Max and I had plugs in our ears, so we didn't hear her screeching at us from the back deck. In fact, we didn't hear or see her at all until she had tottered across the muddy prairie in her high heels to where we stood and smacked us both on the side of our heads.

"Why the hell don't you ever answer the goddamned phone?" she yelled at Max. "You've got to go! You can't wait anymore; you've got to get out of here now!"

We removed the earplugs and looked at her, surprised.

"They'll be coming soon," she said. "You've got to go. Today!"

"What?" Max asked. "Who? The police?"

"No, not yet. It's the insurance company. They hired a private detective. He's been talking to Serge and he spent two hours yesterday talking to *me!*"

Max's face went pale and he rubbed his forehead.

"Damnit," he muttered, and then marched back toward the house, Jane and I following close behind. Inside, he paced around the living room and listened as Jane recounted her meeting with the private investigator.

"He knows it wasn't Serge," she said. "At least he knows it wasn't Serge alone, and he suspects that I know who the others are."

"What did you tell him?" Max asked.

"Not much. I was good about that. I played dumb, but it wasn't easy to keep that up for two hours. He knows that Serge was my teacher, so it's only a matter of time before he knows about you, if he doesn't already. He's even been poking around Paris, asking questions. You know everyone who works there has seen us together! You've got to go!" she cried.

"I can't," Max said, lighting a new cigarette from the butt of the one he'd just finished. "Not just yet."

"But you have to!" Jane yelled, standing up and grabbing him by the shoulders.

"Maybe you better," I added. I was suddenly very aware that the game was nearly over. The summer was at an end.

"I can't!" Max cried, waving his hands. "I don't have enough money! I—I need more money!"

"How much have you got?" Jane asked.

"Only about twenty."

"Thousand?"

"Yes."

"And that's not enough?"

"No, *chérie*, it's not. Twenty thousand probably wouldn't even get me to Paris, Texas, and as you know I need to go much farther than that. It's not like I can just go down to the travel agent and buy a ticket on the Concorde. I don't even have a passport, for Christ's sake. The old Max must be hidden away before the new one can emerge from the cocoon. That all costs money!"

He looked over at Jane, as if she might have the money he needed in one of the pockets of her purse. She let out a laugh.

"Oh, sweetie, everything I've got—and I do mean everything—is tied up in my shop. I haven't even got three hundred!"

"Can't you borrow something?" he asked, his voice cracking. She thought about this for a minute.

"I'll see what I can do," she said, "but I don't think I could get anywhere near the amount you're looking for, and I certainly couldn't get it in time. You have to go!"

"What about the egg?" Max asked, an eager, frenzied look on his face.

"Oh God!" Jane said, and turned and shook her head.

"No, no, no, now listen," he said, running over to the cellar stairs. "What if we broke it up, sold it for parts? The gold and the jewels will surely fetch something!"

And before either of us could say a word, he had disappeared into the cellar to retrieve the thing. Jane closed her eyes and shook her head again. She stubbed out her cigarette and paced around the sofa.

"I've really gotta pee," she proclaimed. "Where's the loo again?"

"There's one under the stairs," I said, and pointed her back toward the foyer. She clicked down the hall and I heard the bathroom door shut. I was nervous. Everything was happening so fast. We were going to get caught, I felt sure, and then what? My worries about what would happen to me at the end of the summer seemed almost trivial now, completely usurped by the present crisis. We had to get him away, but how? My head was spinning.

I spied Max's box of cigarettes on the coffee table. I had never smoked, but from watching Max and Jane, and even Lana, it was evidently something to do when one is nervous. Maybe it would have some calming effect, I thought, so I took one out of the box and lit it, inhaling deeply, just as I'd seen them do. Almost immediately I felt the pain in my throat and for the next several moments I doubled over, coughing violently. When I sat back up, I was surprised to see Wayne standing at the entrance to the room. He was staring straight ahead, his mouth open.

Oh boy, I thought, dropping the cigarette on the floor and quickly stamping it out. *I'll catch hell for this!*

I looked up at Wayne, and tried to appear contrite, but then I realized that he wasn't looking at me at all. I followed his gaze, back over my shoulder, and saw Max, a stunned expression on his face, holding the egg. For several moments no one moved, no one said a word. Then Wayne broke the silence.

"Hey!" he exclaimed. "That's the . . . the one that's been on the TV!" His expression darkened and he added, "But . . . what? I don't . . ."

"I can explain," Max said, but there was terror in his eyes. Again, they stood for what seemed a very long time. Neither one saying a thing.

"It's n-n-not what you think," Max sputtered, but the guilt in his voice made it all too clear that the situation was just as it appeared.

"But . . . *you* took it?" Wayne sputtered, his eyes wide with disbelief.

"No! No, no, no," Max protested. "No. We just, uh, found it. We found it."

There was another horrible silence after this. Max was struggling to think of something to say. Wayne's expression changed again, this time from one of bewildered disbelief to outrage.

"I'm calling the police!" he said, but just as he was about to turn there was a dull thud and Wayne crumpled to the floor. Behind him stood Jane, holding my clarinet in her hand like a baseball bat.

"Oh my God!" she cried and dropped the clarinet to the floor. She covered her mouth with her hands and stared, horrified, at Wayne's body. Max set the egg down and we both ran over to him. There was a big gash on the back of his head, but he was still breathing.

"I didn't . . . He's not . . . dead, is he?" Jane asked, her voice still muffled by her fingers.

"No," Max said. "But he's out."

"Oh my God," she shrieked. "I just saw him, and saw you, and saw the egg, and then he said police!"

"No," Max said, getting up and taking her firmly by the shoulders. "You did the right thing. But how did he get in?"

"I don't know," Jane said. "It's that fucking door. I must have left it open when I came in! Oh how stupid!"

"I was right here," I cried, pointing to the sofa. "I didn't even hear him come in!"

We all stared at Wayne and wondered what to do. Of course it was Max who eventually came up with a solution.

"Okay," he said, as calmly as he could. "Okay, let's get him tied up. We'll stash him in the cellar for now."

Jane and I exchanged horrified glances. Neither one of us made a move.

"If you have a better idea," Max shouted, "you have about two seconds to tell it to me! He's just knocked out, not dead. He'll wake up soon and when he does we'll really have trouble."

"We're not going to . . . kill him?" I asked.

"No," Max said. "No. I don't know. I don't know what we're going to do, but we need to get him secured so we can have time to think up what we're going to do. Now move! Go get some rope from the garage. Jane, help me get him downstairs."

We did as we were told. I headed out to the garage, but I couldn't find any rope. My hands were shaking as I opened and closed the drawers of the workbench, but my eyes weren't really seeing the contents. During the shoplifting and the burglaries, I'd been nervous. In those situations something could have gone wrong, but there was usually an easy way to fix it or at least a way to escape. This time I couldn't see any quick fixes, and the avenue of escape seemed to be narrowing with every tick of the clock. I was afraid, as I had not been afraid since that night in the van with Doris. Everything was suddenly so random and unplanned, like carrying around a bomb with a broken timer, never knowing when it would go off, but aware all the same that it *will* go off.

Finally, I found some string and the remainder of the roll of duct tape we'd used on the cook and the butler. I took these and hurried back inside.

Max and Jane were struggling to carry Wayne's thick body. Max's shirt had ridden up and I saw that he still had his pistol stuck in the waistband of his jeans. That frightened me, but I didn't say anything about it. I ran over to help lift Wayne and together the three of us carried him downstairs to the cellar. We sat him up in the only chair and secured him to it with the duct tape. He was beginning to stir.

"Go get some Rohypnol," Max ordered, "and a glass of warm water."

I nodded and bounded back up the cellar stairs and then up the main stairs to Lana's bedroom. I went to her nightstand and found the bottle, as big as a mayonnaise jar, filled with the pills. James had prescribed them for Lana to help her sleep. After he left and she realized he would not be coming back, she took one of his prescription pads and forged several of them for herself. I shook five of the pills into my hand, replaced the jar, and went back down the stairs to the kitchen. I got a mortar and pestle from the cabinet and ground the pills into powder. Then I took the pestle and a glass of water down to the cellar.

Wayne was almost completely immobilized. His hands and feet were secured to the chair with duct tape and the pretty Hermès scarf Jane had been wearing was now serving as a blindfold. I brought the pills and the water over to Max.

"How many are in here?" he asked, looking down at the powder in the pestle.

"Five."

Max looked at Wayne, trying to assess his weight. He then shook half the powder into the glass of water and looked around the cavernous room for something to stir it with.

"Where am I?"

It was Wayne. We all froze and looked over to the chair. His head was lolling from side to side and it was evident from his expression that he was in pain.

"What the . . . ?" he muttered, trying to move his hands and feet. "Why can't I move? Help! Help!"

Max stood up and took the gun from his waistband. Jane and I, clutching each other, moved back against the wine rack. Max held the barrel up under Wayne's double chin.

"Shhhhh," Max whispered.

Wayne, realizing it was a gun, began to swallow rapidly.

"Play along and you won't get hurt."

"Oh God! Dillon? Help! Help!"

"Shhhh. Shh, shh, shh," Max said, and his voice was almost soothing.

"Are you thirsty, Wayne? I'm going to give you something to drink, okay?"

Wayne gulped again and his forehead began to perspire.

"Bring me the glass," Max said, looking at me. I disentangled myself from Jane and got up. The powder was still sitting undissloved at the bottom. I took the pen from Max's French notebook and used it to stir the liquid noisily until none of the powder could be seen. Then, with a trembling hand, I gave it to Max. He instructed Wayne to open his mouth and drink, assuring him that it was not poison, but just something to help him sleep. Much of it dribbled down the front of his shirt but enough of it went into him to do the job. Once he had finished, the three of us sat silently listening to him blubber. After about twenty minutes, his head began to loll from side to side. Five minutes later he was snoring.

The silent wait had been good for all of us. Like Wayne, we were much calmer. At first the situation had, like an avalanche, caught us off guard. It was dramatic and frightening as it barreled down over us, but now the drama had stopped. We had punched out a little snow cave for ourselves and bought some time, but we still had to decide which direction to dig—before the oxygen ran out.

We went upstairs, and Max and Jane began smoking furiously. Max stood by the sliding glass door, staring out into the field behind the house. Jane paced from one end of the room to the other. I sat on the couch, absently opening and closing the egg, watching the silhouettes appear, and then disappear, and wondering if maybe the thing hadn't been cursed. No one spoke. I noticed a large bulging brown envelope on the floor near the spot where Wayne had fallen. I got up, retrieved it, and cut it open with my pocket knife. Inside there were probably twenty or so color brochures for different military academies.

So that was why he had come, I thought to myself. He'd realized Lana had never received the first batch, so he'd brought her another.

I fanned out the brochures on the table before me. They all had attractive uniformed young men on the covers, and immediately brought to mind Max's libidinous description of Bible camp. Maybe it wouldn't be that bad, I thought. Probably better than prison, which is where I felt sure all three of us were headed.

I thought about all that had happened in such a short time and I tried to make some order of it. Serge was in trouble. Max was in trouble. Jane and I were on the verge of being in trouble. Wayne was being held hostage in the basement, and soon, Lana would be home. It all seemed hopeless.

"Okay," Jane said stubbing out her cigarette. "What are we going to do?"

"Well, first we've got to get rid of the car," Max said, moving back into the room. "But I'm not quite sure how we should go about doing that in the daylight. Jane, do you remember that place everyone used to go in high school for parties?"

"Waterton Canyon?"

"Yeah. There's never anyone up there, right? I mean, it's still pretty deserted."

"What are you thinking?"

"Well, there're all those wastewater ponds from that Martin Marietta plant, remember? The ones with all the no-swimming signs. Suppose we dump the car in one of those?"

"I guess that would work," she said, "but that begs the question, what the hell are we going to do with Wayne?!"

Once again, we all fell into ponderous silence. The furious

smoking and the pacing recommenced while I sat in the middle of it all thumbing through the colorful pamphlets.

At the Waco Academy, we take pride in molding boys into men.

Discipline. Academics. Morals. Patriotism: the four pillars of life at The Jonesbourough School.

Aim for excellence! The Bosworth Preparatory School.

These places probably wouldn't be fun, I thought, but in contrast to the whirlpool of chaos and uncertainty I found myself in, they did hold an odd appeal just then: controlled, ordered environments with a decisive someone in charge who knew exactly what he was doing.

"I've got it!" Max shouted. Jane and I looked up at him expectantly.

"We need a way to keep Wayne silent about what he's seen, right?"

We nodded.

"Well, short of killing him, what is the best way to do that?" he asked, looking from one of us to the other.

"Blackmail?" Jane ventured.

"Precisely!" Max said, punching his palm.

But almost instantly the problem arose: what to use to blackmail someone who has nothing in his character that society at large would see as shameful? We all returned to the cellar and examined Wayne carefully: there was his criminal bad taste in clothing, his shamefully ugly mode of transportation, his disgraceful hairstyle—but those were just the opinions of the three of us as we stood there smoking and assessing him. We went back upstairs to discuss it. No, what we chose would have to be something that he himself would be ashamed of. Something that he would never want anyone to know about. Something really wrong. We tried to think like Wayne.

"If we could show that he'd voted for a Democrat," Jane said.

"If we could record some of his sermons and then play them backward and show that they had satanic references," I added.

"If we could get him in bed with a prostitute," said Max.

We fell silent again, all trying to think of some way to frighten Wayne into forgetting he had ever seen the egg.

"Okay, I've got it!" Max said, jumping to his feet and snapping his fingers. Jane and I looked up. I didn't like the way Max was eyeballing me, or the wicked grin spreading across his face. He looked like a cannibal sizing me up for the pot. He disappeared once again down the cellar stairs. Jane and I exchanged glances and both rolled our eyes. When Max emerged it was with a devilish grin on his face and the Polaroid camera in hand.

Chapter Twenty-one

Some would say that losing your virginity at the age of fourteen is just wrong, and many would agree that losing it with someone of the same sex makes it even worse. Now, if that same fourteen-year-old was to lose his virginity with a member of the same sex who was nearly three times his age, and was, also, the assistant pastor of the Church of the Divine Redeemer, you'd be hard-pressed to find anyone who didn't think it despicable. And that is exactly what Max was hoping for when he proposed that I pose with Wayne for a series of provocative Polaroids.

"We can't make him do that!" Jane cried, pulling me away after he'd explained his plan.

"I had thought of having *you* do it," he said to Jane, "But that didn't seem, well, seamy enough. I mean, you are, after all, a woman, and Wayne is a bachelor. If you two took pictures of yourselves, it would definitely be naughty, but it's not really blackmailable, is it?"

"Oh, God!" Jane groaned, slapping her forehead with her palm.

"I'd do it myself if I thought it would work," Max offered. "You both know that. But it's not bad enough. We're both still adults,

Wayne and I. It's not illegal the way it will be if Dil does it. Don't you see?"

I saw. The baton was being thrust toward me. I could cross my arms and refuse to accept, or I could take it and run. I looked over at Wayne's blobby body, duct-taped to the chair. He was asleep, his mouth wide open and drooling.

"If you don't want to Dil, that's fine. We'll think of something else," Max said and then added, almost under his breath, "although I don't know what."

I knew if I protested he would not make me do it (he never really made me do anything that summer), but I'd been watching Max closely throughout this latest ordeal and had noticed something in his eyes that I'd never seen there before: fear. For the first time, my hero, the one I idolized and adored in spite of everything he'd pulled over the past few days, was truly frightened. It was distressing. I hated to watch it and wanted to do whatever I could to get rid of it, to make it stop, to make him feel at ease again.

"How do we start?" I asked, solemnly stepping forward to join the ranks of Isaac, Iphigenia, and all the other sacrificial lambs.

"I don't want any part of this!" Jane said, stomping back up the cellar stairs.

It really wasn't so bad. The worst part about it was having to take off my clothes and be naked in front of Max, but he was so preoccupied trying to untape, undress, and then pose Wayne's ample body, that he didn't seem to notice me.

We decided to make it appear that Wayne was taking the pictures for his own perverse pleasure, so my role was to be largely passive. Max tried to hold Wayne up so that it looked as though he were the one using the camera, but Wayne was heavy and Max was nervous and scared, so it did not go smoothly. Max could hold Wayne, or he could hold the camera, but he could not do both, and when he tried, one or the other inevitably fell to the floor. Max's third attempt was his last. Wayne had been placed in a kneeling position, straddling me as I lay on my back. Max had his arms under Wayne's arms, and was trying to hold the camera in Wayne's hands. He had it pointed down at Wayne's flaccid penis resting on my chest and was peering through the viewfinder, about to snap the picture, when suddenly Wayne's weight began to shift and he fell to the right. Max tried to stop him, but his arms and Wayne's got tangled in the camera strap and all three—Max, Wayne, and camera—went tumbling down. The camera bounced twice on the concrete and then broke apart, pieces of it scuttling along the floor and coming to rest under the wine racks.

No one moved for a few moments. Wayne was still unconscious, my legs were trapped under Wayne's body, and Max, well, Max just lay there. Then I heard him laugh. It started out small. A tiny little chuckle at the funny absurdity of the situation, but soon the volume increased and I could feel his laughter as it shook Wayne's body beneath him. A moment later Max got up. He grabbed Wayne by the arm and rolled him over on his back, freeing my legs. I got up and wrapped myself in the blanket. Max continued laughing, pointing at Wayne and then at the pieces of the camera, all the while cackling and clutching his stomach. He leaned his back against one of the racks and lowered himself to the floor. His expression changed slightly and his laughter subtly changed to crying. Soon he was wailing like a baby, holding his head in his hands as if he thought it might break.

I was uncomfortable. I felt I was seeing something too personal, too intimate, and I took a step back into the shadows.

"Oh, God, Dil," he cried, and beat his head with his fists. "What am I gonna do? Why doesn't anything ever work out! It all goes along fine for a while, but then there's always something, some Wayne, or Meredith, or some goddamned worthless egg to come along and screw it all up! I try and try, but I'm never safe. I can never relax. I go from one mess to the next, to the next but I never fucking get on solid ground!"

He paused and stared into the darkness. Then he shook his head slowly, still holding it in his hands.

"And I'm tired, Dil. I'm so tired."

I stepped over Wayne's body and knelt down next to Max.

"You'll be okay," I said rubbing his shoulder, aware of how trite I sounded. "You *will* get out of here. You'll get to France and things will get better. You'll land on your feet," I chirped. "Just like Vautrin."

But the comparison to his fictional counterpart did not seem to make him feel any better. In fact, it had the opposite effect: he pulled away from me as if I'd pushed him, and shook his head in disgust.

"Shit!" he said, fishing in his shirt pocket for his cigarettes. "Vautrin is a fake, Dil! A fucking fake!" he cried, punching his hand into his fist.

Of course he's a fake, I thought, *he's fictional.* I stared at Max, confused, and waited for him to elaborate.

"When you took off yesterday," he said, looking at me through teary eyes, "after the, uh, after we fought . . . Well after you left, I stuck around and finished the book."

I said nothing, waiting for him to continue.

"You'll be sorry to hear," he said in a bitter tone, "that your beloved milquetoast, Lucien, gets carted off to prison and then hangs himself."

I was sorry to hear it, but life was much more interesting than fiction just then, so the fate of Lucien seemed small and unimportant. Again, I said nothing and waited for Max to continue.

"But, I'm sure you'll be less than sorry to hear that Vautrin got thrown in jail, too."

He was silent for a long time after this, so I offered a prompt.

"Did the police know it was him?" I asked. "Or was he still disguised as the priest?"

"Oh, they were pretty sure it was him," Max replied, shaking his own thoughts from his head and focusing on the story, "but they couldn't prove it. You know how well he covered up his past and made a new future. Well, the cops tell Vautrin about Lucien being dead, and at first he doesn't believe it. He's smart. He knows that they know he was in love with Lucien and he thinks it's a trap to get him to confess. Then they take him to see the body, and, well, it's pretty much all downhill after that. He loses it. He goes all soft!" Max said, his voice both angry and sad, like one betrayed. "He confesses everything and, and . . . and then he joins the police! Actually jumps the fence and becomes one of them! He sells out! It's all such bullshit!"

Max let his head fall onto his forearms. It lolled from side to side a few times but then was still. He looked exhausted, like a toy when its battery has worn down, and I wondered if he had fallen asleep. The doorbell rang. His head shot up, and there was a renewed look of terror in his eyes. A few seconds later the cellar door was opened and Jane stumbled back in.

"It's the police!" she cried. She vaulted over Wayne to where Max was seated and crouched down next to him, clinging to his arm. They looked like two hunted animals, and I suppose, in a way, that's exactly what they were.

"I'll go," I said, ditching the blanket and putting my own clothes back on. "Stay here and be quiet."

"Wait!" Max cried, pulling himself up. "Wait, what'll you tell them?"

"I don't know yet," I said, as calmly as I could. "I'll handle it. Just be quiet."

The bell rang a second time and the sound was like a shock of electrical current to Max and Jane. They stared, and shook, and did not protest as I went up the stairs and closed the door behind me. I saw the padlock on the stair, where it had remained, unused, since Max's arrival. On impulse, I picked it up and clicked it into place. I then went up the remaining steps and walked over to the front door. I opened it and saw two uniformed policemen standing on the porch. They smiled and looked past me into the house. They asked for Max.

"We'd just like to ask him some questions."

"You and everyone else!" I said, without hesitation. "You're the third ones today."

Eyebrows were raised.

"Is he here?" they asked again

"No," I said, and shook my head. "He's not."

They said nothing. The older one held my gaze for a minute, and I knew he was trying to see whether I was telling the truth. I gazed back, a smile more enigmatic than that of Jackie Kennedy on my lips.

"Do you mind if we come in and have a look?" the younger one asked. The older one frowned slightly, but said nothing.

"I don't know . . ." I replied, with the cautious tone of a children's safety film. I knew I was a little too old to go that route, but I did so anyway. "I really don't think I should," I said. "My mom's still at school and I'm not supposed to let strangers in when she's not here. She gets home about five though, if you want to come back."

They looked at each other, slightly confused and annoyed, unable to really argue against their own philosophy. The older one spoke.

"About five, you say?"

"Yes, if she doesn't get stuck in traffic. Sometimes she's a little later."

"Okay," he said, looking at his watch. "Maybe we'll pop back by about then."

They nodded good-bye and turned and walked back to where the squad car was parked in the driveway. I closed the door and then sprinted up the stairs and peered out the window on the landing. They were still sitting in the car not moving and I wondered if maybe they intended to just sit and wait until Lana came home. I tried to think of what to do if that was the case. But a moment later, I heard the engine turn over and watched as they backed into the cul-de-sac and drove away.

I gave myself a minute to relax on the stairs and took a few deep breaths. Then I went down to the main floor, got the screwdriver from the kitchen drawer, and went back down to the cellar door. When I opened the door, the whole room was dark.

"It's okay," I said. "They're gone."

I heard footsteps and then Max pulled on the light. He and Jane stood in the middle of the room staring at me expectantly. Wayne was not to be seen.

"Will they come back?" Max asked.

"Yes. At five o'clock. Probably before then. You need to go."

"We were just discussing that," Jane said, encircling Max with her arms and giving him a hug. She had been crying as well.

"Jane's going to get rid of Wayne's car," Max said, tossing her the keys to the Oldsmobile.

"I'll be back as soon as I can," she said, and ran past me up the stairs. "I'll park it at that twenty-four-hour supermarket at the bottom of the hill and then walk back up."

"What's the plan with Wayne?" I asked. "Where is he?"

Max led me over to the small crawl space beneath the basement stairs. Wayne's chair had been moved there and he'd been dressed and taped back into it.

"I need about two days, I figure," Max said. "So if you can keep him drugged and hidden for that long . . ."

"Are you sure that's enough time?" I asked.

"No, but I don't think we can keep him any longer without people poking around. If you can keep him two days, that's great. Just do the best you can. He'll probably have to pee . . ." Max laughed, "I guess you'll have to handle that somehow."

I nodded and closed the door on the sleeping Wayne.

"I'll keep him there as long as I can."

"When he does come out," Max said, "pin it all on me, understand? Everything. Jane had no idea about any of it; and as for you, I forced you to do everything, okay?"

I nodded. I felt myself starting to cry but inhaled as deeply as I could and held it.

For the next twenty minutes, Max and I tidied up the cellar. We packed up a few of his things: some clothes, his guitar, his Berlitz tapes, his notebook, his gun, and of course, the egg. He stuffed them all into the same small bag he'd arrived with and took it out to the car. Then he came back inside, and we waited for Jane to return. I sat there drumming my fingers on the table while Max paced back and forth and smoked. Jane returned about twenty minutes later, out of breath and sweating.

"All done?" I asked.

"Yes," she panted. "All done."

"You wiped off the steering wheel and door handles?"

"Gloves," she said proudly.

"The keys?"

"Dropped them in a storm drain on the way up."

She turned to Max.

"We should go," she said.

He nodded and crushed out his cigarette.

"You'll be okay with Wayne?" Jane asked me. "You know how much of the Rohypnol to give him?"

"Yes, I'll keep him as long as I can. Then I'll untie him, let him wake up, and see what he does."

Jane nodded. It was the plan we'd agreed on, but the results were unpredictable at best.

"Call me if there's any trouble," she said. "Although I don't know what good I'd be."

She gave me a kiss on the cheek and a hug.

"I'll, uh, wait out in the car," she said and then went out to the garage.

Max and I stood facing each other in the living room. The same unfinished mess of a living room into which he had arrived just three months before. I felt as though we should say something significant to each other. We'd reached the part in the movie where the characters utter eminently quotable lines, but we were both silent. Life is terribly unlike the movies sometimes and again there was nothing in my head but trite little clichés: "Take care of yourself," or "Hope to see you again real soon." "Happy Trails."

"You'd better go" is what I said, and then tapped at the face of my watch.

"Yes," he said.

He smiled and extended his hand. I took it and gave it a firm squeeze. He pulled me closer and put his arm around me.

"You're all right, Dil," he said, clapping me on the back. "You're all right."

He leaned back, smiled at me once more, and then turned and went out through the garage door. I heard the motor of the garage door opener, followed a moment later by the throaty purr of the Jaguar's engine. Again, I ran up to the window on the landing and looked out just in time to see them drive off down the hill. As if he knew I was watching, Max stuck his arm out of the driver's side window and gave a sort of salute.

The next two days were surprisingly quiet. Lana came home that evening and I did not even tell her about the police. When they arrived, she answered the door, and told them truthfully that Max was not home. The phone rang, as usual, and, as usual, we didn't answer it. We ate dinner in front of the television and spoke little.

"Max must have gone to another movie," Lana said, looking up at the clock during one of the commercial breaks.

"Probably" I replied and went back to eating my dinner.

When Lana went to bed, I snuck back down to the cellar and gave Wayne another glass of Rohypnol water. I cleaned him up as best I could and then went to bed myself. The next day I stayed home and watched over him. When Lana left, I took a chair down to the cellar and finished reading Balzac. It ended just the way Max had said. I, too, was surprised that Vautrin had joined the police, but the more I thought about it the more it made sense; he was caught, exposed, pinned against the wall. What was he supposed to do? Kill himself? That really would have been out of character. He was smart, so he made the best of it. On the surface, it appeared as if he had sold out, but it was more like a successful marketing campaign. He made his infamy and his knowledge of the criminal world into a commodity. As I closed the book, I found myself hoping that maybe Max could, wherever he ended up, do the same thing.

That night, the police came by again. This time they were looking for Wayne. He had not come home and had not shown up to work for two days. Lana jumped at the chance to enter a new drama, and this time did not hesitate to invite the police inside. Alas, she could tell them nothing, so they did not stay long and they didn't even bother questioning me. When they left, she immediately got on the kitchen phone and stayed there gossiping and speculating with the other parishioners for almost three hours. She did not even notice when I entered the kitchen, filled a glass with warm water from the tap, stirred it noisily, and then disappeared down the cellar stairs. When I returned, several minutes later, and placed the empty glass in the dishwasher, she was still talking. She had seen it all but noticed nothing.

The following day, I decided Wayne should wake up. He had not eaten anything since he arrived, and I was afraid of accidentally overdosing him. Once Lana left, I wrestled his chair into the center of the room and untaped his hands and feet. I gave him plain water to drink and then sat on the steps and waited for him to stir. By three o'clock, he still had not moved. I knew I'd better do something before Lana returned, so I brewed some very strong coffee and, when it had cooled, went back down to administer it. I was halfway down the stairs when I heard him moan. I froze. Some of the coffee sloshed out onto the stairs. More moaning. The coffee would not be necessary. I returned to the kitchen, put the cup in the sink, and then sprinted up to my room. I changed into some loose shorts and a T-shirt, threw my Walkman and a few other things in a small backpack, and then went back down the stairs and out the front door.

I had spent the entire day in the air-conditioned house, so the heat from the late afternoon sun felt wonderful on my skin. I stood basking on the porch and looked out west at the mountains. Then I turned, facing the house again, and approached the rock wall. Without any hesitation, almost without any thought to what I was doing, I began scaling the house. I had not done it since that first day when Max had arrived. It had seemed so difficult then, but now, with a summers' experience under my belt, it was easy. The handholds and footholds were large and obvious. I remembered back to that first day climbing and wondered how I could not have seen them. In about two minutes I reached the roof and pulled myself up and over the gutter.

I knew that in the next few hours things were going to get crazy down below and I didn't really want to be a part of it. At least not for a while. Wayne would wake up and he'd call the police. They'd arrive. Lana would follow, and then slowly the story would be pieced together. When that was done, probably not until much later that night, I would come down again. I would listen and determine what they knew, and then I'd ad-lib some answers and fill in the gaps in the narrative as best I could. Until then, I'd wait.

I took my Walkman out of the backpack and popped in a tape of the Carpenters' "A Song for You." I put the headphones on and lay back on the roof staring up at the afternoon clouds as they traveled across the sky, wondering what the near future held for me. There would be trouble, that much was certain. I would play the role of victim, would paint a picture of Max as an evil Rasputin, and I knew that everyone would believe it. Everyone except Lana. She knew me, and she knew Max, and she would know that the tale I told was fiction. And yet, she would probably be wise enough to keep her mouth shut. After all, trouble for me could mean trouble for her, and I knew she didn't want that. More than likely, she would go along with the tune I played. She would hear my notes and see the wisdom of jumping in and adding notes of her own. I really wasn't concerned about that. No, it was what would happen when the show was over that worried me. When the curtain went down and all the players had gone home, I wondered what Lana would do to me then. There would be more beatings, maybe even more church-going, and then there would be military school.

All summer long I had shuddered to even think of military school, but as I lay there on the roof considering it, I was no longer afraid. Oh, it might be awful; it might even be worse than junior high had been, but it would not be forever. It would be a means to an end, and to get through it, I'd just have to keep focused on the end. That much was clear. It had not been at the beginning of the summer and that was part of the reason I drank. I had thought that life with Lana and the miserable middle-school microcosm I was in was the whole world and I could not see that one day it would all be in the past, a not-so-pleasant memory, but a memory nevertheless. The summer with Max had, if nothing else, expanded my view of the world. It had given perspective to my troubles and shown me, when I stood back and took a look at them, how small and temporary they really were. They might seem horrible and overwhelming at the time, but the real grace in life was to realize that they wouldn't always be that way. I knew then that no matter what happened—if I stayed with Lana and returned to junior high, or if I was shipped off to military school—I would be okay. I possessed the knowledge and the strength to survive, and for that I had Max to thank.